**Jennifer Fallon** lives in Alice Springs, in central Australia, and writes anywhere she can get her hands on a computer. She writes full-time and moonlights in business training and IT as a consultant. Visit her website at www.jenniferfallon.com for more information.

Find out more about Jennifer Fallon and other Orbit authors by registering for the free Orbit newsletter at www.orbitbooks.net

D0494025

# HARSHINI

## THE DEMON CHILD TRILOGY: BOOK THREE

## JENNIFER FALLON

www.orbitbooks.net

ORBIT

First published in Great Britain in August 2005 by Orbit
Reprinted 2005, 2006, 2009

A CIP catalogue record for this book is available from the British Library.

ISBN 978-1-84149-328-2

Typeset in Adobe Garamond by
Palimpsest Book Production Limited, Polmont, Stirlingshire
Printed and bound in Great Britain by CPI Mackays, Chatham, ME5 8TD

Papers used by Orbit are natural, renewable and recyclable
products sourced from well-managed forests and certified
in accordance with the rules of the Forest Stewardship Council.

**Mixed Sources**
Product group from well-managed
forests and other controlled sources
www.fsc.org  Cert no. SGS-COC-004081
© 1996 Forest Stewardship Council

Orbit
An imprint of
Little, Brown Book Group
100 Victoria Embankment
London EC4Y 0DY

An Hachette UK Company
www.hachette.co.uk

www.orbitbooks.net

For Harshini Bhoola
and as always, Adele Robinson

# *Acknowledgments*

Once again, I have quite a few people I'd like to thank for their help and support. Lyn Tranter from Australian Literary Management, Stephanie and everyone at HarperCollins Publishers Australia, Sarah Endacott from Edit or Die for editing and advice and patience.

I would also like to thank Debra Rae-Smith and Fiona McLennan, the whiz-kids of cyberspace at HarperCollins and Voyager Online, who have given me a great deal of support, and quite a few emailed suggestions, particularly in relation to Tarja's fate, all of which I happily ignored . . .

I must again thank the awesomely talented Stephanie Pui-Mun Law for her wonderful covers, and the remarkable character sketches that she has provided for this series.

A special thank you, too, must go to Elle, Stephanie, Woody, Alison and Ryan, the gang from Whitley College, for their input, their friendship and their all-night proof-reading session.

To my children, Amanda, Tracey (TJ) and David, my thanks for their support, their faith, the inspiration they have provided, and for making me feel that I haven't completely failed as a mother.

And finally, to my good friend Harshini Bhoola: it's been a long time coming, but this one's for you.

# PART I

# RETREAT INTO DANGER

# I

Korandellan té Ortyn, the last King of the Harshini, waited until the end of the concert before he left the natural amphitheatre in the centre of Sanctuary to return to his apartment. But first, he congratulated the performers. He admired the clever scenery they had devised, which used a mixture of magic and everyday objects, and graciously thanked them for their efforts. He moved among them, smiling and waving, as the glimmering twilight, that was as close to night as it came in this magical place, descended over the valley. Sanctuary's tall, elegant white spires towered over the hidden city, touched with silver as evening closed in. The people were trying so desperately hard to be happy. He did his best to seem happy for them in return.

There was a brittle edge to the serenity of Sanctuary these days. An edge that Korandellan, more than any other Harshini, could feel. The happiness here was fragile; the cheerfulness an illusion. The Harshini were running out of time. Quite literally. Only Korandellan knew how close they were to the end.

Perhaps Shananara suspected. She fell in beside him,

dressed in the long loose robes that most of the Harshini favoured, which surprised him a little. Shananara had been in and out of Sanctuary a great deal of late, and he was more used to seeing her in Dragon Rider's leathers. His sister had always been more interested in the comings and goings of the human population than he. With the demon child abroad, and the whole world affected by her presence, Shananara was anxious to know what was happening. Slipping her arm companionably through his, she walked with him back to his quarters, waiting until the doors swung silently shut behind them before she spoke.

'Let me help, Koran.'

The king sighed, letting his shoulders slump and his façade of vitality crumble in her presence. He looked haggard.

'No. You cannot help, Shanan,' he told her, lowering his tall frame into a delicately carved chair near the open doors that led to the balcony. The tinkling sound of the waterfall drifted through the open windows. The evening, as usual, was balmy and clear. 'I need your strength for other matters.'

'There won't *be* any other matters if you falter,' she warned. 'Let me carry some of the load. Or do you enjoy being a martyr?'

He smiled at her wearily. She had been out visiting the humans again. Her manner of speech always reflected her journeys among the mortals. 'No, I do not enjoy being a martyr, sister. But if I fail, our people will need you to guide them. If you help me now, you will certainly ease my burden, but it will weaken you at a time when one of us needs to be strong. Only the demon child can lift the burden from my shoulders completely.'

Shananara flung herself into one of the chairs opposite

the window. 'The demon child? That unreliable, spoilt, half-human atheist brat? If that's who you're relying on to save us, brother, we are doomed.'

'You shouldn't speak of her so harshly, my dear. R'shiel will do what she must.'

'She will do what suits her, Koran, and not a damned thing more. I doubt if even the gods know if it will be what she was destined for.'

'Yet it is on her we must rely.'

'Then let me bring her back.'

'Here? To Sanctuary? For what purpose?'

'If you won't let *me* ease your burden, then let R'shiel do it. The gods know she's strong enough. Let me bring her back, Koran. Let her carry the load for a time, enough to let you recover, at least. Then you can take up the burden again and R'shiel can do what she has to.'

The king shook his head. 'Events unfold as they should, Shananara. We cannot interfere.'

'What events?' she scoffed. 'Where is it written that you should destroy yourself holding Sanctuary out of time, while the demon child sits on her hands trying to decide if she even believes we exist or not?'

'You did not speak to R'shiel before she left us. She has learnt much.'

'She doesn't know a fraction of what she needs to know. And who is there to teach her? Brak?'

'I thought you were fond of him.'

'I am, but he's hardly the one I would have chosen as the demon child's mentor. He doesn't even like her. And he certainly doesn't trust her.'

'She will learn what she needs to know in Hythria.'

'But does R'shiel know that? She's just as liable to head in the other direction.'

'You worry too much, Shanan. These things have a way of working themselves out. R'shiel will come to accept her destiny and will learn what she needs in due course.'

'Before or after the Harshini are destroyed, brother?' Leaning forward, she studied him intently, as if she could see through his skin and into his soul. 'Xaphista's minions have control of Medalon. The Defenders have surrendered to Karien. Hythria is on the brink of civil war and Fardohnya is arming for invasion. And you are beginning to weaken. I can see it in your eyes. You tremble constantly and cannot control it. Your eyes burn. Your aura is streaked with black. A flicker, a slight wavering in your hold on the spell that holds Sanctuary out of time, and Xaphista's priests will know where we are. Once that happens, you will be able to count the days on the fingers of one hand before the Kariens are standing at our gates.'

'R'shiel will deal with Xaphista before that happens,' he assured her.

'I wish I shared your faith in her. But how long do we have, Koran? How long can you keep draining yourself?'

'As long as I need to.'

She leaned back with a defeated sigh. 'Then I can only pray to the gods that it will be long enough.'

'The demon child will do what she must.'

Shananara did not look convinced. 'You place far too much faith in that uncontrollable half-breed.'

The Harshini king nodded tiredly. 'I'm aware of that, Shananara, but unfortunately that uncontrollable half-breed is our only hope.'

# 2

The marriage of Damin Wolfblade, Warlord of Krakandar, to Her Serene Highness, Princess Adrina of Fardohnya, took place on a small, windswept knoll in the middle of northern Medalon on a bitterly cold afternoon. It was little more than two weeks since the bride had unexpectedly become a widow.

The sky was overcast and low, the sullen clouds defying the brisk, chilly wind by staying determinedly in place. The somewhat less-than-radiant bride was dressed in a borrowed white shirt and dark woollen trousers. The groom looked just as uncomfortable in his battle-worn leathers. The assorted guests appeared either bemused or amused, depending on their country of origin.

Officiating over the ceremony was a tall, serious looking Defender, who wore the insignia of a captain and quoted the stiff, practical and very unromantic Medalonian wedding vows that were carried away by the wind almost as soon as he uttered the words. This wedding was taking place because the demon child had demanded it, and a quick ceremony – enough to make it legal – was all R'shiel cared about. She had neither the time nor the patience for any pomp or ceremony.

'This is probably a waste of time, you know,' Brak muttered as he watched the ceremony with a frown.

'Why?' R'shiel asked softly, not taking her eyes from the bride and groom, as if they would somehow manage to escape their fate if she looked away.

'This marriage will only hold up if you can get the High Arrion to accept the legality of a Medalonian ceremony as soon as you get to Greenharbour,' he explained.

'The leader of the Sorcerers' Collective?'

'The High Arrion is Damin's half-sister.'

'She's not going to be very happy about this, is she?'

'Even if she wasn't concerned about her brother, as the High Prince's heir, he's doing a very dangerous thing.'

'But worth it, Brak. In the end, it will be the best thing that could have happened. This will force peace between Hythria and Fardohnya. Nothing else we can do will achieve that.'

Brak looked unconvinced. 'There's an awful lot that can go wrong, R'shiel.'

'It'll work.'

He stared at her.

'Trust me, it'll work!'

'I'm surprised Zegarnald is letting you get away with this.'

'I have the God of War's solemn promise that he won't interfere. Besides, he'll think this is likely to cause a war.'

'That's because it *is* likely to cause a war, R'shiel,' Brak pointed out.

'Only in the short term.'

He shook his head at her folly and turned his attention

back to the ceremony. It was almost over. Denjon was calling on the gods to bless the union – Kalianah to bless it with love, Jelanna to bless it with children. He sounded very uncomfortable, but R'shiel had insisted on acknowledging the gods, even in some small measure. Personally, she didn't think it would make much difference, but Damin and Adrina were both pagans and it was what *they* believed that counted. One or both of them might try to wheedle out of it if she left them a loophole.

Denjon declared the union sealed, to the scattered applause of the gathered Defenders and Hythrun who had come to watch. The newlyweds turned to face the crowd and smiled with the insincere ease of those trained from childhood to perform in public. They stepped down from the knoll and began to walk towards R'shiel and Brak. R'shiel shivered, although it was not from the cold.

'Just how much power do the Sorcerers' Collective have, anyway?'

'Politically or magically?'

'Both, I suppose.'

'The magic they wield shouldn't bother you. Politically, however, they're one of the strongest forces in Hythria.'

'So if the High Arrion publicly sanctions this union, the Warlords will accept it?'

'They won't openly object, but don't count on acceptance.'

'Then we need the Sorcerers' Collective on our side.'

'Most definitely.'

R'shiel nodded, her mind already working through how to get the High Arrion on side. And the King of Fardohnya. Brak could deal with him. In fact, she had a sneaking suspicion he was going to enjoy it. Her mind churned with possibilities, as she pondered the problem. The scheming came to her as naturally as breathing – one of the legacies of being raised by the Sisters of the Blade.

'Well, it's done now,' Damin remarked as he and Adrina reached them.

'A true romantic, isn't he,' Adrina complained. 'Do we have to stand around here chatting? I'm freezing. Every time I get married, I seem to be freezing.'

'We should head back to the camp. Denjon had the cooks prepare a wedding feast for you.'

'What a culinary experience *that's* going to be,' Adrina grumbled.

'You're not planning to make this easy, are you?' R'shiel asked.

The princess conceded the point reluctantly. 'Very well, I shall endeavour to be appreciative of the efforts of my hosts.'

'That should be a new experience for you,' Damin remarked blandly.

The Warlord enjoyed living dangerously, R'shiel decided, noticing the look Adrina gave him. She made her excuses, leaving the bride and groom with Brak, and slipped away to speak with Denjon.

'Thank you, Captain.'

'I'm sure I've broken a score of laws here today, R'shiel. Are you certain this was necessary?'

'Positive. It'll keep Hythria and Fardohnya off our backs while we deal with the Kariens.'

'I hope you're right. I'm not sure the marriage of a Hythrun Warlord to a Fardohnyan will help Medalon much. Particularly the Warlord who's spent most of the past decade trying to steal every head of cattle on our side on the border.'

'This Warlord is on our side now, Denjon.'

'I'll have to take your word for that. Although he seems reasonable enough.'

She smiled, wondering what Damin would think of such a backhanded compliment. 'Never fear. Events will strike a balance eventually.'

'I hope you're right, demon child.'

R'shiel had no chance to chide the captain for calling her by that hated name. A commotion ahead of them distracted her as a Defender ran towards them from the line of tents ahead, calling her name.

'What's wrong?' she demanded as the man pushed through the wedding party to reach her.

'It's Tarja,' the young man panted. 'He's awake.'

R'shiel beat everyone else to the infirmary tent. She pushed her way through the flap and ran to the pallet where Tarja lay at the far end of the large tent, straining uselessly against the ropes that held him.

'Tarja?'

He turned at the sound of her voice, but there was no recognition in his eyes. His colour had improved but he had a wild look, as if a battle raged inside him. His dark hair was damp and his brow beaded with sweat. The rough, grey, army-issue blankets that covered him were a twisted tangle.

'Tarja? It's me, R'shiel . . .'

His only response was to tug even harder at the ropes. Already his wrists were burned from his efforts. With a cry of dismay, she reached for them, to ease his suffering.

'R'shiel! No!'

Brak hurried to her side and looked down on Tarja with concern. Damin and Adrina were close on his heels.

'Look what he's doing to himself, Brak! You can't just leave him there, tied up like a wild animal.'

'If you let him go, he's liable to do a lot worse damage to himself,' Brak warned. 'Until the demons leave him, he's better off restrained.'

'Demons?' Adrina gasped in horror. 'You mean he's possessed?'

'In a manner of speaking,' the Harshini shrugged.

'That can't be good for him.'

'It's the only thing keeping him alive,' R'shiel retorted, suddenly in no mood for Adrina's tactlessness. 'How much longer, Brak?'

'It shouldn't be long now,' he said. 'He's awake. That's a good sign.'

'How will the demons know when to leave?'

'Dranymire should sense when they're no longer needed. With luck, when the meld dissolves, all the brethren will follow.'

'With *luck*?' Damin repeated dubiously. 'You mean there's no guarantee they'll all leave?' He stared at Tarja for a moment then turned to Adrina. 'For future reference, my dear, if I ever take a fatal wound in battle and the Harshini offer to heal me by having me possessed by demons, let me die.'

'Never fear on that score, Damin. If you ever take a fatal wound in battle, I'll be more than happy to let you die.'

'Stop it!' R'shiel cried impatiently. 'I'm sick of you both! Go away!'

The pair of them looked quite startled at her outburst. 'I'm sorry, R'shiel . . .'

'Just leave.'

Without any further comment the Warlord and his bride beat a hasty retreat from the infirmary. R'shiel turned her attention back to Tarja, who seemed to have lapsed into unconsciousness again.

'I have to tell you, R'shiel,' Brak remarked as he watched them leave, 'if the fate of Hythria and Fardohnya rests in the hands of those two, we're in big trouble.'

'They need to grow up,' R'shiel agreed impatiently. She had no time for the peculiarities of her friends at this point. She was more concerned about Tarja. 'Isn't there anything we can do for him?'

'Not while the demons still substitute for the blood he's lost,' Brak told her.

'How much longer?'

'There's no way of knowing. But he's strong. If anyone can survive this, Tarja can.'

She watched for a moment, as Tarja's chest rose and fell in even, measured breaths. 'Every day, I keep hoping . . . We've already been here too long. We have to leave. I can't keep putting it off.'

'We have a wedding feast to attend first.'

'Don't remind me.' She pulled the blanket up and smoothed it, then looked at Brak. 'I just hope those two behave, tonight. If not, I'll strangle the pair of them.'

'Don't worry, they won't dare cross the demon child.'

'Are you making fun of me, Brak?'

He smiled. 'Just a little bit.'

She returned his smile wanly. 'Don't you ever get sick of watching over me?'

'Constantly. But it's a task I'll be doing for some time yet,' he replied as his smile faded.

'What do you mean?'

'You've chosen which side you're on, demon child. You don't think Xaphista is just going to stand back and watch while you set about destroying him, do you?'

'You think he'll send more priests after me?'

'You should be so lucky,' he told her. 'A priest you can see. No, I'm afraid he'll be a bit subtler this time. He'll probably try to turn someone close to you against you. Someone you trust. Someone who can get near you.'

R'shiel studied Brak for a long moment then glanced down at Tarja. 'You think he'll turn Tarja against me, don't you?'

'Tarja, Damin, Adrina, one of the Defenders, who knows? Any one of them could become your enemy and you won't know a thing about it until they're pulling the knife from your back.'

R'shiel stroked Tarja's brow gently before she answered. 'Tarja would never betray me.'

'Perhaps not. But trust no one, R'shiel.'

'Not even you?'

Brak smiled thinly. 'Xaphista can't turn me to his cause, or any Harshini for that matter. He began as a demon and he was never bonded to my clan or yours. The Harshini you can trust.'

'But nobody else?'

'Nobody else.'

She stood up, frowning at the idea that everybody she knew was a potential traitor. 'Brak, I *really* don't like being the demon child, you know that, don't you?'

Brak shrugged. 'We all have a destiny we can't avoid, R'shiel.'

'I don't believe in destiny.'

'I know. That's why the Primal Gods are so worried.'

*That* thought actually cheered her a little. 'The Primal Gods are worried?'

'They're worried,' he agreed.

'Good,' she declared petulantly. 'They damned well should be.'

# 3

R'shiel escaped the mess tent and the wedding feast as soon as she could slip away without being rude. She had arranged this wedding and felt that the least she could do was make some attempt to be sociable, although Brak's warning about Xaphista worried her more than she cared to admit. She had found herself studying faces in the candlelight, wondering who the Overlord would suborn. Which familiar face was really her enemy? Whose eyes hid treachery and whose were genuine in their friendship? She escaped the tent with relief, glad finally to be alone. Brak seemed to sense what bothered her and made no attempt to follow.

She paced the large Defender camp, too restless to seek her bed. Since returning from Sanctuary, R'shiel found she didn't need sleep the way she once had. While a useful trait at times, in the darkest hours of the night, when the human spirit was at its lowest ebb, she felt the burden of her destiny keenly. With Brak's caution about potential enemies ringing in her ears, tonight it seemed harder than usual.

But she was not unhappy. In fact, it was frightening

to discover how much she was enjoying herself. She had told Brak she did not believe in destiny, but Joyhinia had unwittingly raised her for this. Every lesson she learnt at Joyhinia's knee was aimed at educating her in the art of survival in the cutthroat politics of the Sisters of the Blade.

R'shiel had rebelled against it as a child. Now she found it not only useful, but almost exhilarating. She frequently told Brak that she hated being the demon child, but there were times when it was intoxicating to have princes and princesses deferring to her. Even the Defenders, who had never treated her as much more than the annoying little sister of one of their officers, now treated her with cautious awe.

For the first time in her life she understood the attraction of power, but was still idealistic enough to hope that it would not corrupt her. R'shiel had not yet reached the point where she was willing to sacrifice *anything* to achieve her goals. But she was prepared to do a great deal. As Brak had said, she had chosen which side she would be on. All that remained now was for her to do what the Primal Gods had created her for – a destiny she had absolutely no idea how she was going to fulfil.

Her thoughts turned to Hythria, and the reason she had agreed to accompany Damin and Adrina south. Originally, she agreed to go with them to aid Damin's cause and to avert potential trouble now that he was married to the daughter of Hythria's most despised enemy. But in the past few days R'shiel had realised she *had* to go south because that was where the Sorcerers' Collective was located. If anybody left alive in this world had the knowledge of how to kill a god, the last human practitioners of magic would. R'shiel had already tasted

Xaphista's lure and although she would never admit it to Brak, she doubted she could hold out against him a second time. She needed knowledge that even the Harshini did not possess. They had no idea how to kill a god. They couldn't even squash a flea.

Several turns around the large camp in the chilly starlight did nothing to ease her turmoil, so she decided to sit with Tarja for a time. In the darkness of the infirmary tent, the smell of lye soap sharp in her nose, she cooled his fevered forehead with a damp rag as he literally fought the demons that possessed him. Tarja drifted in and out of consciousness, but he never displayed even a hint of recognition. He would lie quietly at times, and then jerk against the bonds that restrained him so hard R'shiel wondered that the pallet did not break under the pressure. There was nothing she could do for him but hope. She did not have enough faith in the gods to waste her time praying.

As she watched him, she wondered if Xaphista would choose Tarja as the instrument of her destruction. It would be the cruellest jest he could play on her. She loved him; had loved him since she was a child. But Kalianah, the Goddess of Love, had imposed Tarja's love for her on him. Xaphista had told her that and she had no reason to doubt him. Tarja loved her because the gods willed it. He had been given no say in the matter, nor was he aware that the choice had not been his.

*If Tarja ever learns of the geas, Xaphista will have no need to seduce him*, R'shiel thought unhappily. Tarja's wrath would be enough. She knew that, as surely as she knew nothing she could do, nothing she could say would lessen his fury, should he ever discover what had been done to him.

As dawn slowly lightened the sky over the camp, R'shiel abandoned her depressing line of thought. No closer to finding a solution to the troubles that plagued her, she left the tent to find some breakfast and clean up before her meeting with Denjon and the other captains.

'We have a problem,' Denjon announced by way of greeting when she entered the mess tent. It had, by default, become their meeting place over the past two weeks. Brak and Captain Dorak were already there, sitting at one of the long tables nursing steaming mugs. The tables had been cleared from last night's party and the tent was empty other than for Brak and the Defenders. Captain Linst was sitting at the end of the table, the remains of his breakfast in front of him. None of the men rose as she entered. She had finally cured them of that, at least.

'Only *one* problem? When did things improve?'

Denjon treated her to a weary smile. He was a tall, rangy man, who had been a classmate of Tarja's when they were cadets. He had dark hair and the competent manner R'shiel associated with the Defenders. His proficiency was a credit to Jenga rather than a positive reflection on the Sisters of the Blade who commanded the Defenders.

'Perhaps I should re-phrase that. We have an urgent problem. The rest can wait an hour or two.'

'Where's Damin?'

'Still enjoying his wedding night, I suppose,' Dorak suggested with a grin.

'We can't wait for him,' Denjon shrugged. 'We need to decide what we're going to do with the Karien prisoners. We've sat here far too long and the scouts have just brought news of another troop of Kariens coming in from the north, no doubt looking for their prince.'

'We have to move out,' Linst added. 'We can't take the Karien prisoners with us and we can hardly leave them here to announce what we're up to when the search party finds them.'

The problem of what to do with the Karien knights who had accompanied Prince Cratyn on his quest to find Adrina was one R'shiel had been hoping she would not have to face. When Denjon calmly announced he could 'take care of a couple of hundred Kariens', she had callously hoped they would simply die in battle, saving her the problem of what to do with them afterwards. The Defenders, however, were far too efficient to indulge in such needless bloodshed. They had rounded up the Kariens and taken them prisoner with only a handful of Karien casualties and none at all from their own ranks.

The prisoners had done nothing but drain their resources since that day. The young knight in command, Drendyn, the Earl of Tyler's Pass, was a noisy, inexperienced fellow who seemed stunned and heartbroken when he learnt that Adrina was also in the camp and obviously allied with his captors. For a fleeting moment, R'shiel wished she could do what Joyhinia had tried to do to the rebels. Simply put them to the sword and be done with them.

She had no more chance of getting the Defenders to follow that order than Joyhinia had in Testra.

'What do you suggest, Denjon?'

'I was hoping you'd have a suggestion,' he told her with a shrug. 'You seem to have an answer for everything else these days.'

R'shiel frowned. 'You think I can just wave my arm and solve all your problems for you?'

'That's what the Harshini do, isn't it?'

'That is your prejudice speaking, Captain,' Brak warned. 'It does not help your cause to let it get in the way.'

Denjon turned on the Harshini but R'shiel intervened before things could escalate into a full-blown argument.

'Why can't we just release them?'

'Because they'll be on our trail within hours.'

'No, they won't. Their Crown Prince and their Duke are dead. They'll have to go home to return the bodies to Karien, at least. They may send out a party to hunt us down later, but it won't be this lot.'

Denjon looked thoughtful. 'You may be right, R'shiel, but I'm not sure I want to risk finding out the hard way that you're wrong.'

'What if I can guarantee they'll head home?'

'What are you thinking of doing?' Brak asked suspiciously. 'Coercing them?'

'No, of course not!'

'Then how do you plan to make nearly four hundred Karien knights turn on their tails and slink home?' Dorak asked. 'And they have the three priests with them who were accompanying Lord Setenton. *They'll* demand retribution, out of spite if nothing else.'

'Don't you see? As soon as the search party realises that Cratyn is dead, they will turn around and head straight back to Karien for guidance from the Overlord, dragging Drendyn, his knights and their priests behind them.'

'It's a nice thought, R'shiel,' Brak agreed. 'But the captain is right. You won't dissuade the priests so easily. You'd be better off just killing them outright.'

'How long do we have, Denjon, before the Kariens get here?'

'A day at the most, if we want to be gone before they

arrive. Two days if we plan to make a fight of it. I would advise against that. The end result will just be more damned Karien prisoners we have to worry about when the next search party comes looking for *them*.'

She nodded slowly. 'Brak, can Tarja be moved?'

The Harshini frowned. 'I wouldn't advise it, but it won't threaten his life, if that's what concerns you.'

'I don't think we have much choice in the matter,' she announced, figuring that if she sounded decisive, nobody would guess how uncertain she was. 'You should leave for Fardohnya, anyway. Can you get there on your own?'

Brak was watching her closely. If anyone suspected her uncertainty, it would be him. 'Don't worry about me, R'shiel. The demons will see me safely to Talabar.'

'Good. Denjon, you might as well give the order to break camp. Now that Damin and Adrina are married, we need to get to Hythria.'

'And the Kariens?' Denjon asked.

'I'll deal with them.' She glanced at Denjon and frowned. 'Do you have any questions?'

'I have one,' Linst replied. 'Who put you in charge of the Defenders?'

R'shiel turned on him impatiently. 'What Defenders, Linst? You ceased being Defenders the moment you stood back and did nothing when I killed Cratyn. You have defied your orders and taken two hundred Kariens prisoner. If you want to go back to being a lackey for Medalon's new masters, there's another couple of hundred heading this way. Perhaps you'd like to surrender?'

Linst glared at her. 'Just remember, R'shiel, we are following the Lord Defender's orders. He was the one who wanted us to fight the Kariens. I'll take orders from him, but I'll be damned if I'm going to sit back and let you order us around for some heathen purpose.'

'My *heathen purpose* is to throw the Kariens out of Medalon, Captain.'

'There's no point arguing among ourselves,' Denjon interceded. 'We've no choice, in any case. We have to move on. We can sort out the details once Tarja wakes up.'

'*If* he wakes up,' Linst added pointedly.

'He *will* wake up,' R'shiel insisted. 'And when he does, perhaps you'll decide you have a backbone, after all, Linst.'

She did not wait to hear his answer. She stormed from the tent, a part of her simmering with anger; another part of her grateful for the excuse to leave. On the way out she collided with young Mikel, the boy who had followed Adrina from Karien. He squealed in fright at her sudden appearance, landing on his backside in a puddle of icy mud, dropping the tray he carried. He seemed to do that a lot, she recalled, but was too preoccupied to do more than mutter an apology as she strode past the child.

Brak caught up with her near the infirmary.

'Don't you start on me,' she warned, before he could say a word.

'I wasn't going to. I'm on your side, remember?'

R'shiel slowed her pace a little and looked at him. 'I'm sorry. They just make me so angry sometimes.'

'I noticed.'

'I shouldn't let them get to me like that, should I?'

'Of course not, but you don't need me to tell you that. What I'd really like to know is what you're planning to do about those priests.'

She shrugged. 'I destroyed their staffs. How much trouble can they be?'

'A lot. They may not be able to threaten *you* any longer, but they still hold a great deal of sway over their people.' R'shiel didn't answer him. His faded blue eyes darkened for a moment and he shook his head. 'You're not going to kill them, are you?'

'No. I'll think of something else.' She resumed her angry pace and continued on towards the infirmary. An icy wind blew across the plain, stirring dust eddies on the scuffed ground and making her ears ache. She missed her long hair.

'Well, you'd better come up with something quickly,' Brak called after her. 'It'll take a miracle to turn that lot and time is of the essence.'

Suddenly she stopped and turned. 'That's it! Brak, you're a genius!'

He stared at her in confusion. The solution suddenly clear, she ran back, kissed his cheek and hugged him briefly. 'You're right! It's going to take a miracle!'

'What are you talking about?'

'I haven't time to explain,' she said, relief making her giddy.

'What are you thinking of doing, R'shiel?' Brak demanded, grabbing her arm to prevent her escaping.

'I'm going to work a miracle.'

'They won't fall for anything so transparent. Any miracle you conjure up will be dismissed as Harshini magic. You won't fool anyone, not even a bunch of knights as inexperienced as Drendyn and his friends.'

'Then I'll find someone they *will* believe in,' she said, pulling her arm free of him.

'Who? Adrina?'

'Of course not! I'll use . . . someone else . . . someone they'll trust . . .'

'Who?' Brak repeated suspiciously.

R'shiel glanced around, more to avoid meeting Brak's suspicious gaze than in any real hope of finding an answer to her dilemma. Her eyes alighted on the Karien boy, muttering miserably to himself as he picked up the shards of broken dishes that had fallen from his tray when R'shiel bumped into him.

'I'll use him,' she declared, pointing at Mikel.

# 4

Adrina's first thought on waking the morning after she married Damin Wolfblade was: *Gods, what have I done?*

She had thought the same thing on waking in Yarnarrow the morning after she married the late, unlamented, Crown Prince of Karien, too. *There is a disturbing pattern emerging here*, she decided.

'Good morning.'

Adrina turned towards the voice. Damin was already up and dressed and pulling on his high leather boots. She was extremely suspicious of anybody who could be so alert, so early in the morning.

'What's so good about it?'

Damin grinned. It was one of his more annoying habits. He seemed to find most of what she said amusing. In Fardohnya, her moods affected the whole palace. Lords and Ladies tiptoed around her. Even in Karien, they had trod warily to avoid incurring her wrath.

'Are you always so unpleasant first thing in the morning?' he inquired.

She sat up on the pallet, drawing the blankets up to

hide her nakedness. 'Why, in the name of the gods, did I marry you?'

Damin stamped his feet into his boots and reached for his sword-belt. 'Because the demon child ordered you to. And you are a grasping, conniving little bitch,' he added pleasantly.

'And your motives are *so* much more honourable,' she retorted.

'Naturally,' he agreed. 'I just want to stay alive long enough to be High Prince of Hythria, one day.'

'Pardon me, Your *highness*.'

He laughed, which annoyed her even more, and walked to the tent flap. He stopped and turned before he left. 'I sent your little Karien friend to fetch you some breakfast. He should be back soon.'

'Where are you going?'

'I'm supposed to be meeting with R'shiel and the Defenders and I'm already late.'

'Well don't try blaming your tardiness on me.'

'I wouldn't dream of it, my dear.'

'And stop calling me that! I am not your *dear*.'

His only answer was more laughter as he ducked through the entrance. Adrina flopped back onto the pallet angrily. When she left Cratyn, she swore she would never allow herself to be forced into marriage again; swore she would never allow a man that much control over her. She had made that promise to herself last autumn.

The winter wasn't even over and she had broken it already.

When there was still no sign of Mikel or Tamylan an hour later, Adrina gave up waiting and dressed herself, determined to give both her slave and her page a piece of her mind. Did they think that now she was married, that absolved them of their duties?

There was going to have to be a few things cleared up before too much longer, she decided. Her status, for one thing. She was a princess in her own right, more royal than Damin in fact, who was merely the nephew of a prince. *Her* father was a king. Of course, being a woman was something of a hindrance to her claim to the throne, although there were many who would be anxious to lay claim to any son that she might bear.

Except R'shiel. The demon child was impatient and had been raised in a society where women ruled. She had no time for Adrina to bear a son and raise him to manhood. She wanted to unite Hythria and Fardohnya and she wanted to do it *now*. She did not care about the patriarchal traditions of Fardohnya, any more than she cared whether or not Adrina wanted to marry Damin. Their union would force peace on the two southern nations and that was the only thing the demon child cared about. It did not seem to concern her that more than likely, when they reached Greenharbour, the other Warlords would hire assassins to kill either Adrina, or Damin, or both of them.

Hablet's rage on learning of her marriage did not bear thinking about.

On the other hand, if the demon child's ambitious plan succeeded, Adrina would know more power than she had ever imagined. As she thought about that possibility, Adrina began to wonder if she was going about this the wrong way. Damin seemed, if not exactly fond of her, then at least anxious to share her bed. And even Adrina was willing to admit that after a lifetime of paid *court'esa* and the pathetic attempts of her last husband to consummate their marriage, Damin was a pleasant change. *Too* pleasant, in fact. Once they reached Hythria, she would insist on her own quarters and make sure they could be locked, she decided firmly. If she couldn't keep him out of her bed by willpower alone, then perhaps a physical barrier would help.

That raised another uncomfortable thought. She had fled Karien with little more than the clothes on her back. The herbs she kept hidden in her trunk were still back in Karien and she had fallen into bed with Damin Wolfblade in a moment of blind and foolish weakness. She had done nothing since then to prevent conception and in the confusion of their escape, had lost track of the days since her last moon-time.

She would have to speak to Tamylan. Regardless of what the demon child wanted, Adrina had no intention of bringing a child into this world who could be used as a political pawn.

When Adrina finally emerged from her tent it was to discover the whole camp in turmoil. Everywhere she looked the Defenders were pulling down tents and hurrying to and fro, shouting orders and packing up their gear, obviously determined to demolish their campsite as quickly as possible. The Defenders ignored her in the confusion as she wandered through the camp, sidestepping men and piled up equipment. When she finally reached the officers' mess tent, one of the few not in danger of imminent destruction, she poked her head inside. The cooks were busy preparing lunch and paid her no attention until she addressed them directly. Even then, she had to ask twice.

'Where is Lord Wolfblade?'

The closest cook looked up and shrugged. The man beside him jerked his head in a generally northward direction. 'He went off with the heathens. One of them is leaving, I think.'

The heathens, presumably, were Brak and R'shiel. She did not bother to thank the man, but followed his directions until she reached the edge of the camp. She spied Damin with Brak, then R'shiel and young Mikel, of all people, some fifty paces away. She had opened her mouth to call out to them when a remarkable thing happened.

One minute they were standing there talking, the next they were surrounded by little grey demons who seemed to pop out of thin air. There were too many to count and they clustered around Brak, vying for his attention like small children visiting with a favoured uncle. Mikel backed away from them warily, but the adults did not seem in the least concerned. Brak squatted down and spoke to one of the demons, who listened intently with big, liquid black eyes. The little creature nodded, then waddled a small distance away. Without any signal that Adrina could see, the other demons suddenly turned and ran to join the one Brak had spoken to.

Adrina blinked as the demons clustered around their leader and began to dissolve. That was the only word Adrina could think of to describe what was happening. They seemed to become fluid, as one by one they flowed together until the towering form of a dragon took shape, with metallic green scales and delicate, silver-tipped wings that glittered under the sullen sky.

When the dragon was complete, Brak reached up and scratched the bony ridge over its plate-sized eyes. With a final word to R'shiel he climbed onto the back of the magnificent beast. With a couple of powerful beats of its massive wings, the dragon was airborne, banking slowly to the left as it headed south.

Damin turned then and saw her.

'Brak asked me to say goodbye,' he told her when he reached the place where she was standing, open-mouthed, as she watched the dragon dwindle into the distance.

'That was . . . astonishing . . .' she managed to say.

'Well, let's hope your father is just as impressed,' R'shiel added as she and Mikel came up beside them.

'A dragon landing in the courtyard of the Summer Palace should get his attention,' Adrina agreed with a faint smile. Then she turned to Mikel. Even the sight of the stunning demon-melded dragon had not made her forget the boy had been lax in his duties. 'Where have you been, child? Lord Wolfblade sent you to get my breakfast.'

'I—' Mikel began, but R'shiel came to his defence.

'I asked him to help me with something,' she explained. 'You might have to find yourself another page for a while, Adrina.'

R'shiel took Mikel's hand and walked back towards the camp, leaving Adrina wide-eyed and more than a little put out.

'Did you have a hand in this?' she demanded of Damin.

He shrugged and looked almost as puzzled as she was. 'It's the first I've heard of it. But it's not a bad idea. I'm going to have enough trouble explaining away a Fardohnyan bride when we get to Hythria, without having a Karien page to worry about.'

'I can't just abandon the child!' she protested.

'Isn't that what you were planning to do with him when you first crossed the border?'

She glared at him, annoyed that he was right, even

more annoyed that he had guessed her intentions. 'It's not the same thing.'

'Of course not,' he agreed drily.

'Don't you dare take that tone with me!'

'Then don't treat me like a fool,' he retorted. 'Are you still hungry? You've missed breakfast, but I'm sure we could prevail upon the cooks for an early lunch.'

'I will not be patronised like a small child!'

'Stop looking for a fight, Adrina. Did you want to eat or not?'

Adrina was about to explode with fury when her stomach rumbled complainingly. Damin heard it clearly and laughed at her. 'I'll take that as a yes. Come on, you'll fight better on a full stomach.'

'This is intolerable! I am not going to spend the rest of my life having you laugh at me.'

Damin's amusement faded and he looked at her closely. 'Then drop this spoiled princess act. There doesn't seem much point any more.'

'It's not an act!'

'The hell it isn't.'

'You don't know the first thing about me.'

'Don't I?'

'No!'

'Shall I tell you what I do know about you, Adrina?' he asked, suddenly more serious than she had ever seen him. 'You were smart enough to keep the Karien Crown Prince out of your bed so you couldn't conceive an heir. You ordered your troops to surrender rather than see them slaughtered. You rode as hard as I ever pushed my own men without a complaint, because you knew your life depended on it.

'You are not who you pretend to be, Adrina, and it

defies logic that you keep on pretending you are a fool. You're an intelligent woman, yet you insist on hiding it behind tantrums and childish, idiotic demands. I don't know why you do it. Perhaps it's because you grew up in a court where a smart woman was a dangerous one. The truth is, I don't really care. But if you want to survive as High Princess of Hythria, then you'd better learn to use that brain of yours for something other than causing mischief.'

His words stunned her into silence. She had no answer, could think of nothing to say. Never for a moment had she suspected that Damin's suspicion and mistrust was based on how clever he thought she was.

He waited for a moment, expecting her to retort with some sarcastic rejoinder. If her silence amused him, he did not let it show.

'Come on,' he said finally. 'I missed breakfast too.'

## 5

Mikel had to run to keep up with R'shiel's long-legged stride. Although she had him by the hand, she paid him no further attention as they wound through the chaotic camp. With his free hand he wiped his nose, which was tingling in the brisk wind. He was still too much in awe of the demon-melded dragon he had just witnessed to be concerned where R'shiel might be taking him.

The order to break camp had only been issued a few hours ago, but already most of the tents were packed, only the larger infirmary and mess tents and those belonging to the senior officers remained standing. The Defenders were keen to be gone from this place and anxious to avoid the approaching Kariens. Mikel had seen enough to understand that it was not fear of the Kariens that prompted the Medalonians' haste, but that they wanted to avoid the inconvenience of taking even more prisoners.

Mikel's entire system of beliefs had been stretched beyond credulity in the past few weeks. First Princess Adrina had betrayed the prince. Then Prince Cratyn had proved to be as callous and vicious as any other man in his desire to murder his wife for her treachery. His own brother Jaymes had joined the Hythrun and his best friend Dace had turned out to be the God of Thieves. Then, with hardly any objections, Adrina had married Lord Wolfblade.

And now the fabled demon child had commandeered his services. This tall, impatient young woman whom demons followed around like puppies and whom everyone treated with a great deal of trepidation.

'My lady?'

'Yes?'

'What did you want me to do?'

R'shiel stopped suddenly and smiled down at him. 'I want you to help me with something, Mikel. Something magic.'

'Is it going to get me into trouble?'

The demon child laughed softly. 'I have to convince the Kariens they want to go home, and that means turning even the priests from the Overlord's path for a time. Are you afraid?'

Mikel frowned. 'I don't think so. I've turned from my God. I let you kill my Prince. I've honoured the God of Thieves. I don't think I'm much of anything, any more.'

R'shiel placed a comforting hand on his shoulder. 'Mikel, I think you'll find that you are far more worthy than you imagine.'

Mikel wanted to believe her. She was the demon child, after all. Perhaps she knew things he did not. But it seemed unlikely.

'If you say so, my lady.'

R'shiel smiled again but did not answer for a time. When she spoke again, her question took him completely by surprise. 'Mikel, who did the Kariens follow before Xaphista came along?'

'The priests said they worshipped false gods,' he told her, 'just as Hythria and Fardohnya still do.'

'Yes, but there must have been one that was predominant. Zegarnald has a pretty firm grip on Hythria and Jelanna seems to be the most popular goddess in Fardohnya.'

'The only one I ever heard of was Leylanan,' Mikel replied after a moment's thought.

'What is he the god of?'

'She, not he. Leylanan was the Goddess of the River.'

'I thought that was Maera?' R'shiel said.

'Leylanan was the Goddess of the Ironbrook River. Maybe Maera is the Goddess of the Glass River.'

R'shiel was silent for a moment then shook her head. 'No, she won't do. I need someone else.'

Mikel wasn't sure he understood, or even if R'shiel was addressing him. She sounded as if she was simply thinking aloud.

'Do you really think you can turn the priests from the Overlord, my lady?'

'I have to.'

Mikel had the impression that once set on an idea, R'shiel was determined to make it happen. He had no idea what she was planning, and certainly no idea what his role would be.

'Lord Laetho used to say that you've more chance of making a Karien dance a heathen jig naked in the moonlight than you have of turning him from his God,' he offered helpfully.

'Maybe I should call on the God of Music, then,' R'shiel grumbled, obviously not pleased that things were not going according to plan.

'Do the Harshini *have* a God of Music?' he asked curiously.

'Gimlorie is the God of Music, Mikel, and he is as insubstantial and ephemeral as music itself. When I was in Sanctuary, the Harshini would call on him sometimes. His song is the most beautiful thing I have ever heard. It touches men's souls . . .'

Mikel stared at R'shiel as a slow, devious smile crept over her face. 'Music of any kind is frowned upon in Karien, my lady. It's a sin,' Mikel added.

R'shiel looked down at him and smiled. 'Not any more, it isn't.'

She grabbed his hand suddenly and led him away from the direction of the infirmary tent, leaving him even more confused.

'My lady?' he ventured, as he hurried along beside her through the organised chaos that was all that was left of the Defenders' camp. It seemed as if most of it had vanished into the supply wagons while they were talking.

'You don't have to keep calling me that, Mikel. My name is R'shiel.'

'It wouldn't be proper, my lady. Where are we going?'

'We're going to summon the God of Music, Mikel.'

'Why?'

R'shiel looked down at him and smiled reassuringly. 'He's going to teach you how to sing.'

Mikel didn't know whether to be frightened by R'shiel or not. She had never done him any harm; in fact she had virtually ignored him up until this morning, when she suddenly decided she needed him for some yet-to-be-revealed task. She was all but dragging him towards the tents where the Hythrun Raiders were accommodated.

'Almodavar!'

The savage-looking Hythrun turned at the sound of her voice.

'Divine One?'

'Please don't call me that. Where is Mikel's brother?'

'Young Jaymes? Down with the horses helping Nercher if he knows what's good for him,' the captain replied. 'Has he done something I should know about?'

'No. But I'd like to see him. Can you send him to me?'

The captain nodded and turned to give the order to fetch Jaymes. Mikel glanced at R'shiel curiously.

'What do you want with Jaymes, my Lady?'

'You're going to learn a song, Mikel. Jaymes is going to be there to make sure you don't get lost in it.'

'I see,' Mikel said, nodding sagely, although in truth he understood nothing at all.

## 6

By early afternoon, the Defenders were ready to move out. That morning, the camp had been the size of a small town. Now there was nothing left but a large area of trampled grass to mark their passing. He knew they had been setting up and pulling down the camp each day while they travelled north from the Citadel. The late Lord Setenton enjoyed his creature comforts and would have it no other way, but in the two weeks they had spent camped on the plain they had settled in so comfortably, Damin found it hard to believe they could dismantle it all with such speed.

His own Raiders took less time to organise, but they were fewer and had been travelling much more lightly than the Defenders. Almodavar had had them ready to leave hours ago. What kept them here now were the Kariens.

His men formed a mounted ring around the captured knights, bows strung, arrows at the ready, waiting for one of them to break. Damin didn't know why they were holding the Kariens here while the Defenders went on ahead, and a part of him was afraid to ask. He knew as well as anyone the dilemma these prisoners posed. That the Defenders were leaving them behind did not augur well for their future.

Karien they might be, but Damin held no personal grudge against them. They all seemed woefully young and inexperienced to him. The oldest of them could not have been more than twenty. He prayed fervently that R'shiel did not expect him to slaughter these children in cold blood.

'What are we waiting for?'

Adrina rode up beside him with her slave close behind. She was wrapped in a warm cloak against the cold and looked anxious to get moving. She had been remarkably quiet since their conversation on the edge of the camp this morning. That worried Damin a little. She was undoubtedly plotting something and it probably involved him and a lot of blood. He should have kept his big mouth shut.

'We're waiting for R'shiel, I think. And for the Defenders to move out.'

'Where is the demon child, anyway?'

Damin shrugged. 'Nobody's seen her for hours.'

Adrina looked at the nervous Kariens. They had been pushed into a tight cluster, ringed by the Raiders and to a man they wore expressions of uncertainty. Damin could imagine what was going through their minds.

'What's going to happen to them?'

'I don't know.'

'You're not going to . . .'

'Kill them? I wish I knew.' He turned in the saddle at the sound of hoofs and found Denjon and Linst riding towards them at a canter. The red-coated Defenders reined in when they reached them.

'We're ready to move out,' Denjon informed them.

'How's Tarja?'

'Much the same. He's in one of the wagons with a medic. We'll be setting a hard pace, I'm afraid, but it can't be avoided.'

'How long will it take you to reach the border?'

'About six weeks,' the captain replied. 'We could get there sooner if we dumped the supply wagons, but I'm loath to do that, for obvious reasons. We'll only resort to that if we're being pursued.' The captain glanced meaningfully at the Karien prisoners. 'I hope this works.'

'You hope what works?' Adrina asked.

'R'shiel's grandiose plan for turning the Kariens back,' he said.

'And what is that, exactly?'

'We don't know and I'm not sure we want to,' Linst remarked. 'She asked that we be gone before she does it, so we can only assume it's some heathen ritual she'd rather we didn't witness.'

'Heathen ritual or not, I can't say I'll mind missing it,' Denjon said. Then he reached forward and offered Damin his hand. 'I wish you luck, Lord Wolfblade.'

'You'll need it more than I,' Damin said, accepting the handshake. 'With all your troops and the Kariens concentrated in the north, weather permitting I'll have a clear run down to Hythria. You're the ones taking the long road.'

'I was thinking more of what happens when you *get* to Hythria,' Denjon said with a grin.

'I'll worry about that when I get there.'

'Then I'll look forward to meeting you again on your side of the border. For all our sakes I hope it goes well for you, my lord. And for you too, Your highness.'

'Thank you, Captain.'

Damin glanced at Adrina curiously. Her thanks sounded genuine. There was no hint of her usual sarcastic tone. Something was seriously wrong with her.

Denjon and Linst wheeled their mounts around and cantered back towards the long line of red-coated Defenders. They watched them leave in silence, watched Denjon ride to the head of the column, and heard the faint sound of the trumpet signalling their advance as it was whipped away on the icy wind.

'So what happens now?' Adrina asked after a while.

Damin shrugged. 'We wait for the demon child.'

When R'shiel arrived more than an hour later, she was on foot and the two Karien boys were with her. Damin and Adrina both dismounted when they caught sight of her. She was chatting to Mikel and Jaymes as they walked across the trampled grass towards them, the three of them apparently in a fine mood and the best of friends. When she reached them, she was smiling broadly.

'The Defenders got away all right then?' she asked.

'About an hour ago,' Damin informed her. 'Where have you been?'

'Communing with the gods,' she told him with a grin. 'Let's do something about these Kariens, shall we?'

Damin grabbed her arm as she turned towards the prisoners. 'What are you going to do, R'shiel?'

'You'll see.'

Without waiting for his reaction she pulled her arm free and taking Mikel's hand, walked toward the Kariens. Jaymes followed after them. The lad had filled out since he had been training with the Hythrun. At fifteen he was the size of a full-grown man. Any animosity that had existed between the brothers seemed to have been put to rest. That odd turn of events bothered Damin almost as much as what R'shiel might be planning.

Almodavar turned and dismounted at R'shiel's approach. Damin and Adrina threw their reins to Tamylan and hurried after her on foot. The Kariens, sensing something was about to happen, began to grow restless. Those who had tired of standing and were sitting on the cold ground climbed to their feet. The priests pushed to the front of the group, tracing the star of the Overlord on their foreheads as they regarded the demon child with intense suspicion.

'Where is Lord Drendyn?' R'shiel called to the Kariens as she stopped before them. The knight in question pushed his way through the crowd and stepped in front of her belligerently. He was sandy haired and sweating, despite the cold, and looked hardly older than Jaymes.

'I demand you release us immediately and hand over the Crown Princess Adrina so that she may be returned to Karien.'

Damin suspected the young knight's bravado was inspired by fear. His Raiders, with their loaded bows and fearsome reputation, still ringed the Kariens. He had only to raise his arm and there would be a massacre.

'As you wish,' R'shiel replied. 'Lord Wolfblade, be so kind as to ask your men to withdraw. Tell them to muster over that way, upwind from us.'

At a nod from Damin, Almodavar gave the order. The Raiders lowered their weapons, replaced arrows in their quivers and wheeled their mounts around. Drendyn looked stunned by her sudden capitulation.

'Is this some sort of trick?'

'Not at all, my Lord, you are free to go. There is a party of Karien knights headed this way. They should be here in a day or two. The Defenders have confiscated your horses, unfortunately, but they have left you sufficient food and water to last until you're rescued.'

'And our princess?'

'Ah, now that's a different matter. She's not actually your princess any longer. Adrina is now a Princess of Hythria.'

Drendyn's eyes widened in horror. 'Your highness? Is this true?'

Damin glanced at Adrina, who looked very uncomfortable. 'I'm sorry, Drendyn . . .' Adrina said with a helpless shrug. To Damin's surprise, she appeared genuinely upset that she had hurt the young man.

'And you can give your king a message from me, too,' he added, turning to the distraught young earl. 'Any attempt to return the princess to Karien will be taken as an act of war.'

'But they murdered Prince Cratyn!' Drendyn cried to Adrina then turned on Damin furiously, taking a step towards him, ready to fight for his princess's honor. 'What have you done to her?'

'That's far enough, my Lord,' Almodavar cut in, his sword pressing into the young earl's tabard. Drendyn halted abruptly, looked down at the blade aimed squarely at his heart and wisely took a step backward.

'Hythria will pay for the life of my prince. And my princess!' he shouted, albeit from a safer distance.

'Perhaps,' Damin agreed. 'But not today, my young friend.'

'Enough of this,' R'shiel declared impatiently. 'Damin, I suggest you move back. I have something I wish to do before we leave.'

'Something you don't want us to see?'

'Not at all. You can watch if you like, but I'd rather you didn't hear it.'

'The Overlord will protect us from your evil, demon child,' the priest Garanus warned.

Captivity had not been kind to the priest. His shaven head was covered in black stubble and his cassock was rumpled and dusty. The priests who stood behind him had fared no better. Damin considered his threat rather hollow. Without their staves the priests were simply ordinary men.

'The Overlord has abandoned you, Garanus. Why else would he let you fall prisoner?'

'We will not listen to your blasphemy!'

'Suit yourself,' R'shiel said with a shrug. 'Damin, you should leave now.'

'What about Mikel and Jaymes?' Adrina asked, almost as wary as Damin about what the demon child was planning.

'They'll be fine with me.'

Damin still had no idea what she was up to. With some reluctance, he did as she asked. Taking Adrina's hand he headed back to where Tamylan was waiting with the horses. Almodavar mounted and followed them at a walk. Damin swung into the saddle and turned to watch as R'shiel stood facing the Kariens.

'What is she going to do?' Adrina asked as she settled into her saddle and gathered up her reins.

'You know as much as I do.'

'Drendyn was the only person in Karien who treated me like a human being,' she added, staring at the gathering with concern.

That explained her apology to the young knight.

'If she was planning to kill them, she would have done it by now.' It was a hollow reassurance at best. For all he knew that was exactly what R'shiel was planning.

'Or she would wait until there were no witnesses,' Almodavar pointed out.

'She said something about not listening,' Adrina said. 'What could she possibly say to them—'

As if in answer to her question a voice reached them. It was high, pure and perfect and the song it sang touched the very core of Damin's soul. It took him a moment to realise that it was Mikel singing. He could not hear the words; the wind tore them away before he could make them out, but he sat there, rigid, as the lilting notes washed over him in haunting snatches. The song was both enticing and entrancing. It slithered into his brain like sweet wine being poured into an empty cup. It warmed and chilled him at the same time. Visions of a land he didn't know filled his mind and he found himself yearning for it with a passion that took him by surprise. The song made him want to laugh and cry simultaneously. He wanted to hear more. It was fear and comfort on the same breath. Love and hatred intermingled. He never wanted it to end.

'Damin! We have to move! Now!'

It was Adrina who jerked him back to reality. He glanced at the prisoners and realised that whatever remarkable effect the song had on him, the effect it was having on the Kariens was a hundred times more powerful. As he turned his mount and urged him into a gallop, wisps of the song followed him with tantalising fingers.

Then the tenor of the music changed and no longer did he wish to drown in the beauty of the song. Now it was much more strident, its beauty marred by dark, shadowy images that chased him until they were far enough away that the music no longer reached them.

Once they were safely out of range, they turned and looked back at the Kariens. R'shiel stood before the captive knights, but they could not make out her expression from this distance. Mikel stood beside her, singing to the Kariens in that glorious, unnatural voice that seduced and tormented at once.

Jaymes seemed unaffected, his hand resting on his brother's shoulder, as if he was holding him down against the wind, but the rest of the Kariens were transfixed. Some men were weeping, some were frozen to the spot. The priest Garanus was on his knees, his hands over his ears. The young knight Drendyn was staring at the boy as if he was experiencing some sort of religious ecstasy. All around him, his men seemed to be in the throes of either torment or rapture.

'What was that? What is she doing?' Damin asked.

'The Song of Gimlorie,' Adrina told him, her eyes fixed on the Kariens, her voice filled with awe.

'That's simply a legend,' Almodavar scoffed.

'No. It's real enough. My father tried to get some of the priestesses to perform it in Talabar once. He thought it would guarantee him a legitimate son. None of the temples would even consider the idea, and he offered them a fortune in gold to do it. They all claimed it was too dangerous.'

'So how did Mikel learn it?'

'R'shiel obviously had a hand in that.' Adrina turned to him then, her expression thoughtful. 'You know, if the legends are correct, he who sings the Song of Gimlorie is a channel for the gods.'

'I can well believe it,' Damin agreed, thinking of the effect that even catching part of the song had on him.

They waited in silence after that, until R'shiel ordered Mikel to stop singing. Mikel sagged, as if the song had drained him completely. His brother gently gathered the unconscious child up in his arms and together with R'shiel walked back across the plain towards them.

# 7

Despite Adrina's confident assurance that landing in the main courtyard of the Summer Palace was bound to get Hablet's attention, Brak chose to make a less dramatic entrance into Talabar. He landed his demonmelded dragon some distance north of the capital on a warm, muggy afternoon three days after he left Medalon, and set out for the city on foot.

He was not well prepared for the journey, though he wasn't worried about his lack of resources. Once he shed his winter layers of clothing, he turned onto the road and began heading south towards the sprawling pink metropolis, secure in the knowledge that several hundred years of living on his wits left him well equipped to handle anything a Fardohnyan could throw at him.

Brak had eschewed his Harshini heritage for many years, but he was not averse to using a little magic when it was for a good cause. As his *only* cause these days seemed to be aiding the demon child, he felt justified in taking a few liberties with his power that would have horrified his full-blooded cousins.

Since he had no local currency and was not looking

forward to walking all the way to Talabar, he prevailed upon the Lady Elanymire to meld herself into a large uncut ruby. He then traded the ruby to a merchant from a passing caravan, whose eyes lit up with greed when Brak offered him the gem for a horse, a saddle, some basic supplies, and a small bag of coin.

Any guilt Brak may have felt over the transaction vanished when he saw the state of the merchant's slaves. They were underfed and miserable, their bare feet blistered from trudging the gravelled road in the heat. Even the richly dressed *court'esa* who sat on the seat of the gaily-covered lead wagon wore a look of abject misery.

Brak rode away on his newly purchased horse content that the merchant deserved everything that was coming to him. The following morning, Lady Elanymire popped into existence on the pommel of his saddle, laughing delightedly at the expression on the avaricious merchant's face when he discovered his prized ruby had vanished.

Fardohnya had a timeless quality about it. The people were still dusky, smiling, dark-haired souls who seemed, if not content, then accepting of their lot in life. It always struck him as odd that the Fardohnyans were so cheerful. Perhaps it was because their king, while grasping, devious and deceitful, at least understood that a happy population was a quiet one. Hablet wisely confined his more outrageous excesses to his court and Fardohnya's neighbours.

Slaves waved to him as he passed them in fields of rich black loam as they planted carefully tended green shoots of altaer and filganar before the onset of the spring rains. The grains were native to Fardohnya and the staple diet of much of the population. In Brak's experience, they would grow anywhere there was enough heat and water.

Famine was unheard of in Fardohnya; another reason the people didn't seem to mind what their king was up to. It is easy to be forgiving with a full belly.

Talabar came into sight the third day after Brak had traded his demon-melded ruby. Built from the pale pink stone of the neighbouring cliffs, it glittered in the afternoon sun, hugging the harbour like a woman curled into the back of her sleeping lover. Flat-roofed houses terraced the hills surrounding the bay, interspersed with palm-shaded emerald green parks and the tall edifices of the many temples that dotted the city. It was a beautiful city, not so stark and white as Greenharbour, or so grey and depressing as Yarnarrow. Only the Citadel in its heyday could rival its splendour.

It had been many years since Brak had been here. The last time he'd travelled incognito, another faceless soul in a vast city that thought his race extinct. The time before that was when Hablet's great-grandfather was king. He had been known as Lord Brakandaran in those days – feared and respected by kings and slaves alike. He hadn't much liked being known as Brakandaran the Halfbreed, but it was a useful persona at times and, he hoped, in certain circles at least, it had not been forgotten.

Brak rode through the gates of the city without being questioned. The guards were more interested in those bringing wagons, which the soldiers searched with varying degrees of enthusiasm, depending on the wealth of the merchant and the size of the bribe they would collect to turn a blind eye. Corruption was something of an institution in Fardohnya. No self-respecting merchant expected to do business without paying somebody something.

He rode through the crowded streets and let the feel of the city wash over him. One could learn much from the atmosphere of a crowded market place, a boisterous tavern or a bustling smithy. He picked his way past the glassworks, where furnaces glowed red in the dark, cavernous workshops; past the noisy meatworks where the butchers sang their thanks to the Goddess of Plenty before slashing the throats of their hapless victims with an expert flick of their wickedly sharp knives.

Talabar felt much the same as it always had. He could detect nothing out of the ordinary.

His horse shied from the smell of fresh blood that drained from the slaughterhouses into Talabar's complex underground drains. From there it ran into the sea to feed vast schools of fish, who gorged themselves on the unexpected bounty, only to head lazily back out to sea where the fishermen waited with their long hemp nets.

The streets widened as he entered the clothing district, although the traffic did not thin noticeably. The clackety-clack of the looms in the busy workhouses filled the air like a pulse. A few streets later he was forced to dismount. He smiled as he led his gelding past a heated argument between a merchant, whose wagonload of baled wool had overturned and spilled across the street, and a very large, irate seamstress who was denouncing the poor fellow and his drunken habits loud enough to be heard back in Medalon.

Brak swung back into the saddle and soon entered a relatively quiet residential area. The streets were paved and the houses, although built close together, were those of prosperous merchants. They were not quite wealthy enough to own estates close to the harbour, and preferred to live near their places of business in any case. Their houses were in good repair, and many of them had slaves sweeping the pavement in front of the houses, or beating rugs from wide balconies that looked out over the street, and were shaded by potted palms and climbing bougainvillea.

By mid-morning he reached the most salubrious part of Talabar, closest to the harbour and the Summer Palace. A hundred generations of Fardohnyan kings, anxious to curry favour with the gods, had dedicated themselves to building ever more impressive temples in this city. Jelanna was Hablet's personal favourite, so her temple had received the bulk of the king's largesse. It had been faced with marble since Brak saw it last and an impressive pair of fluted columns now supported an elaborate portico carved with cavorting demons at the entrance. It had done him little good, Brak knew. Despite almost thirty years of trying, he had yet to produce a legitimate son, although he had sired enough bastards to fill a small town.

Finally, Brak turned into a discreet, single-storey inn that sheltered almost directly under the high pink wall surrounding the Summer Palace. A slave hurried forward to take his mount in the shaded courtyard and he tipped the lad generously. There were slaves that owned more wealth than their masters in Fardohnya, and one could, if one chose to, purchase one's freedom. Many did not. There was a degree of job security in being a slave that was hard to beat in the uncertain world of the free man.

The interior of the inn was dim and cool, the entrance separated by a whitewashed trellis from the low hum of conversation emanating from the taproom. The owner hurried forward, took in Brak's travel-stained appearance, noticed the jingling purse tucked in his belt, did a quick mental calculation, then bowed obsequiously.

'My lord.'

Brak was quite certain he looked nothing like a nobleman in his current state, but the innkeeper was covering himself against the possibility that this new arrival was a gentleman of means.

'I require rooms,' he announced.

'Certainly, my lord. I have a vacancy in the north wing. It is closest to the palace walls. One can hear the joyous laughter of the princesses at play, if one listens closely.'

Brak thought that highly unlikely. 'I also need to contact someone from the Assassins' Guild.'

'Did you want anyone in particular?'

'I need to speak with the Raven.'

The little man's eyes narrowed. 'The head of the Assassins' Guild does not meet with just anybody, my lord.'

'He'll meet with me,' Brak assured him confidently.

'You know him then?'

'That's none of your business.' Actually, Brak had no idea who now held the post, and did not particularly care. The Assassins' Guild was simply the best source of intelligence in Fardohnya.

'Of course not, my lord!' he gushed, wringing his hands. Only the wealthiest of noblemen could afford to deal with the Assassins' Guild. Brak had just gone up considerably in the innkeeper's estimation. 'Forgive me for being so forward. I will show you to your rooms at once. If there is anything I can do . . .'

'You could be quiet, for a start,' Brak remarked coldly, already annoyed by the man.

'Of course, my lord! What was I thinking? Be quiet . . . Oh . . .' The innkeeper clamped his lips together when he noticed the look on Brak's face.

'That's better. Now, if you could show me the room? I want a bath too. And some lunch.'

The man nodded, wisely saying nothing further. With a snap of his fingers another slave hurried forward to show Brak to his rooms.

Much to Brak's surprise, the contact from the Assassins' Guild was a woman. Fardohnya was notoriously patri-archal and it was rare for a woman to hold any posi-tion of note. He was not even aware that they had changed the rules to admit women to the Guild. She was small and slender, the long, pale-green robe she wore concealing what Brak was certain would be a body in superb physical condition. It was hard to judge her age; she might have been twenty, or perhaps forty. Brak suspected the latter. Her eyes were too knowing, too cautious and too world-weary for her to be in the first bloom of youth.

She came to his rooms after dinner, knocking softly on the whitewashed door. He opened it cautiously and looked her up and down. On the middle finger of her left hand she wore the small gold raven ring of the Guild. While he privately considered it the height of arrogant stupidity to announce one's profession so openly, partic-ularly for an assassin, that he recognised the ring and admitted her without question went a long way to estab-lishing his credentials. He'd had a discussion once, with a previous Raven, about the foolishness of wearing some-thing so obvious, but humans liked their symbols and apparently the custom was as strong as ever. *Foolish humans.*

'What do you want with the Raven?' the woman asked, without preamble, looking around the room.

'I wish to speak to him.'

'The Raven doesn't speak to anyone.'

'He'll speak to me.'

She finished her inspection of the room and turned to look at him. 'So Gernard said.'

'Gernard?'

'The innkeeper.'

'Ah . . . can I offer you some wine?'

'No.'

She walked across the room and threw open the doors that led to the gardens, taking a deep breath of the fragrant air from the riot of flowering greenery. Brak was sure she was more interested in making certain they were not over-heard, than she was in botany.

'So, tell me,' she demanded, turning back to him as she stepped away from the open doorway, 'what is so special about you that the Raven would grant you an audience?'

'I am Brakandaran.'

She studied him for a moment in the twilight then laughed. 'Brakandaran the Halfbreed? I doubt that.'

'You require proof?'

'Oh, I'm certain you have proof,' she chuckled. 'Some mirrors and wires rigged to convince me of your magical powers. You have, however, neglected one minor point.'

'And what is that?'

'Brakandaran, if he was still alive, would be in his dotage now. It's been what . . . fifty years since he was here last? You can't be more than thirty-five. Forty at the most.'

'I'm half-Harshini,' he pointed out. 'I don't age like a human.'

She smiled. 'Very good! You even have an answer for

that one. I still don't believe you, but I do appreciate attention to detail.'

Brak found himself warming to the woman. She was sharp and not at all unattractive. But he was going to have to convince her, and probably the hard way.

'Very well, then,' he shrugged. 'You name the proof. Something I cannot possibly have anticipated. We can even go somewhere else, so that you can be assured I'm not using – what did you call them – mirrors and wires?'

'I really don't see why I should bother.'

'Can you afford to be wrong?'

She thought on that for a moment, then shook her head. She turned away from him, as if in thought, reaching into her robe. 'Proof, you say? Something unexpected?' She spun around, raising her arm. 'Try this!'

The quarrel from the small crossbow took Brak by surprise. He had guessed she was up to something, but had no time to react. Elanymire saved him. She popped into existence in front of him and snatched the missile from the air, chittering angrily at the woman.

The assassin dropped the weapon in surprise at the appearance of the little demon. 'How . . . ?'

'The demons live to protect the Harshini,' he pointed out with a shrug. He bent down and picked the demon up, stroking her leathery skin, trying to calm her. She took a very dim view of anyone trying to hurt a member of her clan and was all for vaporising the woman where she stood.

The assassin stared at him for a moment, as he stood there soothing the angry demon and then dropped to one knee. 'Divine One.'

Brak rolled his eyes. 'Oh, get up! I am *not* divine. But

I *do* want to see the Raven. Now that we've established who I am, do you think we could arrange it?'

She stood up and met his eyes.

'See *her*,' she corrected. 'The Raven is a woman. Her name is Teriahna.'

'Fine,' Brak agreed impatiently. 'Let's go see her, then.'

'You have seen her already, my Lord. I am Teriahna. I am the Raven.'

# 8

The first thing Tarja remembered on waking was that R'shiel was in danger. The thought hit him like a body blow and he jerked upright, only to discover he was tied to the wagon bed on which he lay. He could not understand how he came to be there. Nor did it make any sense that he was obviously moving. The wagon jolted beneath him, hitting a bump in the road and he cried out as his head slammed into the wagon bed.

'I think he's awake.'

Tarja was confronted by the odd spectre of a strange bearded face he did not recognise, which stared at him from the wagon seat. He struggled to sit up, but the ropes hampered his movement. The wagon halted and the man swung his legs around and squatted down beside Tarja, staring at him with concern.

'Captain? Sir? Do you know where you are?'

'Of course I don't know where I am,' Tarja croaked. All he could see was a leaden sky, the sides of the wagon and the face of the Defender bending over him. His voice was hoarse and he was thirsty enough to drink a well dry. 'Water. Get me water.'

The trooper hurried to fetch a water skin. Tarja coughed as cold water spilled down his parched throat.

'Am I a prisoner?' he asked.

'Not that they've told me, sir.'

'Then why the ropes?'

'Oh! Them? That was to stop you hurting yourself, sir. Soon as Cap'n Denjon gets here, we can untie you.'

'Denjon? Denjon is here?'

'Yes, he's here.' Tarja turned to the new voice and peered at the familiar face studying him over the side of the wagon. Denjon grinned at him. 'Welcome back.'

'What's happened? Where are we? Where's—'

'Slow down, Tarja,' Denjon cut in. 'Untie him, Corporal.'

The trooper did as he was ordered and quickly released the ropes that bound him. Tarja tried to sit up, appalled at the effort it took. He glanced around and was astonished to discover himself in the midst of a Defender column that snaked in front and behind the wagon as far as he could see. He did not recognise the countryside around him. They were no longer on the undulating grasslands of the north, but advancing through the lightly wooded plateau of central Medalon. The Sanctuary Mountains loomed too close to the west. Tarja shook his head in confusion.

'How are you feeling?'

'Weak as a kitten,' Tarja confessed. 'And completely lost. What's happened?'

'I'll explain what I can, but one thing at a time. We're about to make camp for the night. I'll fill you in over dinner.'

'Where's R'shiel?'

Denjon shrugged. 'On her way to Hythria, as are we,

my friend. Which reminds me. She gave me this before she left.' He reached into his red jacket and withdrew a sealed letter. 'She said I should give it to you when you woke up. It might explain a few things.'

He handed the letter to Tarja and remounted his horse, shouting an order to make camp as he cantered off. Tarja broke the seal on the letter anxiously, hoping the contents would throw some light on the confusion that was threatening to overwhelm him. He vaguely remembered a battle. He must have dreamt he had taken a sword in the belly, but nothing explained what he was doing tied to a wagon under an open sky, surrounded by Defenders.

The letter was written in R'shiel's impatient scrawl.

*Tarja*, it began without preamble. *If you are reading this, it means you survived. You were wounded trying to help me, and I tried to save your life. The Harshini part of me helped heal your wound, and the demons should do the rest. Brak says they'll leave you when you're well.*

He read the paragraph twice. Most of what she had written made no sense. He had been wounded, it seemed, and she had used her magic to heal him. He could not understand the part about the demons, though. Shaking his head, he read on.

*I have gone on ahead to Hythria with Damin and Adrina. I want their marriage to bring peace to the south, but I must support Damin in Hythria. I might learn about my destiny there, too. I'll explain why it's so important when I see you. Founders, how I hate being the demon child! I wish I could have stayed with you . . .*

*I sent Brak to Fardohnya to tell King Hablet that his daughter is now the future High Princess of Hythria. That might stop him invading Hythria through Medalon come spring.*

Tarja smiled. Damin and Adrina were married. He wondered what R'shiel had threatened them with to make that happen.

*You must know by now that I killed the Karien Prince and Lord Terbolt the morning after you tried to rescue me, so the Kariens will probably want my head even more now.*

*We've arranged to meet you all in Krakandar. From Damin's side of the border you'll be able to plan retaking Medalon. The thousand men you have now is too few to do anything but annoy the Kariens, but with Hythrun help, we'll make those Karien bastards pay for invading Medalon.*

*Denjon is on our side, but be careful of Linst.*

*R'shiel*

R'shiel had killed the Karien Crown Prince? Had she learnt nothing since their days in the rebellion? He read the letter again, wishing he could recall something – anything – of the past weeks. But Tarja's memories stopped abruptly at the point where he had fallen in battle and there was nothing in the intervening period but a black, featureless abyss.

Sitting around a small fire later that evening, Tarja got the rest of the story from Denjon and Linst. His head was reeling by the time they finished telling him of R'shiel's confrontation with the Karien priests, of her abrupt decision to accept the legacy of her Harshini blood and everything else that had happened since then.

They told him of the wound that almost killed him but could not explain either the absence of any evidence of the wound, or why he had lain unconscious for so long, other than they had instructions from R'shiel to restrain him for his own protection. Denjon spoke with awe of the demon-melded dragon that had taken Brak south, and of his uneasiness over the unknown fate of the Karien prisoners they had left behind.

'So that's about all there is to tell,' Denjon concluded with a shrug. 'When Lord Wolfblade told us that Lord Jenga had ordered you to mount a resistance against the Kariens, and with Lord Terbolt and the Karien Prince dead, it seemed prudent to follow the Lord Defender's orders.'

Tarja studied Denjon in the firelight. 'I'm not sure he planned for us to flee to Hythria.'

'We're risking our necks for you, Tarja. A bit of gratitude wouldn't go astray,' Linst grumbled.

'You don't sound very happy about this, Linst.'

'*Happy*? Of course I'm not *happy* about it. But I'm even less happy about taking orders from those Karien bastards, so here I am, ready to fight alongside a thousand other deserters. You know, Tarja, until you came along, nobody even thought of breaking their Defenders' oath. Now it's a bloody epidemic.' He threw the remains of his stew onto the fire and stood up. 'I have to check the sentries, although why we cling to Defender discipline is beyond me. It's not as if we're ever likely to be welcomed back into the Corps, is it?'

He stalked off into the darkness, leaving Tarja and Denjon staring after him.

'He always was a stickler for the rules,' Denjon remarked in the uncomfortable silence that followed.

'How many of the others feel like him?'

'Quite a few,' Denjon replied. 'He's right about one thing, though. It isn't easy for a Defender to walk away from his oath.'

'I never asked you to follow me, Denjon.'

The captain laughed humourlessly. 'No, *you* didn't. But

R'shiel set half the camp on fire just by waving her arm around, then turned on us, bursting with Harshini power and asked us what we were planning to do. Taking your side seemed the prudent thing to do at the time.'

He frowned. Something else bothered him about R'shiel, some feeling or emotion he could not place. A vague uneasiness that lingered on the edge of his mind, just out of reach.

'So, how far are we from Testra? That is where you're planning to cross the river, isn't it?'

Denjon nodded. 'Less than a week. Now you're up and about, we can make better time. Do you think you can sit on a horse?'

'I'm damned if I'm going to spend any more time in that wagon. I can ride.'

'Good. We've picked up quite a few of the Defenders you left the border with along the way. We number close to thirteen hundred now.'

'Thirteen hundred against the Karien host isn't many.'

'I know,' Denjon agreed. 'But that's where your Hythrun friends come in. With their help, we might have a chance.'

Sleep eluded Tarja for a long time that night. Waking from weeks of unconsciousness to find everything so radically changed was extremely disconcerting. He tossed and turned on the cold ground as the stars dwindled into dawn, trying to pin down the uneasiness that niggled at him like a tiny burr. Everything Denjon had told him, he reviewed over and over in his mind. But what bothered him came from another source. Something else was wrong . . . or different. Something that he could not define.

All he knew for certain was that it centred on R'shiel.

\* \* \*

After a full day in the saddle, Tarja realised how weak he was, but he was consumed by a restless energy that made it impossible for him to take the rest he needed. He could not understand the reason for his restive mood and the blank, dark hole in his memory unsettled him more than he was willing to admit.

All he could think of was getting to Hythria. His mind raced, making plans and rejecting them as he tried to figure the best way to hamper the Karien occupation force. The fact that he had no idea what sort of assistance they would receive from the Hythrun once they crossed the border made his task almost impossible. Damin might only be able to spare him a few centuries of Raiders, or he might be able to bring the full weight of the massive Hythrun war machine to his aid. There was simply no way to tell.

He drove Denjon mad when the other captain gave the order to make camp each evening, insisting they had at least another hour of daylight. Denjon was amused the first night, patient the second, and told him bluntly to mind his own business the third.

But Tarja's recovery seemed to bolster the morale of the men. He had been a popular officer once, known as a promising officer, a fair man and tipped to be the next Lord Defender. To see him back among them, wearing his red jacket and brimming with nervous energy, revived the spirits of men who up until then had had little more to do than contemplate their new status as outlaws.

Five days after Tarja woke, they were within sight of Testra. Tarja suggested sending an advance party forward to reconnoitre in the town, while the bulk of their force waited out of sight to avoid drawing attention to their number, although Denjon seemed certain that news of their desertion could not have reached this far south yet.

'We can't risk riding into Testra in force,' Tarja insisted.

'Yesterday you were all for riding through the night to get here. Now you want to add another day to the trip while you go sightseeing,' Linst complained.

'I don't *want* to wait,' Tarja corrected. 'I just think it would be stupid to reveal ourselves until we know we're in the clear. Besides, there's still a garrison in Testra. If they've heard of the surrender, they might want to join us.'

'Reluctant as I am to spend another day on this side of the river,' Denjon said, 'I'm afraid I agree with Tarja.'

Linst glared at both of them for a moment then shrugged. 'As you wish.'

When he left them, Denjon turned to Tarja. 'Do you think he's having second thoughts?'

'You can count on it,' Tarja agreed. 'Who's in command in Testra?'

'Antwon, I think.'

'I know him. He won't like the idea of surrender.'

'Not liking the idea of surrender is not the same as being willing to desert,' Denjon pointed out.

'Still, it's worth sounding him out. Every Defender we get out of Medalon now is another man we can put into the field later on.'

'Aye. And you'd best get some rest. You look ready to drop.'

'I'm fine.'

The practised lie came easily to him now. It was much simpler than trying to explain that he couldn't sleep, couldn't stop his mind from running around in circles, or prevent the confused images that flashed in front of his eyes, catching him unawares.

Something had happened to him. Something to do with R'shiel and her damned Harshini healing. But whenever he thought of R'shiel, a myriad conflicting and seemingly impossible memories surfaced. Some of them were real memories, he was certain of that. Others were like a nightmare. They were the ones where he imagined R'shiel in his arms. The ones where he loved her – not like the sister he had grown up believing her to be – but as her lover.

The absolute certainty that he would never feel that way towards his sister was the only thing that kept him sane.

## 9

'The main wharf looks new.'

Teriahna chuckled softly at Brak's comment. They were walking along the waterfront of Talabar amidst the morning bustle of the busy port, for no better reason than the privacy such a public place offered. The sun beat down on them and the wharves were crowded with frazzled-looking merchants and bare-chested, sweat-sheened sailors shouting boisterously at each other as they unloaded their cargoes.

'Ah, now there's a story behind that,' she told him as they sidestepped a gilded litter carried by four muscular slaves. 'The Princess Adrina tried her hand at sailing Hablet's flagship, the *Wave Warrior*, so the story goes, and ended up ramming the dock. If you believe the rumours that's why Hablet packed her off to Karien.'

'And if you don't believe the rumours?'

'Then he married her to Cratyn because Adrina, more than any of his children, is cast in the same mould as her father. If he was up to something nasty and needed an ally in Karien, Adrina would be the one for the job.'

Brak did not offer any further comment on Adrina.

He had not told Teriahna the news he carried from Medalon. As far as anyone in Fardohnya knew, Adrina was still in the north. That Cratyn was dead, Adrina now married to Lord Wolfblade and that Hablet's eldest base-born son was a casualty of the Karien-Medalonian war, was news he would prefer not to break until Adrina was safely across the border into Hythria, where Damin could protect her from her father's wrath.

'So, what do you know to be *fact* about Hablet's treaty with Karien?'

'Not much more than anyone else, I'm afraid,' she admitted. 'He gave them the Isle of Slarn, we know that for certain, and there's been no shortage of timber for shipbuilding since the Princess left. According to the treaty, he's supposed to attack Medalon from the south come the northern spring, and he's certainly mustering his army for an invasion.'

'But?' Brak asked, sensing there was more she had not told him.

'But he's got his officers studying Hythria, not Medalon.'

'You think he seriously intends to invade Hythria?'

'He's never likely to have a better chance. He can't go over the Sunrise Mountains – Tejay Lionsclaw makes certain of that. The Hythrun defend their ports too well to risk a naval invasion, and until the Kariens declared war on their neighbour, Medalon had the Defenders to deter him from taking that route. But with the Defenders tied up on their northern border, and the Warlord of Krakandar up there with them, Hythria is wide open.'

Brak nodded. Adrina had said almost the same thing.

'Why is Hablet so determined to invade Hythria?' Brak

asked. 'It can't just be greed. He's richer than any man alive.'

Teriahna seemed amused by the question. 'Don't you know? It isn't wealth that drives Hablet, it's fear.'

'Of what?'

'He doesn't have a legitimate heir.'

'That's not a reason to invade Hythria.'

'It is if you're afraid that your next heir is likely to be Hythrun.'

Brak stopped and stared at her, afraid she had already heard about Damin and Adrina, but then he realised that even if she had, Hablet had been planning this invasion long before the two of them met. 'How could that be?'

'Hythria and Fardohnya have not always been separate nations, Brak. You should know that.'

'Fardohnya split from Hythria before I was born,' Brak pointed out. 'And believe me, I was born a very long time ago.'

'They formally became separate nations during the reign of Greneth the Older Twin,' she reminded him. 'That was about twelve hundred years ago.'

Brak nodded. 'Greneth was the twin brother of Doranda Wolfblade, as I recall.'

'Ah, you do know your history then. Well, the split was quite amicable by all accounts. Greater Fardohnya, as it was known then, was a huge country; much too vast to govern effectively. Hythria was the largest province, governed by the Wolfblade family. Greneth married his sister Doranda to Jaycon Wolfblade, gave them Hythria to rule as the High Prince and Princess.'

Brak found himself impressed by Teriahna's knowledge, but no closer to the knowledge he sought. 'I still don't see . . .'

'Then let me finish,' she chided. 'As part of the agreement to separate the two nations, Greneth signed a pledge that in the absence of a male heir to the Fardohnyan throne, the eldest living Wolfblade would automatically inherit the crown. The agreement has never been revoked.'

'I've never heard of it before.'

'Well, until now, there's been no need to worry about it. Hablet is the first Fardohnyan king in twelve hundred years who's failed to get a son.'

'How many others know about it?'

'Enough that Hablet is worried. When your king keeps producing daughters, people start going through the archives. We only stumbled across it recently ourselves. Like you, we were curious about Hablet's obvious obsession with Hythria.'

'I'm still not certain I understand what he hopes to achieve by invading Hythria.'

'He needs to destroy the Wolfblade line. If there is no living Wolfblade, there is no heir. If there is no heir he can legitimise one of his bastards.'

'Wouldn't it be simpler, not to mention cheaper, to hire one of your assassins?'

'Are you kidding? Do you have any idea what we charge for assassinating a High Prince? Trust me, an invasion, even a prolonged one, would be cheaper.'

Brak smiled, not entirely certain she was joking.

'Anyway,' Teriahna continued, 'he tried that, and we refused. Call it professional ethics, but we draw the line at kings and princes. The death of a ruling monarch tends to create unrest and draws unnecessary attention to the Guild and that's bad for business. We are strictly apolitical.'

'What a comforting thought,' he remarked wryly.

She smiled. 'I forget you are Harshini, sometimes, my lord. Does all this talk of killing distress you?'

'Not as much as it should,' he admitted. 'So how long has Hablet known about this forgotten law?'

'A long time, I think. He made Lernen Wolfblade an offer for his sister Princess Marla when he first took the throne. You can imagine Lernen's reaction. He agreed to the offer at first and then changed his mind and married Marla to some rustic Warlord from the north of Hythria, just to add to the insult. Hablet has never forgiven him for that either.'

'So, for the sake of a forgotten law and a thirty-five-year-old insult, Hablet is going to invade Hythria?'

'That's about the strength of it,' she agreed. 'If Damin Wolfblade and Narvell Hawksword are killed protecting Hythria, which is a real possibility, and Lernen dies, which is also likely to happen sooner rather than later, according to my sources, there are no more male Wolfblades and Greneth's pledge is void.'

'Marla has other sons.'

'Stepsons,' Teriahna corrected. 'She has only two natural-born sons and neither of them has an heir. If they die, the Wolfblade line is at an end.'

'And if her daughters have sons?'

'Then they'd have as much claim as Hablet's daughters, no more. The pledge specifies a Wolfblade male and even Narvell's claim is tenuous, because he took his father's name when he became the Warlord of Elasapine.'

'You seem remarkably well informed on the matter of Hythrun bloodlines.'

'It's my job. Besides, I've been looking into the matter lately. The Guild might be apolitical, but we are hardly politically naive. The machinations of kings and princes affect us closely. We have a vested interest in keeping things stable.'

'Hence your reluctance to assassinate them.'

'I see you understand our position.'

Brak nodded, wondering how much he should tell Teriahna. For that matter, it would not be long before she learnt of it anyway. Once Damin reached Hythria, the news would spread like a grass fire.

They had reached the end of the wharf and took the carved stone steps up to the paved road that circled the harbour. Brak glanced over his shoulder, surprised at the distance they had covered. He had been so engrossed in the conversation he hadn't noticed.

'Are you hungry? There's a tavern not far from here that serves the best oysters in Fardohnya.'

Brak nodded his agreement distractedly. The Raven led the way a little further up the road to a small tavern with an arched entrance, over which was carved the words 'The Pearl of Talabar'. The tavern was cramped, but clean and cool and Teriahna was obviously well known. The owner hurried forward to greet them and showed them to a private booth in the back that gave them a clear view of the rest of the room.

'Now,' she said decisively, once they were seated. 'I have answered your questions. I think it's time you answered a few of mine.'

'If I can.'

'What are you doing in Talabar?'

'I don't suppose you'd believe me if I said I was sight-seeing?' he asked with a faint smile.

'No, I don't suppose I would. Nor do I think you sought out the Guild to kill someone for you. So there has to be another reason.'

'There is.'

She let out an exasperated sigh. 'Well? Do I have to drag it from you?'

He smiled. 'I've come from Medalon.'

'Medalon? That's an odd place for a Harshini to be.'

'Not really. The Harshini who survived the Sisterhood's purges still live in Medalon.'

'Everyone believes the Harshini are extinct. Except you, of course. You are thought to be the last. And we all thought you long dead.'

'The Harshini are not dead.'

'So where are they?'

'I like you, Teriahna, but I don't trust you that much.'

She nodded, her eyes glittering mischievously in the gloom. 'I didn't seriously think you'd tell me, but it was worth a try.'

The conversation stopped as the tavern keeper arrived with two platters of chilled oysters. Teriahna tucked into her meal with gusto, slurping the oysters from their shells with obvious relish. The tavern keeper left with a small, indulgent smile at the Raven. She caught his look and smiled.

'I grew up around here. Mornt is an old friend,' she explained, wiping her chin.

Brak picked up a shell and tipped the juicy contents down his throat. Teriahna was right. Seasoned with something he couldn't identify, it was delicious.

'Rumour has it the taste is the result of the oyster beds being in a direct line of Talabar's sewage outlet.'

Brak almost choked on the oyster as she burst out laughing.

'I'm kidding, Brak. Mornt has a secret recipe that he guards with his life. We've been offered a small fortune to torture the information out of him. We refused, naturally, and let Mornt learn of our refusal. Now we eat here for free.'

'A small price to pay for your life. I never realised the tavern business was so cutthroat.'

'You'd be surprised what we get asked to do.'

'No doubt.'

She swallowed another oyster. 'So, you come from Medalon and the first thing you do is seek out the Assassins' Guild. Why?'

'You're the best source of intelligence in Talabar.'

'Flattery is not an answer. Just where were you in Medalon exactly?'

'The northern border.'

'So how goes the war? Are the Defenders winning? They ought to. They deserve their reputation, by all accounts.'

'Medalon has surrendered, Teriahna.'

She made no attempt to hide her shock. '*What?* Why would they surrender?'

'It's a long story, and one I have no intention of trying to explain. But the fact is, Medalon has surrendered and is now in the hands of the Kariens.'

'Gods!' she muttered with concern. 'I knew I should have kept some people in the north. Hablet's not going to be happy when he learns of this. He was hoping the Kariens would keep the Defenders occupied for years.'

'I've other news that's going to please him even less. Tristan is dead. He was killed in the only major confrontation between the two armies.'

She shook her head. 'Now that's bad news. He would have made a good king if Hablet could have found a way to legitimise him.'

'It's not the worst of it,' he warned.

'You mean there's more? I can't think of anything that would upset Hablet more.'

'Prince Cratyn is dead too.'

'I doubt he'll lose much sleep over *that* news.' Then she frowned. 'So Adrina is a widow now?'

'Not exactly.'

'Gods, Brak! Getting anything out of you is like pulling teeth! What do you mean, *not exactly*?'

'She's remarried,' he said, keeping his voice deliberately emotionless. 'To Damin Wolfblade.'

Teriahna laughed. 'Is this your idea of getting even for that comment about the sewage pipes?'

He did not answer. The silence was heavy as Teriahna realised that he was serious.

'Dear gods! How did that come about?'

'The demon child ordered it.'

'The *demon child*? Now I *know* you're joking.'

Once again, he let the silence speak for him. The Raven studied him closely for a moment, then pushed her platter away. 'This is no joke, is it? There really is a demon child? Who is he?'

'She. Her name is R'shiel.'

'That's a Medalonian name.'

'That's right.'

'The demon child is *Medalonian*? Gods! That's a strange turn of events – an atheist who's descended from the gods. So, what gives the demon child the right to interfere in something that is likely to destabilise every nation on the continent?'

'She's on a mission from the gods – quite literally. I believe her eventual plan is to bring peace to every nation on the continent, not destabilise them.'

'Then she has an odd way of going about it.'

'You think so? If what you've told me is true, it seems the perfect solution. Hablet has no son, which makes a Wolfblade his heir. That heir is now married to his eldest daughter.'

'Oh, I agree, it's a solution none of us would have imagined, but how do you think Hablet is going to take the news? He wants to obliterate the Wolfblade line, not welcome their favourite son into his family.'

'Well, he's going to have to get used to the idea. Can you get me into the palace to see him?'

'Probably, although I don't suggest you use your real name. Hablet is no more likely to believe Brakandaran the Halfbreed still lives than I did.' Her expression grew serious as she leaned forward and lowered her voice. 'You have to understand, Brak: it suits a lot of people to believe the Harshini are gone. They represented a way of life that is long past, and while kings publicly lament their passing, privately they are rather pleased the Harshini aren't around to act as their conscience any more. Especially kings like Hablet.'

'Then perhaps,' Brak suggested ominously as he finished the last of his oysters, 'it's time Hablet acquired a conscience.'

## 10

The storm was loud outside, battering against the walls
of the tavern where Mikel and Jaymes were staying with
R'shiel. Although the low-ceilinged taproom was warm,
the fire smoked badly. Their new Medalonian mistress
did not seem to notice the choking haze, the bad food,
or the watery ale. She was deep in conversation with
another young woman she had arranged to meet here,
who she had introduced earlier as Mandah. The two of
them had their heads close together as they talked,
although Mikel sensed there was little friendship between
the women. Mandah was a year or two older than R'shiel,
with long blonde hair, pretty eyes and an air of calm
serenity about her that Mikel had never encountered
before.

They had been on the road for weeks now, pushing
hard to cross the Hythrun border before word of their
flight reached the Citadel – or worse, the Kariens. This
night, in a run-down tavern in the small, poor village of
Roan Vale, was the first break in their relentless journey.
R'shiel had come here to meet with Mandah, to organise
the remainder of the pagan rebels to join them in

Krakandar. At least, that's what he'd heard her telling Lord Wolfblade. The rest of their party was camped several leagues from the town, sheltering around an isolated farmhouse they had commandeered.

'My lady?'

R'shiel looked up from the mug of ale she was nursing. 'Yes, Jaymes?'

'The innkeeper says your rooms are ready. Shall I take your saddlebags up?'

'If you like.'

Jaymes glanced across at Mikel, then picked up R'shiel's bags and headed for the staircase at the back of the room. Mikel ate the strange-looking stew the inn provided, and listened as one of Mandah's men came in to report.

'The road to Bordertown is blocked by a rockslide,' the man said. 'You can either winter here in Roan Vale, or attempt to go further east, through Lodanville, and cross the border there.'

'Winter here? I don't think so. How long will it take if we go through Lodanville?' R'shiel asked with a frown.

'It will add at least a week, my lady.'

'It can't be helped, I suppose. I'll have to speak with Lord Wolfblade, but I think we'll have no choice but to turn east in the morning.'

The rebel bowed and crossed to a table on the other side of the room, where he joined his companions and gave them the news. They did not look happy. One of them complained that the demon child was going to lead them through every village in Medalon before they reached the border. But it was a half-hearted complaint. They knew as well as anyone that the weather was to blame for their delay.

Mikel swallowed the last of his stew and moved around

to the other side of the hearth, where the smoke seemed less suffocating, wondering why these rebels seemed so ambivalent. He always imagined that the Medalonians were like the Kariens – united under one purpose. In reality, there were more factions than he could count. There were the Defenders, and the Sisterhood, and the pacifist pagans, and the pagan rebels . . . and somewhere in amongst all that was the rest of the population, caught in the middle of the power struggle.

'Psst!'

Mikel jumped at the sound and looked behind him. In the darkness beside the hearth, under the woodpile, two large, liquid black eyes stared out at him.

'What are you doing here?' he hissed. 'Go away!'

The demon blinked, but did not move.

'Begone!' Mikel commanded in a firm whisper. That was what R'shiel said when she wanted the demons to leave. It must have something to do with her being Harshini. It had absolutely no effect when Mikel tried it. The demon simply cocked its head to one side with a look of blank incomprehension on its leathery face.

Mikel looked around nervously. Although the tavern was full of pagan rebels, Mikel didn't know them well enough to trust their reaction if they spied the creature. 'You have to leave!' he insisted, this time speaking Medalonian, hoping the demon might understand that language. 'Go back to R'shiel!'

At the mention of R'shiel, the demon began to chitter excitedly.

'Be quiet!'

'Who are you talking to, Mikel?'

Mikel spun around guiltily. 'No one, my lady. I – I thought I heard something in the woodpile.'

'Probably rats,' R'shiel murmured. 'Have you eaten?'

'Yes, my lady.'

'Then go and get some sleep, Mikel. We're leaving at first light.'

He climbed to his feet without looking back at the woodpile and crossed the room until he was standing before R'shiel. 'Do you mind if I check the horses first, my lady?'

R'shiel smiled at him distractedly. 'If you like.'

Mikel let himself out into the battering rain and ran the short distance to the stables. Lightning streaked the sky as the rain hammered down. He was shivering and soaked to the skin by the time he pushed the large wooden stable door shut behind him.

'It's a sour night to be out and about, lad.'

Mikel started at the voice and spun around, squinting in the darkness. The voice belonged to an old man sitting on a haybale. He was wrapped in a tattered dark cloak, smoking a long pipe that gave off a sweet-smelling and vaguely familiar scent. Mikel studied him suspiciously. He looked like some sort of vagabond who had taken shelter from the storm, too poor to afford the inn.

'Who are you?'

'A friend.'

'I don't know you.'

'Oh, yes, you know me, Mikel.'

'How do you know my name?'

The old man smiled and rose to his feet with a grace that belied his age. He stepped closer to Mikel, his long white hair flowing over his shoulders like a silken waterfall. His eyes were piercingly bright in the gloomy stable.

'No matter, lad. I merely wanted to see that you are well.'

'Why would you care?'

'I care about all my people,' the old man said with a smile.

Despite his suspicions, Mikel found himself drawn to the man. There was something about him, some seductive quality he could not define, which made him want to throw himself into the old man's arms and lose himself to the security and warmth of his presence.

'What do you want?'

'Nothing,' the old man shrugged. 'A moment of your time perhaps. A chance to talk. You travel with the demon child, I see.'

'Who told you that?' Mikel demanded.

He smiled. 'Nobody told me, Mikel. I can feel her presence. You are very privileged to be counted among her friends.'

Mikel's chest swelled a little at the compliment. 'R'shiel trusts me.'

'I'm sure she does. It is a rare honour indeed. But don't you worry that she is leading you into danger?'

'R'shiel is just trying to . . .' His voice trailed off, as he realised that he actually had no idea what R'shiel was trying to do.

Smiling, the old man sucked on his pipe for a moment.

'She's helping her people,' Mikel said with determination.

'She is trying to destroy your God.'

'Which god?'

The old man sighed. 'It is a sad world indeed if you have to ask that question, Mikel. R'shiel is trying to destroy the Overlord. She was created for that purpose.'

'Why would she want to do that?'

'That is not important,' the old man shrugged. 'Merely

that you are aiding her. Don't you worry for your eternal soul?'

'But the other gods said—'

'Ah, yes. The other gods. Well, who am I to deny what the other gods have said? All I can do is warn you, I suppose.'

'Warn me about what?'

'You are aiding the demon child. When the time for retribution comes, your God will remember that you turned on him.'

Mikel opened his mouth to object, but the words would not come. He *had* turned on his God. He had honoured Dacendaran, the God of Thieves, and was personally acquainted with Kalianah, the Goddess of Love. And Gimlorie, the God of Music, had taught him how to sing.

'I didn't mean to,' Mikel said in a small voice that was almost drowned out by the storm.

The old man smiled and opened his arms wide. 'Xaphista forgives you, my son.'

Mikel ran to him, sobbing. Wrapped in the warm embrace of the old man, he felt such an overwhelming love for his God that everything he had done in the past seemed insignificant. The Overlord was the one true God – the only God. He could not understand how he had ever lost sight of that fact.

After a long while, his tears ran out and he looked up into the eyes of the old man.

'What must I do?' he asked.

Mikel returned to the tavern in a state of elation. His whole being was filled with love for his God, his mind focused only on the task before him. The rain had eased as he let himself into the smoky taproom, and his small hand clutched his dagger. He was filled with purpose and the secure knowledge that this was *right*.

R'shiel still sat at the table talking with Mandah, although they had been joined by another man. He could hear what they were saying, but the voices were muffled as if he was listening through a waterfall.

'The Defenders are planning to cross the Glass River at Testra,' R'shiel was telling them. 'If you meet them on this side at Vanahiem, you can tell them which way we went. Hopefully, by the time they cross the river, the roads will be clear and they can get straight through to Hythria.'

The innkeeper must have overheard them. He hurried forward, pushed Mikel out of the way and bowed to R'shiel, his expression horrified.

'Forgive me, my lady, if I misunderstood you, but surely you're not planning to bring these men through here?'

'Why not?'

'But the Kariens will be pursuing them! We'll be slaughtered if they think we were harbouring traitors.'

Mandah looked up at the overwrought tavern keeper with a smile. 'Woran, you've been harbouring rebels here since before I was born.'

'That's not true! This is a respectable establishment.'

'This is a flea-ridden, rat-infested hovel,' the man at the table laughed.

'But if the Karien priests should hear of it . . . And what of the other people here in Roan Vale? Can't you send the Defenders by another route?'

'It will be all right, Woran,' Mandah assured him.

Mikel moved closer to the table. The dagger felt warm and comforting in his hand. Mandah spied him and frowned. 'Look at you, child, you're drenched!'

R'shiel looked up at him with a shake of her head. 'Go stand by the fire, Mikel. You'll catch your death if you sleep in those wet clothes.'

Mikel didn't answer. He stared at the demon child, seeing nothing but the woman who was destined to destroy his God.

'Mikel? What happened to you?'

He turned slightly to find Jaymes standing behind him. His brother seemed a stranger. Everyone in the room seemed to be a stranger.

'Come on,' Jaymes said. 'Let's go dry you out.'

Mikel let Jaymes lead him to the fire without resisting. He looked over his shoulder at R'shiel, but she had resumed her conversation with Mandah and the other rebel. The dagger burned with unfulfilled longing in his grasp.

'What were you thinking?' Jaymes asked as he peeled Mikel's sodden cloak from his shoulder. 'Look at you! You're blue with cold and stiff as a board.'

The demon who had been hiding in the woodpile chittered at him in concern as Jaymes shook out his dripping cloak. Mikel stared at the creature for a moment in confusion. Its appearance made him lose his train of thought and he suddenly began to notice how cold and wet he was. He moved closer to the fire and glanced across the room at R'shiel. She caught sight of him out of the corner of her eye and smiled.

He smiled back with the odd feeling that he had meant to do something important, but could not for the life of him remember what it was. He realised then that his hand was still clutched around the hilt of his dagger, his grip so tight that his fingers were cramping.

Mikel let it go, wondering why he was holding it.

# PART 2

# THE MEN WHO WOULD BE KINGS

# II

Krakandar turned out to be nothing like Adrina imagined. She had somehow developed the impression that Damin's home was some sort of isolated, rustic abode with minimal amenities and barely literate servants, all scurrying about in rat-infested, thatch-covered huts. Well, perhaps that *was* an exaggeration, but she was unprepared for the large, walled city that confronted her some six weeks after she fled the border with Damin and Tarja.

Krakandar's population numbered close to twenty thousand. The city had been carefully planned and was laid out in a series of concentric rings. Not only that, but it was, even to the untrained eye, impregnable. There were three rings, each one protected by progressively more complex defences. The inner ring housed the palace and most of the government buildings, including a huge store, which was filled as insurance against a siege each year at harvest time. Just prior to the harvest, the past year's grain was distributed to the poor, and come harvest, Damin explained, the warehouses were filled again for the following year. The central ring was mostly housing, the residences progressively more imposing the closer one got to the inner ring. The vast outer ring was the home to the markets and industries of the city.

Built on a small hill, the palace commanded a view of the entire city, which sprawled across the surrounding slopes with geometric precision. The city was well maintained and constructed of the local dark-red granite, which they quarried not far from the city and formed one of Krakandar's major exports.

Damin told her this as they rode towards the city, the pride in his voice taking her by surprise. He obviously loved his home, and as they rode under the massive portcullis that protected the main gate, it was apparent the citizens of Krakandar loved their Warlord in return.

Almodavar had sent word ahead that they were coming and for entirely selfish reasons, Adrina was looking forward to finally reaching their destination. More than a month in the saddle, living off trail rations and what meat they had been able to hunt along the way, had left her tanned and fit – but desperate for the trappings of civilisation. She had even managed to put on a bit of weight, she thought with despair. When Krakandar came into view, all she could think of was a hot bath, clean hair and the smell of something else besides leather and horses.

As word spread through the city that the Warlord had returned the citizens of Krakandar lined the streets to catch a glimpse of him. It was only a few at first but as the news ran ahead of them, the crowd grew larger. The people stopped working and pushed forward to see him, waving and calling out to Damin, who returned their greetings with a grin, obviously delighted by the warmth of this welcome. Adrina rode behind him, with R'shiel at her side, unaccountably put out by his popularity. The demon child was looking about her with wide-eyed wonder. She could be utterly ruthless when the need arose, but she still showed traces of the young girl underneath when it was least expected.

'Well, the peasants seem fond of him,' Adrina remarked sourly.

R'shiel laughed. 'You really are determined to make this as difficult as possible, aren't you?'

'*I'm* making things difficult? Don't try blaming me, R'shiel. This was your idea, not mine.'

'He adores you, you know.'

Adrina looked at Damin's back and scowled. He was waving to the people, calling out a greeting to a familiar face in the crowd. 'Damin loves himself, R'shiel,' she retorted. 'And his horse. He would probably be upset if anything happened to Almodavar, but that's about as far as it goes. He likes you because you are the demon child and your friendship will help him claim his throne. His only interest in me is political.'

R'shiel raised her brow with a quizzical expression. 'Is that what those noises coming from your tent were? *Political* negotiations?'

Adrina frowned, trying to think of some cutting rejoinder. Then the silliness of the conversation struck her and she smiled reluctantly. 'All right, I admit I've been . . . negotiating . . . more than is wise, but there wasn't much else to do for entertainment, was there?'

'I'm sure you could have found something a little less dangerous if you wanted to, Your highness. Honestly, you're as bad as Damin. I should wave my arm and do something Harshini to make you both see sense.'

'Why don't you?' she said aloud, but she had wondered

before why the demon child had not simply called on her power to bend them to her will.

'Just between you and me, I don't know how.'

'But you're the demon child! Doesn't that make you omnipotent?'

'Omnipotent, maybe, but it doesn't mean I know very much about my powers. Brak says I lack finesse.'

'R'shiel, can I give you some advice?'

'If you think it will do any good.'

'When you've turned someone's life upside-down, killed their husband, ordered them to marry an enemy prince and told them to risk their life by announcing the fact to the entire world, please don't tell them you don't know what you're doing. It's very unsettling.'

R'shiel smiled, but did not answer as they rode under the portcullis of the second ring.

The ride through the central ring took even longer. The crowd had grown so large that troops had been sent out from the palace to hold the crowd back so that Damin's party could have a clear path. The palace guards surprised Adrina. Unlike the Raiders Damin had with him on the border, these men were uniformed in dark-red leather breastplates embossed with a large hawk.

'Captain?' she asked, looking back over her shoulder at Almodavar. 'Why is the palace guard wearing a hawk? I thought Damin's emblem was a wolf?'

'It is, your highness. The hawk is the emblem of Elasapine. They are Lord Hawksword's men.'

R'shiel laughed aloud when she heard. 'I don't believe it! Zegarnald actually did what I told him!'

'You *told* the God of War what to do?'

R'shiel nodded, looking inordinately pleased with

herself. 'I wasn't really sure that he would. I asked him to turn Damin's brother back, in case we didn't make it here before your father tried invading Hythria.'

'His brother? Dear gods, you mean there's more of them?'

'It's his half-brother. Don't worry, Adrina. If Damin dies, I won't make you marry him.'

'I'll hold you to that,' Adrina promised.

As they rode on towards the inner wall, Adrina looked around, surprised at the affluence of the city and the people. Even the beggars in the streets of the outer ring had looked quite healthy under their rags and their professional air of misery. Here in the residential district, mothers held up their babies for Damin's blessing, plump slaves fanned their masters and mistresses as they leaned over their balconies, and more than a few young ladies, noblewomen, peasants and *court'esa* alike, called out quite preposterous proposals, which Damin acknowledged with a laugh. One woman standing on the balcony of a very elegant, red-brick house, bared her breast and called out a suggestion that made even Adrina blush. Somewhat to her chagrin, Damin actually responded with a promise to take her up on her offer some other time.

'The man has no morals,' she muttered.

'That's a bit rich, coming from you,' R'shiel remarked with a grin.

'You'd never catch me making a public spectacle of myself like that.'

'Of course not. You prefer to *negotiate*, don't you.'

Adrina was feeling sufficiently put out that she did not deign to answer as they rode through the massive iron-reinforced gates into the inner city.

\* \* \*

The noise of the crowd behind them faded as they rode forward, the clatter of the horses' hoofs loud on the cobbled pavement. The road opened out into a vast courtyard, surrounded on three sides by impressive buildings. To the left and right of the square were the government buildings, three storeys high, gracefully symmetrical and uniform. In front of them lay the sweeping steps of the palace itself, lined with troops wearing the silver tabard-and-diamond symbol of the Sorcerers' Collective.

Damin slowed his horse and glanced around, taking in the troops lining the steps and then looking up at the walls, which were lined with as many men wearing the hawk emblem of Elasapine or the rampant kraken of Krakandar as there were the Wolfblade livery.

'R'shiel.'

The demon child rode up beside him. 'Is something wrong?'

'I don't know. Are you ready to be the demon child? I have a feeling I might need her.'

'No, but don't let that stop you.'

He treated her to a faint smile then turned to Adrina. 'How about you? Are you ready to face the High Arrion?'

'The High Arrion!'

'Her guard wouldn't be here without her,' Damin pointed out. 'If we're going to do this, we might as well make it look plausible.'

Adrina opened her mouth to make some sarcastic comment, then suddenly thought better of it. Damin considered her intelligent. Perhaps his sister, arguably the most powerful woman in Hythria after Princess Marla, would think the same thing. It would be a nice change.

'I'm ready.'

She urged her horse forward until she rode on his left.

R'shiel unconsciously sat a little taller in the saddle on Damin's right, as if the girl who had gaped at the sights of Krakandar a short while ago had been put aside, and the demon child had taken over. It was interesting, Adrina thought, and more than a little disturbing, the way she did that.

Three figures appeared at the top of the palace steps as they approached. Adrina knew the woman on the left. They had met before, on her only other visit to Hythria. Dressed in black, the diamond-shaped symbol of her office winking in the sunlight, Adrina recognised her as Kalan, High Arrion of the Sorcerers' Collective, Damin's half-sister. The man on the left looked sufficiently like Kalan to be her twin, so she guessed this was Narvell Hawksword, the Warlord of Elasapine, although his gold-chased breastplate, with its swooping hawk, would have given away his identity.

The woman in the middle was shorter than the man and woman who flanked her, but carried herself as if the world lay at her feet, waiting for her command. Adrina envied her poise. Her fair hair was flecked with silver but her skin was unlined. She studied Damin and the two women who rode beside him with dark, watchful eyes.

Damin dismounted at the foot of the steps and, without waiting for Adrina or R'shiel, took them two at a time until he reached the top. He swept the older woman up and hugged her.

'Mother!'

Adrina hesitated and glanced at R'shiel, but the demon child had obviously not heard of the fearsome reputation of Princess Marla of Hythria.

'Put me down, Damin! You smell like a horse!'

Damin laughed and turned to Kalan, who took a step backward. 'Don't you dare touch me! I agree with mother, I can smell you from here!'

'Fine greeting I get! Months away from home and all you can do is complain about how I smell.'

'Don't worry, brother. Within a day they'll have you drowned in perfume and then it'll be your men complaining about the stench,' Narvell chuckled.

Damin embraced his half-brother warmly then held him at arm's length for a moment. 'It's good to see you, Narvell. I don't know what you're doing here, but you're a welcome sight. I damned near fell off my horse when I saw your troops marching out of the palace gates to hold back the crowd. Did you get greedy while I was gone and invade me?'

'We can discuss what he's doing here later,' Princess Marla announced abruptly, then turned her piercing gaze on Adrina and R'shiel. 'In the meantime, you can introduce me to your companions.'

Damin knew better than to argue with her. He turned and beckoned R'shiel forward. 'Princess Marla, Lady Kalan, Lord Hawksword, may I introduce Her Royal Highness, Princess R'shiel té Ortyn.'

Adrina wasn't sure who was more surprised at the declaration of her full title, R'shiel or the trio on the steps. Kalan's jaw dropped. Narvell looked puzzled. Marla stared at her openly then arched her brow elegantly. 'Té Ortyn, did you say? I only know of one té Ortyn family.'

'Then you understand the importance of our guest,' Damin replied meaningfully with a glance at the troops who lined the steps and could hear every word they said.

Marla's eyes narrowed. She understood exactly. 'Of course. Forgive me. You are most welcome, your highness.'

'Thank you,' R'shiel replied, looking rather uncomfortable. Damin would receive a tongue-lashing later, Adrina suspected. R'shiel was not fond of her status as the demon child – and was even less keen to be reminded that her father had been a Harshini king. A few months among the Harshini had not completely eradicated a lifetime of prejudice instilled in her by the Sisters of the Blade.

'And this,' Damin announced, holding his hand out to Adrina, 'is my wife.'

'Your *wife*?' Kalan gasped. It was plain she recognised Adrina.

She accepted his hand and stepped up beside him. 'Adrina, I'd like you to meet my mother, Princess Marla; my brother, Narvell; and I believe you already know my sister, Kalan.'

'Adrina?' Marla remarked, looking Adrina over coldly. 'That's a Fardohnyan name and I only know of one Fardohnyan Adrina. Please tell me this is not the one I've heard of?'

'Perhaps we could continue this discussion in private?' Damin suggested, before his mother could get too worked up. Adrina was a little taken aback by her reaction. She was hardly expecting a warm welcome, but Princess Marla seemed quite appalled. She wisely remained silent, letting Damin deal with his mother.

'I think we'd better,' Narvell agreed. He waved his arm and men rushed forward to take their horses. Almodavar dismissed his men and they were led inside to the marble-floored foyer of the palace. Tamylan and the two Karien boys looked a little lost until Almodavar took them under his command and ushered them away.

Marla led the way into the palace, her slippers silent

on the highly polished floor. Eventually they reached a pair of ornately carved doors at the far end of the main hall. She threw them open and marched inside, turning as soon as Narvell closed the doors behind them.

'So, you are Adrina of Fardohnya?' she accused without preamble.

'Yes, your highness, I—'

'I thought you were married to Cratyn of Karien?'

'I was, but—'

'How in the name of the gods did you happen to marry my son?'

'I—'

'Mother!'

'Have you lost your mind, Damin!' Marla demanded, turning on him. 'Whatever she did to trap you into this marriage, it must be undone immediately! I will not jeopardise everything we have worked for, just because you were taken in by some Fardohnyan whore!'

'If you would let me explain . . .'

'*Explain*? You think you can offer any explanation that will satisfy me? And while you're at it, you might like to think of what you're planning to tell your uncle and the Warlords! Lernen will have a fit when he hears of this. I can't begin to think of what the Warlords are going to say!'

'Mother—'

'All my life I have done nothing but try to secure your throne. It was bad enough your abandoning your province to go chasing off to Medalon. Your unauthorised and ill-timed treaty with the Defenders had the Warlords howling for your blood. And now, after I spend months trying to win them over on your behalf, you throw it all away for the sake of a woman. And a foreigner at that!' She turned suddenly and glared at Adrina. 'No, not just any foreigner! You had to go and marry the most notorious harlot on the whole continent!'

Adrina looked to Damin for support. He sat on the edge of the gold-inlaid desk, listening to his mother's rage with barely concealed amusement. It annoyed her intensely that instead of defending her he thought it was funny.

'Are you finished yet?' R'shiel asked quietly, from the back of the room. She had been studying the books in the bookcases that lined the walls of the library, but now she turned to them, the command in her voice impossible to deny.

Marla glared at her. She was not used to having her authority challenged.

'And who are you to tell me what to do?'

'I am R'shiel té Ortyn.'

'So you claim!' the princess scoffed. 'You're no Harshini! What right do you have to use the name of the Harshini royal family?'

'Lorandranek was my father.'

'That's absurd!' Kalan declared. 'You're human. If Lorandranek was your father, that would make you the . . .' Her voiced trailed off as she realised what she was about to say.

'Yes?' R'shiel prompted.

'It's not possible!'

'You of all people, should know that it *is* possible,' Damin pointed out.

'What are you talking about, Damin?' Narvell asked.

'Tell him, Kalan.'

Kalan glanced at her twin and shrugged. 'If this young woman is really who she claims to be, then she is . . . the demon child.'

Narvell looked impressed by the news, but Marla was not so easily persuaded. '*This girl*? The demon child? Damin, they must have fed you something in the north that affected your reason. You surely don't believe it, do you?'

'R'shiel *is* the demon child, mother. She was placed in my care by Zegarnald himself.'

Kalan stared at him with astonishment. 'You spoke to the God of War?'

'In the flesh.'

'He spoke to me, too,' Narvell admitted. 'It's why I turned back.'

'This is unprecedented.'

'Everything about me is unprecedented,' R'shiel remarked. 'So, if we're through with the histrionics, perhaps we can start again. Princess Marla, I think you owe your daughter-in-law an apology. She's really not that bad. As for you, High Arrion, you and I need to have a talk. Damin, can you do something about rooms for us? Your mother was right about that much at least – we all stink like horses. Perhaps once everyone has had a chance to clean up and calm down, we can sort this out like rational human beings.'

Princess Marla stared at R'shiel with undisguised horror, although whether it was because she found herself face-to-face with a legend, or simply R'shiel's high-handed manner, Adrina couldn't tell.

## 12

Damin knocked on the door of the rooms adjacent to his that his Chief Steward had allocated to Adrina and opened it without waiting for an answer, a little surprised to find it unlocked.

The room had been his mother's once, on the rare occasions she had lived at Krakandar when he was a child. It was furnished in her impeccable taste: the rooms airy and light; the rugs imported from Karien; the crystal made in Fardohnya; the red granite floors polished to perfection. Not a piece of the whitewood furniture was out of place; not a vase or lamp did not belong here.

He followed the sound of voices through the sitting room and into the dressing room beyond. Adrina was standing before the full-length mirror, examining herself critically. She was dressed in a long, sleeveless robe that fell softly to the floor in a cascade of emerald silk. Her slave was moving about in the next room, tidying up after her mistress' bath. She turned sharply as she caught sight of her husband in the mirror.

'Damin!'

'I didn't mean to startle you.'

'Don't you know how to knock?'

'I did knock.'

'Oh . . .' She straightened her gown and studied him for a moment. 'There's something different about you . . . I know what it is. I've never seen you so clean. You almost look civilised.'

Damin had not given much thought to what he wore. A white silk shirt, trousers and polished boots hardly seemed to warrant such admiration. But compliments, even backhanded ones, were a rare thing from Adrina, so he chose not to make an issue of it.

'Do you have everything you need?'

'Yes, thank you. Your sister sent along the dress. I don't know who it belonged to before me, but it's an adequate fit.'

'Well, if you need anything, just ask Orleon, my Chief Steward. He'll see that you get it.'

'Thank you.'

'I'll have a seamstress sent to you tomorrow. You're going to need a suitable wardrobe.'

An uncomfortable silence settled on them as Damin wondered how to broach the subject he'd come here to speak about. Adrina was a volatile and unpredictable woman. He had no way of knowing how she would react to what he had to say.

'I'm sorry about my mother. She shouldn't have spoken the way she did.'

'We both knew this wasn't going to be easy, Damin. Her reaction was nothing less than I expected.' She smiled suddenly, her eyes glinting. 'I will console myself with the thought of my father's reaction when he hears about it. I imagine your mother will seem quite reasonable by comparison.'

'That's true,' he agreed, relieved things were going so well. 'But, I do have a favour to ask.'

'A favour?'

'We caught Marla off-guard today. You may not have heard the worst of it. It would be . . . easier . . .'

'If I bite my tongue and let her insult me?' Adrina finished for him.

'Something like that.'

He expected her to explode at that point, but to his astonishment, she nodded her agreement. 'Don't worry, I'll behave.'

'You *will*?'

'Don't sound so surprised. I plan to survive this farcical arrangement, Damin, and to do that, I'll need your mother on my side. You'd be surprised how charming I can be when the mood takes me.'

Actually, Damin wouldn't have been surprised at all. She could be very disarming when she wanted something. 'Well, if you can win Marla over, you'll have the whole of Hythria at your feet.'

'That's the plan,' she agreed. 'And in the meantime?'

'In the meantime, you should be safe enough here in the palace. I'll have Almodavar hand-pick your body-guards. You have to promise you won't try leaving the palace without them.'

Adrina scowled, but nodded. 'I suppose.'

'I've already arranged for a message to go to the Assassins' Guild,' he added. 'I plan to hire them before someone else thinks of it. They are very loyal employees.'

'You mean they stay bought.'

'It's the same thing in the end.'

She sighed, as if the realisation that life would be

difficult for some time to come had just dawned on her. Damin could not fathom her mood.

'Well, if you've everything you need, I'll see you at dinner. I'll have Orleon send someone to show you the way.'

'Damin,' she called as he turned to leave. 'Why are your mother and the High Arrion here in Krakandar? I know R'shiel arranged for Zegarnald to turn Narvell back, but that doesn't explain the other two.'

'I don't know,' he admitted, a little surprised that she'd asked. He reminded himself, yet again, not to underestimate his wife.

'Well, I suggest you find out. I may not be an expert on Hythrun politics, but I do know the High Arrion doesn't do anything without a good reason, and I suspect your mother hasn't made an impulsive move in her entire life.'

It was a remarkably accurate assessment, considering her short acquaintance with his family. Damin wished for a moment that he could trust her. She would make a daunting High Princess – if she didn't try to murder him first.

'We'll find out what's behind their presence soon enough. Once Marla has gotten over the news about you.'

'Well, if she doesn't like the idea, tell her to take it up with the demon child,' she told him, picking up a silver-backed hairbrush. She turned her back to him and began brushing out her long dark hair.

He had been dismissed.

Damin let himself out of Adrina's rooms, thinking on what she had said about his mother and sister. She wasn't far off the mark. Marla did nothing without thinking it through. As for Kalan, Adrina was right about her too. The High Arrion would not leave Greenharbour without a very good reason. His unease at finding his palace steps lined with silver-uniformed soldiers from the Sorcerers' Collective still lingered.

'My lord?'

Damin turned to find Orleon coming towards him at his usual, unhurried pace. The old man was as much a part of Krakandar Palace as the stones in the walls. He never aged noticeably that Damin could see. He still seemed the same, grey-haired, eagle-eyed watchdog that he'd been when Damin was a child.

'Yes, Orleon?'

'You have a visitor, my lord.'

From the slight tone of reproach, Damin could guess who it was. 'Where is he?'

'In the Morning Room, my lord. I suggest you go there now, while we still have the silverware.'

Damin grinned at Orleon's expression and changed the direction he was headed. The Morning Room was on the ground floor, and he took the broad marble steps two at a time, anxious to see his visitor. When he threw open the door, the man in question was holding up a small statue to the light, examining it with the critical eye of an expert.

'It's not worth your attention,' Damin told him, as he closed the door behind him. 'You'd get more for the candelabra.'

The fair-haired man slowly replaced the statue on the mantle before he turned to Damin.

'Perhaps. But that's inscribed with the Krakenshield crest. Too easy to trace it back to its source.'

'When has that ever bothered you?'

The man smiled and crossed the room, catching Damin in a crushing bear hug, before holding him at arm's length to look at him closely. Older by two years, but of a much slighter build, his clothes were expertly cut of expensive silk and he wore them with the cavalier air of a nobleman. His blue eyes were bright with intelligence and a level of animal cunning that Damin had often envied as a child. He looked prosperous and happy. *Business must be good,* Damin thought, not altogether pleased by the thought.

'Welcome home, Damin. It's good to see you.'

'It's good to see you too, Starros. How's business?'

'It'll be better now that you're home.'

Damin moved to the sidetable, shaking his head. 'I'm sure you mean it as a compliment, old friend, but telling me that my return is going to favour Krakandar's criminal element, really doesn't thrill me.'

He pulled the stopper from the decanter and poured two cups of wine, handing one to Starros with a smile. The thief frowned as he accepted the wine.

'You know what I mean, Damin. All these troops from the Sorcerers' Collective and Elasapine filling up our streets is no good for my people.'

'Maybe I should invite them to stay.'

'Maybe you should invite them to leave,' Starros corrected.

Damin looked at him curiously. 'Perhaps you'd better fill me in.'

They settled into the heavily padded chairs on either side of the hearth. The fire burned low – more glowing coals than flame – but it gave off enough heat to take the chill out of the air. Damin carried the decanter with him, certain he would need another drink before Starros was through.

'The Collective troops arrived about a month ago. Kalan made quite an impressive entrance, and then declared the city under the Collective's protection. Your mother arrived before her by a few days, and Narvell and his henchmen got here last week.'

'Why did Kalan place the city under the Collective's protection? That only happens when a Warlord dies without an heir.'

'You'll have to ask Kalan, I'm afraid. I tried to get in to see her, but she doesn't entertain the likes of me since she became High Arrion.'

Damin frowned, wondering what was really going on. He'd had no chance to speak to Kalan alone since he arrived, and she had not sought him out. Even more worrying was Kalan's refusal to see Starros. The leader of the Thieves' Guild was – so rumour claimed – Almodavar's bastard son. He had grown up here in the palace with them and was counted among their closest friends. Even if she could not acknowledge her friendship with Starros openly, she had never refused to see him before.

'What else has been happening since I left?'

'Not much. Things were pretty quiet until your mother got here. But then things always get sticky once she turns up.'

Damin smiled in fond remembrance. 'You remember that time she arrived from Elasapine and we'd gone fishing in the fens?'

'The time she found me beating the stuffing out of you in that bog?' Starros laughed. 'I remember. Gods, we must have looked a sight. All mud and blood and black eyes.'

'You were *not* beating me,' Damin corrected. 'I was letting you win.'

'You were bawling your eyes out like a baby!'

'I was not!'

'You were so! And I'll never let you forget it, either. It was the only time I ever beat you in a fair fight, Damin Wolfblade.' Starros finished his wine and held out his cup for a refill. Damin shook his head and smiled. It wasn't really worth arguing about. He leaned over and filled the cup without getting out of his chair. Starros sipped the wine appreciatively. 'So, I hear you've taken a bride.'

'That's right.'

'A Fardohnyan?'

'That's right.'

'Well, you always did like to live dangerously. Is she pretty?'

'Very.'

'Worth the trouble?'

Damin grinned. 'I haven't decided yet.'

Starros chuckled softly. 'And the rumour that you have brought the demon child to Hythria? Is that true?'

Damin lowered the cup from his lips and stared at Starros. 'Where did you hear that?'

'I have my sources,' the thief told him smugly.

'I'm serious, Starros. How did you hear about it so soon?'

'Soon? Hell, we've known about it for weeks!' He looked at Damin, his smile fading.

'Who told you?'

'It's really bothering you, isn't it? Nobody told me, not in the way you're thinking. It was a bit odd, actually. About six or seven weeks ago, an old man appeared in the city. Didn't bother anyone at first, just roamed the streets trying to convince the working *court'esa* that their eternal souls were in danger if they didn't renounce their way of life. He stood on a few street corners and gave speeches that nobody listened to. You know the type. We average about one prophet a month in a good year, so we paid him little attention.'

'But—' Damin prompted, certain there was more to the story.

'Do you remember Limik the Leopard?' Starros asked.

'Tall fellow? Scarred hands?'

Starros nodded. 'He burned them as a child.'

'Didn't I have him flogged once for beating his wife?'

'That's the one. Hard case through and through.'

'I remember him,' Damin said. 'What's he got to do with the old man?'

'I'm getting to that. I sent Limik out on a job . . . oh, about three weeks ago, I think. A certain merchant in Felt Street had a bad habit of leaving his wife's jewellery laying about the house. In our profession, that sort of carelessness can't be allowed to go unpunished.'

'Of course not,' Damin agreed wryly.

'Anyway, Limik's an old hand at that sort of thing, so I sent him out to teach our merchant friend a lesson. He did the job and was on his way back to the Guild when he bumped into the old man.'

'What happened?'

'Limik went back to the house, confessed his crime to the merchant – who didn't even realise he'd been robbed – and from that day on, he followed the old man around like a puppy, telling anyone who'd listen that he'd denounced Dacendaran, and was now a follower of another god.'

'Which other god?'

'He didn't say. But he used the word "sin" a lot.'

Damin frowned. 'That sounds like Xaphista.'

'Not even Limik, in the throes of religious ecstasy, is stupid enough to use that name out loud in the streets of Krakandar,' Starros said. 'But after that day, the old man changed his tune. He started talking about you. Said you'd allied yourself with the godless ones – I guess he meant the Medalonians – and that you were consorting with the demon child. Next thing you know, Kalan turns up with her troops and places the city under the Collective's protection.'

'Where is this old man now?'

'Gone,' Starros shrugged. 'As soon as I got word you were on your way home, I sent my people out to find him. He's dropped out of sight. Vanished as if he was never here.'

'And Limik?'

'The day after the old man vanished, Limik robbed three houses and a tavern. He claims he can't remember a thing. Threatened to knife me for even suggesting he'd ever confess to any crime, let alone turn away from Dacendaran.'

Damin stared into his wine for a moment. 'So, what's your theory?'

'I don't have one, Damin. Strange old men and inexplicable religious experiences are not my line of business. That's what we have a High Arrion for.'

Damin nodded, more than a little concerned. 'I'll mention it to Kalan.'

'You might want to mention it to the demon child, too.'

'Why?'

'Because along with reforming thieves and prostitutes, the old man was trying to find someone willing to kill her.'

## 13

'Damin!'

Still brooding over Starros' disturbing news, Damin was startled out of his reverie by R'shiel. He turned as she ran the length of the broad hall, skidding on the polished floor as she neared him.

'What's wrong?'

'Nothing. I need to see Kalan, and Orleon told me she's in the Solar. As I have no idea what a Solar is or how to find it in this rabbit warren you call a palace, I was hoping you could show me the way.'

'Of course,' he said, offering his arm. She took it lightly and fell into step beside him. Her hair was damp from her bath, but she still wore the Harshini leathers she favoured so much. At least he *thought* they were made of leather. They never seemed to get dirty the way other, ordinary clothes did.

'So, have you spoken to Adrina?'

'Yes. She's being remarkably cooperative. It has me worried.'

R'shiel laughed. 'Enjoy it while it lasts, Damin.'

'You know, the annoying thing is, she's actually very

smart underneath that obnoxious attitude of hers. But I still don't trust her.'

'You should. She does love you, you know.'

'Adrina? Don't be absurd. She loves flirting with danger. And power. And herself.'

'She said much the same thing about you.'

Damin looked at R'shiel, shaking his head. 'Stop trying to create romance where there is none, R'shiel. You wanted us to marry and we did, but don't think you can ease your own guilt by inventing some relationship between us that doesn't exist.'

She studied him thoughtfully for a moment then shrugged. 'As you wish.'

They walked in silence after that, through the long, wide halls of the palace, each of them certain that the other was wrong.

Kalan greeted them as they stepped into the Solar. 'Demon child; Damin.'

'My name is R'shiel.'

'It would be improper of me to address you so informally, Divine One.'

R'shiel sighed. 'Whatever.'

The room had been added to the palace by Damin's paternal grandmother and was roofed in clear glass tiles. The far wall was also glassed, and opened out into the palace gardens, which were looking rather forlorn, Damin noted with a frown. The furniture here had been cleverly wrought from iron, brightly coloured cushions relieving its convoluted lines. Damin never used the room much. As children they had avoided it. It was too easy for some passing palace courtier to see inside and discover what mischief they were up to.

'There are a few things I need to ask you,' R'shiel explained.

'Then I'll leave you two in private,' Damin said. Getting caught between the High Arrion and the demon child was not something he relished.

'I think you should stay, Damin,' Kalan suggested. 'I imagine this concerns you as much as anyone.'

'I don't think . . .'

'Stay, Damin,' R'shiel ordered. 'There's nothing I need to ask the High Arrion that you don't already know about.'

'Before I answer your questions, Divine One, perhaps you'd like to start by telling me what absurd Harshini plot you've cooked up that required my brother to betray his country by marrying that Fardohnyan harlot.'

'While we're all so busy with explanations, you can tell me what *you're* doing here with an occupation force,' he retorted. For some reason, Kalan's insistence on referring to Adrina as 'that Fardohnyan harlot' was starting to aggravate him.

'Damin, calm down,' R'shiel advised then turned to the High Arrion. 'Don't judge Adrina too harshly, Kalan. She has a good head on her shoulders and your brother loves her.'

'Not that I noticed.'

'Then you're not as observant as I thought,' R'shiel shrugged. 'Please sit down. This could take a while so we might as well be comfortable.'

'If you're planning to convince me this is a good idea, then we could be here all night,' Kalan remarked as she sat down on the chaise near the fireplace. The clouds moving in front of the sun shadowed the room. It made her expression hard to read.

'There was a time when the Hythrun did not question the Harshini.'

'That time is long past, demon child. The Harshini abandoned us and we learnt to survive on our own. Nothing personal, mind you – the Harshini presence in Greenharbour has been most welcome these past few months – but why should we submit to your people again?'

'Because without the Harshini all Hythria will continue to be is a pack of squabbling Warlords, each trying to kill the others to gain more territory,' Damin said. 'Hythria is better than that.'

'That's very noble of you, Damin. You hope to appeal to my patriotism in lieu of my political instincts, is that it?' Kalan smiled, as if the very idea was laughable.

'No, it's your political instincts we're relying on.'

Kalan turned to R'shiel. 'What do you mean?'

'I have to destroy Xaphista, Kalan. I'm hoping you can tell me how.'

'You think the Sorcerers' Collective is privy to such secrets?'

'It's hardly something I can ask the Harshini.'

Kalan smiled faintly. 'I suppose not, but don't get your hopes up, Divine One. There may be something in the archives that I'm not aware of, but even in ancient times, the gods weren't renowned for documenting the instructions for their own demise and leaving them lying about where a mortal could find them. And even if we have the knowledge you seek, with Hythria on the brink of civil war, I've neither the time nor the inclination to aid you in such an undertaking.'

'On the brink of civil war?' Damin scoffed. 'Aren't you exaggerating just a little, Kalan?'

'You don't know the half of it, brother,' she scowled.

'You wanted to know what I was doing here? Well, I'll tell you. I'm here because the Warlord of Dregian Province tried to have you declared dead and your province gifted to his younger brother. Krakandar is currently under the protection of the Sorcerers' Collective. I occupied your city because without me, you wouldn't *have* a city.'

'Cyrus tried to have me removed?' The idea was laughable.

'It's worse than that. He's publicly calling you a traitor.'

'Let him! Who would believe him anyhow?'

'A lot of people. You left Krakandar all but unguarded, and even the lowliest beggar in the street has heard the rumours that Fardohnya is planning to invade us. You made a treaty with Medalon without consulting anyone. You sent Narvell to Bordertown to help the Defenders. It might have been different if you'd sent him to guard your border, but you didn't. You sent him into Medalon. And now you return home like nothing is wrong, bringing with you the daughter of our worst enemy as your bride. The wonder is not that Cyrus has accused you, Damin. It's that nobody has acted on it until now.'

'I have to get to Greenharbour,' he said, thinking of several rather painful and exotic things that he would like to do to the Warlord of Dregian Province. 'I'll put that obnoxious little upstart in his place. What's Lernen been doing while all this is going on?'

'Fretting,' Kalan told him. 'He's not been well lately and Cyrus has his ear. He knows what Lernen likes and, more importantly, what he fears. You've no idea the damage he's done in your absence.'

R'shiel was looking at him with concern. He did not realise how dangerous his expression was until he caught a glimpse of himself in the glass.

'Don't do anything hasty, Damin.'

'What I plan to do to Cyrus will be very, very slow, R'shiel.'

'I don't have time for you to start a war, Damin.'

He smiled coldly. 'Don't worry. It'll be a nasty little war, but a short one.'

'How long ago did all this happen?' R'shiel asked Kalan, sparing Damin an exasperated look.

'Over a month ago. I've been here since the Feast of Jonadalup. Mother came here as soon as she realised Krakandar was under threat. Narvell arrived six days ago.'

'But now that he's back, you can release Krakandar and return to Greenharbour, right?'

'No. We'll have to go back to Greenharbour so Damin can petition the Convocation of Warlords for the return of his province.'

'Petition the Warlords!' Damin exploded angrily. 'The hell I will!'

R'shiel shrugged philosophically. 'Then we'll go to Greenharbour.'

'R'shiel—'

'Damin, we have to get this sorted out quickly. Medalon is under Karien control and I can't do anything about it until I've found out how to deal with Xaphista. If that means sorting out your damned Warlords, then that's what we'll do.'

'What's the hurry?' Kalan asked suspiciously. 'Xaphista has been the dominant power in the north for centuries. A few more months one way or the other won't make much difference.'

'It's not just the Overlord. I promised to help the Defenders retake Medalon. There's a thousand Defenders headed this way,' Damin told her.

'You're bringing Defenders onto Hythrun soil? Damin, how *could* you?' she cried in horror.

'They come as allies,' R'shiel reminded her.

'There is no such thing, as far as the Warlords are concerned. If those Defenders step one foot into Hythria before this is resolved, there will be nothing I can do to save you, Damin. You will lose Krakandar, the High Prince's throne and probably your life.' The High Arrion turned to R'shiel, her eyes burning with anger. 'You are responsible for this too, I suppose?'

'Sort of,' R'shiel admitted.

'And how does this fit into your grand plan to destroy Xaphista?'

'If we don't turn the Kariens back from Medalon, Hythria is next, Kalan. I can hardly destroy him if he's getting stronger, rather than weaker. We need the Defenders and every man the Hythrun can muster. Only then can we restore the Primal Gods to millions of people who now worship Xaphista.'

'What do you mean, you're going to weaken Xaphista by restoring the Primal Gods to Karien?'

'What did you think I was going to do? Hunt Xaphista down and then throw fireballs and lightning bolts at him? Unless you've got some handy little scroll with precise instructions on how to do that tucked away in your archives, the only way I can seriously threaten the Overlord is to shake the faith of his believers. And I can't do that while he's rampaging through the continent, conquering everything in sight. The Defenders must be helped. Medalon must be freed.'

'And how do you plan to restore the Primal Gods?'

'That's where you come in.'

Kalan stared at her, wide-eyed. 'I fail to see . . .'

'The Sorcerers' Collective is the closest thing to an organised religion that I have to work with,' R'shiel explained, a little impatiently. 'The Kariens are used to being organised. It's how Xaphista maintains control. I can't just destroy his Church. I have to *replace* it.'

'Since the withdrawal of the Harshini our power has been eroded considerably.'

'I know. But Brak told me that the Sorcerers' Collective once sent out their emissaries to every corner of the continent. He said they could travel through a war zone with impunity.'

Kalan nodded. 'They were protected by their black robes, their diamond-shaped pendant and the deep respect the people had for our fellowship.'

'Those days are long past,' Damin warned. 'Anyone caught wearing the diamond pendant in Fardohnya these days is imprisoned as a Hythrun spy. In Medalon they're liable for deportation. In Karien, they're burned at the stake.'

'I can change that. *We* can change it. But I need your help, Kalan. I need access to your archives. I need Hythria united and at peace with Fardohnya, and we need Hythrun help to push the Kariens back. And I need the Collective. Only then can I face the Overlord with a chance.'

Kalan nodded as the ramifications dawned on her. 'Assuming we can save Damin's province and bring our troops to aid Medalon, how do you propose to convert the Kariens?'

'I don't wish to tip my hand by revealing that.'

Damin glanced at her askance, wondering if her reticence was deliberate or she simply didn't have a clue.

Kalan's eyes narrowed suspiciously. 'Yet you *demand* my cooperation?'

'I'm *asking* for it, Kalan. If I wanted to demand it, I would ask one of the gods to appear and make it a divine edict.'

'Then let me see if I understand you. You want me to return to Greenharbour and announce that the Collective sanctions the marriage of the Hythrun heir to Hablet's daughter. You then, I assume, want me to issue some sort of dire threat to the Warlords who oppose this union, to make them toe the line. And while you're scrabbling through my archives looking for something that probably doesn't exist, you want me to get them to release Krakandar back to Damin and convince them that a thousand or more Defenders pouring over our border is an act of friendship, not war.'

'That would help,' R'shiel agreed.

'And you? Having dragged half the world to the brink of war, what will *you* do, exactly?'

'Hand you and your Collective more power than they've known for centuries,' the demon child told her.

Kalan sat, silent and thoughtful for a moment. 'You make a powerful and tempting offer, demon child.'

'You're not likely to get another like it.'

Kalan looked down at her hands again before meeting R'shiel's eye. 'You may, of course, have access to our archives. They are as much the property of the Harshini as they are ours. As for the rest of it . . . I cannot give you an answer now. I must think on this. What you ask is unprecedented. And I wish to speak with my mother.' She glanced up at Damin. 'You are aware of this plan, I assume?'

He nodded. 'So is Adrina.'

'Well that explains this absurd marriage, at any rate.' Kalan rose to her feet and brushed an imaginary speck of dust from her long black robe. Her fair hair fell forward and when she looked up for a moment she appeared much younger and more innocent than she truly was.

'I will give you my answer when I have come to a decision. Damin; demon child.' She bowed politely and left the Solar.

Damin turned to R'shiel, shaking his head. She met his look, puzzled by his expression. '*What?*'

'I was just thinking how well you manipulate people, R'shiel.'

'You sound like you don't approve.'

'I never said I didn't approve. I just can't handle never knowing what you're going to do next.'

'You might find it's better that way,' she suggested with the ghost of a smile.

Damin doubted that, but decided against pursuing the matter. 'R'shiel, do you see Dacendaran much?'

'I haven't seen him since we left the Karien border.'

'Can you speak to him?'

'I suppose.'

'Can you ask him if anyone has been interfering in his followers?'

'If you want. Why?'

'I'm not sure. I just heard something that bothers me a bit, that's all.'

'I'll ask him if you think it's important.'

'That's just it,' he admitted. 'I don't really know if it is, or not.'

## 14

R'shiel would have liked to explore Krakandar, but her status as the demon child was a significant obstacle. She had naively hoped that her identity could be kept secret until they reached Greenharbour. She'd had a vague notion that she would confront the Council of Warlords, tell them to behave because she, the demon child, commanded it, find the secret to destroying Xaphista in the Collective's archives, then return to Medalon with a Hythrun army at her back. The chances of that happening now seemed remote. It had not occurred to her just how much the legend of the demon child meant to these pagans, or how much Damin planned to exploit it. The news had spread and a crowd had gathered outside the gates of the inner city, hoping to catch a glimpse of her.

Although raised as the daughter of a Quorum Member, R'shiel had never been the subject of public speculation before and she found it extremely disconcerting. Her status as a Novice, and later a Probate in the Sisterhood, had meant she had led a fairly normal life, such that it was, until circumstances and her own rebellion had conspired to forever change its course. She was not trained to deal with being a public figure, at least not on this scale.

It was Adrina who came to her rescue. Born and bred to be in the public eye, she seemed to know what to do without thinking about it. In fact, she seemed quite determined to teach R'shiel everything she could – as if it gave her a purpose in life, other than avoiding her mother-in-law.

Thinking of Adrina made R'shiel think of Damin. Now that she had met his mother and sister, she understood what fascinated Damin about Adrina. He had grown up surrounded by intelligent, powerful women, and Adrina was everything he admired. Of course, he was too dense to realise it, just as Adrina was too stubborn to admit how she felt about Damin. The pair of them made R'shiel want to scream with frustration. But at least they were doing what was required of them, and if they were too pig-headed to work out how they felt about each other, that was their problem, not hers.

A knock at the door was a welcome diversion from her woes. She called out a command to enter and was startled to find that her visitor was Princess Marla. R'shiel leapt out of her chair as the princess swept into the room.

'You are comfortable here?' Marla asked, glancing around the room to ensure that everything was as it should be.

'Very comfortable, thank you, your highness.'

'We must talk, demon child. I have many questions for you.'

R'shiel nodded, unsurprised. She'd been expecting this ever since she had spoken to Kalan.

'Of course. Won't you have a seat? I can order some refreshments if you wish. Mikel!'

The boy appeared from the next room at her command. 'My lady?'

'Fetch us some wine, Mikel.'

The boy bowed awkwardly and hurried from the room. R'shiel turned back to the princess who was staring at her suspiciously.

'I won't be drinking wine with you, my girl,' she announced. 'I plan to keep my wits about me.'

'Water, then?'

'That will do.'

Marla seated herself beside the fire as R'shiel poured water from a silver pitcher into a matching cup for the princess.

Winter in Krakandar was much milder than in Medalon, so the fire was banked low, more for the convenience of not having to light it later than from any real need for warmth. She handed the cup to Marla and took the chair opposite.

'So, what is it you wanted to ask me?'

'You are very blunt.'

'I was raised to speak my mind.'

'By the Sisterhood, Damin informs me.'

'That's correct.'

Marla did not look pleased to have her information confirmed. 'So it's true then that you are Joyhinia Tenragan's daughter?'

'She fostered me. My real mother died giving birth to me.'

'I cannot understand how the Harshini allowed Lorandranek's child to be raised by their mortal enemies.'

'The Harshini didn't know of my existence until recently. When they did learn of it, they sent Brak to find me. I can see you're concerned, your highness, but imagine how I feel. I was raised to despise the Harshini. Nobody was more shocked than I was to discover the truth.'

'Yet you appear to have adapted well.'

'Out of necessity. Not by choice, I can assure you.'

Marla took another sip of water, studying R'shiel over the rim of her cup. 'And so, having accepted who you are, you have decided to meddle in the internal affairs of every nation on the continent.'

'There's no point in being half-hearted about this,' R'shiel pointed out with a faint smile. 'I'm supposed to destroy Xaphista. I can't do that without affecting anyone else.'

'And this marriage? How did you get Damin to agree to it? Did you ensorcel him? Did that Fardohnyan woman?'

'Damin might be under Adrina's spell, your highness, but it has nothing to do with magic.'

'It's obvious he's under some sort of spell!' Marla snapped. 'He is beyond reason where she is concerned. I have never seen him so intransigent over a woman. He insists that she will one day be the High Princess of Hythria.'

'And so she shall.'

'The Warlords will never accept a Fardohnyan.'

'They will, in time.'

'We may not *have* time,' Marla told her. 'My brother is dying, demon child. It is only a matter of time before he succumbs to the diseases that consume him. One cannot indulge in the type of activities in which he finds pleasure without eventually paying the price. We do not have years, or even months, for the Warlords to grow accustomed to the idea of a Fardohnyan High Princess. We may only have weeks, and that is simply not enough time.'

'Then you will have to use your considerable powers of persuasion, won't you?'

Marla scowled. 'You haven't persuaded *me* yet.'

'I don't need to. It is done.'

'I will have it annulled.'

'I will have it ratified by the Harshini. I will have the gods put in an appearance if necessary. You can't fight me on this, your highness. I have considerably more resources than you when it comes to divine intervention.'

The princess did not look pleased. 'Even if I agreed to this absurd arrangement, one cannot trust a Fardohnyan, particularly one of Hablet's brood.'

'You don't think Adrina wants peace?'

'I think that young woman wants her father's throne, and that's the only reason she married my son. Have you any idea of the power you have handed her?'

'I'm quite sure Adrina knows a son of hers is likely to be king.'

'I'm not talking of that!' Marla said impatiently. 'This has nothing to do with any child she might bear. Hablet has no legitimate sons. Under ancient law, that makes Damin his heir. My son would have had the Fardohnyan throne in any case, and now you have interfered and that grasping little harlot will become Queen. Just how long do you think my son will survive after that?'

R'shiel leaned back in her chair, stunned by the news. 'I didn't know.'

'Of course you didn't know. But you can bet Adrina knows. Why else would she marry Damin with barely a word of protest?'

'Has it occurred to you that she might love him?'

'Don't be ridiculous! She wouldn't know the meaning of the word.'

'I think you're wrong, your highness. I don't think Adrina knows anything about Damin being the heir to her father's throne.'

'Then you are as blind as my son.'

R'shiel thought back over her conversations with Adrina. Nothing she had done or said would seem to indicate that she knew of any law that would make Damin the heir to the Fardohnyan throne. Even Kalan had given no hint that she knew of such a law. But that did raise another interesting question.

'Does Damin know about this law?'

'He does now! It's a tragedy he didn't learn of it sooner.'

'Why didn't you tell him sooner?'

'I only learnt of it recently, myself. My youngest stepson is a member of the Assassins' Guild. The Guild was approached by one of Hablet's lackeys to murder my sons, Damin and Narvell. They refused the contract, but decided to look into the reasons behind Hablet's obsession with the destruction of the Wolfblade line.'

'Then I don't see the problem. Damin is still heir to the Hythrun and Fardohnyan thrones. With Adrina at his side, won't that just make his claim to the Fardohnyan throne that much stronger?'

'Of course it does, that's my point. There will be no stopping Adrina now. With Damin at her side, she can claim her father's throne. Once she's done that, all she needs to do is dispose of my son and she will rule Fardohnya *and* Hythria. If the child she is carrying turns out to be Cratyn's, then she can lay claim to the Karien throne as well!'

'Child? *What* child?'

Marla shook her head in despair. 'You don't know? By the gods, it's as plain as the nose on her face. Adrina is with child, R'shiel. Surely you noticed! I for one would be very interested to learn whose child it is.'

R'shiel really had no idea. She wondered if Adrina knew, or even suspected. It was possible, of course. She and Damin had been lovers for several months. The child could only be his. If she had been pregnant when she left Karien, her condition would have been patently obvious before now.

'If what you say is true, then the child is Damin's. I can promise you that.'

'Bah! Who knows with a woman like that? It could be Almodavar's, if she was bored enough. I just pray Damin doesn't learn of her condition before I can prove the truth of the child's parentage.'

'You've not told him about it, then?'

'And have him lose what little sense he has left regarding that woman? I don't think so. And I would appreciate it if you said nothing to him either. At least until I can find the evidence I need to convince him how foolish he's being.'

'I'll not say anything about Adrina's condition,' she agreed, in an effort to appear cooperative, 'but only because I think you're on a fool's errand. The only thing you are likely to prove is that Damin is the child's father.'

'My son? Get a child on that Fardohnyan whore? Never!'

Marla's blind prejudice where Adrina was concerned was beginning to wear on R'shiel. 'Your highness, I really think you should reconsider your attitude towards Adrina. She is married to your son and if you're right about her condition, she carries your grandchild. Don't you think life would be a lot easier if you made an effort to get along with her?'

'I don't trust her,' Marla replied stubbornly.

'You've hardly given her a chance.'

'I see no reason why I should.'

'You should, because I say you should,' R'shiel declared.

'I'm not going to be ordered around by a slip of a girl who thinks she can bend the world to her will . . .'

Marla's voice tapered off as R'shiel reached for her power. She didn't do anything with it, she simply let it fill her until her eyes darkened and turned completely black. She stared at Marla unblinkingly, her black eyes like orbs of burning onyx, her silence a threat in itself. There wasn't much point in being the demon child if you couldn't lay down the law every now and then, especially when being reasonable wasn't getting her anywhere.

Marla fell to her knees. 'I am sorry, Divine One. I did not mean to doubt you.'

'Then you will do as I say,' R'shiel commanded, borrowing just enough power to fill her voice with an irresistible compulsion. It was not a coercion, but it *was* enough to scare the wits out of the princess. 'You will treat Adrina in a manner befitting her status as your daughter-in-law and you will give this marriage your full support. If not, you will answer to the gods.'

'It shall be as you command, Divine One.'

'Then be gone from my presence,' she added dramatically, 'while I am still in the mood to indulge you. And do not speak to me of this again.'

Marla scrambled to her feet rather inelegantly and was gone from the room in a matter of moments. R'shiel let go of the power and laughed. The look on Marla's face alone had been worth it. All she could do now was hope that she had frightened the princess sufficiently for her to toe the line.

'Was that Marla I just saw running out of here?'

R'shiel looked up as Adrina slipped into the room. She studied the princess closely, but if her belly was swollen, it was impossible to tell in the long loose gown she was wearing.

'It was. I'm afraid I indulged in what Brak would call a "tasteless and theatrical display of power" to get my point across.'

Adrina frowned. 'Well, I hoped it worked. That woman really doesn't like me.'

'I think you'll find her a little more cooperative from now on. How are you feeling?'

'Fine,' Adrina replied with a puzzled look. 'Why do you ask?'

'Are you pregnant, Adrina?'

The princess paled and took the seat so recently vacated by her mother-in-law. 'What do you mean?'

'I *mean*, are you pregnant? It's a simple enough question.'

'I'm not sure.'

'How can you not be sure?'

'Very well, I have my suspicions, but as I don't *want* to be pregnant, I've done nothing to confirm them.'

R'shiel smiled. 'You mean you hoped it would go away if you didn't think about it?'

Adrina glared at her for a moment, then shrugged. 'It's stupid, I know.'

'Marla thinks you are.'

'Wonderful! That's all I need.'

'Does Damin have any idea?'

'Of course not! He's a man. They never notice that sort of thing. And it doesn't really show yet.'

'Don't you think you should break the news to him before someone else does?'

'And give him the idea he has some sort of claim over me? I don't think so!'

'Adrina, it's his child too. And you *are* married to him.'

'That's beside the point.'

'That *is* the point.'

'R'shiel, don't you understand what will happen when I tell him? The first thing he's going to do is surround me with so many bodyguards I'll be lucky if I can see daylight through them. Then he's going to lock me away somewhere "for my safety" so that the child will be protected. Then he'll strut around crowing like a rooster because he's proved his manhood.'

R'shiel laughed. 'So what are you going to do, Adrina? Carry on as if nothing is amiss while your belly swells to the size of a large melon?'

'I don't know what I'm going to do, I . . .' She stopped mid-sentence, interrupted as Mikel slipped through the door.

'What is it, Mikel?' R'shiel asked, puzzled by the expression on the child's face.

'The High Prince requests your presence in the Great Hall, my lady. You too, your highness.'

'The *High* Prince?' Adrina asked curiously. 'You mean Prince Lernen is *here*?'

'No, your highness, it's Lord Wolfblade. He requests you attend him. The news has just come from Greenharbour. High Prince Lernen is dead.'

Adrina turned to R'shiel, her eyes wide with shock.

'Long live the High Prince Damin,' R'shiel murmured softly.

## 15

'We have to move from here and the roads are still blocked,' Tarja announced, leaning over the map that Denjon had spread out on the table in the cold, dank cellar of the tavern in Roan Vale.

'Move? We only just got here,' Linst pointed out testily, shifting the lantern on the table so he could study the map more easily. The ventilation was poor in the crowded cellar and the lantern smoked badly. Tarja squinted through the stinging haze and scowled at the other captain.

'Take a look outside, Linst. Between your men, those who joined us in Testra and the men I got away from the border, there's close on two thousand men out there now. We're too big a target. We can march some of the men across the border, the rest we have to break into smaller groups – less than twenty men to a squad. Each squad can operate independently, their only orders to get to Hythria. We can muster them at Krakandar. Damin may even appreciate the fact that we didn't march over his border like an invading army. And we have to do something about stopping the Kariens crossing the river.'

'Let them loose in squads? How do you expect to maintain discipline?' Denjon asked.

'I don't. We're going to have to rely on their training.'

'What about provisions?'

'We'll split up what we have here, after that they'll be on their own. You'd be surprised how helpful a sympathetic population can be.'

'Is that how you survived in the rebellion?' Linst asked. There was an edge of reproval in his tone that Tarja didn't much care for.

Tarja nodded. 'It's the reason you could never really break us. Each squad operated on its own. It didn't know where the rest of the squads were, what they're planning, or who was in them. It's like a serpent with a hundred heads. Cut off one and the others will continue to function. If they're captured, they can't betray anyone but their own small group.'

'No Defender would betray his comrades,' Linst objected.

'Any man can break under torture. The trick is minimising what each man knows, to protect the rest of the force.'

'I still say we should fight them head on. This sneaking around, running away to Hythria, it reeks of dishonour.'

'Fight them head on? Our pitiful force of two thousand men? Do odds of five hundred to one appeal to your honour that much?'

'I would rather die an honourable death.'

'Well, I wouldn't,' Denjon laughed, trying to ease the tension. 'I'd rather live, if it's all right with you.'

Tarja smiled briefly then turned to Linst. 'You need to make up your mind, Linst. You can't have it both ways. Either you're with us, or you're against us.'

'Us? Don't you mean *you*, Tarja? Isn't that what all this

is really about? You've gone pagan, haven't you? And you expect us to fight to save the damned Harshini from the Kariens.'

Tarja straightened and turned to Linst. 'Who said anything about the Harshini?'

'Who *said* anything? Your damned sister, or whatever she is these days, is one of them! Don't think me a fool. How long have you known they were in hiding? How long have you been protecting them?'

'You have no idea what you're talking about.'

'Then enlighten me, Captain. Tell me how you came to be in the company of two Harshini, one of whom we always considered your sister. Tell me how you survived a wound that would have killed any other man. Tell me why we are risking our necks. Is it really to save Medalon? Or is it because you know the Kariens will ensure the Harshini are eradicated completely this time?'

Tarja fought down the urge to throttle Linst where he stood. He was not the only Defender who felt that way. He was merely giving voice to a sentiment that was rapidly spreading through their forces, a situation not helped by the pagan rebels who had flocked to their banner. Tarja swallowed his annoyance and took a deep breath. This problem had to be dealt with, and the sooner the better.

'What I think about the Harshini is irrelevant, Linst. So is what the Kariens plan for them. My only concern at the moment is to get across the border so we can mount a counter-attack. There are no Harshini here and I'm not expecting any. But there *is* a Karien army marching on the Citadel, and a First Sister who is issuing their orders. We can decide what to do about the Harshini when we've gotten rid of the Kariens. Until then, I don't intend to waste my time arguing with you about it.'

Before Linst could answer, the cellar door opened and Mandah entered, followed by a civilian dressed in rough farmer's clothing. The man looked at the Defenders with barely disguised suspicion then turned to Tarja.

'Good to see you again, Cap'n,' he said, revealing a mouth full of broken teeth.

'You too, Seth. What news do you have?'

Seth had been a rebel long before Tarja had joined their cause. Tarja knew him for a reliable and steady man, not prone to flights of fancy the way the younger men were.

'The Kariens moved south from the border 'bout two weeks ago. They're headin' straight for the Citadel by the looks of things.'

'And the Citadel? Any news from there?'

'Aye. There's been a stack of new laws issued. Not bad ones, mind you, but odd, if you know what I mean.'

'Odd, how?' Denjon asked.

Seth glared at the officer, but did not answer.

'You can trust him, Seth,' Tarja assured the rebel.

Seth hesitated for a moment longer before he spoke. 'There's a Karien advising the First Sister. Squire Mathen, they call him. Word has it he's the one issuing the laws. The First Sister is just a puppet.'

'More than you know,' Tarja murmured, thinking of what Brak had told him about the spell cast by the Karien priests and whose mind now occupied Joyhinia's body. 'What sort of laws is he issuing?'

'He's started a program to "redeem" the *court'esa* and made it an offence for any man or woman with children to spend their wages in the "houses of exploitation" as he calls 'em.'

'He's outlawed the *court'esa*?' Denjon asked in surprise. 'The Sisterhood legalised them two centuries ago.'

'Not outlawed 'em exactly. The First Sister now reckons there are too many children going hungry 'cause their parents spend all their money on "pleasures of the flesh", rather than food for their kin. The law was passed with barely a murmur of protest.'

'Why issue a law like that?' Linst asked.

'It's the first step to outlawing prostitution completely,' Tarja said. 'In Karien it's an offence punishable by stoning. Our people wouldn't accept the Church of Xaphista being imposed on them, but if they make new laws that sound reasonable enough, before you know it, they'll be building churches in every damned village in Medalon.'

'Aye, you're right, Cap'n. All the laws seem good on the surface, but they're only a step away from worshippin' the Overlord.'

'That's the danger of them,' Tarja agreed. 'Is there any other news?'

Seth nodded grimly. 'They're gonna hang Sister Mahina.'

'When?' Tarja asked.

'Restday next, I think.'

'Then we still have time to rescue her!' Denjon declared.

'Don't be an idiot,' Linst said. 'That's exactly what they'll be expecting. Even if you could get to the Citadel in time, which is unlikely, Garet Warner will have the city locked up so tight, you won't be able to sneak a table knife through the main gate, let alone a squad of armed men.'

'Tarja? What do you think? Mahina was a friend of yours, as well as the only decent First Sister we've had in a century.'

Tarja did not answer for a moment. 'Linst is right, Denjon. We'd be walking into a trap.'

'So you're just going to let them hang her?'

'We have two thousand men here that we need to disperse and the Karien army moving through Medalon. Mahina knew the risk she was taking when she returned to the Citadel, and she'd be the first to tell us not to throw everything away trying to be heroic. I'm sorry, Denjon. Nobody wants to save her more than I do, but we simply can't risk it.'

Denjon shook his head, but he could not deny Tarja's cold practicality.

'Then we shall have to settle for avenging her death instead.'

'And avenge it we will,' Tarja promised. 'Every damned day until the Kariens are gone from Medalon.'

Tarja looked down at the map, rubbing his eyes, which felt as if they'd had handfuls of sand thrown in them. Denjon and Linst were gone and he was alone in the smoky cellar, going over the plans they had made, looking for faults and finding none. It was a useless exercise, but it was better than trying to sleep.

'Tarja?'

He looked up as Mandah entered the cellar carrying a tray. She hadn't changed much in the year since he'd last seen her. She was still as calm as her brother Ghari was fierce, still as thoughtful, and still as infuriatingly devout in her belief that the gods would take care of everything. Her fair hair was tied back in a loose braid and she was wearing an apron over her homespun trousers. She had been waiting for them, here in Roan Vale, and had appointed herself housekeeper to the senior officers and none of them had objected. Mandah was the sort of woman who could make herself indispensable with remarkable ease. Denjon was quite taken with her.

'You didn't eat at dinner, so I brought you something.'

'Thanks. Just put it there on the table. I'll eat it later.'

She put down the tray but made no move to leave. Tarja looked up at her. 'Was there something else?'

'I thought you might like to talk.'

'Some other time, Mandah. I'm busy.'

'You're always busy. You don't eat. You don't sleep. What's wrong?'

He laughed humourlessly. 'What's *wrong*? Have you looked outside lately?'

'That's not what's bothering you, Tarja. You could organise those men out there in your sleep. If you ever did sleep, that is. Is it Mahina?'

He had forgotten she was there when they spoke with Seth. 'That's a part of it.'

'And what about the rest of it?'

'I don't want to talk about it, Mandah.'

'You'll have to get it off your chest sooner or later, Tarja. It's eating you up.' She hesitated for a moment and then added in a small voice, 'Is it R'shiel?'

He looked up sharply. 'Why do you ask?'

'Because you haven't mentioned her once.'

'Is that such a surprise? I've had quite a bit to do lately, in case you hadn't noticed. Besides, what do you care? You never liked her, anyway.' He didn't mean to sound so harsh, but she had cut too close to the truth for comfort.

'It doesn't matter if I like her, Tarja. She is the demon child.'

'So everyone keeps telling me.'

Mandah walked around the table to stand beside him. She placed a tentative hand on his shoulder. 'Do you want to talk about it?'

'No,' he said bluntly, shaking off her arm.

'You'll have to eventually, Tarja.' Her eyes were full of pain at his rejection. 'You can't keep on like this. You're on the brink of exhaustion. How much use will you be to any of us if you can't think straight?'

He pushed aside his annoyance and made an effort to be civil. His mood was hardly Mandah's fault. 'Look, I appreciate your concern, Mandah, but there is really nothing to tell. Thanks for the food, and I promise I'll eat it later.'

He smiled at her, hoping it didn't look nearly as false as it felt, and turned back to the map. Mandah did not move. Tarja studied the terrain with great concentration, wondering what it would take to get her to leave.

'Ghari told me you and R'shiel were lovers,' she said after a long moment of strained silence.

Tarja slammed his palms down onto the table so hard, the tray jumped. Mandah leaned away from him, her eyes suddenly fearful.

'Ghari had no reason to lie, Tarja.'

'Damn it, Mandah, it's none of your business!'

'Is that what's bothering you?'

He took a deep, calming breath before he turned to her. 'You wouldn't understand.'

'Then explain it to me.'

Tarja looked at her for a moment then shrugged. She was not going to be put off easily. 'How much did he tell you?'

'Enough.'

'Then I don't need to explain anything.'

'Tarja, if you really love her . . .'

'Ah, now that's the problem, you see. I remember loving R'shiel as if there were no other woman in the world. But it's like the memories belong to someone else. I don't feel like that now, and I can't ever imagine feeling like that, yet I can remember it, clear as day.'

'Can you remember when you first felt that you loved her?'

'Almost to the instant,' he told her. 'It happened at the vineyard near Testra. One moment I wanted to strangle her, the next moment I was kissing her.'

'And do you remember when you stopped feeling that way about her?'

'I only remember waking up in a wagon with a head full of memories I thought were simply nightmares, at first.'

'It sounds like a geas,' she said thoughtfully.

'A *what*?'

'A geas. A spell, if you like.'

'Magic? Oh, well that's just bloody wonderful!' he snarled.

'Look, I'm no expert, but it seems the only logical explanation.'

'Mandah, where I come from you don't use the words *magic* and *logic* in the same sentence.'

'The two are not mutually exclusive, Tarja.'

'I'm sorry, Mandah, but I don't hold with your belief in the powers of the gods. You'll have to come up with a better explanation if you're trying to make me feel better.'

'I would have thought you'd seen enough to believe in their power by now, Tarja. Your determination to ignore what you've witnessed with your own eyes is just as illogical as you pretend my faith in the gods is.'

Tarja had a bad feeling he was stepping onto dangerous ground discussing theology with Mandah. 'Look, even if I conceded that such a thing was possible, why would they bother? And why, if they did put a . . . what did you call it . . . a geas, on me, would they take it off again?'

Mandah thought for a moment before answering. 'Do you know how R'shiel healed you, Tarja?'

'She used her Harshini magic.'

'That's true. The same magic you claim you don't believe in. But you may not know the whole of it. You were possessed by demons. They melded to form the blood you lost while you recovered.'

'Demons? Founders! I had a *demon-meld* inside me? How do you know that?'

'R'shiel told me. She wasn't sure what it would do to you. I think it destroyed the geas.'

He shook his head and stared back at the map. This was too incredible, too fantastic to be real.

'That's what it sounds like to me,' Mandah persisted. 'The gods sometimes put a geas on a person, to make them act the way they want. The demon-meld might have broken it, which is why you woke up thinking you could never have felt that way about R'shiel. And why you never questioned how you felt about her while the geas was on you.'

'Why would anybody, god or man, put a spell on me to make me love R'shiel?'

Mandah shrugged. 'Who can guess the mind of a god? But think about what has happened since then. Would you have rescued her from the Kariens? Would you have done half of what you did, if you were not driven to keep her by your side? Perhaps it was the gods' way of protecting R'shiel.'

'I am getting pretty bloody sick of your gods, Mandah.'

She smiled. 'You have served them remarkably well for an atheist.'

'I wasn't planning to serve them at all.'

'One cannot avoid one's destiny, Tarja, and like it or

not, you are tied to the demon child.' She smiled comfortingly. 'Try not to let it bother you. If it was a geas, then you're not responsible for how you felt about her. You shouldn't feel guilty for feeling that way, or that you don't feel that way any longer.' She placed a hand on his shoulder. 'Let it go, Tarja. And get some sleep.'

'Later,' he promised, turning back to the map.

Mandah hesitated for a moment, perhaps hoping he would confide in her further, but he had already said more than he intended. After a while he heard the door snick shut behind her as she let herself out of the cellar.

Once she was gone, Tarja swore softly under his breath for a time, cursing every pagan god he could name.

## 16

In the days that followed the news of the death of High Prince Lernen, all of Krakandar seemed to be in turmoil. The streets were draped with black and the gongs in the temples rang almost constantly, tolling the death of the High Prince. At night the city was a blaze of light as the citizens placed candles and lanterns at their doors to show Lernen's soul the way to the underworld, should he stumble into their street on his journey there. After three houses caught fire in the Beggars' Quarter, Damin declared the official mourning period at an end. He understood his subjects' need to follow tradition, but he didn't want his city burned to the ground for the sake of a man that very few genuinely lamented.

Rogan Bearbow, the Warlord of Izcomdar, had delivered the news. His province bordered Damin's to the south and although the two had never been close, he was politically astute enough to ride north to Krakandar to see if Damin was in residence, before choosing which side he would take. That he would eventually *have* to choose a side, Damin was certain. Along with the news that Lernen had been dead for close on a month came the news that Cyrus

Eaglespike, the Warlord of Dregian Province, had laid claim to the High Prince's crown. Apparently his ambitions had grown from merely removing Damin from Krakandar.

Marla was livid when she heard the news, but Narvell was unsurprised. Cyrus was a distant cousin and long an enemy of the Wolfblade family. His mother, Alija Eaglespike, had devoted her life to securing the throne for her son. It didn't surprise them to hear Cyros had taken up her cause. Damin was less worried than he might have been otherwise, knowing that regardless of Cyrus' tenuous claim to the High Prince's mantle, *he* had the demon child on his side.

Just how useful an ally she was became evident the first time she met Rogan Bearbow. Older by several years than Damin, he was a tall, aloof man; who ran his province with harsh efficiency and kept the other Warlords at bay by lining his highways with the crucified bodies of any enemy Raiders foolish enough to cross his borders.

R'shiel had entered the Great Hall with Adrina at her side. Amidst the courtiers crowded into the hall standing in small clusters discussing the implications of the High Prince's death, her skin-tight leathers looked out of place. R'shiel didn't seem to care. She strode purposefully towards Damin, leaving Adrina to follow at a more dignified pace.

'Is it true?' she asked, interrupting his conversation with Rogan.

Damin nodded. 'Rogan had a messenger bird from Greenharbour nearly ten days ago.'

R'shiel turned on the Warlord. 'Why did you take so long to send word?'

'Excuse me, young woman, but who are you to question me?'

'I'm sorry, Rogan, I forget my manners,' Damin said

distractedly. He was watching Adrina out of the corner of his eye as she approached them, terrified she might do or say something that would embarrass, or worse, endanger them all. 'Rogan Bearbow, Warlord of Izcomdar, allow me to introduce Her Royal Highness, R'shiel té Ortyn, the demon child.'

'The *demon child*? This is some sort of jest, yes?'

'This is some sort of jest, no,' R'shiel retorted. 'What's happening, Damin?'

Before he could answer, Adrina reached them. To his astonishment, she curtsied solemnly before him. 'My condolences on the loss of your uncle, your highness, and my congratulations on your elevation.'

Damin stared at her in surprise. There was not a trace of sarcasm in her tone, nor a hint of irony. She stood up and met his gaze, her expression grave.

'And who is this delightful creature?' Rogan asked, quite impressed by her regal bearing.

'This, Lord Bearbow, is my wife, the Princess Adrina.'

Adrina smiled demurely at the Warlord and offered him her hand. He bowed and kissed her palm in the traditional manner, studying her closely.

'You are not Hythrun, I judge, your highness.'

'And you are very astute, my lord. I am not Hythrun, I am Fardohnyan.'

Rogan looked at Damin frowning. 'You have taken a Fardohnyan bride?'

'I—' Damin began, but R'shiel cut in before he could answer.

'He has taken the bride I chose for him, Lord Bearbow. If you wish to object, I can arrange for you to discuss the matter with the gods. Did you have a particular favourite, or will any one of them do?'

Rogan stared at her, his eyes wide, as it dawned on him that she truly *was* the demon child. R'shiel's impatient bearing, her entire dismissive attitude that discounted titles and bloodlines, was a sharp reminder that she was not an ordinary mortal. The fact that her bearing had more to do with being raised among the Sisters of the Blade than with her status as the living embodiment of a pagan legend was something that Damin found rather ironic.

Rogan dropped to one knee in front of R'shiel. 'Divine One.'

R'shiel rolled her eyes, but fortunately, Rogan's head was bowed and he didn't see it. When she spoke, her voice betrayed nothing about how she truly felt.

'Arise, Lord Bearbow. I have no need of your worship.'

'We may have need of your sword, though,' Damin remarked as the Warlord climbed to his feet.

'Is there trouble?' Adrina asked.

'My cousin, Cyrus Eaglespike, has claimed the throne.'

'Then we must make all possible haste to Greenharbour and take it from him, Your Highness.'

Rogan smiled grimly at her words. 'This Fardohnyan wench has teeth, I see.'

Damin grimaced as Adrina looked him up and down, her green eyes cold. 'I am not a "wench", my lord, I am a Fardohnyan princess of the Blood Royal. Your loyalty to your High Prince does not entitle you to insult me.'

'I'm sorry, your highness,' Rogan mumbled, quite taken back by her reprimand. 'I meant no offence.'

'Then I shall forgive you on this occasion, my lord. My husband has need of loyal Hythrun such as you. I would not weaken his hand by insisting you be put to death for something so trivial. Not this time.'

Damin held his breath, waiting for Rogan to explode. Did she have *any* idea of what she was doing? Damin knew he could count on Narvell, and probably Rogan's sister, Tejay Lionsclaw from Sunrise Province bordering Fardohnya, but Rogan could go either way. Threatening to hang him for insulting his wife was hardly the way to win him over. But the expected explosion did not eventuate. If anything, Rogan looked shamefaced.

'I thank you for your forbearance, your highness,' he replied with a bow. 'And now, if you will excuse me, I must pay my respects to Princess Marla and offer her my condolences.'

They stood back to let him leave. As soon as he was out of earshot, Damin turned on his wife.

'What in the name of the gods are you *doing*?' he hissed.

Adrina seemed unfazed by his anger. 'Securing your throne.'

'By *threatening* him?'

'Rogan's a barbarian,' she said with a shrug. 'He understands open threats. Subtlety would be wasted on him.'

'And you worked that out after *how* long?'

'Not here, Damin,' R'shiel warned, glancing around the hall. 'Besides, I think Adrina's right. Rogan appreciates strength. She may have done you a favour.'

Damin realised at that moment that he was in serious trouble. Adrina was bad enough. R'shiel, when the mood took her, was even worse.

Together, they were impossible.

Princess Marla set the whole palace in motion to prepare for the journey south to Greenharbour. Kalan left Krakandar the day after Rogan arrived, anxious to return to the capital and gain a measure of control over the situation. No High Prince could be crowned without her approval.

She was furious that Cyrus Eaglespike would attempt to claim a throne he knew well was not his while she was out of the city. He was a cousin, certainly, but the kinship was distant. Kalan considered him less a threat than an ambitious fool.

Damin was not so sure. Cyrus would not have claimed the title unless he thought he could hold it, which meant the Warlords of Pentamor and Greenharbour were probably supporting him. With Narvell and Rogan both here in Krakandar, that only left Tejay Lionsclaw, who might not even be aware of the death of the High Prince. Damin had dispatched several birds and two human messengers to inform her, hoping that her constant battles with the Fardohnyan bandits in the Sunrise Mountains did not mean she was out of touch. He needed her in Greenharbour.

Damin was almost as certain of her support as he was of Narvell's. He had sided with Tejay when her husband died and left her with four small sons, a province to rule and an heir that was only five years old. She was Warlord of Sunrise Province because, against all the objections of the other Warlords, Damin had prevailed upon Lernen to grant her the title, rather than hand it to some ambitious young stud who had little thought for the strategic importance of the province. That had been ten years ago, and the first time he had challenged the Convocation of Warlords. Although tactically sound, his interference had proved politically unwise. He had tipped his hand too early and warned the Warlords what sort of man was heir to the throne. He'd been dodging assassins since he was a small child, but after that day the only place he'd felt truly safe was here in Krakandar. *And Medalon*, oddly enough.

'Damin?'

He turned from the window as Adrina entered the study, almost welcoming the distraction. Adrina had been in an odd mood lately, although he could not fault her behaviour. Rogan was quite enchanted by her, which Damin found amazing. Adrina was a much better judge of character than he had given her credit for. It would have been so much easier if he could trust her.

'Adrina.'

'Your mother seems determined to pack the entire palace.'

'You're not fighting with her again, are you?'

'No. We just avoid each other. It's easier that way.'

'Is there anything you need?'

She crossed the room and came to stand beside him, looking out over the winter-browned gardens. 'We need to talk.'

'Then unlock your door tonight.'

She had locked it every night since they had been in Krakandar, offering no reason for her sudden desire to sleep alone. It disturbed him to discover how much that bothered him.

'I'm not going to talk to you in bed, Damin. I want to see your face in the cold light of day.'

'This sounds serious.'

'It is, and for once in your life, I need *you* to be serious.'

He nodded, careful to keep his expression solemn. 'Very well. What did you want to talk about?'

'I want to know how long you've known that if my father has no legitimate male heir, his throne falls to you.'

'Ah,' he said uncomfortably. 'You've been talking to R'shiel.'

'How long, Damin?'

'I could ask you the same question.'

'I asked first.'

'The truth? I learnt of it the day after we arrived in Krakandar. Marla told me.'

'You didn't know before then?'

'I swear I had no idea.'

She searched his face for some hint that he was lying. 'I believe you, I suppose.'

'You're too kind, your highness.'

Adrina scowled at him. 'Don't start, Damin.'

'I'm sorry. Was that all you wanted? I really should be meeting with Almodavar and Narvell. It's not that I doubt Brak, but I'm not convinced your father won't attack come spring and I have to make arrangements for the arrival of the Defenders, assuming they get here. It won't do our alliance any good if my people start loosing arrows at them the moment they cross the border.'

'No, that's not all. I have something to tell you.'

'Let me guess. You want a divorce?' he asked with a grin.

Her eyes blazed dangerously. 'By the gods, I wish I'd never agreed to this marriage. You are a child, Damin Wolfblade, in the guise of a man. You are incapable of taking anything seriously! How in the gods' name you expect to rule Hythria, I have no idea!'

He was surprised by her vehemence, and a little guilty. It wasn't often that she spoke to him like this. It was foolish to deny her the opportunity now.

'I'm sorry, Adrina. That was uncalled for. You've been keeping up your end of the bargain, and I do appreciate it. You've got Rogan wrapped around your little finger and Narvell would probably throw himself on his sword if you asked him. Even Kalan was forced to admit that once they meet you, the other Warlords might eventually come around.'

'You didn't mention your mother.'

He shrugged. 'The best you're ever likely to get from Marla is begrudging acceptance.'

'I could live with that if I thought you trusted me.'

The comment puzzled him. 'Trust you?'

'You treat every word I utter with suspicion. You have done since the day we first met.'

'Not without just cause,' he pointed out. 'You lied to me then. For all I know you're lying to me now. How long have *you* been aware of the law that made me heir to Hablet's crown?'

'What are suggesting?'

'For all I know, you could have been planning this for years. You managed to manipulate Cratyn into taking you to the border. You betrayed him, fled to Medalon and gave your real name to the first Defender you met, almost guaranteeing I would come after you. All you had to do was get rid of Cratyn, marry me, wait till your father dies and I take his throne, then have me killed. You'd rule Hythria and Fardohnya.'

'That's preposterous! I didn't kill Cratyn.'

'No, that was the demon child. The same demon child who decided we should be married.'

'You think *R'shiel* is part of some twisted plan I have to rule the world? You're insane!'

She turned away angrily and began to walk towards the door, but he caught her arm and pulled her back. He couldn't hide his grin.

'You can be so gullible sometimes, Adrina.'

She punched his chest angrily. 'Dammit, Damin! Can't you ever stop fooling around? Have you any idea what's going on around you? You're about to ride into Greenharbour to claim your crown from a usurper. You're likely to have assassins dogging your heels and a civil war on your hands and all you can do is play stupid, childish games!'

'I know what's going on, Adrina,' he assured her, suddenly serious. 'I've had assassins dogging my heels since I was born. I was twelve years old before it was judged safe enough to let me sleep without an armed guard at the foot of my bed and that was only because Almodavar was convinced I was skilled enough to kill a full grown man. But I can live with the threat of assassination and the gods know I can deal with war well enough, but I'll tell you something that might surprise you. I wish I could trust *you*. I wish I knew what you were really after. I wish there was some simple way I could be sure about you.'

'You've never given me a chance, Damin,' she accused.

He was still holding her arm and when he pulled her to him, she did not object. She looked so open, so honest, so ingenuous, he almost believed her, and he truly wanted to believe her. But if he was wrong, it might cost him his life, although at that moment, holding her so near, her lips so close he could feel her breath on his, the prospect didn't bother him nearly as much as it should have.

'Sire, Lord Hawksword asks that when you . . . Oh, I do beg your pardon, your highness!' Almodavar stood at the door, clearly embarrassed to find them in such an intimate embrace.

Adrina stepped away from him with a fleeting look of regret, then turned to the captain. 'It's all right, Almodavar.

I was just leaving. I'll speak to you later, Damin. When you have more time.'

'Adrina?'

She hesitated at the door. 'Yes?'

'What did you want to tell me?'

'It's not important. Some other time perhaps.'

'I'll see you later, then?'

She nodded. 'If you wish.'

When she was gone, Damin turned his attention back to the organisation of Krakandar's defences, unable to shake the feeling that Adrina had left something very important unsaid.

## 17

Teriahna was waiting for Brak in his room when he returned from his evening meal. He was quite partial to the spicy fare of Fardohnya, and had lingered over his dinner, enjoying the feeling of repletion that comes with a good meal accompanied by an excellent wine. For a fleeting moment he regretted his indulgence, but even had she searched his room, there was nothing for her to find here.

He did not bother to ask how she had got past the locks. Those skills were taught to apprentice assassins. Besides, he was expecting her. She had promised to arrange to get him into the palace in the guise of a visiting lord from southern Fardohnya, come to court to find a royal bride. Brak had been surprised by her choice of disguise, but she had assured him that with so many daughters to dispose of, Hablet would see any man willing to take one of them off his hands, particularly if he was an insignificant, powerless lord who lived far, far from Talabar.

'Any luck?' he asked as he closed the door behind him. She was sitting near the window, staring out over the gardens. The heady scent of frangipani filled the room, as it did every night once the sun went down. The room was shrouded in shadows and she did not turn when he spoke.

'Lernen Wolfblade is dead.' She looked at him then, her eyes curious in the gloom. 'Does this alter your plans?'

'I'm not sure. What happened?' He lit the lantern on the table and dragged the only other chair in the room to the window beside her.

'He died of the pox, by all accounts. But that is neither unexpected nor surprising. What *is* interesting is that it happened nearly a month ago.'

'And you've only just heard of it? Who kept it quiet? The Sorcerers' Collective should have been tolling the bells of every temple in Hythria from the moment they heard the news.'

'The High Arrion isn't in Greenharbour. She's in Krakandar. There was a great deal of unrest because of Damin Wolfblade's alliance with Medalon. She went north after Princess Marla to sort it out.'

'So Marla was out of the capital when it happened, too? That's not good.'

'Not good for Damin Wolfblade, perhaps, but it proved a stroke of good fortune for Cyrus Eaglespike. He's named himself High Prince.'

'Without the sanction of the High Arrion? How long does he think that can last?'

'He's got the Warlords of Greenharbour and Pentamor on his side. It's a foregone conclusion that Narvell Hawksword will support Damin's claim, but there is still Rogan Bearbow and Tejay Lionsclaw to consider.'

Brak nodded thoughtfully. He had been away from the politics of the southern nations too long. There was a time when he didn't need the Assassins' Guild to provide his intelligence.

'Why has it taken the news so long to reach you? I would have thought you'd have heard about this within a day of it happening.'

'Normally, I would expect to,' she agreed. 'However, in this case, someone went to a great deal of trouble to stop the news getting out.'

'Cyrus Eaglespike?'

'Or his cronies. This isn't the act of an opportunistic man. This has been very well thought out. I'd say they've been planning it for some time.'

'Perhaps. Has King Jasnoff heard about Cratyn's death yet?'

'I don't think so. It's possible the news hasn't even reached Yarnarrow yet. It's winter in Karien, and travel will be difficult.'

'They could have sent a bird.'

'Even carrier pigeons fall prone to bad weather, Brak.'

'And your spies in Krakandar? What do they tell you?'

She smiled innocently. 'What makes you think I have spies in Krakandar?'

'If you don't, it would be the only place in the south that you have none.'

'You know far too much about us for an outsider, my lord.'

'And you seem to be avoiding the question.'

Teriahna shrugged. 'I don't mean to. In truth, there's not much to tell. Damin Wolfblade arrived in Krakandar, he stayed a week or more, learnt his uncle was dead and left for Greenharbour a few days later. Adrina is with him, certainly, and so is your demon child. The news of *her* presence set the city talking, I'm told, so much so that it somewhat overshadowed the news that Damin had taken a bride. Between the demon child and the death of the

High Prince, she's managed to keep a fairly low profile. The news is out, but it's a poor third to the other rumours currently on offer. Oh, there was one thing I neglected to mention. Damin Wolfblade contacted the Guild in Hythria.'

'Who does he want them to kill?'

'Nobody. He sent a message saying that whatever price the Guild – either in Hythria or Fardohnya – was offered to kill either him or Adrina, he would double it if we refused the job.'

'I always thought he was a smart lad. Can you get me in to see Hablet? This is becoming urgent.'

'If he's finished mourning.'

'Hablet is *mourning* Lernen Wolfblade?' Brak asked sceptically.

The Raven laughed. 'In public. He's probably locked himself in his rooms and is throwing a party. But he is a king, and one has to be seen to do the right thing.'

Brak fell silent, wondering how the death of the Hythrun High Prince would affect R'shiel's plans. It was a singular waste of time, as he actually had no real idea of R'shiel's ultimate plans. He was here on trust, and that was not an emotion that came easily when dealing with the demon child.

'May I offer you some advice before your audience with our esteemed monarch, Brak?'

'Of course.'

'Hablet is a very devout man in his own way, but he despises the Harshini. He has no wish to learn they still exist and no desire to welcome them back into his court. He finds he gets along very nicely without them.'

'Glenanaran and the others have been in Greenharbour for months. It's no longer a secret that the Harshini survive.'

'True, but neither is it common knowledge. Oh, people

have heard the rumours, and some even believe them, but their belief is based on faith not fact. You won't get a very warm reception when Hablet realises who you are. He'll see your presence as the thin edge of the wedge. When you deliver your news about his daughter, he'll take it as a sign that the Harshini are already interfering in Fardohnya. Be very careful.'

'I can take care of myself.'

'I've no doubt of that,' she said. 'But it is better to be warned.'

'I appreciate your concern, my Lady.'

Teriahna leaned forward, studied him closely for a moment, then smiled. 'Do you, Brak?'

There was something in the way she spoke; something in the shift of her body that set warning bells ringing in Brak's head. She placed her hand gently on his thigh. Then she abruptly shed any pretence of subtlety and the invitation in her eyes was so blatant she might as well have cried it aloud.

'Do you really appreciate me, Brak?' she asked softly.

Brak smiled ruefully and lifted her hand from his thigh, placing it quite deliberately on the arm of her chair.

'Yes, I really do appreciate the help you've given me, Teriahna,' he said.

'I see,' the Raven replied, nodding her head thoughtfully. 'There's someone else, isn't there?'

'What do you mean?'

She laughed softly. 'Do you know how I came to join the Assassins' Guild, Brak? I was a *court'esa*, and a damned good one, too. I was recruited by the Guild for a very special job. The rest, as they say, is history. But just because I've changed careers, it doesn't mean I've lost the skills I started out with.

'There *is* someone else. I can see it in your face, plain as day. Who is it? Some impossibly perfect Harshini back in Sanctuary? Some lucky farm girl in Medalon?'

Her assumption took Brak completely by surprise. He had taken no lovers since L'rin in the Grimfield, back when R'shiel was a prisoner there. Since then he had been so consumed by his task of protecting the demon child, he'd had no time to think of his own pleasure.

'There's no one else, Teriahna.'

'Perhaps you're not even aware of it yourself,' she shrugged.

Brak laughed at the very idea. 'You think that after several hundred years I wouldn't notice if I'd fallen in love?'

'I think after several hundred years, you're so used to *not* being loved, you wouldn't know what it felt like if it ran up to you and hit you on the head.'

'You think so?'

'Yes, I do,' she chuckled. 'But don't let it bother you. I'm sure it will work itself out. As for me? Well, I like to try new things. Sometimes I succeed, other times I don't.'

'New *things*?'

'I'm sorry. I've offended you, haven't I?'

'No. I just don't find myself referred to as a *thing* too often.'

Teriahna's smiled faded. 'You should try a stint as a *court'esa* some time, Brak. Then you'd truly know the meaning of the word.' She looked away, suddenly uncomfortable that she had spoken so freely. Rising hastily to her feet, she pushed the chair back along the polished floor with a scrape of wood against wood. 'I really should be going. I've spent far too much time away from my other duties. I'll bring your audience clothes around in the morning.'

Brak remained seated, guessing that she would prefer

it that way. Teriahna walked to the door, stopping with her hand on the latch.

'There was one other thing I meant to tell you,' she said, turning back to look at him. Her manner had reverted to its usual professional mien. 'I had a message from Starros, the head of the Thieves' Guild in Krakandar. He said there was an old man there who was stirring up the population against the demon child. I don't know if it's important, but I thought you'd like to know.'

'Why would Starros send you a message about some old man in Krakandar?'

'He thought it might have been one of our people on a contracted hit. It's not inconceivable that someone might want the demon child eliminated and that they would be prepared to pay handsomely for the job. And it wasn't a message so much as a reprimand. He was rather put out that I might have sent someone into his city without advising him first out of professional courtesy.'

'Did he say anything else?'

'No. Just that the old man had been preaching on street corners, subverting his people and making a general nuisance of himself. Starros thought our plan was to incite a riot of some sort and for the demon child to be killed in the ensuing chaos.'

'That doesn't sound like your style.'

'It's not. Crowds are much too hard to control. Particularly when you've worked them up into a brain-less mob. Whoever the old man was, he certainly isn't one of ours.'

'It's probably nothing to be concerned about.'

'I agree, but I thought I should let you be the judge. I'll see you later, then?' She turned her back to him and opened the door.

'Teriahna? Just out of curiosity, if someone did contract you to kill the demon child, would you take the job?'

She closed the door again and turned to him with a sly smile. 'That would depend on how much they offered me.'

'What price would you set on the demon child's life, my Lady Raven?'

'What would *you* pay for it?' she retorted.

He laughed humourlessly. 'The ultimate price.'

'You'd pay with your life?'

'I already have.'

She nodded thoughtfully. 'Then I have the answer to my question, Brak. There is someone else. It is the demon child.'

## 18

Tarja knew exactly how he planned to strike his first blow against Medalon's new masters, a plan as simple as it was fraught with danger. He also knew it would meet considerable opposition, so he kept silent until they were ready to leave Roan Vale, hugging his idea to himself as he pulled his cloak against the chill wind.

They waited in the small village for the remainder of their troops and the rest of the rebels to catch up with them. His meeting in Testra had gone well, and although Antwon could not bring himself to desert, he gave any Defender under his command who wished to flee the advancing Kariens leave to follow Tarja. Consequently, the force Tarja now had gathered to cross the border into Hythria numbered over two thousand. It still wasn't enough to take on the Kariens, but it was a start.

'We should be ready to move at first light,' Denjon reported that evening, as Tarja stood poring over the map in the cellar. It was a singular waste of time. He had studied the map so often these past few days that every line and contour was burned into his brain.

'Now if only this damnable rain would stop, so we could get through to Hythria.'

'Aye. My scouts tell me there's not a navigable road for miles. They're either flooded or so boggy we're going to have to walk most of the way.'

'And every day the Kariens are getting closer to the Citadel.'

'Well, look on the bright side,' Denjon shrugged. 'The Glass River's so full they'll not be able to cross it for a while.'

'I'd prefer it if they couldn't cross it at all,' Tarja said.

Denjon's eyes narrowed. 'That sounds suspiciously like a suggestion.'

'Actually, it was. Where are the others?'

'Linst is organising the supply wagons. Dorak is trying to beat some sense into your rebel friends. They're not being very cooperative.'

'That's because they don't like taking anything from the Defenders,' Mandah explained as she closed the cellar door behind her. 'Least of all orders.'

Tarja nodded, satisfied that they would not be disturbed for some time. He stabbed his finger at the map and looked at Denjon and Mandah.

'We have to stop the Kariens crossing the Glass River.'

'You said that already,' Denjon said, folding his arms across his chest.

'There's only three ways they can cross,' Tarja continued. 'They can build rafts and float themselves across, which is far too time consuming and dangerous. They can commandeer what trading vessels and river boats they can find, or they can use the ferries at Testra and Cauthside.'

'They won't find many river boats,' Mandah said. 'Most of them have sailed south for the Gulf. They know what's coming.'

'Then that just leaves the ferries,' Denjon agreed. 'How do you plan to stop the Kariens using them? We don't have enough men to fight them off.'

'We're going to have to sink them.'

Mandah gasped. 'Sink the ferries? But that would cut Medalon in half.'

'I'm aware of that,' Tarja replied evenly.

'It would stop the Kariens in their tracks, though,' Denjon mused.

Tarja nodded. 'With the ferries gone, the worst they can do is turn south-west and attack Testra. The heart of Medalon is the Citadel, and until they occupy that, theirs will be a hollow victory indeed.'

'It won't be easy, Tarja,' Denjon warned. 'Even if the Kariens don't try to stop you, our own people will. You'll destroy their livelihood along with those ferries.'

'I know, which is why I'm only taking a few men. We'll backtrack to Vanahiem, cross over to Testra, and then make our way overland to Cauthside. Hopefully we can take out the Cauthside Ferry before the Kariens reach it.'

'Then take the Testra Ferry out on your way back?' Mandah asked.

Tarja nodded and glanced at Denjon.

'That will take you weeks,' the captain said with a shake of his head. 'The Kariens will be in Cauthside long before you.'

'The logistics of moving an army the size of the Karien host are considerable,' Tarja reminded him. 'They can only move a few leagues a day, or be forced to break their army up into smaller units. The latter is unlikely. They'll stay together, thinking their impressive size will cow the Medalonians into submission.'

'That's a bit optimistic,' Mandah remarked with a thin

smile. 'The vast majority of Medalonians live south of the Glass River.'

'You'll be cutting it fine,' Denjon said with a frown.

'I'll hand-pick the men who accompany me. We've some good men out there and none of them come from the river towns or have family whose livelihood depends directly on trade across the river. It'll ruin the merchants and families who depend on it for their wages and I don't want any second thoughts when it comes to the crunch.'

'And the Hythrun? What do you want me to tell them?'

'I'll leave that to you,' Tarja shrugged. 'Once you get to Hythria, you and Damin can start planning the conquest of Medalon. There's not much we can do until we find out how many men he can spare us, at any rate. I'll join you as soon as I can. In the meantime, you can send out some other squads with orders to do whatever they must – cajole, threaten or destroy – to stop the river boats from docking on the western bank. I want every boat on the river – even those moored on this side too – safely out of reach of the Kariens.'

'You know, given enough time, the Kariens will find a way across. They've engineers and boat builders aplenty and there's more than enough timber on the other side of the river to build rafts to move their troops across.'

'I'm counting on the change of seasons. By the time the Kariens have constructed their own transport, the Glass River will be even more swollen than it is now with the spring melt from the Jagged Mountains. It'll be far too dangerous to attempt a crossing until the flood waters have subsided.'

'I'll come with you,' Mandah announced abruptly.

'Don't be stupid,' Tarja retorted without thinking.

'But I was a Novice once,' she explained. 'I know how to behave like a Sister of the Blade. Disguised as a Sister I can commandeer the ferry and once aboard you can take it out into the middle of the river, set fire to it, then swim ashore once it's well and truly ablaze.'

'That may even work,' Denjon said thoughtfully.

'It's too dangerous.'

Mandah laughed softly. 'Dangerous? Tarja, I was fighting in the rebellion long before you came along and nothing much has changed that I can see. Why is it too dangerous for me and not for you?'

Tarja was unable to answer her. He could hardly admit his bravery had more to do with his desire to escape his own thoughts than it did from any innate sense of honour. Turning back to face the Kariens meant not having to continue south. It meant not having to face R'shiel for a little while longer. He was afraid to admit how much that thought relieved him.

'She has a point, Tarja. You'll raise less suspicion travelling with a Sister than you would if you travel alone.'

'Then it's settled. I'm going with you,' Mandah declared.

'Are you really so anxious to throw your life away?' he asked her with a frown.

'I don't plan to throw my life away, Tarja, and I wasn't aware that this was a suicide mission.' Her eyes challenged him to deny her accusation.

Tarja looked away first. 'No, I'm not planning a suicide mission. You can come if you wish. We'll be riding hard though. It won't be easy.'

'If I'd wanted "easy", Tarja, I would have stayed with the Sisterhood.'

\*   \*   \*

Later that evening, Tarja sat in the taproom of the Roan Vale tavern finishing his meal, wondering why Mandah had accused him of planning a suicide mission. He didn't feel suicidal. But neither did the prospect of dying unduly concern him. As he pondered the matter, he realised that the only thing he felt about death, when he consciously thought about it at all, was apathy. He did not hunger for death. He did not particularly hunger for life. He simply didn't care.

'Do you mind if I join you?'

Tarja looked up at the old man who had spoken and glanced around the room. The taproom was filled to capacity and the only spare seat was the empty bench opposite him. He wondered for a moment if the others were avoiding him.

'Suit yourself,' he replied with a shrug.

The man sat down with his foaming tankard and smiled at Tarja. He had long white hair and a disturbingly familiar air about him that Tarja couldn't quite place.

'You look troubled, my son.'

'These are troubling times.'

'And you bear a heavier burden than most, I suspect.'

Tarja shrugged but did not offer a reply. He had no wish to fall into conversation with this old man, whoever he was.

'I hear you flee Medalon to join the demon child?'

Tarja looked up sharply. 'Where did you hear that?'

'The rumours are everywhere,' the old man told him. 'There's not a Defender here who isn't whispering the news to his comrades.'

*That's true enough*, he thought. *Too many of these men were there when R'shiel revealed her power. It's long past the point of being a secret.*

'Well,' the old man continued, taking a sip of his ale, 'one can hardly blame you for being worried.'

'Who says I'm worried?'

'Every line on your face proclaims it, Captain.'

'Thanks for your concern, but you needn't be worried on my behalf. We have everything under control.'

'I'm sure you do,' the old man agreed solemnly. 'But nothing will ever be certain while the demon child lives.'

Tarja studied the old man suspiciously. He was not so full of his own troubles that he did not recognise a threat to R'shiel when he heard it.

'What's that supposed to mean?'

'I mean nothing,' he shrugged. 'It just seems to me that the Kariens would be much more amenable if they weren't facing the threat of the demon child. Isn't she supposed to destroy their God? How would you feel if you thought someone was trying to destroy everything that you held dear? One doesn't have to be on their side to understand what drives them. I just think it odd that the Defenders are going to such pains to protect the very one whose presence caused this conflict in the first place.'

'R'shiel didn't start this war.'

'Didn't she? Isn't her existence what prompted the Kariens to act? You killed their Envoy because he was trying to take R'shiel to Karien, didn't you? Why do you defend her? If Medalon means so much to you, why not simply hand her over and be done with it? She's your greatest bargaining chip, yet you refuse to play it. Is she so important to you that you are willing to risk your entire nation to protect her?'

'You don't know what you're talking about, old man,' Tarja scoffed, unwilling to admit that his logic made frightening sense. Could it really be that simple? Could they end this conflict now by trading R'shiel to the Kariens? Would their enemy withdraw for something so easily arranged? Tarja shook his head, unable to believe that he could even consider betraying her.

The old man looked at him closely, as if he could read Tarja's internal conflict. Then he smiled and shrugged and took another swallow of his ale.

'You must forgive me, Captain. I let my mouth run away with me at times. I'm just an old man who sees things a little differently from younger men. What would I know? I wish you luck in your quest.'

'Luck has nothing to do with it,' Tarja replied, pushing away the remains of his stew. For some reason he had lost his appetite.

'I just hope the demon child appreciates the sacrifice you have made for her, Captain.'

The old man downed the rest of his ale and climbed to his feet. Tarja watched him as he threaded his way through the crowd to the door, disturbed to discover how easily the seeds of doubt and treachery planted by the old man had found fertile ground inside his troubled mind.

## 19

Slaves lined the walls of the Main Hall of the Summer Palace, moving the languid air about with large rattan fans, although at this time of year the temperature was quite bearable. It was an impressive chamber, crowded with courtiers and supplicants awaiting the chance for an audience with their king. The potted palms provided the perfect backdrop for the clusters of schemers and syco-phants who always seemed to find their way into any royal court, regardless of where it was or who was in power. Hablet held open court here each morning when he was in residence, and made a point of putting in an appearance, even if he never actually heard a petition.

Brak moved among the jewelled and pampered crowd, dressed in the garish yellow silk trousers and embroidered vest Teriahna had provided for him. She had claimed, with a perfectly straight face, that it gave him an air of 'rustic nobility'. He assumed she meant he looked like the provincial lord he was pretending to be. He privately suspected he looked like an idiot.

Eventually he spied the man he was searching for and pushed his way through the courtiers to confront him.

Hablet had yet to arrive and his Chamberlain, Lecter Turon, was busy openly collecting the bribes that would ensure one a place at the head of the queue. Brak had no intention of parting with a single coin to see Hablet. He had far better currency to deal with.

'My Lord Chamberlain?'

The eunuch turned to Brak and looked him over with a practised eye, taking in his air of 'rustic nobility' and dismissing him as inconsequential with a single glance.

'Can I be of assistance, my lord?' he asked rather impatiently.

'I wish to see the king.'

'As does every other man here,' the eunuch sighed.

'I was told you could arrange it.'

'Ah, now that can be difficult. The king is a very busy man.'

'I could make it worth your while.'

Lecter's eyes narrowed greedily. 'Such a consideration would be expensive, my lord.'

'Then the Raven was mistaken when she said you could help me.'

Lecter paled, his bald head shining with sweat. 'The Raven?'

'Did I forget to mention that she recommended you? The Raven seems to know quite a lot about you, actually, Chamberlain Turon. I wonder why that is?'

The Chamberlain looked decidedly uncomfortable with the notion that the head of the Assassins' Guild was taking a personal interest in him. 'I will do what I can, my lord, but as you may have heard, the king is in mourning for his cousin, the High Prince of Hythria.'

'I'm sure he's devastated,' Brak agreed wryly. 'But I won't need more than a moment of his time.'

'May I inquire as to the nature of your business with the king?'

'I have news for him that would be best delivered in private.'

'Please wait here, my lord. I will see what I can do.'

It wasn't long before Turon returned and beckoned Brak forward. Brak followed him through the curious and envious stares to the delicately carved doors at the end of the hall. He knocked once and entered without waiting for an answer.

'Your majesty! Allow me to introduce Lord . . . what was your name?'

'Brakandaran.'

'Lord Brakandaran! From . . .' Lecter looked at him questioningly.

'I come from Sanctuary,' Brak said.

Up until that point, the king had been sitting behind his elaborate gilt desk, reading from a parchment scroll in front of him, utterly disinterested in his guest. At the mention of Sanctuary his head jerked up and he stared at Brak with bright, birdlike eyes.

'Where did you say?'

'Sanctuary.'

'Which one?'

'There is only one, your majesty.'

'Lecter! Leave us!'

Hablet's tone left no room for argument. The Chamberlain hurried to do as he was bid. As the door closed, Brak stepped further into the room and looked around with interest. The doors to the balcony were open and he could hear faint childish voices from the lush gardens below. The king's private chamber had barely changed since he last stood here confronting Hablet's great-grandfather.

'You look human,' Hablet accused as soon as they were alone. His voice was anything but friendly, but at least he made no pretence of not understanding who Brak was.

'I'm only half Harshini. It's an advantage at times.'

'Brakandaran, did you say your name was? Not Brakandaran the Halfbreed, surely? I thought you'd be long dead by now.'

'As you can see, I'm not dead.'

'What do you want? If you're here to petition my court for a place for one of your damned sorcerers, you're wasting your time. I'll not have the Harshini spying on my every move for that degenerate in Hythria.'

'That degenerate in Hythria is dead,' Brak pointed out. 'I was led to believe you were mourning him.'

'Ha! Dancing on his grave, more like it. Is that why you're here? Now that Lernen is dead, you've decided to come to me for protection? You should have come here first, in any case. It was a grave insult to Fardohnya, the Harshini king sending his people to Lernen's court without coming here first.'

'You just said you didn't want any Harshini in your court.'

'That's not the point. You should have offered. I have served the gods faithfully. I deserve it.'

Brak knew it was hopeless trying to argue with such a man. 'Your majesty, the decision to allow the Harshini to return to the Sorcerers' Collective was not mine to make. I might point out, however, that if you hadn't rounded up every member of the Sorcerers' Collective and had them thrown in gaol when you assumed the throne, my king *might* have considered sending someone to Fardohnya. As it is, you've a lot of explaining to do.'

Hablet tugged on his beard unhappily. 'They were Hythrun spies.'

'And the others you killed when you inherited the crown? What was their crime?'

'You've been around long enough to know what happens in Fardohnya when a new king takes the throne. Why quibble about it now?'

'Your barbaric practices don't concern me, Hablet. Interesting though, that they were never practised when there were Harshini in the Fardohnyan court.'

'That's because the Harshini are so damned squeamish. Now, did you want something in particular, or are you just going to stand there and chide me for things I did thirty years ago?'

Brak's eyes darkened and he waved his arm, drawing a chair from the side of the room across the polished floor with an uncomfortable screech. When the chair magically arrived at his side, he sat down and leaned back, smiling at the Fardohnyan king.

'Thank you, your majesty. I will have a seat.'

Hablet's eyes widened. He had never been confronted with true Harshini power before. His day-to-day dealings with the gods involved bribing the temples and praying for a legitimate son.

'What do you want?'

'You and I need to have a talk about your heir.'

'I'll name my heir when I'm good and ready,' Hablet declared. 'And no black-eyed bastard from Sanctuary is going to make me appoint someone I don't want.'

'I wouldn't dream of it, your majesty, however circumstances have arisen of which you are not aware, and they will radically affect your choice.'

Hablet squinted at him 'What circumstances? Ah! I

have it! You've discovered that stupid law about leaving my crown to a Wolfblade, haven't you? Well you can go back to Sanctuary and tell Lorandranek, or whoever the hell sent you here, that Talabar harbour will freeze in high summer before I let a Wolfblade set foot in Fardohnya, let alone sit on my throne.'

'I wasn't sent by Lorandranek, your majesty. He's been dead for over twenty years. Korandellan is King of the Harshini now.'

'I don't care if the damned First Sister of Medalon is king!'

'I was sent here by the demon child.'

'The demon child? Are you drunk? The demon child is a legend made up to frighten children. Lorandranek never sired a half-human child.'

'Perhaps if you hadn't been so hasty throwing the Sorcerers' Collective out of Fardohnya, you might know that he did.'

'Who is he then? Where is he?'

'Her name is R'shiel.'

'A girl?' Hablet laughed with genuine amusement. 'Why would the gods invest such power in a female?'

'Perhaps they don't share your prejudice.'

'Perhaps they're not as smart as they think they are,' the king scoffed.

'I don't suggest you say that in Jelanna's hearing,' Brak warned. 'Maybe that's why the Goddess of Fertility has denied you a legitimate son. She must know what you think of women.'

'Don't you threaten me with my beliefs,' the King warned. 'I am a faithful servant of the Goddess.'

'So I've heard,' Brak agreed with a wry smile.

'So, this demon child . . . this *girl* . . . sent you here

to tell me who to name as my heir?' Hablet laughed scorn-fully. 'I don't know what's funnier – that she thinks she can dictate to me, or that you actually thought I would listen to you.'

'You'd better listen to me, Hablet,' Brak warned. 'There will be no legitimate son for you. Your heir will be as the law decrees – it will be Damin Wolfblade.'

'Over my dead body!'

'Exactly,' Brak pointed out simply.

'I'd rather give my crown to that simpering Karien idiot Adrina married than name that Hythrun barbarian my heir.'

'That might prove difficult,' Brak murmured, but Hablet wasn't listening to him.

'Anyway, you're mad if you think the people of Fardohnya would ever accept a Hythrun King!'

'They would accept a Fardohnyan Queen.'

'Oh! So now you want him to marry one of my daugh-ters, I suppose!'

'No need,' Brak said, with a smug smile. 'The demon child has already taken care of that minor detail.'

Hablet stilled warily. 'What do you mean by that?'

'Ah, now those would be the circumstances I spoke of,' Brak said, brushing a fleck of dust from his yellow silk trousers as he deliberately drew out the silence.

'*What* circumstances?' Hablet demanded.

'Cratyn is dead, your majesty. Your daughter has remarried.'

'*Remarried*? Who?'

'Perhaps you'd like to hazard a guess?' he suggested. He was rather enjoying Hablet's discomfort.

'*No!*' the king cried, leaping to his feet, his face almost as crimson as the silk-panelled walls. 'I'll not tolerate this!

I'll disown her! Damn it, I'll invade Hythria and bring her back!'

'Your House is now united with the House of Wolfblade. You will honour the peace between your Houses and do no such thing. As the Wolfblade House is the ruling House in Hythria, it is now beyond your reach. You can't invade them and you can't make war on them.'

'This is intolerable!'

Brak smiled serenely. 'I'm sure you'll learn to live with it.'

'Get out! Get out of my palace! Get out of my country, for that matter! Take your damned Harshini manipulations and your demon child and get the hell out of Fardohnya!'

Brak drew on enough power to blacken his eyes again, rose to his feet and loomed over the Fardohnyan King.

'You *will* abide by the law. You *will* name Damin Wolfblade your heir and you *will* give your blessing to his marriage to Adrina.'

'Never!'

'Then be prepared for the consequences, Your Majesty,' Brak warned. 'You defy the demon child at your peril.'

## 20

It was obvious that Cyrus Eaglespike and his cronies were in control of Greenharbour. The streets, while not exactly deserted, were unnaturally free of the normal bustle of commerce that one would expect in the greatest trading port in the south. There were no soldiers from the Sorcerers' Collective in evidence and no sign of the Palace Guard either. Although the guards made no move to prevent Damin and his force entering the sparkling white city, their breastplates were embossed with a soaring eagle.

R'shiel looked around with interest. She rode at Damin's side at the head of a column made up of three centuries of Krakandar Raiders. Narvell Hawksword followed Damin's men with three hundred Elasapine Raiders, while further back, Rogan Bearbow rode at the head of his own entourage. Between them they had brought close to a thousand men south to claim the High Prince's throne. Adrina was riding in the coach a little further back in the column with Princess Marla. She had refused to ride since Krakandar, although she declined to give a reason. Damin was convinced it was simply to make things more difficult for him. R'shiel knew the reason but figured it wasn't her place to say. Besides, she had promised Marla she would say nothing yet. No doubt Adrina was being subjected to her mother-in-law's intense scrutiny as they travelled together. R'shiel wondered with a faint smile just who would emerge the victor from that small, but important, skirmish.

'This doesn't look promising,' Damin murmured.

'Who normally guards the city?' R'shiel asked with a glance over her shoulder at the wary guards who fingered their sheathed blades with itching fingers as they passed through the city gates.

'The Collective.'

The further they rode into the city, the more deserted the streets became. News of the arrival of the Warlords of Krakandar, Elasapine and Izcomdar ran before them like flame on a line of lamp oil and the citizens of Greenharbour wisely kept to their homes, out of the way of a confrontation that was likely to get very ugly.

'Damin, I may not be a tactical genius, but is this a good idea? Riding openly through Greenharbour when you know your cousin has claimed the throne?'

He shrugged. 'Greenharbour is neutral territory.'

'Nine hundred Raiders isn't very many.'

'That's all I'm permitted to bring into the city. Three centuries for every Warlord, no more. It's the law.'

'The law didn't stop your cousin claiming the throne. What makes you think it's going to stop him breaking the rules about the number of troops he can muster in the city?'

'I can't risk marching into Greenharbour openly flaunting the law. It would be playing right into Cyrus' hands. Besides, you won't let anything happen to me.'

'You're relying on *my* power to save you? Adrina was right, you do enjoy living dangerously, don't you?'

'Adrina said that, did she?'

'Yes.'

'What else did she say?'

R'shiel rolled her eyes impatiently. 'Why don't you ask her?'

'I'm asking you.'

'You're a damned fool, Damin Wolfblade.'

He didn't answer her; didn't have a chance to. She stilled suddenly, her whole body tensing as the familiar prickle of magic ran over her skin like a million tiny ants wearing hobnailed boots.

'What's wrong?' Damin asked, watching her curiously.

'Someone is drawing power. A lot of it.' Her face was a mask of concentration as she tried to pinpoint the source. Finally she stood in her stirrups, looking out over the white, flat-roofed houses and then pointed towards the harbour. 'It's coming from that direction.'

'The harbour?'

'No. I don't think so. But close to it.'

'Then it's probably the Sorcerers' Collective you sense. Perhaps it's some of the sorcerers—'

'No!' she declared emphatically. 'What I can feel isn't someone chanting spells. This is Harshini.'

Damin shrugged. 'That would mean it was one of the Harshini who returned to the Collective last winter. I doubt it's anything to be concerned about. If it's Harshini magic you can sense, then they're bound to be on our side.'

She sat down again and looked at him. 'How do you figure that?'

'You are the demon child. You ride with me.'

'You don't understand, Damin. This isn't one Harshini drawing their power that I can feel. It's several of them and they are drawing every drop they can handle.'

'Then it could mean trouble.'

'Founders, Damin! Do you practise being so dense?'

He grinned sheepishly. 'I'm sorry. Explain it to me.'

'I think the Harshini are under attack. It's the only explanation.'

Damin reined in his stallion and brought the column to a halt. His grin faded and was replaced by a look of consternation. 'Someone is *attacking* the Harshini? That's inconceivable. This is Hythria, not Medalon or Karien. We honour the . . . R'shiel!'

She wasn't listening to him. Instead she spurred her horse forward to the end of the paved street where the rise of the land enabled her to look out over the rest of the city. What she saw made her gasp with astonishment.

Greenharbour lay before her, a sea of whitewashed buildings glaring under a sky of sapphire silk.

The city curved around the crescent-shaped bay. To the left was the forest of tall masts that marked the vast wharves of the city. To her right was a magnificent white palace, its domed spires gilded and almost too bright to look upon. Above the palace was a glittering dome of radiant, shimmering light enveloping the temples and palaces that R'shiel thought must be the Sorcerers' Collective. She could just make out the outlines of the buildings inside the dome as it waxed and waned with the fading strength of the Harshini who held it in place.

Legend held that two centuries ago, the Harshini who defended the Citadel from the Sisters of the Blade had done the same thing. But if several hundred Harshini had not been able to hold a protective dome in place long enough to save the Citadel, there was little chance the few Harshini in Greenharbour could hold this one longer than a few more minutes.

'What in the name of the gods is *that*?' Damin gasped as he reined in beside her.

'The Harshini trying to protect themselves,' she explained. 'Look down there.'

Damin looked in the direction of her pointing finger. The streets surrounding the dome of light were crowded with soldiers. Although they were too far away to make out their individual escutcheons, R'shiel could easily guess whose troops they were. They were massing in the main avenues leading to the Collective, simply waiting for the strength of the Harshini who protected it to fade. She glanced over her shoulder at the men Damin, Narvell and Rogan had brought into the city. They were easily outnumbered three to one. The other two Warlords were riding up the street towards the head of the column. R'shiel left Damin to deal with them and turned her attention back to the dome of light. Even in the short time she had been watching it had faded somewhat.

'What's going on?' she heard Rogan Bearbow demand of Damin behind her. She did not wait to hear his answer. Spurring her horse forward, she headed for the harbour at a canter. Whatever politics were involved in the battle for the High Prince's throne, the Hythrun had no right to endanger the peaceful Harshini.

R'shiel had no plan in mind. Her only thought was that the dome was fading and the Harshini trapped inside were in danger. She could not reach the Harshini through the impenetrable barrier, but when it collapsed the soldiers massed in the streets surrounding the Collective would overrun them. She smiled grimly to herself as she rode, wondering how life could change so drastically in such a short time. Two years ago, had she heard there were Harshini under attack, she would have applauded the forces ranged against her despised enemies. Now she was riding to their rescue, heedless of any danger she might be placing herself in. ·

That thought had a sobering effect, and she slowed her horse to a walk. *What am I doing? I can't just ride up to the gates of the Collective and demand the enemy disperse.*

R'shiel looked around and discovered she had ridden into an area of the city that was filled with government buildings. At least she guessed that's what they were. They had an aura of bureaucracy that R'shiel knew well. The buildings were several storeys high and a number had impressive entrances flanked by fluted marble columns. They surrounded a broad circular plaza dominated by a fountain that spewed forth its cascade from the mouth of a beautifully sculpted water dragon. R'shiel studied the creature curiously for a moment. She had heard of the remarkable beasts that populated the warm waters of the Dregian Ocean, but she had never seen anything like the creature in the fountain. It had a large dorsal fin, wide-set eyes and a long, elegant tail that ended in a broad, flipper-like paddle.

She had little time to admire the artistry of the fountain, however, as the sound of horses moving towards her caught her attention. At the far end of the paved plaza a number of mounted Raiders appeared, a tall, middle-aged man riding at their head. His blond beard was neatly trimmed, his leather armour gilded. The soaring eagle of his House was picked out in precious stones that glinted in the sunlight falling across the plaza.

Behind her, R'shiel could hear Damin and his party

forming up. She sat alone and exposed astride her horse in the centre of the plaza as the opposing forces arrayed themselves on either side. An unnatural silence descended, only the splashing of the fountain and the creaking of leather harness disturbing the morning.

'Cousin!' Cyrus Eaglespike called loudly, moving forward at a walk. 'I never thought to see you alive again!'

'That's pretty bloody obvious!' Damin called back as he rode out to meet the pretender flanked by Narvell and Rogan.

R'shiel watched them approaching with a frown. She didn't have time for this. The dome of light flickered in the distance.

'It warms my heart to see that the reports of your death were . . . overstated, cousin,' Cyrus declared with vast insincerity as he neared the fountain.

Damin, Narvell and Rogan reined in on the other side of the fountain. 'I'm sure it does, cousin. That would explain what you're doing here with so many troops.'

'We acted to contain the potential civil unrest brought on by the news of our uncle's death.'

'Lernen was my uncle, not yours, Cyrus. Your relationship to the Wolfblade family is so tenuous it barely exists.'

'Actually, it's not as tenuous as you might think, cousin. Once Kalan ratifies my claim . . .'

'The High Arrion? Ratify *you*?' Rogan Bearbow declared hotly. The mere thought obviously offended him.

'Is that why you're attacking the Harshini?' R'shiel demanded.

Cyrus seemed to notice R'shiel for the first time. He smiled patronisingly. 'Who is this, Damin? Some piece of Medalonian entertainment you picked up north of the border? Or is this the wife that we've been hearing about?'

R'shiel's eyes darkened with anger as she drew on her power. Cyrus' eyes passed over her contemptuously for a moment, then suddenly locked on her face as he saw her eyes blacken.

'Mother of the gods!' he cried. His horse reared, the gelding reacting to the proximity of a Harshini drawing on her power. Even the mounts that Damin, Rogan and Narvell rode began to toss their heads nervously, although they knew her scent well enough not to fear the unfamiliar but instinctive urge they felt to respond. Her own horse was not concerned, having been with her long enough now to recognise and welcome the touch of the magic that it had been born to serve. R'shiel suddenly understood why the majority of the troops surrounding the Collective were infantry. With the Harshini inside the Collective drawing so much power, the Hythrun sorcerer-bred cavalry mounts would be uncontrollable.

'Cyrus, call off your troops. Now.'

Damin spoke with quiet assurance, as if he had no doubt as to the outcome, should the Warlord refuse.

'Who are you?' Cyrus demanded of R'shiel.

'I'm the last thing you will ever lay eyes on if you don't withdraw,' she informed the startled Warlord. The power filled her, hungering for release. Cyrus' mount was becoming increasingly restive and he was fighting to maintain his dignity and his seat at the same time.

The pretender turned on Damin angrily. 'What sort of trickery is this?'

'This isn't trickery, my lord, this is the demon child. I suggest you do as she says. She's not noted for her patience.'

If Cyrus had heard that Damin was married, then he certainly must have heard that the demon child rode with him. The Warlord debated the issue for a long, tension-filled moment, then angrily waved his arm. A rider broke from the ranks at the entrance to the plaza and cantered forward.

'Take a message to Lord Foxtalon and Lord Falconlance,' Cyrus ordered through clenched teeth. 'Tell them to order the troops to withdraw.'

'Sir?'

'You heard me!'

With a puzzled look, the captain nodded and wheeled his mount around. Cyrus turned back to R'shiel, his expression a mixture of contempt and fear.

'Satisfied?'

'For now,' R'shiel agreed, although she did not let go of the power. The dome was fading fast, its light failing as fatigue consumed the Harshini holding it in place. Now she was drawing on her own power, she was even more aware of the drain on the Harshini inside. A few more minutes and they would have to let it go completely. She bit her bottom lip in frustration, wishing she knew how to lend them her strength. Brak and her tutors at Sanctuary had never taught her how. Perhaps they had not thought she would ever need a reason to link her power to another Harshini. Or maybe she couldn't link with a Harshini unless they were a té Ortyn like her . . . Maybe it was too dangerous . . . She shook her head to clear it of the useless thoughts and turned her attention back to the matter at hand. What she could and couldn't do with her power was a problem for some other time. Right now it was enough that Cyrus believed she knew what she was doing. 'Aren't you supposed to have some sort of election to confirm the new High Prince?'

'The Convocation would already be under way, but

for the interference of the Harshini, who prevented us entering the Sorcerers' Palace.'

'You can't hold a Convocation without all seven Warlords,' Damin pointed out.

'Actually, cousin, I merely need a majority.'

'Which you don't have,' Narvell reminded him.

'A situation that will be remedied as soon as Tejay Lionsclaw arrives.' Cyrus looked to Rogan with a frown. 'I see you have chosen whose bed to lie in, Lord Bearbow. I'll remember your choice when I'm High Prince.'

'That's an empty threat, Lord Eaglespike. You don't have the numbers.'

Cyrus smiled with oily contempt. 'You might be surprised, my lord.'

The two men glared at each other like lions facing each other over a recent kill. R'shiel sighed impatiently.

'Founders! I've had enough of this! Damin, how soon can we hold this Convocation?'

Damin didn't answer her. He was glaring at Cyrus with such venom that R'shiel was afraid he was going to call his cousin out, right here in the plaza. Despite how satisfying it would be to witness him beat the arrogance out of Cyrus, she knew this had to be resolved legally. Damin could vent his anger later, once he was High Prince.

'Damin!'

'What?'

'I said, how soon can we hold this Convocation?'

'As soon as Lady Lionsclaw arrives.'

'Fine. Send someone to fetch her. In the meantime, I want every Raider off the streets. The Collective can go back to guarding the city. I assume you all have sufficient control over your men that you can keep them out of trouble until this is sorted out?'

Cyrus opened his mouth to object then decided against it as R'shiel turned her black-eyed gaze on him.

'Very well, we have a truce until the Convocation,' he agreed reluctantly. 'But don't think this has changed anything!'

'Damin?'

'A truce,' he agreed, almost as reluctantly as Cyrus.

'Fine, that's settled then. Now get rid of these soldiers!'

'This is not finished, demon child!' Cyrus hauled his reins around sharply, taking his anger out on his horse as he rode at a brisk canter back to his men. Behind him, the dome of light wavered and shimmered brightly for a moment, as if sprinkled with a billion tiny stars, then it faded away to nothing as the Harshini finally succumbed to exhaustion.

'That was close,' Narvell muttered.

'We'll sort him out soon enough, brother,' Damin promised savagely.

'Aye,' Rogan agreed. 'And the more painfully the better.'

R'shiel glared at them impatiently. 'You're all as bad as each other,' she snapped, then turned her horse and continued towards the Sorcerers' Collective – and hopefully the answers she sought.

## 21

The weather was bitterly cold as Tarja and his squad rode north as hard as they could push their horses without them foundering. The small band of saboteurs made good time retracing their journey of a few weeks ago, staying close to the Glass River, camping at night under whatever meagre shelter they could find. Their good fortune lasted until a day south of Cauthside, when a savage thunderstorm forced them to take shelter in an abandoned boathouse next to the remains of a small dock jutting precariously into the swift flowing water.

When they arrived, Tarja found a surprise for which he was completely unprepared. The boathouse was already occupied by a score or more Fardohnyans; the remnants of Adrina's Guard who had fled the border with them. Damin had given them supplies and maps, and ordered the Guard to make for Fardohnya weeks ago. What they were doing here, this far north, when they should have been almost home by now, completely baffled Tarja. Getting the story out of them proved something of a trial too, as none of the Fardohnyans spoke Medalonian, and nobody in his troop had more than a passing acquaintance with their native language. In the end, they conversed in Karien, as it proved the only language they had in common.

Second Lanceman Filip, the young man who had surrendered the Guard to Damin on the northern border, told the story. They had taken Damin's advice and headed for Cauthside and the ferry there, only to discover the town crammed with refugees. Not only could they not converse with anyone in the town, their mere presence had caused no end of trouble, some people mistaking them for Kariens. Explaining they were Fardohnyan, not Karien, had done little to help their cause. The townsfolk had turned on them. They'd been forced to fight their way clear of the town rather than risk the remainder of their small band in a civil riot. Filip and his men were now hiding in the boathouse while they waited for their wounded to recover sufficiently so they could continue south to Testra and attempt to cross the river there. They had lost three men getting out of Cauthside.

Tarja allowed the men to light a fire with what dry fuel they could find, satisfied that the weather offered them adequate protection from accidental discovery. The fire cheered the troop considerably. Even the Fardohnyans seemed a little more spirited. They sat around the small blaze, his own men discussing tactics and speculating on what their captain had in mind, the Fardohnyans talking softly among themselves.

Tarja stood by the small window looking out over the dark water, uncaring of the rain that splattered his face. He could hear the low murmur of conversation over the storm outside and knew he would have to decide quickly what to do with the Fardohnyans. It was also time to tell his troop what he was planning.

Mandah was still the only person in his small squad who knew exactly what he had in mind. She was right when she claimed that she knew how to behave with the careless arrogance of a Sister of the Blade. Disguised as a Blue Sister she had commandeered the ferry in Vanahiem with remarkable ease. He hoped she could do the same in Cauthside with as little effort.

Before he'd acquired an additional twenty-four Fardohnyans, the plan had been to burn the ferry then swim to safety. If the rain kept up like this, they would have no chance of burning anything. Nor would they be able to risk swimming the river.

'Tarja?'

He turned as Mandah walked up beside him, hugging a borrowed Defender's cloak around her against the cold. She reeked of damp wool, her fair hair hanging limp and wet against her head, yet her eyes were bright with the excitement of the adventure.

'You should stay near the fire and dry off,' he told her.

'I'll be all right. I've been checking the Fardohnyan wounded. The one in the corner with the belly wound, I'll be surprised if he makes it through the night. The others should be fine to travel when we leave tomorrow.'

'So you think we should bring them with us?'

'They've a better chance of getting home eventually if we do.'

He shook his head but didn't answer, thinking she would have said the same if they were stray cats.

'Is something wrong?'

'No. I was just thinking about tomorrow. It won't be easy if this weather keeps up.'

'Is there anything I can do to help?'

'Can you stop it raining?'

'I could pray to Brehn, the God of Storms, but I'm not sure he would listen to me. You need the demon child if you wish to speak directly to the gods.'

'Well the demon child isn't here, is she?'

'Is that such a bad thing?'

He looked at her for a moment then shrugged. 'No, it's not such a bad thing, I suppose.'

Mandah laid a gloved hand on his arm and smiled encouragingly. 'You're far too hard on yourself, Tarja. Come to the fire and get warm. You won't stop the rain by staring at it.'

She was trying so hard to cheer him. He didn't have the heart to deny her. Mandah could not bear to see any creature in pain, human or beast. He thought of R'shiel: of her temper, her anger and her willingness to manipulate others to get her own way. There was no comparing the two women and it hardened his suspicion that the memories that haunted him could not possibly be real. The old man in the tavern had summed it up neatly. They were doing this for R'shiel. He was still trying hard to convince himself she was worth it.

'Pity I *can't* stop the rain by staring at it,' he replied, making an attempt to sound light-hearted. Then he glanced over his shoulder at the men around the fire. 'It's time I told the men what our mission is, anyway.'

Mandah took his arm as they approached the fire. The others moved aside a little to make room for them. The Fardohnyans withdrew to the corner of the boathouse, sensing that this did not involve them. Tarja squatted down and glanced around the circle, satisfied he had picked the right men. There were few Defenders in his squad. Those he had left to Denjon and Linst. The men he had chosen were rebels for the most part, men he had fought with before; men who understood how to frustrate a numerically superior enemy without confronting them head on.

'We're going to burn the Cauthside Ferry,' he announced as they looked at him expectantly. 'If we're not back in Testra within a month, the commander of the Testra garrison will destroy that ferry, too. If all goes well here, we'll destroy it ourselves, once we've completed our mission and are back on the other side of the river.'

'You think that will stop the Kariens getting to the Citadel?' Ghari asked.

'No. But it will delay them for a time.'

The rebels looked anxiously at each other. Ulran, a small, dark-eyed man from Bordertown, and the best knife-fighter Tarja had ever met glanced around the gathering, gauging the mood of his companions before he spoke.

'That's going to hurt more than the Kariens, Tarja. There's a lot of people who depend on those ferries.'

'How much trade do you think there's going to be once the Kariens get across the river?' Torlin asked. The same age as Mandah's brother Ghari, he was one of the rebels captured in Testra who had followed Tarja to the northern border. Slender and surprisingly quick-witted, he would have made a good Defender.

'Torlin's right,' Rylan agreed. He was one of the few Defenders in the squad – solid and dependable. 'The Kariens are foraging their way south. They'll strip Medalon clean. There won't be anything *left* to trade by the time they've passed through.'

Ulran nodded his reluctant agreement. 'I suppose. It just seems a pity to destroy a perfectly good ferry, that's all.'

'Well, if you're feeling so noble, Ulran, you can come back and build them a new one after the war,' Harben suggested with a grin. Harben worried Tarja a little. His enthusiasm for destruction was matched only by his refusal to take anything seriously. He reminded Tarja a little of Damin Wolfblade.

'I've a feeling we'll all be in our dotage before that day comes,' Ulran retorted, then turned back to Tarja. 'So, we burn the ferry. How?'

As if in answer to his question, the night was lit by jagged lightning, accompanied by the rattle of thunder. The rain began to fall even more heavily, pounding on the battered shingles of the boathouse so hard that Tarja could barely hear himself think. He looked up, shook his head and looked back at his men.

'I was hoping one of you would have a bright idea.'

The wounded Fardohnyan that Mandah was so concerned for died not long after midnight. By dawn the following day the rain had not let up, but Tarja could not afford to delay, so they hastily buried the dead soldier in the soft ground, packed up their makeshift camp and rode on. After a lengthy conversation with Filip in Karien, it was decided that the Guard would wait on the south side of the town while Tarja and his men sank the ferry. The Fardohnyans would offer cover in case of pursuit and together they would head back to Testra and the ferry there once the job was done. Tarja's men had shaved and now wore Defender uniforms and Mandah sat astride her mare in Sisterhood blue. They were stiff with the cold and soaked to the skin by the time they split from the Fardohnyans and turned towards the northern river town.

Cauthside was normally a quiet town, but now it was

filled with refugees fleeing the advancing Kariens. When Tarja had last seen it over two years ago, he was with the late Lord Pieter and his entourage. That fateful journey had led to most of the trouble he now found himself in, he thought sourly. The town had been preparing for the Founders' Day Parade. Streets he remembered decked out with blue bunting were now crowded with lost souls, waiting a chance at the ferry to get to relative safety on the other side of the river.

'Tarja, what will happen to these people?' Mandah asked as they dismounted and led their horses towards the landing through the press of bodies. 'They'll be stranded once we've . . . you know.'

'It can't be helped,' he told her. 'Better a few stranded souls on this side than the Kariens in control of the Citadel.'

'There's more than a few people here, Tarja. There must be thousands of them.'

Tarja nodded, but found himself rather unsympathetic to their plight. These were the camp followers who had ridden on the heels of the Defenders hoping for a profit from the war. He did not intend to feel guilty because things hadn't turned out as they planned.

'You can't help them, Mandah.'

She nodded reluctantly as a child of about eight or nine with large, sad grey eyes ran up alongside them, tugging hopefully on Mandah's blue sleeve. She was clutching a bedraggled, tan-coloured puppy to her chest and both of them were shivering.

'Are you here to save us, Sister?'

Mandah looked down and shook her head. 'I'm sorry, child. I'll—'

Tarja grabbed her arm and pulled her away before she

could say anything else, or offer to adopt the puppy, which was the sort of thing Mandah was liable to do when left to her own devices.

'You're supposed to be a Sister of the Blade.'

'That doesn't mean I have no compassion.'

'No, but it does mean you keep your damned head down,' he reminded her. 'We've a job to do, Mandah. You've already adopted a score of lost Fardohnyans. You'll have to save orphans and stray dogs some other time.'

'But—' she protested indignantly.

'That's an order,' he told her harshly as he shouldered his way through the crowd. 'Now do as I say. Keep your head down and don't make eye contact with anyone . . . or any*thing*.'

'You're a heartless fiend, Tarja,' she hissed as she followed the path he cut through the throng. 'How can you just stand by and watch—'

'Mandah!' Ghari warned from behind, saving Tarja the need to scold her further. He glanced back at his men to make sure they were still behind him. The young woman glared at him but said nothing, obviously offended. They pushed on through the crowded streets and into the small town square, which had the look of a refugee camp. There were hundreds of tents set up, crowded close together, their pegs driven into the gaps in the cobblestones.

'This is madness,' he muttered, mostly to himself, as he surveyed the square. A drizzling rain had begun to fall again and the air was biting, even through his Defenders' cloak. He glanced over his shoulder and beckoned Ghari forward. The young rebel threw his reins to the man beside him and pushed his way between the horses to Tarja's side.

'What's wrong?'

'I don't know yet. You and the others stay here. Mandah and I will make our way down to the river and see what's happening. We'll never lead the horses through this.'

Ghari nodded and took their reins. Tarja took Mandah's arm and led her through the chaos, stepping over guy ropes, small children, washing lines and smoking cook fires that hissed defiantly at the rain that threatened to extinguish them. The landing was not far, but the closer they got, the thicker the crowd grew, until they reached a wall of densely packed bodies that no amount of pushing and shoving could penetrate.

Being taller than average, Tarja could see over the heads of the crowd. What he saw did not please him. The ferry was halfway across the river, loaded almost beyond capacity with passengers, sluggishly making its way against the current to the other side.

'What do you see?' Mandah asked, her view blocked by a solid wall of bodies.

'The ferry is making a crossing. It'll be hours before it returns and even then we'll have no hope of getting near it.'

'What are we going to do?'

'We'll have to fall back on my other plan.'

'What's your other plan?'

'I'll tell you as soon as I think of it,' he said with a frown.

By mid-afternoon the ferry had returned to Cauthside. Tarja waited with growing impatience as the barge made its way laboriously across the rains-wollen river under a sky as dark as tarnished silver. The crowd grew restless as it neared the bank, surging forward as the refugees tried to push to the front of the line. Short of taking to the crowd with swords and cutting their way through (and even then he wasn't certain that would work), there was no way they could get near the landing.

More frustrated than angry, Tarja pushed his way through the mob and walked back to where Mandah and the others waited under the eaves of the local inn. His expression told them what they wanted to know, even before he got close enough to speak.

'So, how do we get near the ferry?' Ghari asked.

'We don't. We'll have to think of something else.'

'If we had a ballista, we could set it alight with burning pitch,' Rylan suggested.

'A *ballista*?' Harben asked. 'And to think I had one in my pocket and left it behind because I didn't think we'd need it!'

Tarja frowned at the young man's flippancy. 'If you can't offer anything useful, Harben, be quiet.'

Harben had the sense to look contrite. Tarja called the men to him and they huddled together under the thin shelter of the inn, suggesting and rejecting ideas as they tried to think of a way to get close enough to the landing and the ferry. In the end it was Harben who suggested the solution, and he acted on it before Tarja could stop him. The young rebel pushed his way into the crowd in his red Defenders uniform and began shouting.

'They're coming! They're coming! The Kariens are here! Flee! Run for your lives! The Kariens are here! The Kariens are here!'

It was not long before the mob took up his cry. The effect was instantaneous and disastrous. Those at the back of the crowd broke away and began to run from the landing back towards the square. Those closest to the landing lunged forward, pushing the front ranks into the icy river.

Everyone was shouting, pushing, shoving to get clear.

'Stop him, Tarja!' Mandah gasped. 'Someone will be killed!'

But it was too late to stop the panic Harben's reckless cries had triggered. Instinct quickly replaced common sense. Fear replaced reason. The crowd became a heedless mob. Tarja was pushed back against the wall of the inn as the crowd spilled into the square, trampling tents, cook fires and anything else that got in their way. Their cries echoed through the town, panicked and desperate.

'The Kariens are coming! The Kariens are coming!'

'The Kariens!' Mandah shouted, echoing the hysterical cries of the mob. Tarja grunted as a sharp elbow jabbed him in the ribs and he turned to chide her for contributing to the chaos. But she wasn't looking at him. Her eyes were fixed on the entrance to the square. 'Oh gods, Tarja, they're here!'

Tarja turned to look in the direction of Mandah's pointing finger. At the entrance to the square a column of armoured knights was ploughing into the chaos, their pennons flapping wetly in the damp air. Whether the knights had intended to run down the people before them, or simply had not had time to stop their heavy warhorses, Tarja couldn't tell. In any case, the effect was the same. Harben's cries of impending doom had proved horribly prophetic.

'Back this way!' he yelled, as he pulled Mandah along the wall to the corner of the inn. The narrow lane behind the tavern was cluttered with debris and fleeing refugees. Tarja pushed his way through, using his size and height to shove less motivated souls out of his way.

'I was right!' Harben chortled gleefully as he leapt over a pile of garbage and raced ahead. 'The Kariens are here!'

'Get to the horses!' Tarja shouted after him. Harben waved to indicate he had heard the order and ran on. Tarja glanced over his shoulder to assure himself the others were following. Mandah stumbled beside him, her long skirts hampering her steps. Once past the inn he dragged Mandah into a small lane between the Heart and Hearth inn, and the livery next door.

'Get rid of the jackets,' he ordered as the others followed them into the lane. He tore off his own distinctive red jacket and stuffed it behind a barrel full of rain-water placed to catch the run-off from the roof of the inn. The air was icy, but it was vastly preferable to being identified as a member of the defeated Medalonian army.

'We'll never get past them,' Ghari predicted as he shoved his jacket down beside Tarja's.

'We're not going to try. But sinking that ferry just changed from a good idea to an imperative.' The others nodded their agreement. With the Kariens quite literally on their heels, all objections were forgotten. 'Mandah, you and Ghari follow Harben and get the horses ready. Borus, you and Torlin scout the north side of town. Find out if this is just an advance party, or if we really do have the Karien host just over the next hill. Paval, you ride back and warn the Fardohnyans that when we leave here, we'll be running and we might have half the damned Karien army on our heels.'

The men nodded and slipped away. Mandah looked as if she might object, but Ghari gave her no chance. He grabbed her arm and headed back out into the lane behind the inn in the direction Harben had gone.

'And the rest of us?' Rylan asked.

'We're going back to the ferry. Kariens or not, it still has to dock. If we're ever going to have a chance at it, it will be in the next few minutes, before the Kariens take control of the town. We need to sink that ferry and get out of Cauthside before the Kariens arrive in force, or it's going to be a *very* long war.'

They retraced their steps back to the square and turned towards the landing, pushing against the flow of the crowd, which had thinned considerably since the appearance of the Karien knights. The square was a shambles of flattened tents, distraught mothers and screaming men trampled by the fleeing mob. Then there were the dozen or so knights who had ridden through them, milling about in the centre of the square, almost as confused about what had happened as the refugees.

The ferrymen waited a little offshore, afraid to land, yet unable to hold for long against the current. They pulled on a rope as thick as a man's thigh that stretched from one side of the river to the other, clinging to it grimly to hold the boat steady. Tarja judged the distance between the ferry and the riverbank and realised it was too far to jump. He glanced up as a crack of thunder rumbled over the river. The sky was so low he felt he could almost touch it. Back in the square the Kariens were still too disorganised to even notice the ferry, let alone realise its strategic importance.

'They can't hold the ferry in that current much longer,' Cyril noted.

'It's going to rain again any moment,' Tarja added. 'At least we'll have that small measure of cover.'

'Aye,' Cyril agreed as thunder shook the ground. Jagged lightning brightened the dull afternoon for an instant. 'Those knights will rust if they don't get indoors.'

Tarja glanced at the older man, wondering if he was trying to be humorous, but his expression was grim. 'If we can't destroy the ferry, we may have to settle for cutting it adrift.'

The rope that secured the ferry on this side of the river was tied to a massive pylon sunk deep into the ground about ten paces from the landing. To cut through it would be time consuming and dangerous. The rope was wet and they had only their swords, which, although razor-sharp, were not designed for such a task. Even if they could attempt it unnoticed, it would take several long, exposed minutes to sever the rope, and the ferrymen who waited anxiously to haul the barge ashore were unlikely to let them attempt such a feat without objection. Surrender or not, the river was their livelihood. Crouched by the edge of a small warehouse, Tarja debated the issue for a moment then turned to his squad.

'Lavyn, take Byl and Seffin and go pick a fight with the ferrymen. I want them too busy to notice what we're up to. Cyril, you stay here with the others and keep an eye on those knights. If they pay us no attention, stay out of their way. If they look like going anywhere near that ferry, call them out. Insult their mothers, if you have to. Whatever it takes to keep them off our backs.'

'And remember,' Ulran added with a grin, 'if you truly want to insult a Karien, make sure you mention his god, his mother and at least one dog.'

Tarja shook his head at the knife-fighter, but allowed himself a small smile. 'Ulran, you're with me.'

The small man grinned and produced a wicked, serrated dagger from the side of his boot. The blade was nearly as long as his forearm. 'You think this might do the trick?'

Tarja nodded, more relieved than surprised to find Ulran carrying such a vicious weapon. His sword would have been as blunt as a butter knife after hacking through so much wet hemp.

'Let's move!' he ordered. The men slipped away to their assigned positions and Tarja followed Ulran down the slight slope towards the landing. The three men he sent to distract the ferrymen were ahead of them, shouting aggressively at the unsuspecting river-folk as they approached. Their words were drowned out by another bellow of thunder as Tarja drew his sword and turned his back to Ulran to protect him while he cut through the massive line.

Lightning split the clouds for a moment and then icy rain began sheeting down, blurring Tarja's vision and soaking him in seconds. He glanced over his shoulder at Ulran, who was sawing the rope, wiping the rain from his eyes as he worked. A strand unravelled and then another as he hacked at the rope, the weight of the ferry pulling it as taut as a harp string one moment, slackening the next, as the ferry rocked against the current. Somewhere over the rain he could hear angry shouting, but if it was the men on the ferry, the boatmen Tarja had sent the others to distract, or the Karien knights, he could not tell. He couldn't see more than a few paces in front of him. All he could do was stand on the balls of his feet, his sword at the ready, hoping that if they were attacked, he would see it coming.

Ulran sawed frantically at the rope as time slowed to a crawl. Tarja risked another look over his shoulder. Half the rope was severed now, but it was taking much too long.

'Hurry, Ulran!'

'You think you can do this any faster?' the rebel shouted over the downpour as another strand unravelled. He was panting heavily with the effort of sawing through the wet hemp, his muscles bunched under his wet shirt, his lips blue with the cold.

The shouting seemed closer and Tarja turned back in time to see a Karien knight riding down on them. Cyril had fallen near the edge of the square, the puddle he lay in red with blood. He could not make out the rest of his men through the sheeting rain, but the spectre of a massive Karien warhorse loomed over him as one of the knights, suddenly realising what they were attempting, rode straight at them.

'Out of the way!' Tarja shouted.

Ulran slipped and fell as he scrambled to get clear. Tarja swung his sword like an axe and struck the taut rope with every ounce of strength he could muster. The Karien was almost on him, the sound of hoofs on the cobbles almost louder than the rain. He swung again, wincing as the blow jarred his arms to the shoulder. The Karien was only a heartbeat away and still the rope held. Tarja swung one last time and the rope finally gave way under the strain of the ferry pulling against it. Rain swallowed the shouts of the panicked ferrymen as it whipped free; the barge suddenly swinging into the current, at the mercy of the hungry river.

Tarja barely had time to turn as the Karien rode him down. He had no time to recover his fighting stance or bring his sword around. He saw the blow coming, saw the flat of the Karien's blade aimed at his head and knew there was nothing he could do to stop it.

Pain blinded him.

Then there was blackness as unconsciousness swallowed him whole.

## 22

There had been some dissension over whether or not Damin should be allowed to take up residence in the High Prince's Palace, his opponents fearing that his possession of it might imply their tacit agreement to his claim. Marla had put an end to the argument by pointing out that the palace actually belonged to the Wolfblade family, therefore she had a perfect right to be there and invite whoever she wished to guest with her.

That had been yesterday. Cyrus Eaglespike was evicted as the Wolfblades reclaimed their palace. Adrina had been shown to her apartments, the same quarters she had used when she visited Greenharbour for Lernen's birthday almost three years ago, and seen nobody since.

She paced the sumptuous rooms impatiently, striding past tall, diamond-paned doors that opened out onto a balcony overlooking the harbour. They allowed what little cooling breeze there was to sigh through the room, gently billowing the sheer curtains that screened the windows against insects. The screeching gulls circling the fishing boats grated on her nerves. The air was humid, worse even than Talabar.

Adrina hated not knowing what was going on. She knew there had been some sort of confrontation with Cyrus Eaglespike, and that R'shiel had somehow temporarily defused the situation, but other than that she was completely in the dark.

The door opened and Tamylan slipped into the room, bearing a tray with a silver jug beaded with condensation. She placed the tray on the gilded table by the door, then turned to her mistress.

'You should be resting, your highness. You look exhausted and there is more than yourself to consider now.'

'I can't rest,' she declared, stifling a yawn. 'What news?'

'Not much, I fear. The city seems quiet. R'shiel has gone to the Sorcerers' Collective to meet with the High Arrion and the Harshini.'

'Where's Damin?'

'With Lord Bearbow and Lord Hawksword. I believe Princess Marla is with them also.'

'So I'm to be excluded from their council, am I? Where are they meeting?'

'Adrina, I really don't think you should—'

'I don't recall asking what you thought, Tam. Where are they meeting?'

'Downstairs in the throne room.'

'Then I think I shall join them,' she announced. Squaring her shoulders, she marched to the door and flung it open, only to have her way blocked by two heavily armed Raiders wearing Damin's wolf's head crest. 'Out of my way!'

'I'm sorry, your highness,' the taller guard said. 'Lord Wolfblade said you weren't to leave this chamber.'

'Don't be absurd! I'm his wife, not a prisoner! Stand aside!'

'Lord Wolfblade was very specific in his orders, your highness.'

'Actually, I told them to tie you down, if necessary.'

Adrina turned to find Damin coming towards her, his boots clicking on the mosaic floor. He was unshaved and still dressed in the same clothes she had seen him wearing yesterday. He had probably been up all night. Damin looked almost as tired as she felt. She quashed a momentary pang of sympathy for him, preferring anger to compassion.

'How dare you treat me like a prisoner!'

'It's for your own protection, Adrina. Until I'm certain the palace is secure, I don't want you wandering around.'

'You don't want me to know what's going on, more like it.'

The guards stood back to let Damin enter, tactfully closing the door behind him. Tamylan curtsied to him and he nodded absently in acknowledgment.

'Can I get you anything, my lord?'

'Something to eat, Tam,' Damin replied wearily. 'And something cold to drink. Have it sent up here.'

Tamylan curtsied again and let herself out of the room before Adrina could countermand the order.

'You seem to be getting very familiar with my slave.'

'I believe Tamylan has finally decided that I may not be an ogre, after all.'

'You haven't convinced me yet.'

He smiled tiredly. 'Are you all right?'

'What harm can come to me here, locked away like a bird in a cage? Of course, I might die from boredom, but don't let that bother you.' She resumed her pacing as Damin flopped onto the chaise near the open balcony doors.

'I'm sorry, I didn't mean to give the impression you were a prisoner.'

'Ah . . . now let me think . . . I'm stuck in this room. There are guards on the door. I'm not allowed to leave. How silly of me to think all that meant I was a prisoner.'

'My uncle has been dead for nearly two months now, Adrina. That's two months that Cyrus Eaglespike has had access to this palace. We've already discovered at least three rooms that were rigged with assassination devices.'

She stopped pacing and turned to him. 'But you said the Assassins' Guild was on our side.'

'They are. That's how we found the devices. Cyrus hasn't got access to the Guild, but there are some gifted amateurs out there. This is a big palace. It will take days before we're certain they've found every nasty little surprise Lord Eaglespike has left for us.'

Adrina found herself regretting her outburst. Perhaps he really was concerned for her welfare. On the other hand, he may simply be using it as an excuse to exclude her.

'You didn't invite me to your council,' she accused with a bad feeling she sounded like a petulant child.

'That was Marla's idea, not mine.'

'You're a Warlord and a High Prince. Don't you think it's time you stopped listening to your mother?'

'If I listened to my mother, Adrina, you *would* be a prisoner.'

She did not doubt he spoke the truth. 'What's going on, Damin? I've a right to know.'

He nodded. 'That you have. How much have you heard?'

'Only that you confronted your cousin and that R'shiel did something to him.'

'Actually, it was more the threat of what she *could* do that encouraged Cyrus to see reason. When Kalan returned to Greenharbour ahead of us, Cyrus tried to get her to ratify his claim to the throne and sanction the Convocation, even though he had only three Warlords to attend. Kalan refused naturally, so he tried to storm the Sorcerers' Palace. He didn't count on the Harshini. They threw up some sort of protective dome that he couldn't penetrate. They'd been under siege for days. R'shiel says we arrived just in time.'

'And what is the demon child doing now?'

'I don't know for certain. As soon as we took possession of the palace, she left for the Sorcerers' Collective. I haven't seen her since.'

'Has something happened?'

Damin shrugged. 'Who knows? R'shiel has all of us dancing on strings like puppets in a show that only she can see.'

'Yet we all dance willingly enough,' Adrina said with a frown. 'So what happens now?'

'We wait for Tejay Lionsclaw. Until she arrives, we can't hold the Convocation.'

'Is she on her way?'

'She should be.'

'You sound uncertain. Isn't she on your side?'

'I would have said yes a few days ago, but that was before I learnt that Cyrus Eaglespike married his daughter Bayla to Tejay's eldest son last spring, while I was in Medalon.'

'So the person who holds the casting vote is tied to your opponent by marriage. That's not a very comfortable position to be in.'

'Decidedly uncomfortable,' Damin agreed.

'How are you going to ensure that she remains in your camp?'

'I haven't worked that out yet. Any suggestions?'

The question took Adrina by surprise. That Damin actually wanted her opinion was flattering. In fact, that he had bothered to come here at all, to acquaint her with the situation and ask her advice was the last thing she expected.

'You need to discover the quality Tejay Lionsclaw admires most in a leader and make sure you have more of it than your cousin,' she advised. 'That, or give her something she wants. Something that nobody else can give her.'

He laughed sourly. 'That's easy! All I have to do is give her the secret of the explosive powders your damned Fardohnyan bandits use against her in the Sunrise Mountains. If I could do that, she'd swear the allegiance of her House to mine for an eternity.'

'My father guards that secret more closely than his treasury.'

'I know. We've tried everything we could think of for years to discover it.'

Adrina hesitated before she spoke again, aware that her next words would mean she was taking an irrevocable step in a direction she had not planned to go. But she was tired, mentally and physically. Her surrender seemed inevitable and the energy it took to sustain her defiance was needed elsewhere.

'You haven't tried asking me.'

Damin looked up at her in astonishment. '*What?*'

'I said, you haven't tried asking me.'

'I heard what you said, Adrina,' he told her, rising to his feet. He stood too close. She wished he had stayed seated. She didn't like looking up at him. 'Are you telling me that you know the secret of the explosives?'

She could not tell if he was angry or just surprised.

'That's exactly what I'm telling you.'

'Why didn't you tell me this before?'

She took a step back from him. 'You didn't ask.'

He turned away from her and walked to the open doors. The set of his shoulders was stiff and angry. He was silent for a time then he turned back to her.

'Why tell me now? Why the sudden change of heart?'

'You always suspect me of having an ulterior motive, don't you?'

'That's because you usually *do* have an ulterior motive, Adrina.'

She was honest enough to not deny the charge. 'Our fates are bound, Damin, whether we like it or not. I cannot go on fighting you forever.'

'You seem to be doing just fine, so far.'

The door opened and Tamylan returned before Adrina could respond to the charge. Her slave didn't seem to notice the tension in the room. She curtsied hurriedly then turned to Damin. 'My lord, Princess Marla requires your presence urgently. She has news of Lady Lionsclaw.'

Damin nodded then turned to Adrina. 'We'll finish this discussion later.'

He strode from the room, angry and annoyed, before she had a chance to answer.

Tamylan closed the door behind Damin and leaned against it, staring at Adrina suspiciously. 'Did you tell him?'

'No.'

'Adrina . . .'

'I keep planning to, Tam, but the timing never seems right.'

'You can't keep it a secret much longer.'

'I know,' she sighed.

Tamylan crossed the room and took her arm gently, leading her to the chaise.

'Well, I suppose there's no point in worrying about it now. Why don't you lie down? You need your rest and he said he'd be back. You can tell him then.'

Adrina nodded, aware that she was almost swaying on her feet with fatigue.

'He's mad at me again.'

'He'll get over it.'

'I told him about the gunpowder.'

'Was that wise?'

'I thought . . . oh, hell! I don't know what I thought. He makes me so angry!'

'No angrier than you make him,' Tamylan pointed out with a shrug. 'Now stop fretting and come and lie down.'

Adrina sighed wearily. 'What would I do without you Tam?'

'I'm sure I don't know, your highness.'

Adrina smiled and lay back on the couch. She would tell Damin when he returned – about the gunpowder and the child.

'Tam, did Marla say what the news was? About Lady Lionsclaw?'

'No, but she seemed excited rather than upset, so I suppose the news is good.'

Adrina closed her eyes for a moment then opened them again, looking at Tamylan with concern. 'If I go to sleep, you'll wake me when he comes, won't you?'

'Of course.'

'You seem to like him now. You used to think he was a barbarian.'

'I still do,' the slave told her. 'But I've decided the demon child is right about one thing. I think he really cares about you, Adrina. That rather improves my opinion of him.'

Adrina closed her eyes again. The humidity and the strain of the past few weeks caught up with her in a wave of fatigue. 'Do you think he'll be happy when he learns I'm with child?'

'He'd better be,' Tam replied sternly.

'You're going to make a wonderful nurse, Tam.'

'Rest, your highness.'

Adrina didn't answer. By the time Tamylan had gently closed the door behind her, she had let the torpor overtake her and drifted off to sleep.

## 23

When Adrina woke, it was dark. She experienced a sharp pang of bitter disappointment when she realised Damin had not come back. *Well, what did you expect?* she asked herself grumpily. *It's not as if he actually* wants *to spend time in your company.* Tam had not lit the candles yet and the room was full of dancing shadows. Moonlight reflecting off the still waters of the harbour painted flickering patterns on the ceiling. She lay still for a moment, wondering what had woken her, then heard the noise again in the corridor outside her room.

Curiously, Adrina climbed to her feet and crossed to the door, placing her ear against the warm wood. The noise grew louder, the unmistakable sound of shouting and the clang of metal on metal. She stepped away from the door in puzzlement. It sounded like a fight. Was the palace under attack?

The door burst open suddenly and the light from the passage outside momentarily blinded her. She screamed as the room filled with armed men. Arms grabbed at her and a mailed hand was clamped over her mouth, stifling her cries. She struggled against the man who held her then suddenly relaxed as she remembered the child she carried. If she struggled too hard she might cause it harm.

'Are you sure that's her?' one of them asked.

'Aye.'

'Then let's get out of here. Make certain they're all dead out there,' he added, jerking his head towards the corridor.

A Raider slipped through the door, his sword drawn. Adrina cringed as a high-pitched and unmistakably female scream followed a few seconds later. She twisted her head around and caught sight of a blue skirt puddled on the tiles near the door, the familiar slippers stained with the blood that pooled around them.

*Tamylan!*

'Get her to the balcony,' the man in charge ordered. 'The boat is waiting.'

Adrina struggled as they dragged her across the room, her heart beating so hard she thought it might burst through her chest. She turned her head, trying to keep Tam in her line of sight, willing the feet to move, to give some indication that she was still alive. The man sent out to finish off the guards slipped back into the room and closed the door behind him, cutting off her view. Adrina sobbed into the mailed hand still covering her mouth.

*Tamylan!*

They dragged her through the open door and out onto the balcony. A Raider was lowering a rope over the edge, down to the dark waters of the harbour below. His leather breastplate was embossed with a soaring eagle. The Raider who seemed to be giving the orders checked the rope was secure then turned to Adrina.

'Sorry about this, your highness.'

The man holding her suddenly released his hand from her mouth, but before she could scream a mailed fist hit her in the jaw. The pain blinded her for a moment and she struggled to stay upright.

The second blow was more effective. By the time she realised she had been struck again she was unconscious.

The next thing Adrina knew, she was tied hand and foot, lying in a puddle of icy water in the bottom of a small boat. The sea churned beneath them, and the motion of the boat made her ill, but she was determined not to vomit. She held down the contents of her heaving stomach by sheer force of will. Spitting out a mouthful of sour blood and stale salty water, she lifted her head to see where she was. In the darkness she could make out little but the bare feet of the sailors who pulled on the oars, and the booted feet of the Raiders who had kidnapped her.

One of them looked down and noticed she was conscious. He bent over and pulled her into a sitting position, squinting at her in the moonlight.

'Awake, then, are you?'

'You have a gift for stating the blindingly obvious, my man.'

'I ain't your man, missy,' the Raider replied. 'I'm one of Lord Eaglespike's men.'

'Again, you state the obvious,' she remarked, glancing at his breastplate, proudly embossed with the soaring eagle of Dregian Province. 'Where are you taking me?'

'Somewhere safe.'

'That's a rather relative term under the circumstances. Untie me at once!'

'Can't do that, your highness.'

'Why not? Are you afraid I'll escape? With all these big, nasty sailors surrounding me? I'm flattered.'

'Lord Eaglespike said . . .'

'Ah! Lord Eaglespike! Did he give orders that I was to be treated like some galley slave you snatched for a bit of sport? Untie me this instant!'

Her tone almost had him convinced. He was reaching for the ropes when another man stopped him, looking down at her with contempt.

'Leave her be, Avrid,' the other man ordered. 'Don't let her trick you.'

Avrid lowered his hands, almost apologetically. Adrina glared at the Raider with all the regal scorn she could muster while sitting in such an inelegant position.

'I promise I will personally see to it that you all die a very slow and painful death. I will supervise your torture and execution myself. I enjoy watching my enemies suffer long, excruciating punishments. I'm Fardohnyan, you know. We have ways of making a man live in agony for weeks without killing him.'

'Shut up!' the Raider ordered, noticing the looks on the faces of the men who could hear her.

Adrina smiled coldly. 'Then, there's always a chance I won't get to do a thing to you myself. Once the demon child hears of this, your days left in this world will be so few even you could count them. Did I mention that the demon child is a friend of mine?'

'I told you to shut up!' The Raider's voice had an edge of panic to it. 'Don't say another word!'

'Am I scaring you?' she asked cheerfully.

The Raider punched her in the face rather than answer her question.

Just before dawn, they reached their destination, a small stone jetty that jutted out into a small churning bay in the shadow of a massive white tower that seemed to grow out of the cliff-face. Adrina was hauled from the boat by another pair of Dregian Raiders and dragged along the slimy dock to a narrow staircase that wound upwards towards a square of yellow light. Shivering in her damp clothes, she shook off the man who was holding her and climbed the steps without assistance, despite the effort it cost her. She was cold and stiff and aching in places she didn't know existed until now. Her head ached, her stomach was queasy and her face felt as if it had swollen to three times its normal size.

At the top of the stairs was a small guardroom where more Raiders waited for her with another man dressed in gold-chased armour. He studied Adrina with concern then turned to the Raider who had hit her in the boat.

'Lord Eaglespike said not to harm her, you fool!'

'She's not hurt bad,' the man replied defensively. 'Nothing's broken. But she's got a mouth on her.'

The young lord turned to Adrina apologetically. 'I'm sorry, your highness. You were not meant to be injured.'

'That's a fairly hollow apology, don't you think?'

'We've brought you here for . . . political reasons,' the young man explained uncomfortably.

'Is that what you call it? Where I come from, we don't usually start our political negotiations with criminal acts.'

'If you'd stayed where you belong and Damin Wolfblade had heeded our warnings, we wouldn't need to commit criminal acts, your highness,' he shrugged. 'I am Serrin Eaglespike, Lord Cyrus' brother.'

'Bully for you,' Adrina replied, unimpressed.

'Lord Eaglespike will be here later. He may wish to speak with you then, or he may wait until Wolfblade has met his demands. In the meantime, you may consider yourself . . . our guest.'

He stood back as Adrina was pushed forward from the small guardroom to a long, narrow corridor. The walls were made of rusted iron bars, each one revealing a damp cell beyond. Most of them were empty, and the occupants of the few that weren't looked up disinterestedly as she passed.

About halfway up the corridor, her escort stopped and unlocked the cell on her left. They pushed her through the door with little ceremony and locked it behind her.

Serrin followed the guards and stood outside the bars, watching her as she took in the small high window, the damp, salt-pitted floor and the mouldy straw that served as a bed. A guard untied the ropes that bound her wrists and she rubbed at the raw skin absently as she looked around.

'Not exactly what you're used to, I imagine?'

'If you want to use your imagination for something fruitful,' she suggested frostily, 'use it to imagine what I'm going to do to you when I get out of here. Have you any idea how long we Fardohnyans can hold a grudge? Do you have any concept of the lengths we are prepared to go to for revenge? Perhaps you've heard of the ancient Fardohnyan tradition of *mort'eda*?'

Rather than looking fearful, Serrin actually smiled. 'You don't think the threats of a woman frighten me, do you?'

'Then what does frighten you, my lord? You'll go to war over this, you know that, don't you?'

'Know it? We're counting on it! Damin Wolfblade will gather up the thousand men he has in Greenharbour and come storming over our border as soon as he hears you are missing.'

'Then why aren't you out there getting ready to face him?'

'We *are* ready to face him, your highness. We have ten thousand men waiting. He'll fly right into our trap like a fox on the scent of fresh chicken blood. If there's one thing you can always count on, it's Damin Wolfblade's reaction to anything that he perceives as a threat to something he loves. He'd rather fight than eat.'

Adrina burst out laughing, despite how much it hurt her split lip. 'This is your grand plan? There's a fatal flaw in your logic, I'm afraid.'

'What flaw?'

'You're assuming Damin loves me.'

'Well, doesn't he?' Serrin asked, a little confused.

'I hate to disappoint you, Serrin,' she said, holding her sides against the bitter laughter that shook her. 'But you've not provoked Damin, you've played right into his hands. He won't care if you send me back to him in little pieces. You've kidnapped the one thing he wants to be rid of!'

Serrin glared at her in disbelief. 'You're just saying that.'

Adrina's laughter had almost reached the point of hysteria. She could not believe they had actually kidnapped her for such a mistaken reason.

'You poor, misguided fools!' she cried, sobbing with mirth. 'Love me? Dear gods, he despises me!'

Serrin turned away and left her alone, his footsteps echoing angrily along the passage. Still crying with laughter, Adrina sank down onto the floor of her cell and hugged her knees. Her mirth abated slowly but the tears did not as the harsh truth of her predicament hit her with full force.

Damin would not risk a civil war for her. She knew that. Even if he wanted to, Marla would prevent him from taking action, or worse, she would convince him to go to war, but not until after her despised daughter-in-law had been conveniently disposed of. There was a chance that R'shiel might come to her rescue, but with everything else that was going on, saving Adrina was probably far down on her list of priorities and the demon child could be as ruthless as Marla when the mood took her.

The worst of her predicament was the dreadful realisation that at that moment, she wanted nothing more than to be warm and dry and safe in Damin's arms somewhere far from this place.

And Tamylan – dear, sweet, loyal Tamylan – had died for her.

She cried anew for her slave, realising now, when it was too late to do anything about it, that Tam had been her one true friend. The loneliness that settled on her seemed worse than her small cell, worse than her bruised and battered face, worse even than the bitter knowledge that she had fallen for Damin Wolfblade and she would probably never get the chance to tell him.

Damin would not come for her. She was certain of that.

He didn't even know that she carried his child.

## 24

The Seeing Stone in the Temple of the Gods loomed over R'shiel, a solid lump of crystal as tall as a man, mounted on a black marble base. Candles set in solid silver sconces lit the altar, reflecting off the Stone with flickering rainbow light. She studied it for some time, hoping to learn its secret.

'It concerns me that the demon child knows so little of the ways of the Harshini.'

R'shiel turned. Kalan was striding towards her down the centre of the echoing temple. Kalan had ordered it cleared whenever R'shiel wished to use it – apparently she thought the demon child needed solitude during her worship.

R'shiel did not correct the High Arrion's assumptions. It was convenient that the Sorcerers' Collective thought of her as Harshini. It wouldn't do at all to remind them she was a Medalonian half-breed raised to despise the gods and everything they represented.

'Concerns *you*? It scares the hell out of me.'

Kalan frowned. 'I wish you were joking.'

'So do I.'

The High Arrion climbed the steps to the altar and stopped beside her, studying the crystal for a moment. 'You sent for me?'

'I need to contact Sanctuary.'

'And you want to know how to use the Stone?'

R'shiel nodded. 'Glenanaran and the others are still unconscious. I'm not sure how to help.'

'We owe them a great deal,' Kalan agreed.

'So, what's the trick with this thing?'

Kalan shook her head in despair. 'This *thing*? Divine One, you have a bad habit of blaspheming every time you open your mouth. I hope the gods are forgiving.'

'I'd settle for them just minding their own business.'

Kalan sighed eloquently but made no further comment. She stepped up to the Stone and laid her hand on it, as if she drew strength from its solid presence, then turned to R'shiel.

'In the old days, before the Sisterhood conquered Medalon, the Seeing Stone was our main link with the Harshini. In those days we had scores of Harshini roaming through Hythria and Fardohnya. Medalon was their home but their teachers were spread out even as far as Karien, before the Overlord came to power. There were five Seeing Stones back then.'

'Five? What happened to them? Where are they now?'

'The Stone in Yarnarrow was taken to the Isle of Slarn, when Xaphista came to power in Karien. The Sisterhood somehow disposed of the Stone at the Citadel. The Stone in Talabar is gone too, but nobody is certain where.'

'And the fifth Stone is in Sanctuary.'

Kalan nodded. 'This Stone was silent for almost two

hundred years, after the Harshini left us. Then Korandellan appeared about three years ago, seeking Lord Brakandaran.'

'He sent him to look for me.'

'And now here you are, seeking to use the Stone to speak with Korandellan. Strange how things turn out.'

R'shiel wasn't sure how to answer that. Kalan had been in a strange mood since they arrived in Greenharbour. Perhaps it was because of the attack on the Collective.

'Can you use the Stone?'

Kalan shook her head. 'I cannot use the stone as you can. All you need do is place your hands upon it, draw on your power and think of whoever you wish to contact.'

'That's all?'

'So I'm led to believe.'

'But you don't know for certain?'

'I am not Harshini, Divine One. I do not have access to the power that you control.'

*Control might be a bit optimistic*, R'shiel thought irreverently, although she did not voice her uncertainty. It was better that the High Arrion thought her omnipotent. She stepped closer to the Stone.

'The staffs that Xaphista's priests use. They have crystals in them too. Are they like the Seeing Stones?'

Kalan looked thoughtful. 'I don't really know. The Overlord uses them to link with the priests, so I suppose they work on the same principle. I've never seen one up close.' She smiled faintly. 'As you can imagine, there is little communication between the Collective and the Overlord's minions.'

'The shaft is black,' R'shiel told her, her voice hardening in remembrance, 'and made of metal. The head of the staff is gold, shaped like a five-pointed star, intersected by a lightning bolt crafted of silver. Each point of the star is set with crystal and in the centre of the star, is a larger gem of the same stone.'

'You speak as if you've seen one.'

'I've had the dubious pleasure of being on the receiving end,' she explained.

'That raises some interesting possibilities,' Kalan said thoughtfully.

'What do you mean?'

'I wonder if the crystals you describe are pieces of the missing Stones? I don't know how they could be, but it's possible, I suppose.'

'If they are, could I use them too?'

The High Arrion shrugged, but she did not dismiss the idea out of hand. 'For what?'

'I don't know, exactly. I'm just curious, I guess.'

'Even if the crystals really are pieces of Seeing Stone, you couldn't really do anything with a staff unless you could get past the pain.'

'Yes, well that does present something of a problem,' she agreed, pushing away the painful memory of Xaphista and the pain his staff could inflict. She had beaten the collar though, and that had been worse than the staff. Perhaps, if she had to, she could do it again. But not easily; and certainly not by choice.

'I suppose you could get around having to touch the staff itself by using another Seeing Stone,' Kalan added thoughtfully.

'Why another Seeing Stone?'

'The Seeing Stones are channels, Divine One. They focus the power of the gods and allow it to be used in a specific manner. The size of the Stone determines its power. Legend has it that the Stone at the Citadel was three times the size of this one.'

'So, what are you saying? That even if the staffs contain pieces of Seeing Stone, they're too small to do anything with?'

'I'm saying they couldn't be used like this one. You couldn't use them to talk to the priests. They would convey nothing more than . . . I don't know, really . . . emotions, maybe . . . vague impressions, at best. And that's assuming you can access a Stone capable of communicating with the chips of crystal in the staffs.'

'What about this Seeing Stone? Or the one at Sanctuary?'

She shook her head. 'The Stone in here is only good for contacting Sanctuary – the Harshini made sure of that before they withdrew, and you can't use the Stone in Sanctuary, because for something requiring that much power, Korandellan would have to bring Sanctuary back into real time. If they are chips from the missing Stones then the Stone that controls those jewels is probably the one on Slarn.'

R'shiel frowned. 'I'm not sure I want to risk Malik's Curse just to satisfy my curiosity.' She'd seen a man with the wasting disease once, on his way from the Citadel to the colony on Slarn. It still gave her nightmares.

'The disease would be the least of your problems,' Kalan pointed out. 'Just getting there would be trouble enough. You couldn't use the demons. The priests would sense you coming from the other side of the Fardohnyan Gulf.'

'Pity the Seeing Stone at the Citadel is lost,' she sighed, glancing at the lump of crystal behind her. 'Do you think the Sisterhood destroyed it?'

'No human possesses the power to destroy a Seeing

Stone, Divine One. It's missing, certainly, but I doubt it was destroyed.'

'Then it might be still in the Citadel? Hidden somewhere?'

The High Arrion did not seem to share her optimism. 'I suppose, although where you would hide something as large as a Seeing Stone is beyond me.'

'I wonder if there are any records in the Citadel's library? The Founding Sisters documented everything. There are even reports on the number of sacks of grain they confiscated when they took over the Citadel.'

'It's worth a try, I suppose, and if it *is* still there, it would be a lot safer than trying to get near the one on Slarn. But the Citadel is under Karien control. How are you going to get inside? And, more importantly, what does it have to do with your quest to destroy Xaphista? Do you have the time to waste answering questions that have no relevance to the task at hand?'

'I suppose not.' She glanced up at the Stone again with a sigh. For a moment, it had seemed like such a good idea, too.

R'shiel had the librarians scouring the archives of the Collective looking for something, *anything*, to help her cause, but so far they had come up with nothing. Dikorian, the Collective's Chief Librarian, was not hopeful either. He knew his archives like he knew his own reflection and had never heard of anything in them that gave even a hint about how to destroy a god. Maybe, with a bit more time . . . she shook her head impatiently, reminding herself of why she had come here this evening. Time was something she didn't have to waste at the moment. 'Right now I have to help Glenaranan and his friends. Will you see that I am not disturbed?'

Kalan nodded. 'Of course.'

The High Arrion stepped down from the altar and began the long walk through the temple across the gorgeously mosaic-tiled floor. Every building R'shiel had entered in Greenharbour had floors like it, their intricate geometrical patterns sometimes so complex they made her dizzy.

She waited until Kalan was lost in the shadows before turning back to the Stone. Pushing away stray thoughts of Seeing Stones and chips of crystal, R'shiel swallowed a lump of apprehension and reached out, placing her palms upon it, then opened herself to the power. She felt her eyes darken, felt the familiar, intoxicatingly sweet energy surge through every cell in her body, and then thought of Korandellan.

*Demon child.*

R'shiel jumped in fright. It seemed hours since she had laid her hands on the Stone. The power filled her and she opened her eyes, which now burned black. Korandellan's image appeared in the crystal against a milky backdrop. He looked haggard.

'Korandellan!'

*You should not sound so surprised, demon child. You are the one who called for me.*

'I . . . I know . . . I just wasn't sure if it would work.'

*You should not doubt yourself, R'shiel. You are capable of so much more than you realise.*

'I'm glad you think so.'

The king smiled indulgently. *How can I help you, child?*

'Glenanaran, Farandelan and Joranara are unconscious. The Collective was attacked and they built a dome of light to protect it. They collapsed just before I got here and we can't wake them. They don't seem injured at all – they just won't wake up.'

His face clouded with concern. *It was unwise of them to draw on so much power. The gods always exact a price for such excess.*

'The gods? You mean they're like this as some sort of punishment?' She could feel her ire rising and fought it down. Linked mentally with Korandellan, it would distress him greatly to be exposed to her anger. 'So what can I do?'

*You must appeal to Cheltaran directly, I fear.*

'The God of Healing? I don't know him.'

*But he knows you, demon child. I'm certain he will heed your summons.*

The image flickered for a moment and R'shiel realised that Korandellan was weakening. The idea alarmed her. Korandellan was as strong in the power as she, and certainly far more skilled. The effort it took to link through the Stone was minimal. It should not be having that effect on him. 'Are you all right?'

*I am tired, that is all.*

'How can *you* be tired? You're the King of the Harshini.'

Your *faith in me is encouraging, R'shiel.* Korandellan could not lie, but he could avoid giving her a direct answer.

'What's wrong?'

He sighed, obviously reluctant to share his burden. *The strain of holding Sanctuary out of time is telling on me.*

'Why don't you just let it go? Nobody knows where Sanctuary is.'

*Xaphista's priests would find us easily, if we were back in normal time. I cannot risk it.*

'But if your hold weakens, they'll find it anyway.'

*Then I must rely on you to remove the threat of the Kariens, and trust you are able to achieve it before I falter.*

Korandellan was not trying to pressure her – it was not in his nature to do anything so blatantly human, but

R'shiel felt it, nonetheless. It simply wasn't fair. She never asked to be the demon child. She certainly didn't want to feel responsible for the survival of the Harshini.

The king smiled. *I fear I have made the burden of your destiny heavier. Do not concern yourself, R'shiel. Things will turn out as the gods will them.*

*Which isn't saying much,* she thought irreverently. 'Is there anything I can do?'

*If you are following a path that leads to breaking the power of the Overlord, you are doing all you can, my dear.*

'Well, I'll try to do it a bit faster,' she offered with a wan smile.

Korandellan nodded wearily. *You will prevail.*

The strain of maintaining the link was telling visibly on the king's face. She took her hands from the Stone and it cleared almost instantly, the milky backdrop returning to the crystalline clarity that characterised the magical talisman. R'shiel sank down onto the floor, sitting with her back to the marble base, her knees drawn up to her chin. She let the power go with some reluctance.

*So, I have to call Cheltaran,* she told herself. That would take care of the wounded Harshini. *Then, if Dikorian can't help me . . . maybe the answers I need are at the Citadel. But I'm running out of time.*

That the Harshini might be imperilled had never occurred to her until now. In fact, she had never really felt that she was working to a timetable. She knew that at some distant point in the future she would finally have to confront Xaphista, but she had always thought the one thing on her side was time. Perhaps she could sneak away after this damned election. Damin was a smart boy, Adrina even smarter. *Surely, between the two of them, they can figure out how to secure his throne without my help?*

She climbed to her feet and glanced around the temple. *What makes it holy?* she wondered idly. *The gods – or the people who worship them?*

'Cheltaran!' Her voice echoed through the cavernous chamber, but no divine being answered her call.

'Cheltaran!' Was there some sort of ritual she should perform to summon him? Zegarnald came when she called, as did Gimlorie. Dacendaran and Kalianah seemed to come and go as they pleased. She had never tried summoning another god.

'Hey! Cheltaran! I need you!'

'Never have I been summoned quite so . . . eloquently, demon child.'

She started at the voice and spun around to find the god standing behind her, leaning against the Seeing Stone, his arms folded across his chest. They did that a lot, she noticed. You called them and they popped up where you least expected them.

'Cheltaran?'

He smiled serenely. In solid form he looked like an older version of Dace, but without the motley clothes or cheeky grin. He wore a long white robe, similar to those worn by the healers of Hythria, but she had expected someone older. A fairly ridiculous expectation in hindsight – these beings were immortal. If they appeared old, it was simply because they wished to.

'Is there some reason you called me? You appear quite well.'

'There are Harshini here who need you.'

'Ah yes. The Harshini who overextended themselves.'

'You know about them?'

'Naturally. I am the God of Healing. All sickness and injury is known to me.'

'Then why haven't you done something about it?' she demanded impatiently.

'Healing is part of every living being, just as, sometimes, allowing nature to take its course is also a part of life. Things happen as they must, R'shiel. I do not interfere without good cause.'

'Well you have a good cause now. I need them up and about.'

'*You* need them? Am I to interrupt the natural order of things at your whim, demon child?'

R'shiel thought about that for a moment, then decided she didn't have time to argue. She nodded. 'That's about the strength of it.'

'I have interfered more since you came along than I have in the past millennium,' the god told her with a frown.

'Then a bit more won't make much difference, will it?'

Cheltaran sighed. 'Very well, demon child. I will do as you ask. But be warned. There will be a reckoning. Nature requires a certain balance. Each time you call on us to disturb that balance, the day of reckoning draws nearer.'

There was something vaguely threatening in his tone that worried R'shiel.

'I don't mean to.'

'I know you don't. But you are the demon child. You are a force of nature in your own right.'

Cheltaran vanished abruptly, before R'shiel could say anything more. She was puzzled by his sudden disappearance, but the reason became clear a moment later, when the doors to the temple flew open and the sound of booted feet pounding on the tiles echoed through the place. She turned as the interlopers emerged into the light.

It was Almodavar, Damin's captain, and a squad of his Raiders.

'My lady! Lord Wolfblade demands you return to the palace at once!'

'He *demands*, does he?' she asked with faint annoyance as she descended the steps from the altar. 'What's the matter now?'

'The palace was attacked. They've taken Adrina.'

R'shiel swore under her breath.

By the time she reached Almodavar, she was running.

## 25

R'shiel was shocked by the devastation when she reached the palace. There was blood on the white marble steps and smeared across the tiled floor of the main hall. The diamond-paned windows that led out onto the balcony and overlooked the harbour were shattered into a carpet of glittering shards that crunched underfoot as she followed Almodavar at a run. There were several bodies lined up near the doors, with shrouds thrown hastily over them. *How many had died,* she wondered? *And for what?*

Almodavar led her to a small passage off the main hall that ended in a door inlaid in gold with the crest of the Wolfblade family. Someone had driven a dagger through the eye of the wolf and it remained embedded in the wood like a silent warning. Almodavar opened the door without glancing at the knife and stood back to let R'shiel enter. The Raiders who had escorted them from the Collective stayed on guard outside.

'What happened?'

Damin looked up at the sound of her voice, obviously relieved to see her. His eyes were hard and she could read the tension in the set of his shoulders. The other

men in the room, whom she guessed were Damin and
Narvell's lieutenants, wore expressions of concern – and
perhaps a little excitement – at the prospect of seeing
some action. The only woman present was Marla, who
paced the floor impatiently as her sons plotted their
revenge. There were maps scattered across the large oval
table, anchored at their corners by anything heavy enough
to act as a paperweight.

'We received a message that Tejay Lionsclaw had arrived
and wanted to meet with us before she entered the city,'
Damin told her. 'As it turns out, it was false. The palace
was attacked while we were gone. We're still counting the
dead.'

'And Adrina?'

'We think they took her by boat,' Narvell added. 'We
found a rope tied to the balcony in her apartments.'

'She could have simply used the confusion to run away,'
Marla suggested tartly. 'I've never trusted that woman.'

Damin glared at his mother. 'I've no time for your
unreasonable prejudices, Marla. Adrina did not run away.'

R'shiel silently applauded Damin. It was about time
someone put Her Royal Highness in her place. She glanced
around the room that Damin had turned into his command
post to avoid meeting Marla's eye. It must have been
Lernen's private sanctuary. The walls were rather distract-
ingly painted with explicit murals that depicted a variety
of sexual positions, some of which R'shiel was certain were
physically impossible. It seemed odd, this bustling war
council being held amidst such decadent artwork.

'Where would they take her?'

'Dregian Castle lies along the coast here,' Damin said,
pointing to the map laid out on the table before him. 'It's
a few hours away by boat, but easily navigated.'

'They'll have her there before we can mount a counter-attack,' Narvell added.

'So what are you going to do?'

'Get her back,' Damin announced matter-of-factly. His outward air of control worried R'shiel a little. The Damin she knew should have been raging like a wounded bull. It was not like him to be so level headed. He glanced at Narvell, not waiting for R'shiel's reaction. 'Have you heard from Rogan yet?'

'No.'

'Damn! I'll need his troops.'

'You're going to attack Cyrus?'

Damin turned to her impatiently. 'Of course I'm going to attack him!'

'You're an idiot.'

The whole room stilled as Damin slowly straightened. His eyes were terrible, his whole being radiating fury. This was the Damin she knew. The rage, the grief, the debilitating fear for Adrina was perilously close to the surface. R'shiel realised she had about a heartbeat to explain herself before Damin lost control completely.

'Don't you see? That's why they took Adrina. They *want* you to attack. Or to be more specific, they want your troops – and Narvell's and Rogan's – out of the city.'

Damin's shoulders relaxed a little. R'shiel breathed a sigh of relief. He was quietly murderous, but not beyond reason.

'You don't know that for certain.'

'No, but they've been rather obvious about it, don't you think? I mean, leaving the rope hanging from her balcony where you can find it? They might as well have hung out a sign. It's a trap, Damin. Cyrus wants you out of the city. Worse than that, he wants you on his territory.'

'Then I plan to see that he gets what he wants,' Damin growled.

R'shiel sighed with frustration, wishing she could make him see what was so obvious to her. 'Even if you took every man you have here in Greenharbour, and Narvell's and Rogan's with them, you've got less than a thousand men. How many has Cyrus got waiting for you?'

'It won't matter.'

'The hell it won't!' she scoffed. 'I don't mean to dent your precious male pride, Damin, but even *you* can be outnumbered. I don't care how good you think you are.'

'If you don't plan to help me, R'shiel, then get out of my way.'

'I'll help you to rescue Adrina, Damin. I'm not going to help you commit suicide.'

'What are you talking about?'

'If you attack Dregian Province, you will be invading Cyrus' province, whatever the provocation. Cyrus will defeat you, and hang your head on his walls *and* he'll have the full force of the law on his side, if I'm not mistaken. I imagine Adrina will live long enough to see your head fall off the block, before she joins you.'

Damin sank down in the chair behind him as the logic of what she was saying finally began to sink in.

Marla looked at R'shiel in surprise. 'You have an excellent grasp of politics, demon child.'

'I had very good teachers, your highness.'

'The benefit of an education by the Sisterhood,' Damin remarked sourly. 'You see treachery where others think only of honour. So, demon child, what do you suggest? That I leave Adrina to the mercy of my enemies?'

'Certainly not! We'll go and get her back. But we won't do it with an army at our heels.'

Damin met her eye for a moment and then nodded in understanding. 'I'll organise a ship. It'll take three days by land to reach Dregian Province, and the gods know what he'll have done to her by then.'

'Then we won't go by land, or by sea, for that matter. But don't worry about Adrina being hurt. Cyrus won't harm her and she's worth nothing to him dead.' She turned to Marla. 'Your highness, can you keep up the illusion that Damin is in the palace?'

'To what purpose?'

'Cyrus undoubtedly has spies everywhere. They'll be waiting for him to move. Narvell, I suggest you and Rogan continue to muster your troops, but take your time about it. While Cyrus thinks Damin is still in Greenharbour preparing to fight, he won't be on his guard.'

'How many men should we take?' Damin asked.

'Two. You and me.'

'You can't attack Dregian Castle single-handed,' Narvell declared, aghast at her suggestion.

'I'm not going to. We shall retrieve Adrina, by stealth rather than force, before Cyrus Eaglespike knows anything about it. We shall then wait for Tejay Lionsclaw to arrive and hold the Convocation as planned.'

'And when Cyrus tries to play his hand, he will find it has slipped through his fingers,' Marla added, with undisguised admiration. 'Damin, you should have married *this* one.'

Damin frowned at his mother but didn't bother to answer her. Instead he turned to R'shiel. 'How do we get out of the palace without being seen?'

'You leave that to me.'

'You worry me when you say things like that.'

She shrugged. 'When shall we leave?'

Damin smiled savagely, his mood improving noticeably with the prospect of doing something useful. 'Now is as good a time as any. Unless you have something better to do.' He jumped to his feet, wearing the same stupid grin he always wore when he was about to fight. It was a male thing, R'shiel reasoned. Tarja did the same thing. 'Narvell, keep an eye on things while I'm gone. And don't let mother bully you.'

Marla looked as if she might protest, but Damin and R'shiel did not wait around to find out.

## 26

'Can we get to the roof?' R'shiel asked as she stepped into the hall. Damin closed the door behind them and looked at the dagger embedded in the door. He jerked the blade free and hurled it to the floor angrily.

'Why do you want to go up on the roof?'

'Because we want to sneak out of the palace Damin, and it might be a little bit obvious if I summon a dragon in the middle of the main courtyard.'

'A dragon? You are going to summon a dragon?'

'If Dranymire agrees to it.'

'I don't know about the roof in this part of the palace, but there is a roof garden in the west wing. Will that do?'

'I suppose.'

She followed Damin as he hurried through the debris of the attack. They were still clearing out the bodies of the guards who had died defending the palace. As they climbed the sweeping marble staircase they met two Raiders carrying a stretcher between them, coming down the stairs. A sheet covered the body on the stretcher, but it did not conceal the blue skirts and bloodstained slippers underneath.

'Damin!'

He glanced at the stretcher and ordered the men to halt. With some trepidation, he peeled back the cover. R'shiel let out a small cry of anguish as she saw who lay beneath it.

'Gods,' Damin muttered. 'Tamylan never deserved such a fate.'

'Tam was Adrina's best friend.'

'She was just a slave, R'shiel,' Damin corrected, gently replacing the sheet and waving the men on.

'She was still Adrina's best friend.'

Damin nodded grimly. 'Come. We have another reason now to deal with Lord Eaglespike.'

When they reached the second landing, R'shiel discovered Mikel sitting on the stairs, tears streaming down his face. R'shiel knelt down beside him, ignoring Damin's impatient sigh.

'Mikel? Are you hurt?'

He shook his head. 'I'm sorry, my lady . . .'

'Sorry? For what? This wasn't your fault.'

'We heard them . . . me and Tamylan . . . we were bringing the princess her dinner. We saw the men in the hall and Tamylan ran at them. She told me to hide. So I did.'

'Then you've nothing to be ashamed of, Mikel.'

'But Tamylan's dead and all I did was hide!' he wailed. 'Now all these people are dead . . . and I don't where Jaymes is . . .'

R'shiel glanced up at Damin helplessly. She had no idea what to say to the child.

Although she could tell Damin was consumed with impatience, he squatted down beside the boy. 'Mikel! Look at me!'

Unable to ignore Damin's commanding tone, Mikel

wiped his eyes and turned to the Warlord. 'Every man under my command knows how to follow orders, even when they don't like them. I don't expect to find them sitting about crying over it afterwards, either.'

'No, sir,' Mikel replied weakly.

'As for your brother, he's alive and well. He was with the party I took to meet Lady Lionsclaw.'

Mikel brightened considerably at the news. 'He was?'

'Yes, he was. Now, pull yourself together, lad, and get your arse down to Captain Almodavar and tell him I said to find you something useful to do. We need every man we've got at the moment and I don't have time for you to sit here bawling like a baby.'

'No, sir.' Mikel squared his shoulders and smiled tentatively at Damin. 'Are you going to rescue the princess, my Lord?'

'If I don't keep getting distracted,' he agreed, with an impatient glance at R'shiel.

She smiled at Mikel, then on impulse she summoned the little demon who seemed so fond of getting Mikel into trouble. He started as the creature popped into existence beside him.

'The demon will stay with you, Mikel, until we get back. But you mustn't tell anybody that we've gone.'

Mikel stared at it for a moment then turned to R'shiel. The demon chittered at him unhappily, sensing the child's misery. 'What's his name?'

'*She* doesn't have a name yet. Maybe you can help her think of one.'

He nodded and sniffed back the last of his tears.

'Off you go, boy,' Damin ordered. He was chafing at the delay.

Mikel fled without another word, the little grey demon

tumbling down the stairs in his wake. R'shiel watched them go and then turned to Damin with a smile.

'You handled him very well.'

'You gave him a pet demon.'

She shrugged. 'It'll keep him company.'

He stared at her for a moment and then shook his head. 'Come on. And I don't care what we find on the next landing, we're not stopping.'

The roof garden was a riot of greenery, intricately laid out paths and fountains that filled the night with their musical splashing. Damin led her to the paved clearing in the centre of the garden and glanced up at the starlit sky.

'Another few weeks and the rains will start.'

'A pity they aren't here now. We could do with a bit of cloud cover.'

'Can't you make us invisible?'

'I'm not even sure how to *ride* a dragon, Damin.'

'But you said—'

'I know what I said. I wish Brak were here.'

Damin glanced at her for a moment then shook his head. 'You really are a bit of a fraud, aren't you?'

'I'm the biggest fraud in the whole world. I have no idea what I'm doing and only the vaguest idea of what I'm *supposed* to be doing. I just have to hope that if I keep pretending long enough, I'll figure out what's going on.' She frowned then, turning to look at him. 'I have to leave soon, Damin. You don't need me to take your throne for you. You have Adrina. She's actually a lot better at politics than I am.'

'You seem to get by,' he noted with a faint grin.

'I've Joyhinia to thank for that.'

Damin wasn't sure how to answer that, so he turned and looked up at the sky again. 'Summon your demons, demon child. I'm sure the gods will watch over us.'

She frowned, wondering if she should mention that his assurance gave her little comfort. Then another thought occurred to her – something that should have been dealt with, long before this.

'Damin, there's something you should probably know. About Adrina.'

'What about her?'

'She's pregnant.'

'I know.'

'You *know*? Who told you? Marla?'

He smiled smugly. 'I am neither blind nor stupid R'shiel. And I can count.'

'Why didn't you say something?'

'It was more fun watching Adrina trying to work up the courage to tell me herself.'

'You can be a real bastard, Damin Wolfblade. You don't deserve her.'

He sighed, suddenly serious. 'No, I think we actually deserve each other.'

'Then you admit you feel something for her?'

'When I heard she'd been kidnapped, I thought I would die, R'shiel,' he admitted, albeit with some reluctance. 'I've never felt that way about anyone before.'

'Not even your horse?' she asked.

'My *horse*?'

'It's something Adrina said once. That the only thing you truly cared about was your horse.'

Damin thought for a moment and then smiled. 'No, I think I actually care about her more.'

'Well make sure you tell her when we get her back.

I'm sick to death of you two. Everyone's life would be considerably easier if you devoted all that effort to making peace instead of war.'

Dranymire responded almost instantly to her summons, although he seemed unimpressed when she explained what she wanted of him.

'Riding a dragon is a skill that takes a great deal of time to learn, R'shiel,' he warned in his deep voice. 'You can't just hop on and hope for the best.'

'But we need to get to Dregian Castle. Tonight. It's three days by road and they'll see us coming from leagues away if we take a ship.'

'Getting there late is better than not getting there at all.'

'Please, Dranymire.'

The little demon cast his liquid eyes over Damin and frowned. 'I suppose you want us to carry him, too?'

'Yes.'

'When next you are at Sanctuary, your highness, you and I need to have a long discussion regarding the nature of the relationship between demons and the Harshini. Specifically, the wanton use of demon melds.'

'And I promise I'll listen to every word. But right now, I need a dragon.'

'You need some discipline,' the demon corrected loftily. 'However, I am in the mood to indulge you, and there are a number of my brethren who will benefit from the experience.'

'Thank you,' she said with relief, bending down to kiss his wrinkled grey forehead. 'I won't forget this.'

'Neither will I,' the demon promised, somewhat ominously.

They stepped back as more demons began to materialise and gather around Dranymire. R'shiel quickly lost count of them. The demons bonded to the té Ortyn family were among the oldest and most numerous of all the brethren, which accounted for the size and stature of the dragon they could form. She watched in fascination as the meld began, demons flowing into each other almost too fast for the eye to take in.

The dragon grew before her until its wings blocked out the stars.

'Climb on, your highness, and try not to fall off.'

R'shiel used the dragon's leg as a step and pulled herself up, surprised at how warm the metallic scales felt under her hands. Damin clambered up and settled himself behind her, his arms around her waist. R'shiel tried to find something to hold onto, but there was nothing.

'You must grip with your thighs,' Dranymire informed her. 'Riding a dragon is simply a question of balance.'

'Balance,' she repeated dubiously, seriously doubting her wisdom in deciding to use a dragon to rescue Adrina. She glanced over her shoulder at Damin. 'You ready?'

'I suppose.'

Dranymire must have heard him. A gust of warm wind rushed over them as the dragon beat its powerful wings and lifted them into the darkness.

## 27

Dregian Castle grew out of a promontory that jutted into the ocean like an upright sword buried hilt-down in the white chalk cliffs. It was a tall, narrow structure, more tower than keep, its white stone pitted and yellowed by years of being assaulted by the corrosive sea air. Unlike Krakandar, the main city of Dregian Province was some distance away from the castle, crowded around a small bay eight leagues to the east of the keep.

Dranymire landed near the woods that ringed a vast open field of cleared ground surrounding the fortress, just as dawn was feeling its way over the horizon.

R'shiel climbed down stiffly from the dragon, her thighs aching from the effort of keeping her seat. Damin appeared to have fared no better than she as he stumbled to the ground. The two of them hobbled about for a few moments, trying to work out the knots in their muscles. Dranymire seemed highly amused by their plight.

'As I said, your highness, riding a dragon is a skill that takes years to acquire.'

'I didn't fall off. Give me some credit.'

The dragon lowered its head and studied her with his

plate-sized eyes. 'Yes. You managed that much. Did you want me to wait for you?'

'For me, yes. Damin's probably going to have to return to Greenharbour by more conventional means once we've found Adrina.'

'I shall await your summons, your highness.'

Looking rather relieved that he would not have to repeat the journey, Damin caught up with R'shiel as she stumbled down the small slope to the open ground below.

'What are you doing?'

'I'm off to rescue your wife.'

'What are you going to do? March up to the draw-bridge and knock?'

'Pretty much.'

'R'shiel!'

She stopped and turned back to him. 'What?'

'You can't do that!'

'Why not?' She smiled at his expression. 'Stop thinking with your sword, Damin. We can't storm the place, so we have to get them to let us in. Once we're inside, I can deal with any opposition.'

'You're not even armed.'

'There you go, thinking with your sword again.' She resumed walking, pleased to discover the exercise was beginning to loosen the stiffness from her thighs. Damin ran to catch up with her.

'So what *are* you planning to do?' he demanded, falling into step beside her.

'Two people walking across a field are no threat to the castle. Even if you're recognised, they'll be so surprised you came alone, that they won't do anything straight away. At worst they'll send for Cyrus.'

'And what do you think he's going to do?'

'Nothing. By the time we're inside, it won't make a difference.'

'You're going to use magic then?' he asked, rather sceptically.

'Of course.'

'But you don't know what you're doing. You admitted as much before we left Greenharbour. You might accidentally harm Adrina.'

'I did learn *something* at Sanctuary, Damin.'

'Not nearly enough, from what I've seen so far.'

'Trust me.'

'I hate people who say that.'

She grinned at him. 'Stop worrying about me and start thinking about how you're going to apologise to Adrina.'

'Apologise? Why should I apologise?'

'Because she deserves one. And besides, an apology is always a good way to make a woman listen to you.'

'And when did you become such an expert on affairs of the heart? You're a child. And a spoiled one, at that.'

'I'm the demon child. I'm omnipotent.'

'I hope you never actually begin to believe that, R'shiel.' She glanced at him, her grin fading. 'So do I.'

The castle was just beginning to waken as they reached it. With an ear-piercing squeal, the gates swung open and they hastily stepped back to let a troop of Raiders thunder past them, heavily armed and armoured. They were too intent on their own business to notice the couple standing in the shadow of the castle wall. Damin watched them leave, his brow furrowed.

'They're getting ready to fight.'

'What did I tell you? Cyrus has probably got his borders lined five deep in Raiders, waiting for you to attack.'

'I hate people who say, "I told you so", almost as much as people who say "trust me".'

She smiled. 'Come on. Let's get inside before they close the gates again.'

R'shiel carefully opened herself up to the power as they entered the cool dimness of the short tunnel that led to the iron-studded gates. She had seen Brak attempt this once and hoped she remembered how it was done. She wove the glamour clumsily as they moved forward, but somewhat to her astonishment, the guards on duty paid them no attention as they walked boldly into the small yard that surrounded the tall white tower. Damin glanced at her in surprise when they were not challenged, nodding in understanding when he noticed her black eyes.

'So we're inside,' he whispered. 'What now?'

'There's no need for whispering, Damin. They cannot see us or hear us.'

'Are you sure?'

'Almost.'

Unconvinced, Damin glanced up at the tower. 'She'll be in there, I suppose.'

'Great deductive reasoning, Lord Wolfblade. Where else would she be?' R'shiel ignored the look he gave her and looked up with a frown. 'How much do you want to bet she's right at the top and we're going to have to climb about a million steps to get there?'

They let themselves into the tower through the main hall, which was littered with the remnants of the previous evening's festivities. The slaves were starting to stir from their places near the cooking hearths, rubbing bleary eyes as they yawned themselves into wakefulness. A few of the more alert slaves were already up and about, righting overturned stools and clearing away dishes stained with congealed fat and limp vegetable remains.

'Looks like it was quite a party,' R'shiel remarked.

'Cyrus would have feasted his troops before he sent them out.'

She glanced around the hall, at the low, vaulted ceiling and the rough stone floor. 'This place is pretty old, isn't it?'

'It's one of the oldest structures in Hythria,' he agreed. 'It predates Greenharbour, I think.'

'Then it probably has dungeons.'

'I suppose.'

'Then we'll check them first.'

'Cyrus wouldn't dare throw Adrina in a dungeon.'

'No, *you* wouldn't dare. Cyrus doesn't care about Adrina, one way or the other. Besides, I've spent all night clinging to a dragon with my thighs. My legs are killing me. I really don't want to climb all the way to the top of this place, just to find out she's a few steps below us. We check the dungeons first.'

Damin nodded his agreement, probably just as sore and stiff as she was. He pointed to a door that led off the hall by the second hearth. R'shiel followed him, stepping over a number of sleeping bodies along the way. She looked about her, unable to entirely believe that the glamour she had drawn around them was actually working.

They made their way down a narrow corridor that curved around the tower and led to another door at the end, this one reinforced with bands of iron. Damin pushed it open slowly, wincing as the hinges squealed in protest.

'They might not hear *us*,' Damin hissed. 'But they're bound to hear *that*.'

'Keep going. If they come to investigate, they'll just think the door hadn't been latched properly.'

Damin obviously didn't share her confidence, but he led the way forward, down a set of damp, narrow steps that reached into the darkness. R'shiel kept her hand on the wall, making her way by feel more than sight. The stone was slimy under her fingers, and in the distance she could hear the faint rush of the ocean as it pounded against the castle's foundations.

She bumped into Damin when he stopped abruptly, pointing to a spill of yellow light coming from the bottom of the stairs. She nodded silently, falling victim to Damin's desire for stealth, even though, protected by the glamour, there was no need for it. They reached the bottom and stepped into another narrow passage, this one lined by barred cells and lit by fitfully sputtering torches. There were guards at the other end of the passage, squatting on the floor, engrossed in their game. The air was surprisingly fresh, heavy with the smell of the ocean and the waves crashing against the cliffs seemed even louder. A faint breeze whispered past them and R'shiel realised that there must be an opening down here that led to the sea. If they had brought Adrina here by boat, then there was a good chance this was the way she had come. With luck, they hadn't bothered to take her any further.

'You check the cells on the left,' Damin told her. 'I'll take the right.'

R'shiel nodded and moved to the first cell, which proved empty. The next housed a sleeping man wearing a shirt tattered by the lash. The third cell she checked also contained a sleeping prisoner, but whether male or female, R'shiel could not tell from the rags piled on the damp floor.

'Adrina!'

Damin's cry made her jump, and she looked at the guards nervously, reminding herself that they could not hear him. She hurried to his side. Adrina was sitting on the floor of the fourth cell on the right, her knees drawn up under her chin, rocking backward and forward on the damp, cold floor, as tears streamed silently down her face. There was a nasty bruise on her jaw and her lip was puffy and split. Her silken gown was muddied and torn, her hair in disarray. Her wounds appeared superficial, though, and the tears were more likely to be for Tamylan than herself. Adrina was not the self-pitying type. But R'shiel had never seen anyone looking quite so miserable.

'Adrina!' Damin called again, grabbing at the bars in anguish.

'She can't hear you, Damin.'

'Where are the keys?'

'The guards have them, I imagine.'

'I'll get them,' he announced, reaching for his sword.

'No, you stay here. I'll get them.'

She walked to the end of the passage and watched the guards for a moment as they wagered on the fall of two crudely carved die. There were three men, all of them lacking the spit and polish of fighting troops. The guard nearest the wall carried a bunch of keys on his belt. She frowned. They may not be able to see her, but they would notice the keys detaching themselves and floating up the hall.

R'shiel didn't want to kill the guards. Doing so would alert Cyrus to their presence. It was possible that the Lord of Dregian Province would have no need to check on Adrina until he thought Damin was ready to attack. With luck, Adrina's escape might go unnoticed for the rest of the day, even longer, if the guards paid little attention to their charges. But whatever she did, she would have to let go of the glamour. Strong she might be, but she was not accomplished enough to do two things at once.

'R'shiel! Hurry!'

She ignored Damin's impatient plea and stepped into the shadows. With infinite care she let the glamour that made them invisible slip from her grasp. As it left her, she concentrated on the gaming soldiers, willing them to sleep. They fell so quickly, she was afraid she had killed them.

Not sure how long unconsciousness would hold the men, she hurriedly removed the keys from the belt of the snoring guard. She ran back to Damin and began trying the keys in the lock.

Adrina glanced up at the sound, able to see them now the glamour was gone, although it took a moment for her to realise who was standing at the door to her cell.

'*Damin?*'

'Adrina!' he cried anxiously, then turned to R'shiel. 'Hurry up!'

'I am hurrying,' she snapped as the lock turned on the fourth key she tried. Damin pushed roughly past her into the cell as soon as the lock snicked open. Adrina flew into his arms, sobbing. He held her so tightly, he lifted her clear off the ground. Then he was kissing her forehead, her neck, her eyes, anywhere he could reach. When he kissed her mouth she cried out in pain and pushed him away.

'Founders, Damin! She's been punched in the mouth.' R'shiel glared at him as he let Adrina go. She examined the wound for a moment, deciding it could wait before she healed it. That way, Damin might show a little self-control. 'Any other injuries we can't see?'

Adrina shook her head, wiping her eyes.

'What about the baby?' Adrina's eyes widened and she stared at Damin in horror. 'Don't worry about him. He knows. Is the baby all right?'

The princess nodded mutely.

'Fine, then let's get out of here.'

R'shiel led the way from the cell then turned impatiently to find they weren't following her. Instead, they stood in the centre of the dim dungeon, locked in an embrace that was as touching as it was inconvenient.

'We don't have time for this!' R'shiel warned as one of the guards began to stir.

Damin reluctantly let Adrina go. R'shiel let out an exasperated curse and turned towards the stairs. The sound of footsteps changed her mind and she hurriedly turned the other way, pushing Damin and Adrina ahead of her, past the sleeping guards. An archway on the far side of the guardroom proved to be the source of the chill ocean breeze. R'shiel pointed to it urgently.

'Down there! I'll follow in a minute.'

They needed no further urging. R'shiel ran back to Adrina's empty cell and locked the door, then returned the keys to the belt of the sleeping guard, smiling to herself. *Let them figure that one out.*

The footsteps drew closer on the stairs and the guard stirred again as she stepped away from him. She glanced around, satisfied that there was no other evidence of their passage and disappeared into the darkness of the archway.

Adrina and Damin were waiting for her. As she suspected, the stairs finished at a small dock, carved into the living rock at the base of the castle. Unfortunately, the dock was empty.

'Now what?' Damin asked, holding Adrina close.

'We need a boat.'

'Great deductive reasoning, demon child.'

She loftily ignored the jibe and turned her attention to the thrashing sea. Even if they had a boat, she didn't like their chances of navigating their way clear of the rocks.

'What's the name of the God of the Oceans?'

'Kaelarn,' Damin told her. 'Why?'

'I think we're going to need his help.'

'You are going to summon a god and you don't even know his name?'

'Got any better ideas?' When neither of them answered her she turned back to face the thrashing ocean. 'Kaelarn!'

The ocean surged below them. Cold spray showered them as the waves swelled. Out of the steely depths a figure appeared, vaguely human in form, but shaped from the sea itself. It rose out of the surf until it loomed over them. R'shiel had to strain her neck to look up at him.

'So the demon child has need of me,' Kaelarn boomed wetly. He had the most unpleasant voice R'shiel had ever heard. It was like someone talking through a bucket of water. She fervently hoped nobody else could hear him.

'We need to get away from this place. We need a boat.'

'A boat? You have demons to meld boats for you, demon child.'

R'shiel glanced over her shoulder as shouts drifted down from the guardroom. The sleeping guards had been discovered. It was only a matter of time before Adrina's absence was noted.

'A meld will take too long.'

'You wish to aid these humans, I presume?' he asked, pointing a watery arm at Damin and Adrina.

'Yes.'

'Is this part of your task to defeat Xaphista, or merely a whim?'

'It is most definitely part of my task.'

'Then I shall aid you, demon child. However, I cannot conjure up a boat. Perhaps this will suffice.'

With a tremendous splash, Kaelarn returned to the ocean. The sea churned and boiled as the god vanished. R'shiel looked about her in frustration. Kaelarn had disappeared and the sea was still facing them, churning savagely as it ate at the rock beneath the castle.

'Well, he was a big help,' she muttered in annoyance.

'R'shiel! Look!' Adrina suddenly cried in delight.

Out of the foaming waves, three red-grey creatures approached, their large dorsal fins slicing through the water. Just like the creature in the fountain in Green-harbour, they had long, elegant tails ending in broad, flipper-like paddles. Their wide-set intelligent eyes looked straight at them as they surfed towards the dock. R'shiel had grown up in landlocked Medalon. She had never seen anything like them before.

'What are they?'

'Water dragons!'

'Are they dangerous?'

Damin laughed at her expression. 'No. They're called the "fisherman's friends". We can ride them.'

'*Ride* them?'

The water dragons edged their way to the dock as the shouting in the guardroom grew louder. Without hesitating, Damin and Adrina slipped into the water and climbed aboard the creatures, grabbing hold of their dorsal fins.

'I can't swim, Damin.'

'Come on! You don't baulk at riding dragons.'

With another glance over her shoulder at the stairs to the guardroom, R'shiel decided she didn't have time to be squeamish. She slipped into the water, gasping as the chill salty ocean filled her mouth. She began to panic as the waves crashed over her, then a warm, solid body pushed her clear of the foam. She grabbed for the beast's fin and pulled herself upright as it plunged through the waves in the wake of the creatures carrying Adrina and Damin.

R'shiel clung to the beast in terror as the castle dwindled in the distance, determined never, as long as she lived, to ask another god for his help again.

## 28

Just on sunset, at R'shiel's insistence, the water dragons left them on a small beach not far from Greenharbour. It was partly because she wanted to give Adrina a chance to recover from her ordeal, and partly because she wanted to get out of the water and back on dry land where she felt she had some control over things. Damin had built a small fire and dried out their clothes and had gone in search of fresh water.

R'shiel healed Adrina's split lip with a touch and watched the bruise on her jaw fade before placing her hand on Adrina's stomach. She could feel the life there, strong and resilient.

'Can you tell if it's a boy or a girl?' Adrina asked hopefully.

'I'm the demon child, Adrina, not a prophet.'

'With my luck it will be a girl.'

R'shiel looked at her curiously, as she let go of her power. 'What's so bad about that?'

'You have to be born Fardohnyan to understand.'

'Your child will be the heir to Hythria, Adrina. They don't seem to suffer the same prejudice against women.'

'Maybe not, but it irks me to think I was never worthy

of my father's throne, simply because I had the misfortune to be born a girl.'

'Is that why you're so annoyed that the throne will fall to Damin?'

She smiled wanly. 'No. That just annoys me on principle.'

'He was ready to go to war over you, Adrina. In fact, he may still have to.'

Adrina sighed forlornly. 'I didn't really think he'd come for me, you know. Or if he did, he'd come charging over Cyrus' borders like some avenging god and play right into his enemies' hands. I suppose I have you to thank for the fact that he didn't.'

R'shiel sat back on her heels, but she did not confirm or deny Adrina's suspicions.

'You told him about the baby, didn't you? That explains why he came for me.'

'He already knew about it, Adrina. And I don't think it made the slightest bit of difference. Damin would have come for you, no matter what.'

The princess shook her head, as if she didn't believe it was possible. R'shiel felt like slapping her.

'There's a spring not far from here,' Damin called, striding across the white sand towards them. 'I'm afraid I've nothing to carry the water in, though.'

R'shiel glared at him. 'Use Adrina's head. It's hollow enough!'

Damin stared at her in shock. '*What*?'

Adrina climbed to her feet, brushing the sand from her tattered skirts. 'R'shiel is angry with me. And you too, I think. That's just her way of expressing it.'

'What did I do?' Damin asked, full of wounded innocence. R'shiel felt like screaming.

'Nothing!' she snapped. 'Nothing at all! That's the whole point.'

'Look, if I did something to make you angry, don't take it out on Adrina.'

'I don't need you to stand up for me, Damin Wolfblade,' Adrina interjected. 'I can take care of myself, thank you.'

'Why shouldn't I take it out on Adrina?' R'shiel asked, ignoring the princess as if she wasn't there. 'It's not as if *you* care.'

'What are you talking about? You know damned well I care what happens to her! What's the matter with you?'

'Since when did you give a damn about me?' Adrina demanded, turning on Damin.

'Since when did you give a damn about *me*?' Damin retorted, forgetting R'shiel momentarily.

'How can you say that?' Adrina cried angrily. 'I've done everything you asked of me and more!'

'What have you ever done besides flaunt your royal superiority?'

'What have *you* ever done for *me*? You held me prisoner! You accused me of trying to murder your uncle. You kept me collared like a slave just for the sheer hell of it! And then you took advantage of me!'

R'shiel knew of Adrina's impressive temper, but it was the first time she had seen it in full flight since the morning Cratyn had tried to kill her. She stepped back from the couple with a faint smile and sat down on the cool white sand to watch the show. They had forgotten she existed.

'*I* took advantage of *you*?' Damin gasped in disbelief. 'You devious little bitch. You came over the border dressed as a *court'esa* and spent the whole time acting like one! Ask

Tarja if you don't believe me. You were all over him like a wet blanket any time he got within five paces of you.'

R'shiel hadn't known about that, but she found herself more amused than jealous at the idea. *Poor Tarja. Fancy having to fight off Adrina when she was determined to seduce him.*

'At least he treated me like a princess! You treated me like a *court'esa*! You kept me collared and bound as if I was bought and paid for.'

'Oh, I've paid for you, Adrina,' Damin said with feeling.

'You think so? I've suffered the insults of your wretched mother. I've entertained your brutish Warlords. I've been kidnapped and beaten and locked in a dungeon. Even my slave was killed because of your damned throne. I've given up my whole life for you, you ungrateful bastard!'

'You manage to act in a civilised manner at a few dinner parties and that's supposed to justify the fact that I'm facing a damned civil war because of you?'

'I didn't cause your measly little war! The miracle is that you haven't gone and gotten yourself killed before now!'

'Well, maybe you'll get lucky again, Adrina, and I will be killed. Then you can go and find some other poor unsuspecting sod to marry you and give you a crown.'

The crack as Adrina slapped Damin's face echoed along the deserted beach with startling clarity. The argument stopped abruptly as Damin stared at her in shock. Even Adrina looked stunned that she had hit him.

For a long moment they stared at each other, not saying a word

'I'm sorry,' the princess said finally, drawing herself up with regal poise. 'I shouldn't have done that.'

Damin hesitated for a moment then shrugged, rubbing the handprint that stood out against his tan in the twilight. 'No. You don't owe me an apology, Adrina. I shouldn't have said what I did.'

'I still shouldn't have hit you,' she insisted.

'It could have been worse,' Damin replied, with a hint of a grin. 'You might have been armed.'

Adrina's eyes blazed dangerously for a few seconds, then she took a deep breath, visibly bringing her anger under control. 'You're lucky I wasn't,' she agreed. Then, with a tentative smile, she added, 'I really don't want to be a widow again so soon.'

'No?'

'No.'

They said nothing for a time, the silence loaded with unspoken tension. R'shiel waited expectantly, then rolled her eyes. 'Oh, for Founders' sake!'

They both turned to stare at her in horror.

'Do you mind?' Adrina asked, quite put out that she had witnessed their altercation. 'This is private.'

'Actually, they could probably hear you back in Greenharbour. But don't let me interrupt you. You appear to be enjoying yourselves immensely.'

'R'shiel, do you think you could maybe . . . go away for a while?' Damin asked, a little more cautiously.

'Are you going to stop shouting at each other? I might as well stay here if I can still hear you anywhere in a five-league radius.'

Adrina looked at Damin searchingly then turned to R'shiel. 'I think I've done all the shouting I need to for the time being. Would you mind, R'shiel? I think we have a few things to sort out.'

'That's something of an understatement,' she agreed.

'Why don't we go and find that spring?' Damin suggested. 'I could do with something to drink.'

'You go on ahead,' R'shiel told them. 'I'll see you later.'

Damin offered Adrina his hand and she took it willingly. With barely a backward glance they walked away, hand in hand.

'They make such a nice couple, don't they?'

R'shiel jumped at the unexpected voice and turned to find Kalianah sitting on the sand beside her.

'I wish you wouldn't just appear like that! Can't you warn me first?'

'What would you prefer? A fanfare?' The Goddess of Love was in her favourite form: a little girl. The slight breeze stirred her fair hair and she was smiling wistfully as she watched Damin and Adrina walk along the shoreline.

'Did you have anything to do with that?' R'shiel asked suspiciously.

'Much as I would like to have interfered, demon child, Damin Wolfblade belongs to Zegarnald. He takes a very dim view of other gods meddling with his followers. They did that all on their own. I'm afraid I can't claim any credit at all.'

Her words reminded R'shiel of something that she had forgotten until now. 'Kali, have you seen Dace lately?'

'No. He's sulking, I think.'

'Why?'

'I don't know. Why do you ask? You're not thinking of becoming one of his followers, are you?'

R'shiel laughed at the mere suggestion that she would ever worship any of the creatures that the Harshini called gods. 'Hardly. It's just something Damin mentioned a while back. He wanted to know if anyone had been stealing his followers.'

'With Dacendaran, it's usually the other way around,' Kalianah chuckled. 'I can ask him if you like. Is it important?'

'I don't really know. Who would want to steal his people anyway?'

'All of us,' the goddess told her. 'It's sort of a game, really. Particularly for gods like Dacendaran and Zegarnald.'

'What do you mean?'

Kalianah looked surprised that she had to explain it. 'Life can't exist without love, which is why the others tolerate me more than most. But you can be human and not be a thief or a warrior. So gods like Dace and Zeggi have to work a bit harder to keep their people.'

'What would happen if nobody believed in the gods any more?'

'I don't know. I guess we'd fade away into the background. You can't kill a Primal God. To kill me, you would have to stop love. While ever there's a fox trying to steal eggs from a nest, or two rams willing to fight over a ewe, Dacendaran and Zegarnald will survive. But the Incidental Gods need humans. They need someone to acknowledge their existence, or they cease to exist.'

'So all I have to do to defeat Xaphista is make a few million Kariens deny his existence?'

'Basically,' Kalianah agreed. 'How are you going to do that?'

'I have no idea,' the demon child admitted with a shrug.

## 29

Once Damin and Adrina were out of sight, Kalianah lost interest in them and vanished without warning. With an impatient sigh, R'shiel scrambled up the sandy bank behind her and made her way through the trees, following her instincts rather than any set path. The night was bright, but even without the moonlight she would have found what she was looking for. Before long she came to a large clearing where Dranymire and the demon-meld rested, still in dragon form. He opened his eyes at her approach and studied her quizzically.

'You said you would call for me.'

'Things got a bit out of hand. I had to call on Kaelarn.'

The dragon shook its massive head. 'That is beginning to develop into a dangerous habit, your highness.'

'Don't worry, after being dragged through the ocean on the back of a water dragon, I'll think twice before I call on the gods again,' she assured him.

'Your mission was successful, then?'

'Very. Now I need your help again.'

'I live to serve, your highness.'

R'shiel frowned at the dragon, certain he was mocking her.

'Can you get a message back to Greenharbour? To Kalan?'

'The High Arrion? Not directly. But we can speak to Glenanaran, and he can pass on your message.'

'Tell her where Damin and Adrina are. Ask her to send a carriage. Preferably one that's closed, so that they can return to the city without being seen.'

'And you?'

'I don't think the answers I need are here in Hythria, so I want to get back to Medalon, and the only way I can do that is make sure Damin's throne is secure. I'm going to find the elusive Tejay Lionsclaw.'

The dragon closed its enormous eyes for a moment, then opened them again. 'Your message is being delivered as we speak, your highness. If you would like to climb on, we can be on our way.'

'How can you have sent the message already?'

'Not all the té Ortyn demons are part of the dragon meld. I have sent Polanymire to Greenharbour on my behalf. Did you expect me to deliver your message personally?'

'No, it's just . . . I thought . . .'

'You thought what?'

'Nothing . . . I just haven't worked out this demon-meld thing yet, I think. Do you suppose Brak has had any luck with Hablet in Fardohnya?'

'The demons say not.'

'Damn,' she muttered impatiently. 'This is what I get for thinking everything was starting to go according to plan.'

'You actually *have* a plan then?' the dragon asked.

He was definitely mocking her now. 'As a matter of fact, I do. But first I need Damin confirmed as High

Prince. And I need to make sure Hythria is allied with Fardohnya. After we've tracked down the Warlord of Sunrise Province, I suppose we'll have to go to Fardohnya. Anyway, I've a feeling I'll need Brak's help once I get to the Citadel.'

'Then that is what we shall do.'

'But what about Damin and Adrina?'

'Staying with them now will serve no purpose if they do not get the aid they need, your highness.'

She nodded, aware that he was right, but feeling a little guilty for abandoning them, nonetheless.

'Can you send a demon to check on them? To see if they're all right?'

'They are in no danger here. But I suppose we can ascertain that they haven't killed each other.'

'That's very big of you, Dranymire.'

The demon did not appreciate her tone. 'I could just as easily *not* send one of the brethren to check on them, demon child.'

'I'm sorry.'

'As you should be. Now, unless you plan to spend the night in this insect-infested swamp, I suggest you climb aboard and we shall find your lost Warlord.'

With some misgiving, R'shiel pulled herself up and settled herself between the dragon's massive wings. As Dranymire and the meld lifted into the sky, she wondered if she should have told Damin and Adrina that she was leaving. She decided it wouldn't matter. Help was on the way, and Dranymire's demon would keep an eye on them until it arrived.

Besides, they probably wouldn't even notice she was missing.

*   *   *

She found Tejay Lionsclaw just on dawn. From her vantage on the dragon's back, R'shiel could make out the dying fires of her campsite. Her column was camped for the night on a plain some thirty leagues from Greenharbour. Dranymire saw them and swooped downward so swiftly that R'shiel almost lost her seat.

The dragon landed in the middle of the camp, scattering cook fires and startled Raiders with equal contempt. Tejay Lionsclaw emerged from her tent, clutching a sword that R'shiel doubted she could even lift. Tall and well muscled, with thick blonde hair, the Warlord of Sunrise Province was a handsome woman. Behind her emerged a boy of about fifteen, clutching the hand of an even younger girl, who was rubbing her eyes sleepily.

'Who are you?' Tejay demanded belligerently.

'I am R'shiel té Ortyn. I am the demon child.'

Tejay studied her for a moment then held up her hand to halt the suddenly nervous troops who were advancing on them.

'The demon child? That's a legend we tell to frighten children.'

'It works pretty well on grown men, too,' R'shiel noted, glancing around at the men who were staring with undisguised terror at the dragon.

Tejay planted the sword on the ground in front of her and stared at R'shiel for a moment before glancing up at the dragon. 'I suppose I must believe you, considering you arrived on the back of a dragon.'

'I thought it might save a lot of explanations.'

'Then you are sadly mistaken, demon child. Nobody lands in my camp in such a fashion without providing an explanation.'

'I come on behalf of Damin Wolfblade. Cyrus Eaglespike has laid claim to the High Prince's throne.'

'That doesn't surprise me, somehow. I've had a great deal of correspondence from him lately.' Suddenly the Warlord smiled and sheathed her sword. 'I've so many of his damned pigeons in my roosts that I was tempted to throw them into the cooking pot. Come, let's talk inside.'

She led the way to her tent, where the boy and girl stood wide-eyed at the entrance, staring at R'shiel's dragon. Dranymire was quite enjoying the effect he was having, R'shiel decided, although she wasn't sure if his smug expression was real, or if she was simply imagining it.

'Divine One, this is my son Valorian and his wife Bayla.'

R'shiel thought the pair too young to be out alone at night, let alone married. She looked at Bayla curiously, but could see nothing of her father, Cyrus Eaglespike, in her. The youngsters bowed hastily as she passed them, following Tejay into the tent.

'Can I offer you refreshment, Divine One?' the Warlord asked, indicating with a wave of her arm that R'shiel should sit. She sank down onto the scattered silk cushions gratefully, her thighs still quivering from riding the dragon.

'Thank you. And you don't have to call me Divine One, my lady. My name is R'shiel.'

'Very well, R'shiel. You may call me Tejay. Bayla!'

Her daughter-in-law's face appeared meekly through the embroidered hangings on the tent. 'My lady?'

'Make yourself useful for once and fetch us some breakfast.' When Bayla disappeared behind the curtain, Tejay sat down opposite R'shiel with a sigh. 'If there is one thing I cannot abide, it is simpering females. And that girl has it down to a fine art.'

'Then why did you let her marry your son?'

'Because she came with a dowry that not even I could ignore. In hindsight, I suppose it had more to do with Cyrus Eaglespike's plans for the throne, than any great love for his daughter.'

'He expects you to support him.'

'Then he has badly misjudged me. I am not so easily bought. I owe Damin Wolfblade for my province and for saving me from the necessity of marrying a man I did not love. That means more to me than a large dowry and an insipid daughter-in-law.'

R'shiel smiled. Perhaps things *were* still going according to plan.

'Does Cyrus know how you feel?'

'I'm not given to artfulness, R'shiel. I have made no secret of where my loyalties lie.'

'Then you need to be aware of what has happened over the past few days. Cyrus used your name to lure Damin out of Greenharbour, then kidnapped his wife.'

'The Fardohnyan?'

'Princess Adrina.'

'It was unwise of him to take a Fardohnyan wife,' the Warlord said with a frown. 'It gave me pause for a time. In fact it came close to costing Damin my loyalty. Fardohnyans killed my husband and I cannot count the people I have lost to them since.'

'His marriage to Adrina will bring peace.'

'Then the peace had better be accompanied by substantial reparation,' Tejay warned. 'So, where do things stand now? Is Damin preparing to attack Cyrus?'

'No. We managed to retrieve his wife by . . . other means. They'll be back in Greenharbour by now.'

'And what of Lords Foxtalon, Bearbow and Falconlance? I've no doubt Narvell Hawksword stands with his half-brother.'

'Rogan Bearbow is on Damin's side. Foxtalon and Falconlance are still allied with Cyrus.'

'Then with my vote, Damin has a majority. Foxtalon will change sides as soon as he realises he's backed a loser, but Eaglespike and Falconlance will not give up so easily. And they have the advantage. Their provinces make up most of the south. We outnumber them in theory, but it will be months before we can muster an army sufficient to defeat them. Our troops are spread out all over Hythria.'

'Cyrus is already prepared for war.'

'You can bet Falconlance is too. The city of Greenharbour might be neutral territory, but it is surrounded by Greenharbour Province – and *that* is owned, lock, stock and barrel, by Conin Falconlance.'

'Then Greenharbour is likely to fall under siege?'

'You can wager on it.'

R'shiel thought for a moment, trying to think of a way to get the scattered armies of Krakandar, Sunrise, Elasapine, Izcomdar and Pentamor (assuming Tejay was right about Lord Foxtalon) mustered. With a sigh, R'shiel decided Tejay was correct in her assessment. It would take far too long.

*Damn it! I don't have time for this!* R'shiel fought back the feeling that this entire trip to Hythria had been a waste of time. She was no closer to finding a way to defeat Xaphista, and was certain now of only one thing: if the solution she sought wasn't at Sanctuary, and the Sorcerers'

Collective in Greenharbour was unable to help her, that left the Citadel. It had been the heart of Harshini power and was the only place left she could think to look for an answer. She was also sure that the Sisters of the Blade would have kept every book, every scroll, every scrap of parchment they had taken when they overran the Citadel. They might despise the Harshini and do whatever they could to obliterate all traces of their existence, but they were too methodical, too pragmatic, and far too sensible to destroy the only documents that might hold the key to the destruction of their enemies. But with Damin likely to encounter an invading force, and Fardohnya poised to attack . . .

R'shiel heartily wished she had kept her nose out of the whole messy situation. And she wished she had never conceived the absurd idea that Damin should marry Adrina to force the ruling Houses of Hythria and Fardohnya into a truce. It had seemed like such a good idea at the time . . . If she was honest with herself, she was willing to admit that her plans had as much to do with annoying the God of War as they did with her ultimate desire to defeat Xaphista. Two nations that had been fighting each other sporadically for centuries suddenly united would be a serious blow to Zegarnald's mammoth ego. Perhaps she was drunk on her own power. Whatever the reason, it didn't help her at present. Her desire to bring peace had actually caused another war.

Brak had warned her that it would. She should have listened to him. Now she had to do something to end it, preferably before it got started.

'What if you had another ally? One who could be in Greenharbour in a matter of weeks with an army that outnumbers your enemies?' suggested R'shiel.

'Who are you thinking of?'

'Fardohnya.'

Tejay laughed contemptuously. 'You think Hablet would send his troops into Hythria for a reason other than conquest?'

'He would if the demon child told him to.'

'I hope your abilities match your confidence, my dear. Besides, the Fardohnyans are even further from Greenharbour than our own troops.'

'But they can sail from Talabar and be in Greenharbour faster than you can get your armies together overland.'

The Warlord nodded, but she was decidedly unhappy about the idea. And sceptical. 'So, you plan to ride your dragon into Talabar and make Hablet send his troops to our rescue.'

'If necessary.'

'I will believe it when I see it.'

They were interrupted by Bayla, who backed into the tent carrying a platter of bread and freshly roasted meat. R'shiel realised how hungry she was as the smell reached her. She had not eaten since before she spoke to Korandellan, and that had been two days ago. Bayla placed the tray on the small table in front of them and managed to bow half a dozen times on the way out. Tejay watched her leave with a look of exasperation.

'The gods alone know what it will take to get some spirit into that girl.'

'She's very young.'

'Which is a blessing. Valorian is quite smitten with her helplessness at present, but it won't last. The novelty will wear off soon enough and then they'll both be unhappy.'

'If it's strong women you admire, Tejay, then you and the Princess Adrina should become fast friends.'

'Me? Befriend a Fardohnyan? I find that prospect even more unlikely than the idea that Hablet would help us for a reason other than territorial gain.'

'You might be surprised, Tejay.'

The Warlord helped herself to a shank of meat and smiled at R'shiel. 'My dear, if I find myself friends with a Fardohnyan princess, and one of Hablet's brood at that, "surprised" won't even begin to describe it.'

## 30

From Tejay's camp, R'shiel flew northward towards Fardohnya. Now that she was assured of the Warlord's support and it seemed that Damin and Adrina were finally fighting on the same side, she figured she could leave the rest of it up to them. Tejay was confident that Cyrus Eaglespike and Conin Falconlance would not attack until after the Convocation, on the slim chance she would support them and give Cyrus the majority he needed to claim the High Prince's throne.

With Tejay's promise to stall things as long as possible, R'shiel calculated that she had a couple of weeks at most before Greenharbour fell under siege. Two weeks in which she must get to Fardohnya and convince King Hablet to gather his fleet and send his army to rescue his daughter and her husband, as their ally, not their conqueror.

*All this when I want to be in the Citadel,* she silently lamented.

But it wasn't just the situation in Hythria that lent her mission urgency. Time was running out on more than one front. Korandellan was weakening and she was worried sick about Tarja. She had received no word of him since crossing into Hythria, and she had no idea of how things stood in Medalon.

Dranymire sensed her urgency and did not complain when she told him their destination. He suggested warning Brak of their imminent arrival, and R'shiel gladly agreed. She was surprised how much she missed Brak, or at least his counsel, and was hopeful he would be able to ease her mind about Tarja. He might even know what was happening in Medalon. And she was certain that she would need his help in getting to the Citadel.

The journey north took four days, and by the time the pink walls of Talabar appeared in the distance, R'shiel felt almost confident that she had mastered the skill of dragon riding. She still ached for hours when she climbed off the beast, but she no longer clung with grim determination to the dragon's back for fear of plunging to her death. As Dranymire had explained, it was simply a question of balance. Besides, after riding a water dragon through the foaming waves of the Dregian Ocean, R'shiel decided that airborne dragons were a vastly preferable method of transport. At least you could talk to them. They didn't just smile at you with stupid, fixed grins, then drag you down under several tons of cold water, just for the sheer joy of it.

Dranymire began to lose altitude while they were still several leagues from the harbour. He headed for a clearing that appeared in the vast canopy of trees passing beneath them in a green blur east of the city. Brak had arranged to meet them here, and her heart quickened a little at the thought of seeing him again. The reason was quite simple and more than a little disturbing. Brak was the only person, Harshini or demon, god or human, who she trusted implicitly. Including, she realised with a frown, both Tarja and Damin.

Her reason for distrusting Damin was fairly straightforward. He had a bad habit of acting first and worrying about the consequences later. If he let her down, it would not be lack of honour, but lack of forethought, that betrayed her. Tarja was a little more complicated. His love for her was imposed on him. It might vanish as abruptly as it had appeared and his anger when he realised how he'd been manipulated could easily turn that love to hatred. She wished she knew where he was, and that he was safe. She desperately wanted to know what he was thinking.

Brak was waiting for them in the clearing when they landed. The humid jungle was alive with the sounds of insects and other creatures she couldn't see, and the trees shook as the unseen beasts leapt from tree to tree. Whatever they were, they seemed unafraid of the dragons and not too bothered by the presence of the Harshini.

R'shiel slithered off the dragon's back, and collapsed inelegantly as she hit the ground. Brak smiled and stepped forward to help her up.

'Not as easy as it looks, is it?'

'I'm getting the hang of the riding. It's the walking around afterwards I'm still having trouble with.' She looked up at him smiling as she climbed unsteadily to her feet. 'I'm so glad to see you, Brak. Do you think we could just sit for a moment?'

'I think you'd better,' he agreed, helping her across the clearing to a fallen log that was slowly being consumed by the jungle around it. She sat down gratefully as Brak turned and bowed respectfully to the dragon.

'Lord Dranymire.'

'Lord Brakandaran.'

'I thank you for delivering the demon child safely.'

'Luck and a modicum of natural ability is the only reason she survives, my lord. I can claim no credit.'

Brak smiled. 'I thank you all the same, my lord.'

'Will you be long discussing your plans? We have been in this meld for days now, and I wish to allow my brethren an opportunity to rest.'

'Dissolve the meld, my lord. We shall call on you later, should your services be required.'

The dragon bowed its huge head towards Brak. 'You may wish to take this opportunity to teach the demon child some manners regarding the brethren, Lord Brakandaran. She is sorely in need of education.'

As soon as he finished speaking, the meld began to dissolve and the dragon disintegrated into a writhing mass of little grey demons that vanished almost as soon as they were free of the meld. Within moments Brak and R'shiel were alone in the clearing.

'What did you do to upset Dranymire?'

'Who knows? As he said, I'm sadly lacking in demon etiquette.' She flexed her knees stiffly and looked up at him. 'You seem pretty good at it.'

'I've had several hundred years of practice.'

'Are you really that old?'

'Don't I look it?'

'Actually, you don't look a day over thirty-five.'

'My family always did carry their age well,' he agreed with a grin, then he sat beside her, his smile fading. 'What are you doing here, R'shiel? I thought you were wreaking havoc in Hythria?'

'I was.'

Brak laughed.

'I don't mean that the way it sounds, Brak! Everything was going along fine until High Prince Lernen up and died on me. Then Damin's cousin claimed the throne and then when we got to Greenharbour, Glenanaran and the others were half dead from trying to protect the Sorcerers' Collective. And *then* Adrina was kidnapped – she's pregnant, by the way – so I had to go and rescue her, and stop Damin launching a suicidal attack on his cousin to defend her honour. If that isn't enough, Korandellan's about to fall over from exhaustion because he's been holding Sanctuary out of time for too long.' She took a deep breath and looked at him expectantly.

'You've been busy. When did you speak to Korandellan?'

'A few days ago. I used the Seeing Stone.'

'My, we have come a long way, haven't we?'

'Don't patronise me, Brak.'

'I didn't mean to. But the news about Sanctuary concerns me.'

'I know. And there's nothing I can do about it until I sort out Hythria and Fardohnya.'

'Why? Does it really make that much difference? Why not leave them to their bickering and do something about Xaphista? Do something about the situation in Medalon?'

'I *am* doing something about Xaphista! At least, I thought I was. That's why I went to Hythria in the first place. As for Medalon, that's where I'm headed next. Tarja will need my help and—'

'Tarja's been captured, R'shiel.'

She swallowed hard as her heart relocated itself in her throat. 'When? How?'

'It happened about a month ago. He sank the ferry at Cauthside but didn't get away quickly enough. The Kariens have been waiting for the flood waters to subside, but they've not been idle. They'll be ready to cross the

Glass River any day now. Tarja is being taken to the Citadel for trial.'

'I'm surprised they didn't kill him,' she remarked tonelessly.

'He's too important. Publicly hanging Tarja in the Citadel will be the Kariens' final and unequivocal declaration of mastery over Medalon. His death will tear the heart out of the resistance.'

'It'll tear the heart out of more than the resistance,' she said softly, then buried her face in her hands, wishing the whole world would just stop for a while and let her catch her breath.

'I'm sorry, R'shiel.'

'I almost wish you hadn't told me.' She straightened suddenly, looking at him curiously. 'How do you know all this, anyway?'

'I have a new friend. She keeps me informed.'

'She?'

'The head of the Fardohnyan Assassins' Guild is a woman.'

'How nice for you, Brak.'

'Now who's being patronising? And you still haven't answered my question. What are you doing in Fardohnya?'

'Trying to undo the damage I caused. Once the Convocation is held, and Cyrus loses the election, Greenharbour will be under siege within a matter of hours. Damin doesn't have the troops to hold out for long, even with the other Warlords on his side. Their armies are scattered all over Hythria.'

'I hope you don't expect Hablet to help. He's being very uncooperative. He ordered me out of Fardohnya, actually.'

'Did you try reasoning with him?'

'One doesn't use the words "reason" and "Hablet" in

the same breath. Not when it comes to the Harshini. Or the delicate matter of his heir. Which reminds me, did you know that if he doesn't get a legitimate son, the Fardohnyan throne falls to Damin?'

She nodded. 'Princess Marla told me.'

'How did Adrina take the news?'

'As you'd expect.'

Brak frowned. 'And you left them alone in Hythria?'

'That was the one good thing to come out of all this. Damin and Adrina have finally worked out what everyone else has known for months. Sometimes humans don't know what they've got until they've almost lost it.'

He smiled. 'That sounds very Harshini, R'shiel.'

She rolled her eyes but did not deny the accusation.

'So, what do you want to do about Hablet?'

'Well, if reason won't work, perhaps a show of force will.'

'I don't like the sound of this.'

'Brak, I need Hablet's army to set sail for Greenharbour within the week. And I need them to go to Damin's aid, not use it as an excuse to invade Hythria. If Hablet won't listen to reason, then I'll scare him into it, but either way, I have to stop the civil war in Hythria before it gets out of hand.'

'Why?'

She didn't answer immediately.

'R'shiel? Your silence is scaring me. Just exactly what are you cooking up in that devious little mind of yours?'

She fidgeted uncomfortably under his scrutiny. 'I don't intend to let Zegarnald – or any other god – profit from my mistakes.'

Brak was silent for a moment. 'Zegarnald wants you to destroy Xaphista, R'shiel. Aren't you overstepping yourself just a tad?'

'Zegarnald wanted me "tempered", remember?' she reminded him bitterly. 'Well, he's only got himself to blame if he forged a two-edged sword.'

Shaking his head, Brak stood up and held out his hand to her. 'One day, when we get the time, along with respect for the demons, I think I need to teach you the concept of leaving well enough alone.'

R'shiel and Brak made no attempt to conceal their presence as they flew towards Talabar. Brak rode his metallic green dragon, which Lady Elanymire and her brethren had formed at his request, while R'shiel rode beside him on Dranymire's golden meld. They made an impressive sight swooping down over the city – two creatures from legend and their Harshini dragon riders flying out of the sun to land in the courtyard of the Summer Palace. By the time they had scattered the startled palace guards and the dragons settled to the ground, the city was in an uproar.

R'shiel climbed down from Dranymire, pleased to discover the short ride had left her capable of walking. 'I hope Hablet is in. We're going to look pretty damned foolish making such an impressive entrance if he's not home.'

'He's home,' Brak assured her, pointing to flags flying proudly over the main entrance to the palace. A tubby, bald-headed man in gloriously expensive silks hurried towards them. His expression was caught somewhere between shock and outrage.

'What is the meaning of this?' he screeched, panting heavily as he tried to block their path. 'You can't enter the palace like this! Who are you? What do you want?'

'Who is this, Brak?' she asked. Both were drawing on

their power and their eyes burned black. Although the courtyard was full of guards, the dragons kept any potential trouble at bay, simply by being dragons.

'Lector Turon, your highness, King Hablet's Chamberlain,' Brak replied in a superior tone.

Brak was quite an actor when the occasion called for it, R'shiel thought. She bit back a grin at his manner and turned her ebony eyes on the eunuch. 'You will take me to the king.'

'The king cannot be disturbed!'

'Come, Lord Brakandaran,' she declared dramatically. 'This underling is of no use to us. We shall find the king ourselves.'

She pushed Lector Turon out of the way and began walking across the paved courtyard with Brak at her side. Lector scurried past them, yelling at the top of his voice.

'Bar the doors! Shut them! Quickly! Protect your king!'

The guards were quick to respond. The doors boomed shut before R'shiel and Brak reached the steps and shook as the locking bar was dropped into place.

'He's an annoying little toad, isn't he?'

'Immensely,' Brak agreed. 'What are you going to do about the doors?'

'What doors?'

She kept walking as the massive, bronze-plated doors blew outward off their hinges. Everyone but Brak and R'shiel dived for cover.

'Impressive.'

'Actually, I wasn't sure that would work,' she admitted, in a voice meant only for Brak. 'Shall we go and find the king?'

'You're enjoying this, aren't you?'

'Aren't *you*?'

He allowed a small smile to flicker over his lips, before he turned back to stare at what was left of the entrance to Hablet's Summer Palace. 'I hate to admit it, but yes, I am enjoying it.'

'Good. I like to see people happy in their work.'

He followed her up the steps to the entrance, stepping over the debris from the explosion. The dazed guards made no attempt to stop them as they strode past.

R'shiel glanced around, wondering where Hablet would be hiding – if he *was* hiding. He might just have the spine to confront her. He was Adrina's father, after all, and she certainly never shied from anything.

Courtiers, slaves and guards stepped out of their path as they strode through the palace. When they reached the throne room, R'shiel resisted the temptation to blast those doors off their hinges, too. She settled for blowing them open, instead. The long narrow hall was crowded with people clinging to each other fearfully, their silks and jewels quivering as they stared aghast at the sight of two black-eyed and obviously annoyed Harshini striding through their midst.

They stopped several paces from the foot of the raised dais where Hablet sat, clutching the gilt arms of his throne with white-knuckled terror. It was the only outward sign of his fear. His expression was one of carefully contrived contempt, rather than dread.

'Who are you?'

'I am the demon child.'

'Well, I don't care who you are, young lady, you'll pay for the damage to my palace.' He turned his royal gaze on Brak with a frown. 'I thought I told you to leave Fardohnya?'

'I answer to a higher power than you, your majesty.'

'Well, I don't!' the king declared petulantly. He reminded R'shiel of Adrina when she was in high dudgeon.

'You will answer to the gods, Hablet,' R'shiel warned, sincerely hoping she would not have to involve them. She wasn't entirely sure they would back her in this.

'The gods will not betray me!'

'Perhaps, your majesty, but they will do what *I* ask of them.'

Hablet stared at her for a moment, weighing up the advisability of defying someone who spoke directly to the gods. He sagged visibly and turned to the Captain of the Guard.

'Clear the hall.'

'Sire?'

'Clear the hall! Everybody out! Now!'

The captain hurried to do as his king ordered. Within minutes they were alone, the doors slamming shut behind the fearful courtiers as they scurried from the throne room.

'What do you want?' Hablet asked once he was certain they were alone.

'I want you to set sail for Hythria, your majesty.'

'Hythria? Your friend here was warning me to stay out of Hythria a few weeks ago, and now you want me to invade it.'

'You're not going to invade Hythria, Hablet. You're going to relieve the siege at Greenharbour.'

'What siege?'

'Your daughter is now the High Princess of Hythria, and her capital is under siege, or at least it will be, by the time you get there.'

'Adrina? That traitorous little ingrate? Why should I do anything to aid her? She betrayed me and married my worst enemy!'

'She married the heir to your throne.'

'I'll die before I let Damin Wolfblade inherit my crown!'

'That's the whole idea, isn't it?'

Hablet glared at her. 'What do I get out of it?'

'You leave this room alive, for a start,' R'shiel warned him in a voice so dangerous that even Brak looked at her askance.

'You can't kill me,' he scoffed. 'You're Harshini.'

'I am the demon child, Hablet. I'm only half-Harshini, and believe me, the human part of me has no qualms about removing people who stand in my way.'

Hablet rubbed his beard thoughtfully then his eyes narrowed. 'If I send my fleet to relieve this siege of Adrina's, I want something in return.'

'You're hardly in a position to negotiate, your majesty.'

'You think so? Try getting my fleet to move past the end of the docks without my help.'

Reluctantly, R'shiel had to concede that he had a point. 'What do you want?'

'I want a son. I want a legitimate son.'

'I can't grant you that.'

'Oh, so there are limits to what you can do? Well, in that case, Adrina and her damned barbarian can rot in Greenharbour and you can kill me now. It won't make much difference either way. If I'm dead, Wolfblade gets my throne, but he won't be in a position to claim it, will he?' Hablet chuckled nastily, daring her to do her worst.

R'shiel considered the matter. If she acceded to his demand – assuming Jelanna agreed to cooperate – then she would lose her ability to unite Fardohnya and Hythria on Hablet's death. On the other hand, all she really wanted to do was get to the Citadel. It didn't really matter who ruled Fardohnya, just so long as they weren't at war with Damin. He couldn't spare any troops to aid Tarja in ridding Medalon of the Kariens if he was embroiled in a war with either his cousin or his father-in-law. Time was of the essence and she didn't have any spare to waste arguing with Hablet.

'Very well. I will speak to Jelanna. That's the best I can do. But the first hint that you are exceeding your mandate, your majesty, and I will personally see to it that your son withers and dies in the womb.'

Hablet nodded. If he believed her threat, he did not appear bothered by it. All he wanted was finally getting the heir he craved. He beamed at her happily. 'I find myself suddenly warming to you, demon child. I shall issue the orders today and we shall set sail for Greenharbour by week's end. I shall place Gaffen in command. He was always fond of Adrina.'

'Gaffen?'

'The second eldest of my baseborn sons. He and Tristan were always finding trouble with Adrina. Speaking of which, you've not mentioned him. I cannot believe he stood idly by while Adrina ran off with a Hythrun Warlord.'

R'shiel glanced at Brak warily before she answered the king.

'Tristan is dead, your majesty, as is most of the Guard you sent north with Adrina. They were killed fighting the Medalonians.'

The king paled. His voice was like ice when he finally spoke. 'What were they doing fighting the Medalonians?'

'I believe it was on Prince Cratyn's orders. It was following their death that Adrina fled Karien.'

Hablet was silent for a long time. His anger was a

palpable thing. 'Once the situation in Hythria is resolved, you will be confronting the Kariens, yes?'

'They need to be pushed out of Medalon, certainly.'

'Then you have found yourself an ally, demon child. No child of mine, baseborn or otherwise, dies in such a manner without a reckoning.'

## 31

The Convocation of the Warlords to elect the High Prince of Hythria finally took place four days after Damin and Adrina returned to Greenharbour. Tejay Lionsclaw had arrived, bearing news that she had met the demon child, and that when last heard of, R'shiel was heading for Fardohnya to speak with King Hablet.

The news did little to ease Damin's mind. It was bad enough that she had vanished without warning, but to learn that she was heading for Fardohnya made things even worse. He knew as well as anyone what was likely to happen should he win the election. Inviting Hablet to come to his rescue, the man who had spent the past thirty years trying to figure out how to invade his country, the man who had tried to hire assassins to have him killed, did not strike Damin as a particularly prudent move.

'You look very . . .'

'What?' he snapped as Adrina walked into his dressing room. 'Foolish?'

'I was going to say dashing, but foolish will do, if you prefer.'

Actually, he felt like an idiot. One of the reasons he

had spent as little time at court as possible was his dislike of dressing in such cumbersome finery. He wore white, the traditional colour reserved for the High Prince, from his knee-high calf leather boots to his gloriously embroidered jacket and short cape that was heavy and uncomfortable and totally unsuited to Greenharbour's humid climate. The gold coronet around his forehead was uncomfortably tight and the ceremonial sword he wore owed more of its weight to its gem-encrusted scabbard than it did to its blade. In a fight it would be as useful as a knitting needle. It was Adrina who insisted he dress the part of High Prince for the Convocation, and she had found a surprising ally in Princess Marla.

She smiled and stepped forward to adjust the coronet, which eased the pressure a little, then she smoothed his fair hair down. 'You look every bit the High Prince.'

'Looking the part won't win me the title.'

'You'd be surprised.'

'Gods, how I hate all this pomp and ceremony!'

'Well, you'd better get used to it, my love.'

The endearment caught him by surprise. 'My *love*?'

'Well, I can't go on calling you the Evil Barbarian Bastard forever, can I?'

He laughed. 'No. I suppose not.'

Adrina sat down on the small settee and curled her legs up under her to watch him finish dressing. Since their return from Dregian Castle, and their argument on the beach, she had been a different person. Or perhaps he was seeing a side of her that she had never shown him before. The change in her scared him, not because of what she had become, but because he was afraid it wouldn't last. The new Adrina was everything he could have wished for in a consort. She was intelligent, charming and determined to secure his throne, whatever the cost. How much of that was because she cared for him, and how much was simply her desire to see Cyrus Eaglespike brought down, he did not dare ask.

'Explain something to me, Damin. Why do you have an election for the High Prince? Isn't it a hereditary title?'

'Yes, but there's frequently been more than one contender. Twins are fairly common in my family, and the first born is not always the most suitable for the job.'

'Twins? Gods, you're not telling me I'm likely to have twins, are you?'

He smiled at her alarmed expression. 'Kalan and Narvell are twins. Even Lernen was a twin, although his brother died in infancy.'

'But didn't Lernen name you as his heir? Surely, in that case, there would be no need for an election?'

'The Convocation is a formality, more often than not,' he agreed. 'It makes the Warlords feel they have a say in things. In this case, however, there are two contenders.'

'How can Cyrus seriously think he's a contender if Lernen named you his heir? I can understand him jumping in when he thought you'd vanished into Medalon, but now that you're back, you'd think he'd just bow out gracefully.'

'Cyrus doesn't do anything gracefully, least of all admitting he was wrong. No, he will fight this to the bitter end. He's come too far to give up now.'

'I wish I could come with you. There are a few things I'd like to say to Lord Eaglespike.'

'Which is why it's a good thing you're *not* coming with me.'

She smiled. The old Adrina probably would have

thrown something at him. 'Just be careful what *you* say, Damin.'

'I won't let him get to me.'

'I don't care if he gets to you. Just don't let him win.'

He reached for her and pulled her gently to her feet. She did not resist. He drew her close and kissed her, still amazed how good it felt to be able to do that without fear of having her slide a knife between his ribs. She laid her head on his chest and he held her for a moment.

'You'd better come back in one piece,' she warned, looking up at him. Her emerald eyes were glistening with unshed tears.

'I'll do my best, your highness.' He kissed her again and put his arm around her shoulder as they walked back out into the main chamber of his apartments. Or rather *their* apartments now – Adrina had moved in the day they arrived back in Greenharbour. Almodavar was waiting for them, dressed in full battle gear. Adrina frowned when she saw him.

'Almodavar! Aren't you ready yet?'

'He's not coming with me,' Damin explained. 'I'm leaving him here to protect the palace.'

'But you need a Guard of Honour!'

'And I have one. But if things don't go his way, Cyrus may make his move before we leave the Sorcerers' Collective. I don't intend to make the same mistake I made the last time. Almodavar is staying here to ensure your safety.'

'You need him more than I do,' she insisted.

'The matter isn't open for negotiation, Adrina.' He kissed the top of her head and let her go. 'I'll see you later. When it's all over.'

She nodded but didn't answer him. Almodavar opened

the door for him and he stepped into the hall without looking back.

'Damin!'

He stopped and turned to her. 'Yes?'

She hesitated for a moment, opened her mouth to say something, closed it again, then shrugged helplessly. 'Be careful.'

He wondered what she had really wanted to say. Whatever it was, she had obviously changed her mind. He smiled mockingly and bowed to her with all the flair of a court dandy. 'As her highness commands.'

She frowned at him then turned to his captain. 'Get him out of here, Almodavar. That coronet is obviously stopping the blood flow to his brain.'

Even Almodavar grinned, which had the unfortunate effect of making him look fiercer than normal. 'This way, my lord.'

Damin straightened up and met her eye. She smiled at him. It was a genuine smile, without guile or artifice. Suddenly it didn't seem to matter what else the day might bring.

The Hall of Convocation in the Sorcerers' Palace was a room used for the election of the High Prince and the confirmation of Warlords. It was a windowless, nine-sided room, not particularly large, but lavishly decorated. Seven of the wall panels depicted the crests of the Warlords of Hythria in mosaic tiles of gold, silver and semiprecious stones. The doors broke the eighth panel, but when closed, they formed the diamond symbol of the Sorcerers' Collective. The panel opposite the door was fashioned from a sheet of solid gold and was embossed with the snarling wolf's head of the Wolfblade House. A massive candelabra suspended from the ceiling, which took two acolytes almost an hour to light, provided the only illumination.

In the centre of the room was a nine-sided table, with nine gilt stools arranged around it. Like the walls, the table was split into panels that were inlaid with the colours of the seven provinces, the Royal House and the Collective. Marla had brought him here for the first time on his tenth birthday to impress upon him the importance of his heritage.

Damin took his seat – not under the Wolfblade crest, but under Krakandar Province, represented by the rampant kraken of his late father, Laran Krakenshield. Although he had never known his father, Damin still mourned his loss at times. By all accounts Laran had been a strong and ruthless man. He could do with such an ally today. He realised that he would need to find a suitable replacement for himself in Krakandar. If he secured the title of High Prince, the province would need a new Warlord.

The other Warlords took their places, all dressed in finery to rival Damin's. In fact, next to Toren Foxtalon's gem-encrusted armour, Damin felt quite ordinary. Cyrus, who was also dressed in white, avoided meeting his eye, as did Conin Falconlance. Rogan simply nodded in his direction. Tejay smiled at him and Narvell didn't look at him at all, too busy scanning the faces of the other Warlords with a threatening scowl. Damin felt a rush of affection for his younger half-brother. It was odd to think that Narvell was feeling protective of him, rather than the other way around.

Kalan was the last to arrive. She was dressed in a simple black robe, her only adornment the diamond-shaped pendant of her office. As soon as she entered, the doors swung shut behind her without any visible effort on her part. Wordlessly, the Warlords took their places. The High Arrion placed her hands on the table in front of her and closed her eyes.

'We meet to elect a new High Prince. May the gods grant us wisdom.'

'May the gods grant us wisdom,' the Warlords echoed with varying degrees of enthusiasm.

Kalan opened her eyes and sat down, then studied the gathering for a moment before continuing. 'According to the will of the late High Prince, Damin Wolfblade is his legal heir, by right of blood. Are there any other candidates?'

Although the statement was one of tradition, all eyes turned expectantly to Cyrus. He nodded slowly and rose to his feet.

'Lord Eaglespike?'

'I offer myself as a candidate, my lady.'

'On what grounds?'

'By right of blood.'

'Your great-great-grandmother was a Wolfblade, Lord Eaglespike. By right of blood, Lord Wolfblade has the stronger claim.'

'I merely mention my blood tie to validate my claim, my lady. My reason for offering my candidacy however, is because I believe Lord Wolfblade has committed treason.'

Terse silence met Cyrus' startling claim.

'That is a serious accusation, my lord.'

'No more serious than the actions of Lord Wolfblade.'

'Can you substantiate your claims?' Narvell demanded, leaping to his feet. 'If not, I suggest you sit down before I decide to—'

'Narvell, shut up,' Kalan snapped, for a moment addressing her twin, rather than the High Arrion addressing a Warlord.

'Kalan!' he objected. She was the older twin by a mere twenty minutes, but she had always been the dominant one.

'Sit down, Hawksword,' Rogan added. 'Cyrus will dig his own grave without any help from you.'

Narvell reluctantly sat as Cyrus turned to Rogan. 'Are you threatening me, my lord?'

'No, Eaglespike, I'm not threatening you. You'll know about it if I do.'

'As I was saying, before I was interrupted,' Cyrus continued, looking pointedly at Narvell, 'Damin Wolfblade has committed treason. He cannot, therefore, be allowed to take the throne, regardless of the will of the late High Prince.'

'Would you care to elaborate, my lord?'

'He made an unauthorised alliance with a foreign power and then he married a Fardohnyan.'

'At least he married,' Tejay remarked with a chuckle. 'Which is more than you can say for poor old Lernen.'

Cyrus did not appreciate her levity. 'This is a serious matter, my lady. You would do well to treat it as such.'

'I'm *trying* to take this seriously, Cyrus, and I would, if this wasn't such a joke.' She turned to Damin. 'What say you, Lord Wolfblade? Is Cyrus right? Did you make an unauthorised alliance with a foreign power? I think we all know by now that you married a Fardohnyan.'

'Guilty on both counts,' Damin replied calmly.

Cyrus stared at him, making no attempt to hide his surprise. 'You admit to your crimes?'

'I don't know that I'd call them 'crimes', cousin, but I

certainly did make an alliance with Medalon and I believe you've already met my wife.' Cyrus still had enough honour left in him to squirm a little under Damin's scrutiny. Damin wondered if he had figured out yet how she had escaped. 'I plead mitigating circumstances.'

'What mitigating circumstances?' Conin Falconlance scoffed. 'What could possibly justify such actions?'

'I was asked to aid Medalon. I was ordered to marry Adrina.'

'By whom?'

'In the former case, Lord Brakandaran of the Harshini asked for my aid. In the latter it was the demon child. As she had been placed in my care by Zegarnald himself, I could hardly refuse, could I?'

Cyrus laughed sceptically. 'You expect us to believe the God of War singled you out and asked you to aid the demon child?'

'Yes.'

'That's preposterous! What proof have you?'

'Call Glenanaran, if my word isn't good enough. You'll take the word of a Harshini, won't you? He was with us when we crossed into Medalon and I'm sure he wouldn't mind calling up the God of War so you can cross-examine him.'

Only Kalan and Narvell knew that he had spoken with Zegarnald. With the exception of Cyrus, the other Warlords seemed quite overawed by the revelation. Lord Eaglespike glanced around the table, shaking his head.

'Am I the only one here who finds this fantastic tale unbelievable?'

'No, you're the only one here with a vested interest in having us deny it,' Tejay pointed out. 'I believe Damin, and when it comes down to it, I'd rather have a High

Prince who speaks to the gods than one who uses my name to perpetrate mischief.'

Cyrus was looking decidedly uncomfortable. He obviously had not expected Tejay to learn of his deception, just as he expected to come to this meeting with Adrina as a hostage.

'Well, Lord Eaglespike?' Kalan asked. 'Shall I call on the Harshini to bear witness to Lord Wolfblade's defence?'

Cyrus shook his head. 'That won't be necessary, my lady. Lord Wolfblade is a man of honour.'

'An honourable traitor? You flatter me, my lord.'

The Warlord ignored the comment and remained standing. 'There is still the issue of his marriage to that Fardohnyan. He may have married her on the orders of the demon child, but that doesn't make the situation any less intolerable.'

'What's your objection, Cyrus?' Tejay asked cheerfully. 'That she's Fardohnyan, or that you can't seem to keep her in your dungeons for more than a few hours without losing her?'

Cyrus kept his temper with admirable restraint. 'Anything I have done, my lady, I have done for the good of Hythria.'

'Then we are of one purpose, my lord,' Damin replied. 'I, too, have only the interests of Hythria at heart.'

'If you only care about Hythria, how can you possibly expect us to tolerate that woman? She is a viper! When she was here in Greenharbour the last time, you claimed she tried to kill Lernen!'

'I was wrong.'

'Wrong? Or simply thinking with your balls?' He glanced around at the others with a knowing smirk. 'I hear she's *court'esa* trained.'

Damin called on every ounce of self-control he owned to stop him leaping over the table and taking Cyrus Eaglespike by the throat.

'You will speak with respect when referring to your High Princess,' he managed to say, despite the effort it cost him to remain outwardly calm.

'She is *not* my High Princess, and will never be!'

'Whether or not Princess Adrina is the High Princess is yet to be decided,' Kalan reminded them, raising her voice slightly. 'Lord Eaglespike, do you have a specific objection to the Princess, or is it simply her nationality that disturbs you?'

'I'd settle for just *one* good reason why we should accept that foreign whore,' Conin Falconlance interjected.

Damin gripped the side of his stool until his knuckles were white, but gave no other indication of his anger. 'One reason? Gunpowder.'

That got their attention.

'Gunpowder?' Tejay gasped. 'Gods, Damin, if you took *all* of his daughters off his hands, Hablet still wouldn't part with that secret.'

'I'm aware of that and so is Adrina. When Hablet signed the treaty with the Kariens, which included sharing the secret of gunpowder, it was sealed by her marriage to Cratyn. She knew he was never likely to live up to his end of the bargain. She was understandably fearful that his refusal might result in the Kariens taking reprisals and the most obvious target would have been her. So she made a point of learning the secret before she left Fardohnya.'

'And she told the Kariens the secret?' Toren Foxtalon asked. It was the first time he had spoken. He had been sitting so quietly Damin thought him asleep, but this news had seemingly woken him from his torpor.

'No. The only person she has shared it with is me.'

'What makes *you* so special?' Cyrus laughed disparagingly.

Damin turned to him and smiled with languid smugness. 'I, too, am *court'esa* trained, my lord.'

Tejay clapped her hands and laughed delightedly. 'Ha! You deserved that, Cyrus! I say let's finish with this pointless argument. We all know how we plan to vote and I doubt that anything said here today has changed any of our opinions. It certainly hasn't changed mine. Order the vote, Kalan!'

Cyrus glanced around the table, calculating his position. He had lost Tejay – that was obvious – and Foxtalon was quite taken with the idea of learning the secret of gunpowder. Narvell had never been in his camp and it was clear where Rogan's loyalties lay. He threw his hands up and sat down heavily.

'Have your damned vote then. This is a farce!'

'Then I will take your votes, my lords,' Kalan agreed with a frown at Cyrus for disparaging the validity of the Convocation. 'Lord Bearbow, how does Izcomdar vote?'

'Wolfblade.'

'Lady Lionsclaw? How does Sunrise vote?'

'Wolfblade.'

'Lord Falconlance? How does Greenharbour vote?'

'Eaglespike.'

'Lord Hawksword? How does Elasapine vote?'

'Wolfblade.'

'Lord Foxtalon? How does Pentamor vote?'

Toren fidgeted uncomfortably, staring determinedly at the table in front of him. 'Wolfblade.'

Damin breathed a sigh of relief. With five of the seven

Warlords on his side he had more than he could have hoped for a few days ago.

'Lord Eaglespike? How does Dregian vote?'

'Eaglespike,' he snapped angrily. 'For all the good it does.'

'Lord Wolfblade? How does Krakandar vote?'

'Wolfblade.' He didn't need to say anything else.

'Then I declare Damin Wolfblade is the High Prince of Hythria. Long live High Prince Damin!'

'Long live High Prince Damin!' the others echoed, with the notable exception of Cyrus and Conin.

Cyrus pushed his stool back and rose to his feet. 'This is a sad day for Hythria, my Lords. You have just handed our nation over to a man who is under the thrall of a Fardohnyan whore. You will live to regret this decision. Come, Conin, let us together commiserate on the death of our nation's independence.'

Lord Falconlance stood and followed Cyrus wordlessly. The doors swung open as they approached, and swung shut behind them when they left the room. The tension flowed out of the room with the departure of the Warlords.

'Anyone care to wager that Cyrus' idea of commiseration involves a civil war?' Rogan asked of no one in particular.

'I don't think I care for the odds, Rogan,' Tejay said.

'Kalan, as High Prince, I want command of the troops belonging to the Sorcerers' Collective.'

The High Arrion did not even hesitate. 'They are yours, Damin, along with anything else you need.'

Rogan smiled. 'You see, there's an advantage to keeping things all in the family. How long do we have, do you think?'

'Until sunrise, is my guess,' Damin replied. 'I suspect they'll be waiting for us when we open the city gates in the morning.'

'Then we won't be opening the city gates,' Narvell predicted grimly.

'What about the harbour?' Tejay asked. 'Cyrus and Conin have enough ships to blockade it.'

'I issued a warning to the fishing fleet this morning before I left the palace. Any boats that want to leave will be gone by now. As for the rest, if the demon child is to be believed, help is on the way. We won't have to hold out for much longer than a couple of weeks.'

'Help? What help?' Foxtalon asked suspiciously.

'The Fardohnyans.'

'The Fardohnyans! You can't trust them!'

'And I don't,' Damin told him. 'But I do trust the demon child.'

'I hope your trust is warranted, Wolfblade,' Rogan warned. 'We are placing a lot of faith in that slip of a girl.'

He smiled at the description. 'That "slip of a girl" has the power to destroy a god, Rogan.'

'She also has the power to destroy us,' Kalan reminded him ominously.

## 32

The siege didn't bother the citizens of Greenharbour at first. If anything, they considered it something of a novelty, a variation from the normal humdrum of their everyday lives. Crowds gathered at the walls each day, hoping for a chance to climb up to the ramparts and see the armies of Greenharbour and Dregian massed below. A few enterprising souls even began charging admission, after doing a deal with the guards on the walls, and they did a roaring trade until Damin got wind of it and had the entrepreneurs thrown in gaol.

By the second week the shortages began, and then the novelty quickly wore off. There was fresh water aplenty, but Greenharbour was a large city and it wasn't possible to store enough to keep the population fed for long. The city housed almost fifty thousand people, and relied on the bounty of the sea, as well as the numerous farms outside the city, for produce. With the harbour blockaded, there was no daily catch, and with the gates closed against the armies of Lord Eaglespike and Lord Falconlance there was no produce getting through. Damin heard reports of a loaf of bread costing a hundred times its normal value.

They fared no better in the palace though, because Damin had distributed most of the palace stores quite publicly on the seventh day of the siege, in the hopes of avoiding a hungry population storming the palace in the belief that food inside was being hoarded for the High Prince and his family.

Cyrus and Conin were carrying out typical siege tactics, he knew. They made no effort to attack the city. They didn't have to. It wasn't the threat *outside* the walls that would undo them, but the internal unrest. Damin had stationed troops to defend the walls of the city, but the bulk of his forces were employed simply keeping the peace. As the siege dragged on, he grew less and less tolerant of the opportunists and malcontents. He had begun by throwing them in gaol. This morning he had ordered three men beheaded for hoarding grain and then selling it at inflated prices. He did not regret their passing. As their heads dropped into the baskets beneath the executioner's block his only thought was, *That's three less mouths to feed.*

He had fifteen hundred Raiders in the city, comprising the three hundred men each Warlord was permitted. The Guards of the Sorcerers' Collective, although competent, had no combat experience to speak of. He had placed the Raiders on the walls and kept the Collective Guards for civil matters. They were well suited to the task. They knew the city and the people knew them. In total, he had two and a half thousand men, but no idea when, or if, help would arrive. There were close to ten thousand camped outside his walls.

A knock at the door disturbed him, and he looked up in annoyance. The elegantly carved desk in front of him was littered with parchment. Lernen never seemed to have to deal with this much work. He was beginning to wonder how his uncle had found time to indulge his wide variety of perversions. Damin had barely found time to eat or sleep since becoming High Prince. For the first time, too, he began to fully appreciate how much his mother had done for the High Prince over the past thirty-odd years. And was more than a little surprised at how willingly she had handed over the responsibility. Garlon Miar, Marla's fifth husband, had remarked to Damin once that he thought Marla sought power for duty's sake, not for personal ambition. In light of Marla's willingness to let her son rule in his own right, Damin was starting to think the assassin may have had the right of it.

'*What*?' he called angrily.

The door opened a fraction and Adrina's head appeared. 'Do you have a moment, Damin?'

'No,' he replied unhappily.

She opened the door all the way and entered the study with the Harshini, Glenanaran, at her side.

Damin rose to his feet with a frown. 'What is it now, Adrina? Are the peasants storming the Sorcerers' Collective?'

Glenanaran smiled, which was the usual Harshini reaction to anything one said in their presence. He was very tall and slender, with long, fair hair held back by a simple leather band. His height was emphasised by the long white robe he wore. His totally black eyes were wide with an innocence and hopefulness that no human could ever hope to emulate. 'No, your highness. But it grieves me to see you so overwrought.'

'The administration of a city under siege is proving to be worse than I could possibly have imagined, Divine One. Being overwrought seems the only appropriate reaction.'

'Don't listen to him, Glenanaran. Damin enjoys feeling sorry for himself.' Adrina smiled at him. She was looking suspiciously pleased.

'What are you up to, Adrina?'

'We have an idea.'

'Actually, the idea belongs to the High Princess, your highness. I am merely the instrument of her desire.'

'Aren't we all,' Damin muttered as he sat down. 'All right. Tell me this grand idea of yours, Adrina. The day can't get much worse.'

'You have to order the fishing boats to put to sea.'

'In case you haven't noticed, Adrina, the harbour is blockaded.'

'I know. The boats can't get past the blockade, but the fish can.'

'What are you talking about?'

'Fish, Damin. You know, those little silver wiggly things that people eat?'

He smiled, in spite of himself.

'What the High Princess means is that we can call the fish into the harbour and your fishing boats can net them without trying to get past the blockade.'

Damin leaned back in his chair and studied Adrina in amazement. 'That is the most brilliant idea I've ever heard.'

'I thought so.'

'And you can do this, Divine One? Doesn't it conflict with your aversion to killing? Those fish will go straight into the cooking pots of Greenharbour.'

'We cannot abide violence, your highness, but we understand the laws of nature. Death is an inevitable part of life. All creatures serve to nourish and feed other creatures. Even humans, when they return to the soil, feed the creatures of the earth, who in turn feed other animals. I cannot say it will make me happy, but neither can I stand idly by while the people of Greenharbour starve.'

'Then I'll order the boats to sea immediately. And get

some troops down to the harbour to avoid a riot when the catch comes in. I cannot thank you enough, Glenanaran. This may mean the difference between life and death.'

The Harshini bowed solemnly. 'I am aware of that, your highness. And now, if I may be excused, I will return to the Collective to speak with Farandelan and Joranara. I will need their help for this task.'

'Of course,' Damin agreed. 'And again, I thank you.'

As soon as he was gone, Adrina walked around the desk and pushed a stack of rolled parchment out of the way, so she could sit on it. Her expression was insufferably smug.

'So, how do you like my first official act as High Princess?'

'Not bad.'

'Not bad! It was a stroke of genius!'

'Yes, it was. But you already know that. I'm not going to inflate that ego of yours any more than it already is by admitting it, though.'

Adrina laughed. Despite the siege, despite Tamylan's death and everything else that had happened to her recently, Damin had never seen her happier. She was finally in her element, he realised. She had power and respect and the ability to use that awesome intellect for something other than causing trouble. Hablet had been a fool not to recognise what he had in his daughter. Then again, he might have actually seen her potential and banished her to Karien where he thought she couldn't threaten him.

Her laughter faded after a while and she became serious. 'It's only a temporary measure, Damin. We can't ask the Harshini to call fish into the harbour indefinitely.'

'I know. But every day we hold out is a day closer to help arriving.'

'You still believe R'shiel will be able to convince my father to send help?'

'If anybody can, R'shiel can. It's simply a question of how long it takes. She knows the urgency of the situation.'

'Personally, I don't see why she couldn't just stay here and throw a few fireballs around like she did in the Defender's camp in Medalon. That would have softened Eaglespike's spine quick enough.'

'She wants peace, Adrina,' he reminded her. 'Besides, throwing fireballs around might cow Cyrus into submission, but it would more than likely burn my city to the ground.'

'And you think a running battle through the streets of Greenharbour is going to be any less damaging?'

'No. But I've some control over the way a battle goes. R'shiel has *no* control over where her magic lands.'

'Do you think she'll ever be ready to face Xaphista?' she asked.

'I hope so.'

'If she fails,' Adrina warned, 'we'll spend the rest of our lives at war. I've lived with the Kariens, Damin. I've heard what they preach. Xaphista won't be content until the whole world is on its knees before him.'

Following the Harshini summons, the fish netted in the harbour kept the city fed for another few days, but that problem was quickly replaced by another, more urgent dilemma, one that even outweighed the threat of imminent starvation. To make matters worse, it was an enemy Damin had no idea how to fight: garbage.

Normally, an army of slaves was employed to remove the refuse of the city and dump it outside in a vast old quarry several leagues away that had been disused for decades. But the garbage wagons were full and there was nowhere to go. Damin refused to let them dump it in the harbour and had ordered the rubbish burned instead. That would have worked if the refuse was dry, but in the humidity of Greenharbour, nothing ever dried completely and the burning could not keep pace. So the garbage piled higher in the streets and ten days after the siege began, Kalan came to him with the first reports of disease spreading through the poorer quarters of the city.

He ordered the affected areas quarantined, but it only served to slow the spread of the disease, not stop it. The Harshini, who were naturally immune to human ailments, worked tirelessly healing the sick, but there were only three of them – not enough to keep pace with the plague. Sorcerers from the Collective worked beside them until they either dropped from exhaustion or succumbed to disease themselves. He had seen Kalan only twice since the outbreak, and both times she had been haggard with fatigue.

He'd had a blazing row with Adrina when she decided that she should go out and help, claiming it would enhance his position as High Prince no end if his wife were seen to be caring for the sick. Her pregnancy was just beginning to show and even if he hadn't been terrified at the thought of her catching something, he was not going to let her endanger their unborn child. She had reluctantly given in, and only then when he reminded her of the danger to their baby. The atmosphere had not been pleasant since. Adrina was like a caged leopard, prowling around the palace, feeling useless and frustrated. But he did not resent her mood – he felt exactly the same way.

On the fifteenth day of the siege, Cyrus sent a message under a flag of truce. The messenger was let in through the postern gate, and proved to be Serrin Eaglespike, the Warlord of Dregian's younger brother. He was escorted to the palace followed by the curious stares of a population weary of the siege and hopeful that the young lord's presence heralded the end of their ordeal.

'My brother offers leniency, my lords,' Serrin informed them as he stood before Damin, Narvell, Rogan, Tejay, Toren, Adrina and Princess Marla in the main hall. He handed Damin a parchment sealed with the Eaglespike crest – Cyrus' formal terms for surrender. Damin didn't even bother to open it.

'In return for what?' Rogan demanded.

'Lord Wolfblade must surrender the city, abdicate the throne, and agree to exile in the country of his choice. You, my lords,' he added, addressing the other Warlords, 'may retain your provinces, provided you agree to swear allegiance to Lord Eaglespike immediately.'

'Cyrus must think we're bored,' Tejay remarked. 'He obviously sent Serrin here for a bit of light entertainment.'

'This is not a jest, my lady.'

'It is from where I'm standing,' Tejay laughed. 'Send him back to his big brother, Damin. Preferably a piece at a time.'

'Tempting though the idea is, Lady Lionsclaw, he's here under a flag of truce,' Damin reminded her. 'If you want to cut him into little pieces, you'll just have to wait until he comes over the wall.'

Serrin glared at them in disbelief. 'Don't any of you take this seriously? You are surrounded and starving and yet you make jokes! You cannot hope to hold out for much longer.'

'What we hope for is not your concern,' Damin told the young man.

'And that is your answer to our terms?'

'This is your answer.' Damin tore the unread document to shreds and threw the scraps at Serrin. 'Go back and tell your treacherous brother and his allies that we do not deal with traitors. Instead of wasting his time figuring out the terms of my surrender, he'd be more gainfully employed putting his own affairs in order. I hear that's the wisest thing to do when one knows that their death is imminent.'

'You will regret this, Wolfblade,' Serrin warned.

'Not nearly as much as Cyrus will,' Damin predicted.

The following day, the bombardment began.

Greenharbour's walls were more decorative than defensive, and the only thing that had kept the enemy at bay thus far was Cyrus' willingness to wait. Once the war engines were rolled into place, however, Damin knew it was simply a matter of time before the walls were breached and the armies of Dregian and Greenharbour poured into the city.

But Cyrus did not attack the walls immediately. The boulders and burning pitch he lobbed into the city landed at random, killing any soul unfortunate enough to be in their destructive path. At first, Damin thought they were merely testing their range, but after two days he realised it was a deliberate attempt to further demoralise the people. The bombardment went on relentlessly, day and night, and the death toll mounted.

They had their own catapults mounted on the walls, but they were much smaller than the weapons Cyrus could bring to bear, and he kept his forces well clear of their range. By the end of the second day under the gruelling attack, the gates were stormed – not by Cyrus, but by a riotous mob desperate to flee a city that was rapidly becoming a death trap. The Raiders were forced to beat back their own people. A dozen or more died in the fracas; some trampled, others killed by the Raiders defending the gates from the mob. Damin ordered a curfew and threatened execution for anyone caught out on the streets without good cause.

It was later that night that he returned to his rooms, hoping to snatch a few hours' sleep before dawn and the next crop of crises emerged. Adrina was asleep when he arrived, and he stood in the moonlit chamber watching her through the flimsy curtain draped over the bed against insects. He'd not seen much of her lately and was a little surprised at how much he missed her. Pregnancy agreed with her, he thought. It was as if the budding life inside her had imbued her with some indefinable inner peace. She had always been beautiful, but now she was stunning. With a faint smile, he thought of the constant stream of potential brides that Marla had paraded before him over the years, glad now that he had held out for something truly worth fighting for.

Although he had made no sound, some instinct of self-preservation must have warned Adrina that she was not alone. Her eyes opened and she started a little, only relaxing when she realised who it was that stood in the doorway.

'I didn't mean to wake you.'

'I wasn't really asleep,' she replied, stretching languidly. 'What time is it?'

'Late. Very late.'

'Then you should get some sleep. We'll still be under siege come morning.'

'I knew I could rely on you to cheer me up.'

She pulled back the curtain so she could see him more clearly. 'You look tired.'

'Really? I only feel exhausted.'

'Was it that bad today?'

He nodded wearily as he crossed the room and sat on

the edge of the bed. Part of him wondered if it was worth taking his boots off. In a few hours the sun would be up and he'd only have to put them on again. Another part of him was trying not to recall the trampled bodies he had seen at the gate.

'I'm beginning to wonder if I should have accepted Cyrus' offer.'

'Surrender? Damin, you can't mean that!'

'I could save a lot of lives.'

'You'd be ending ours.'

'Cyrus offered us exile.'

'And you believe him?'

He saw the look of fierce determination in her eyes and smiled wearily. 'No, I don't believe him. And don't worry, I haven't given up yet.'

'And if you do, it won't be Cyrus you have to fear,' she declared. 'I'll run you through myself!'

He didn't doubt that she meant it. With a yawn he lay down beside her, fully clothed, as she moved across the bed to make room for him. As soon as his head hit the pillow, he felt fatigue wash over him. He closed his eyes with relief.

'Damin, if you're coming to bed, you could at least take your boots off.'

'I haven't got time to sleep,' he murmured. 'I'm just going to rest my eyes for a moment.'

She moved into the circle of his arms and laid her head on his chest. He could smell the fresh scent of her hair and feel the slight bulge of her belly against his hip.

It was the last thing he remembered until Almodavar burst into the bedchamber next morning to inform him that Cyrus was breaking down the walls.

## 33

Cracks appeared with the first hits. The walls were made of fragile chalkstone and had never been designed to withstand a serious attack. When Damin heard the news, he rode out to see the damage for himself. He was no engineer, but even he could tell that they wouldn't last long.

'Call up the Collective Guards,' he ordered Almodavar. 'Have them reinforce the troops on the walls.'

'You want me to take them off riot duty?'

'Riots are going to be the least of our problems shortly,' he said, as the crash of a boulder striking the wall made their horses rear in fright. The crack he had been examining widened alarmingly. A few more direct hits and it would be large enough for a man to walk through.

He turned his horse and cantered back through the streets to the palace, distressed by the devastation the bombardment had caused. There were blackened buildings everywhere he looked; others had crumpled under the weight of the boulders dropped from the sky. He avoided looking at the people. It was too hard to confront the fear in their eyes, the agony of their grief. Cursing himself for a fool, he wondered if he should have attacked sooner – tried to break out of the city and take the battle to Cyrus on open ground, where he at least would have had some freedom of movement.

He should never have put so much faith in R'shiel.

Another boom sounded, and his horse reared again, but this was a different sound to the solid cracking of stone against stone. The noise came again and he looked at Almodavar with a puzzled expression.

'That didn't come from the walls.'

'It sounded as if it came from the harbour.'

Another boom rolled over them as Damin spurred his horse forward. The sounds became more frequent, like a constant wave of thunder. As he neared the palace, the faint smell of smoke was drifting on the still air. But it wasn't ordinary smoke. It had a flavour he did not recognise. He flew from the saddle and ran up the steps into the palace and through the main hall to the balcony overlooking the harbour, gripping the balustrade in astonishment.

The sight that greeted him left him speechless. Three of the ships that had been blocking the harbour entrance were in flames. Behind them were a dozen or more warships. *Fardohnyan warships.* The booming sounded again as flames shot out from the nearest ship, and another of the blockaders fell victim to the Fardohnyan cannon. The ship in the lead headed for the gap in the sinking blockade line and sailed majestically through, her oars dipping and rising in a flawless rhythm.

'The Fardohnyans,' Almodavar remarked unnecessarily.

'They believe in cutting things a bit fine,' Damin agreed, finally finding his voice. The relief he felt was so intense he felt faint with it. 'Where's Adrina?'

'I'm here, Damin,' she said, stepping out onto the

balcony. She was smiling fondly as she pointed to the ship in the lead. 'That's the *Wave Warrior.*'

'Your father's flagship?'

'R'shiel has outdone herself.'

'Does that mean Hablet has come?' Almodavar asked.

'Gods, I hope not,' Adrina muttered, stepping up to the balustrade. 'Do you have a looking glass?'

Almodavar produced one from a pouch on his belt and handed it to her. She placed the tube to her eye and trained it on the ship. Then she laughed and lowered the glass.

'What?' Damin asked impatiently. 'Is it your father?'

'No. It's better than that. He's sent my half-brother, Gaffen.'

Damin refrained from telling her how relieved he was that he would not have to confront her father. They watched the ship sail forward, heading for the dock below the palace. As it neared the wharf the oars banked sharply, turning the ship into the dock.

'Come on. Let's go and greet our new allies. We've about an hour before Cyrus breaks through the walls.'

'That'll make Gaffen happy. He'd be dreadfully disappointed to come all this way and not have someone to fight.'

By the time they reached the dock, the ship was secured and a long gangplank was being shoved out from the tall deck of the Fardohnyan warship. The first man off the ship was a tall, blond fellow who strode purposefully up the dock and swept Adrina up in a massive bear hug. She squealed as her feet left the ground. He put her down then held her at arm's length for a moment.

'You're getting fat,' was the first thing he said.

'I'm having a baby, Gaffen. I'm allowed to get fat.'

Gaffen looked startled at the news. He turned to Damin and eyed him up and down. 'You'd be Wolfblade, I'm guessing. Where's the fight?'

'You guessed correctly. And the fight is just about to start, my lord. They are breaking down the walls as we speak.'

'Then what are we standing around here for?' The Fardohnyan spun on his heel and marched back towards his ship, yelling orders for his troops to disembark as he went. Damin turned to Adrina, looking rather bemused.

She smiled. 'Don't worry. He likes you.'

'How can you tell?'

'He didn't try to kill you. That's always a good start with Gaffen.'

Before he could answer, a messenger came running down the dock towards them, calling for him. The man skidded to a halt and bowed hastily before delivering his news.

'Lady Lionsclaw said to tell you they've broken through, your highness.'

'Where?'

'On the north wall. Near the weaving district.'

'Tell her I said to hold on. I'll be there with reinforcements shortly.'

The courier glanced at the Fardohnyans pouring off the *Wave Warrior* and saluted sharply, suddenly grinning from ear to ear. He ran back the way he came, whooping with delight.

'Seems your brother's arrival has somebody happy today,' Damin murmured as he watched the young man's departure. Then he turned to Adrina. 'I want you to go back to the palace and stay there.'

'Yes, dear.'

'I mean it, Adrina. You're not to stick your nose outside the palace until this is over. With your brother's troops, we could have Cyrus on the run soon enough, but I don't intend to spend the next few hours worrying about what you're getting up to.'

'Don't pussyfoot around, man!' Gaffen declared, coming up behind them. 'Tell her to stay put, or you'll beat her senseless. It's the only thing that works with Adrina.'

'Gaffen, shut up!'

He grinned at his sister then turned to Damin. 'Come on, Wolfblade! Let's go slaughter your enemies. Adrina, get back to the palace now, or I'll throw you over my shoulder and carry you screaming all the way back, and lock you up.'

Adrina glared at her brother, but to Damin's astonishment she turned and strode haughtily back towards the palace without another word. Gaffen noticed Damin's expression and laughed.

'I can see you and I need to have a talk about Adrina when this business is done with, your highness.'

'If I had threatened her with that, she would have killed me.'

'Probably,' Gaffen agreed cheerfully. 'Can you organise someone to get the rest of my ships docked? I've a feeling we'll need every man before the day is out.'

'How many did you bring?' he asked.

'Three thousand. Do you think that will be enough?'

He'd been hoping for twice that many. Cyrus had ten thousand men outside the walls. Between Gaffen's reinforcements and the troops he had in the city they were still outnumbered, but at least the odds were a little better

'It's going to have to be enough,' Damin said, trying not to sound disappointed.

The breach in the wall near the weaving district was contained easily enough, but it was followed by more reports of breaks in the walls from all over the city. By mid-morning, Cyrus had broken through and Damin gave up trying to plug the gaps. He pulled his troops back from the walls and the battle for Greenharbour was well and truly under way.

They fought for the city, street by street, falling back when they had to, surging forward to repel the invaders when they could, but slowly, a street at the time, they were pushed back towards the harbour. The Fardohnyan forces were still not completely disembarked. There simply weren't enough berths to get them all ashore quickly enough.

Gaffen ranted at his commanders to unload the troops faster, but there was little he could do to speed up the process. All they could do was hold out as long as possible, throwing Gaffen's fresh troops into the fray wherever the lines weakened. But they were coming off the ships at irregular intervals. A few of the Fardohnyans had gone charging into the battle without waiting for orders, bolstering lines that didn't need them, while Cyrus' men broke through in other places that were desperate for reinforcements. Another troop had ploughed into the fray and accidentally turned on Rogan Bearbow's men, not realising that they were not the enemy.

By mid-afternoon, Damin was seriously considering evacuating the palace. Cyrus had pushed so far into the city he was almost ready to admit they were losing the battle. Gaffen's troops were disembarked, but they were too little, too late. If he'd had them earlier, before Cyrus first breached the walls, he might have had a chance. As it was, they only filled the gaps. He didn't have the men to take the battle to Cyrus.

Rubbing his temples wearily, he glanced across the room at Adrina's brother, who wore a look of wounded pride as much as anything. Gaffen wasn't used to defeat.

'Perhaps if we turn my ships broadside to the city, we could turn the cannon on them,' he suggested hopefully.

Damin shook his head. 'You'll kill as many of our people as you will theirs.'

'Then we fire the city.'

Damin nodded reluctantly. He had been hoping to avoid it, despite the fact that he'd had Almodavar quietly distributing barrels of pitch throughout the city for days prior to the battle. Setting fire to Greenharbour would stop Cyrus surely enough, but it was likely to destroy much of the city in the process.

'I was hoping to use that as a last resort.'

'Aye,' Gaffen agreed heavily. 'But that moment is approaching rapidly.'

The battle continued without pause as the day wore on. The reports kept coming in, each progressively worse than the last. The sun was resting on the horizon when Damin's stomach rumbled, and he realised the day was almost over. He'd been too busy directing the fighting to eat. Damin hated combat like this. He was a warrior at heart, not a tactician. He would much rather be in the thick of battle, not directing others to do his fighting for him. Tarja was good at that sort of thing. Damin spared his friend a thought for a moment, wondering what had become of him. Was he waiting in Krakandar for aid that would never come? Or had he done something stupid and got himself killed by the Kariens?

Damin doubted he would ever learn the truth. Cyrus was all but knocking on the doors of the palace. It was little more than three hours after Gaffen suggested it that he was forced to concede that they had no other option but to fire the city in the hope of driving the enemy off.

'Gaffen, I want you to take Adrina and whoever else you can find in the palace and get them out of here.'

The Fardohnyan looked at him for a moment and then nodded in understanding. 'And what of you, your highness?'

'I can't order anybody else to do this. If Greenharbour burns, then it will be by my hand.'

Gaffen hesitated for a moment, then called in one of his captains and began giving the orders to evacuate the palace. When he was done, he snatched up his sword from the table where he had been using it to hold down a map of the city.

'Let's go, then!'

'What are you doing?'

'You don't think I'm going to run away with the women and the children, do you?'

'This isn't your fight any longer, Gaffen. I'm not going out to do anything particularly heroic. I'm going to set fire to the city.'

'Well, someone has to watch your back. Besides, you're married to my sister. That makes you family.'

Damin took one look at the expression on Gaffen's face and decided not to argue. In truth, he didn't mind the idea of the big Fardohnyan watching his back for him.

Gaffen was the sort of man who looked as if he could stop an avalanche if he stood in front of it.

'Let's do it, then,' Damin said, pushing away all thoughts of the consequences of what he was about to do. He strode from the command post with an air of grim determination and ordered the horses brought out. He didn't know how far he could get, but the further from the harbour he set the fires, the more people might have a chance to escape.

The sounds of the battle could be clearly heard as he and Gaffen rode out. The streets this close to the harbour were already clogged with people fleeing the advancing horde. They pushed through the crowds for several streets until they broke through into a reasonably deserted street. The fighting had not yet reached this part of the city and it looked oddly peaceful, like a calm oasis in the middle of a raging sandstorm.

That's when he heard the trumpets.

'What was that?' Gaffen asked curiously, his head cocked at the unusual sound.

'I don't know.'

The trumpets came again, drifting on the early evening breeze. Damin listened with a feeling of total bewilderment until he recognised the sound. He last heard it on the northern plains of Medalon and had never, in his wildest imaginings, expected to hear it in Greenharbour.

'Well, I'll be damned.'

He flew from his saddle and headed for the tallest building in sight, which was a gracious, four-storey residence belonging to some prosperous merchant. Gaffen followed him at a run. Damin kicked in the door, ignoring the screams from the merchant and his family sheltering within. He took the stairs two at a time with Gaffen on his heels, and finally burst onto the roof. He ran to the northern edge of the building and looked out over the devastated city.

The sound of the trumpets reached him again, clearly this time. Panting beside him, Gaffen stared at the scene before him with a puzzled look.

'What is *that*?'

Wordlessly, Damin pointed north, at the perfectly formed ranks of red coats preparing to march on the city, too stunned and relieved to speak.

There were two thousand of them at least.

Two thousand fresh, disciplined and well-trained Medalonian Defenders.

## 34

The battle for Greenharbour was ugly, but blessedly short once the Defenders joined the fray. Cyrus' army broke and ran just after sundown. Conin Falconlance and Serrin Eaglespike died during the battle, but Cyrus survived and fled back to Dregian Province with the remainder of his scattered forces to make a last stand.

Damin sent Narvell after him, with Gaffen and a force of Fardohnyans. It wasn't that he thought Narvell needed the help so much as his desire to separate Adrina's half-brother and Tejay Lionsclaw, who would rather have perished in battle than accept help from her despised enemies. She made no secret of her distrust of their new allies, so Damin thought it prudent to put as much distance between Gaffen and Tejay as possible until things calmed down a bit. Gaining entrance to the castle by the same hidden passage that he, Adrina and R'shiel had escaped through, Narvell and Gaffen took Dregian Keep with barely a man lost in the fight.

Conveniently, Cyrus threw himself on his sword rather than face the consequences of his actions. Damin was privately glad that he had. It was always messy, following a civil war, to decide what to do with the miscreants. If he had executed Cyrus, there would always be a small core of resentment among the people that could be fanned into life in the future. If he left him alive, he left him free to plan further mischief. It was better this way. Cyrus' widow and three-year-old son were back in Greenharbour as prisoners, but Damin was inclined to be generous towards them. It was hardly their fault that Cyrus had let his ambitions run away with him, and anyway, he doubted he could bring himself to order the execution of a child, no matter how sound the logic behind the decision.

There were other issues to be resolved, too. Dregian, Greenharbour and Krakandar now needed Warlords, and everyone from Tejay Lionsclaw to the palace gardeners had an opinion on who should be awarded the positions. Although there were numerous candidates among the nobility, it was not uncommon for a Warlord to be appointed from the lower classes. Talent still counted more than bloodlines in Hythria, and Damin was seriously considering looking further afield for the new Warlords. He'd had enough of bored noblemen with delusions of grandeur. A few young bucks who were more interested in holding onto their own provinces than eyeing off his throne would let him rest much easier at night.

Then there was the problem of the Defenders.

Tarja was not with his men, which worried Damin a great deal. Denjon had told him what Tarja had planned to do, but the fact that he had not returned from his mission to sink the ferries on the Glass River was a bad sign. Damin felt he owed the Defenders an enormous debt. With Tarja missing, and with an administrative and political nightmare ahead of him, he was tempted to drop everything, gather up his forces, head for Medalon and leave Adrina to sort out the details here at home. He smiled grimly at the idea. Trusting Adrina was still very new to him. He could not bring himself to tempt fate by handing her that much power.

It was five days since the battle and his hope that things would improve had proved optimistic in the extreme. Although gradually being brought under control, disease still raged throughout the city. There were thousands of homeless, as many wounded, and another five thousand Fardohnyans and Medalonians to feed.

Cyrus had stripped the countryside of what food there was close to the city. Damin had a vast number of his men out scouring the land for grain to tide them over until supplies could be brought in from the outlying provinces. The fishing fleet had put to sea again, which prevented the situation from becoming desperate, but he was so heartily sick of fish for every meal, that he was certain he would never be able to face it again once this crisis was over.

The door to his study suddenly flew open and slammed against the wall. Adrina stormed into the room. The candles wavered in the breeze caused by her anger. She was shaking with fury.

'Do you know what she's *done*?'

'Tell me who "she" is, and I might be able to answer you,' he replied calmly. Adrina's tantrum was a welcome distraction.

'R'shiel!'

'She sent your brother and three thousand men to save our necks?' he suggested.

Adrina actually stamped her foot at him. He fought very hard not to smile.

'He would never appoint me Regent.'

'He will if we make him an offer he can't refuse.'

'Like what?' she asked suspiciously.

'I'll renounce the Wolfblade claim on the Fardohnyan [t]rone. I'll remove forever the threat of Fardohnya having [a] Hythrun king.'

She nodded thoughtfully. 'And in return, he appoints [m]e Regent? You know, that may actually work. But [w]hat of your plans for unity between Fardohnya and [H]ythria?'

'That will be up to you. This child will be as much [y]our brother as Gaffen is. If you manage to get along [w]ith him half as well as you do with your bastard [s]iblings, there'll be no danger of war between us. For [t]hat matter, he'll only be a few months younger than [o]ur child. If we're smart about this, they'll grow up the [b]est of friends.'

'And you'd do this? You'd renounce a throne for me?' [S]he appeared to be putting a rather romantic slant on [s]omething he considered a coldly rational and practical [c]ourse of action. But he didn't correct her.

'Yes. I'd renounce a throne for you, Adrina.'

With a sob, she ran to him, threw her arms around [h]is neck and buried her head in his shoulder. He could [f]eel the slight swell of her belly pressing against him.

'Gods, you're not crying, are you?'

Adrina sniffed and looked up at him with glistening [ey]es. 'No.'

[H]e gently wiped a tear from her cheek. 'If I'd known [th]is was going to reduce you to tears, I wouldn't have [su]ggested it.'

'Nobody ever loved me enough to renounce a throne [fo]r me, Damin.'

'Don't be so bloody obtuse, Damin! She promised Hablet a son!'

'I know. Gaffen told me.'

'You *knew* about this? Why didn't you tell me?'

'I have been rather busy lately.'

'Then what are you doing about it?'

'Nothing.'

'You can't do *nothing*! She has just cost you the throne of Fardohnya!'

'Well, as I never actually wanted the damned thing in the first place, it hardly seems worth getting upset over the fact that I've lost it.'

'How could you not want it?' she asked, genuinely puzzled by his lack of ambition.

'Not everybody shares your desire to wear a crown, Adrina,' he told her. 'Anyway, you were furious at me for being the heir to the throne. Now you're angry because I'm not. Make up your mind.'

She glared at him for a moment then flopped inelegantly into the chair on the other side of the desk. 'I'm in no mood to be reasonable, Damin. Fight with me.'

'I will,' he promised, 'when the occasion warrants it. But in this case, it's not worth it. I've got my hands full holding onto to Hythria. I don't need your father's kingdom as well. The whole idea of splitting Fardohnya and Hythria in the first place was because they were impossible to govern as one nation.'

'We could have done it,' she grumbled.

'*We*? Ah, so that's what this is all about. If I don't become the King of Fardohnya, you don't get to be Queen. I'm sorry, but you'll just have to settle for being the High Princess of Hythria.'

She smiled faintly, as if she understood how childishly

she was behaving. 'You have no idea how good it would
have felt to return to Fardohnya as her Queen. My father
sold me like a side of beef to the Kariens because that's
all I was worth to him. And for no better reason than I
was born a girl. It didn't matter how clever, or well
educated, or politically astute I was.'

'Personally, I think your political acumen had a lot to
do with it,' he suggested. 'You are far too clever for a
disinherited Princess. If I was in your father's position,
I'd have shipped you off to a temple somewhere when
you were five.'

'I think he wishes he had,' she agreed. 'But there's more
to this than me losing my chance to revenge myself on
my father, Damin. Do you know what's going to happen
once this child is born?'

He shrugged. 'You mean other than a very big party?'

'Once my father has an heir, he will remove any threat
to the child's claim on the throne.'

'But there *are* no other claimants to the throne.'

'I have thirteen living baseborn brothers, Damin.
Hablet was quite prepared to legitimise one of them if
he couldn't get a son. Each of them is a potential threat.'

Damin looked at her aghast. 'Are you telling me he'll
kill his own children?'

'He'll kill them and not lose a moment's sleep over it.
This may be hard for you to understand – Hablet loves
every one of his bastards – but they know as well as he
does what fate will befall them should he produce a legitimate heir.'

'You're right. I don't understand.'

'It's tradition. When Hablet was born, his father had
seventeen baseborn children and his three unmarried
daughters put to death. When *my* father took the throne,

every pregnant concubine and *court'esa* in the
executed. His own sister committed suicide a
her love for him. She was hailed as a heroine.'

'And you call *me* a barbarian.'

She shrugged, helpless to make him unders
the Fardohnyan way.'

'Then I'm glad I won't ever have to sit on
that is soaked in so much innocent blood.'

'Don't you see the irony? You would never ha
tenanced such slaughter. I think that irks me m
anything else does. We could have put an end
dreadful custom.' She rose to her feet and smile
sadly. 'I'm sorry to burden you with this, now.
you have a lot to do. Is Gaffen back yet?'

Damin nodded. 'He arrived back with Narv
morning.'

'Then I'll go find him and leave you in peace.
as I've slapped him around a few times for being
pig to me when he arrived, I shall endeavour to m
most of what little time we have left together.'

Adrina walked to the door, leaving Damin sta
her back. It wasn't learning of the fate awaiting her
that disturbed him as much as her quiet acceptan
inevitability.

'Adrina, wait!'

She turned and looked at him questioningly.

'If you can't be Queen, would you settle for

'Regent of Fardohnya? How?'

'Your father's how old? Sixty? Sixty-five?'
suddenly excited as the idea formed in his mi
live another ten years, perhaps, less if we're
son won't be old enough to take the throne
dies.'

'That probably has more to do with lack of opportunity, rather than you being unloved,' he told her with a smile.

'Can't you be serious? Even when I'm *trying* to be nice to you?'

'I'm sorry. You bring out the worst in me.'

She kissed him then leaned back in his arms with a sigh. 'I don't like admitting it, but I suppose I must feel something for you, Damin Wolfblade.'

'Well, I won't tell if you don't,' Damin promised with a smile.

# PART 3

# HOMECOMING

## 35

The high plains of Medalon were a riot of colour, caught in the burgeoning grip of spring. R'shiel reined in her horse and studied the scattered clouds that dotted the pale blue sky. Wildflowers carpeted the plains, and the day was so mild she had shed her cloak some leagues back. As the tall white towers of the Citadel appeared in the distance an odd feeling came over her and she found herself strangely reluctant to go on.

'What's the matter?'

She shrugged and leaned forward to pat the neck of her gelding. He was a sturdy, deep-chested grey they had purchased in Vanahiem. R'shiel missed the magnificent speed and stamina of the Hythrun horses she had grown accustomed to riding, but he had been a reliable mount, if more stolid than spirited.

'I'm scared, I think,' she admitted, thoughtfully. 'I wasn't expecting that.'

'You're only half-Harshini, R'shiel,' Brak reminded her. 'You'll find your human emotions have a nasty habit of jumping out and biting you at the most inopportune moments. What were you expecting to feel?'

'I'm not sure. Some overpowering sense of righteousness, I suppose.'

Brak laughed sourly. 'You have a lot to learn, demon child.'

'I wish you'd stop calling me that. You know how much I hate it.'

'I thought you were growing quite enamoured of the title. You certainly threw it around enough in Fardohnya.'

'In Fardohnya I wasn't likely to be hanged for it.'

He nodded silently. They both knew the risk they ran by returning so openly to Medalon. In fact, even more than the mediocrity of their mounts, it was the need to travel through Medalon by conventional means that had taken them so long to reach their destination. Had they been willing to risk using their power, R'shiel and Brak could have been at the Citadel weeks ago, but they were too deep into Karien-occupied territory to tempt fate by openly using demons.

Hablet had provided them with a ship, which had delivered them to Bordertown. Then they had taken passage on a river boat as far as Vanahiem. With news that the Testa ferry had been destroyed and the river boat captains understandably nervous about approaching the Citadel, it proved quicker and easier to complete their journey on horseback.

R'shiel turned in her saddle at the sound of other horses approaching. Brak followed her gaze and muttered a curse. The road they travelled from Brodenvale was almost deserted this late in the afternoon. Earlier, it had been crowded with refugees fleeing the Citadel and the occasional Karien patrol.

'We'd best get off the road.'

'Founders! They're everywhere!'

Brak urged his horse into the long grass on the shoulder of the road. R'shiel followed him as the approaching patrol drew closer. She gripped the reins until her knuckles turned white as she watched them. The troop of Kariens passed by without sparing them a glance, pennons snapping from the tips of their lances, the armoured knights claiming the road with the arrogant assurance of conquerors who have nothing to fear from their vanquished foes. It was the third Karien troop they had seen in the last few hours. Southern Medalon was still relatively free of them, but the closer they got to the Citadel the more they saw.

'There are no priests with them.'

'They'll be at the Citadel. Mathen probably doesn't want to scare the population into thinking they're going to be forced to worship the Overlord,' Brak speculated.

'But isn't that exactly what they're planning?'

'Undoubtedly, but Squire Mathen is too smart to do it openly.'

'Squire Mathen?'

'Don't you remember him? Terbolt left him in charge of the Citadel.'

'I don't remember much of anything from the last time I was at the Citadel,' she admitted with a frown. 'Except Loclon.'

'Mathen's not a nobleman,' Brak told her as the Kariens moved slowly past them. Behind the knights trundled several wagons carrying loot from some outlying village that had been the victim of their foray out of the Citadel. 'That in itself is a bit odd for the Kariens. But he appears to be a very astute politician.'

'I think I'd prefer a good old fashioned nobleborn moron,' she said, noticing the grain-filled wagons, but she decided against saying or doing anything that would bring them to the attention of the knights. She had learnt that much restraint over the past few months.

'One has to work with what one is given, I'm afraid. Still, we won't have to worry about him too much.'

'Why not?'

'As I said, Mathen's not a nobleman. Terbolt placed him in charge, but I can't see Lord Roache and his ilk tolerating a commoner calling the shots for very long, and unless he's advocating mass conversion, the priesthood won't like him much either. They have no care for Medalonian sensibilities.'

The last of the wagons rumbled by. They waited until the Kariens were some way up the road before they urged their horses back onto the road and followed them at a walk.

'Speaking of the priests,' Brak added. 'You remember what I told you?'

'About them being able to detect us if we call on our power? Yes, Brak, I remember.'

'I mean it, R'shiel,' he warned. 'Don't underestimate them.'

'I dealt with those priests in the Defenders' camp.'

'You faced three of them and caught them by surprise,' he reminded her. 'Once we get to the Citadel, there will be scores of them, and they know the demon child is abroad. I wouldn't be surprised if they have a Watching Coven posted, just waiting for you to slip up.'

'What's a Watching Coven?'

'A group of priests who link through their staves, sometimes up to twenty or thirty of them. A Coven's power could give either of us a run for our money.'

'How can they be so strong? They don't have access to Harshini power.'

'No, they have access to a god who doesn't mind bending the rules.'

'The gods!' she muttered in annoyance. 'It always comes back to them, doesn't it?'

'In the end, yes.'

She smiled grimly. 'Don't worry, Brak. I'll watch myself. Squire Mathen isn't the only one who can get what he wants by subtle means.'

'Oh? You have a plan then?' There was an edge of scepticism in his voice that she didn't much care for.

'I'm going to take a leaf out of your book, actually. I'm going to go straight to the best source of intelligence in Medalon.'

'Garet Warner?' he asked with amusement. 'I thought the first thing you'd want to do when you saw him again would be to run a blade through him.'

'No. Garet helped me as much as he could, I think. I'm not going to kill him. Unless he doesn't want to help us.'

Brak didn't answer her and she could not tell if he approved or condemned her intentions.

They reached the Citadel just on sundown, halting on the slight rise in the road to stare at the scene before them in horrified awe. A blanket of humanity covered the plains surrounding the Citadel: the Karien army camped about the fortress of their newest subject nation. R'shiel could not begin to guess their number, but as far as she could see, the grasslands were thick with tents and men and the panoply of war. Both sides of the shallow Saran River were crowded with them. The bridges curved gracefully out of the plain, the only part of it not swarming with the enemy. A pall of smoke from the countless cooking fires lay over the whole scene, touched with ruddy light by the dying sun, making it look like a painting of some nightmarish vision of a pagan hell.

'Founders!' she swore softly. 'I didn't think there'd be so many of them.'

'Having second thoughts?'

She glanced at him, then smiled. 'No. I figure between you and me, we have them outnumbered, Brak.'

He returned her smile briefly. 'I think I preferred it when you were scared.'

They urged their horses on and rode down through the Karien host that was camped right up to the edge of the road. For the most part, the soldiers ignored them, too engrossed in their own business to care about two unarmed travellers on the main thoroughfare into the Citadel. She avoided meeting their eyes while despair threatened to overwhelm her.

As they crossed the bridge over the Saran River she looked up at the high white walls. Bile rose in her throat. There was a head, or the remains of one, mounted on a pike over the gateway. It had been there for some time. The eyes were empty sockets picked clean by the ravens and the skin of its face hung in strips of desiccated flesh. The hair, or what was left of it, was grey and straggling, but long enough to identify the hapless skull as once having been a woman. With sickening dread, R'shiel wondered who it had been, afraid that she knew. Unless the Kariens had murdered Joyhinia, there was only one woman in Medalon likely to incur such wrath and she had never deserved such a fate.

'Brak,' she said softly.

He followed the direction of her gaze then shook his head sadly. 'Gods!'

'I think it's Mahina.'

He studied it more closely then shrugged. 'There's no way to tell, R'shiel.'

'Loclon is going to die very, very slowly,' she said with frightening intensity.

R'shiel had feared the Defenders on the gate might recognise her, but she need not have worried. There were no Defenders guarding the Citadel. There was, however, a large contingent of Kariens and they were interrogating anybody seeking entrance to the city.

'Let me handle this,' Brak said.

'What are you going to do?' she asked suspiciously.

''Cause a fuss,' he told her as he kicked his horse forward. 'Hey you! Do you speak Medalonian?'

R'shiel cringed as he called out to the guards, wondering what in the name of the Founders he was up to. This was hardly her idea of sneaking into the Citadel.

'Halt!' a Karien trooper called out in Medalonian – probably the only word he knew.

'Halt yourself!' Brak retorted. 'I demand to see whoever is in charge!'

The guard looked at him blankly.

'Where is your superior, young man? I demand to see him at once!'

'Halt!' the guard repeated.

'What's the problem?' The man who spoke was a Defender. He emerged from the gatehouse with another Karien, this one wearing knight's armour. He was very young, just out of the Cadets, R'shiel guessed. She did not recognise him and that hopefully meant he would not recognise her.

'Ah! Someone who understands me!' Brak declared.

'Young man, I demand to be taken to whoever is in charge of this . . . invasion, or whatever you call it, at once!'

The Defender translated Brak's words for the benefit of the Kariens, which explained his posting on the gate. His Karien was quite fluent but he wore a sullen expression. She could imagine how this duty must irk him. The Karien knight said something to the Defender, who then turned back to Brak.

'Why do you want to see Lord Roache?'

'Lord Roache? Is that who's in charge?'

'Yes.'

'What happened to the First Sister?'

'The First Sister is *assisting* Lord Roache and Squire Mathen,' the young Defender informed him in a voice loaded with scorn.

'Well then, I wish to see this Lord Roache, young man, to lodge a formal complaint against the behaviour of these . . . these . . . hooligans who have invaded our country. Do you know what they've done? Do you?'

'I can guess,' the Defender muttered. 'What have they done?'

'What have they *done*? My shop is in ruins! My wife and I are homeless! My servants have all fled in fear and I am on the verge of destitution! I intend to see this Karien fellow and demand compensation.'

The Defender appeared genuinely amused at the idea. 'Good luck, my friend, but I don't like your chances.'

'Well!' Brak declared indignantly. 'We shall have to see about that! Come, Gerterina! Let us go find this Lord Roache person and set him straight on a few things!'

Brak urged his horse through the gate, with R'shiel following close behind. The Defender and the Kariens stood back to let them pass. As the young man explained what they were doing in the Citadel the Kariens roared with laughter, which followed them down the street.

'*Gerterina*?'

He shrugged apologetically. 'It was all I could think of.'

'And *that* was your plan? Make such a fuss at the gate that they'll never forget us?'

'Sometimes it's easier to hide out in the open, R'shiel. People trying to sneak into the Citadel don't start by demanding to see whoever is in charge. We were barely questioned and they didn't even look at you twice.'

She had to admit he was right. 'Brak, why is it that when you do things like that, you're being clever, but when I do them, I'm being reckless?'

'Because I'm older than you. A *lot* older.'

'Well, *Old One*, what are we going to do now?'

They rode at a walk down the cobbled main road that led past the Great Hall to the amphitheatre. The tension in the air was almost solid enough to touch. R'shiel realised that the awful spectre nailed over the main gate was more than just a gloating gesture of barbaric triumph. It was a warning, and one the citizens of the Citadel appeared to have taken to heart. The streets appeared almost as deserted as Greenharbour had been, when she arrived with Damin.

'We need to find an inn and a meal and perhaps some company for the evening.'

'Company?'

'We need to find out what's happening here. The next best source of information in any city, after the assassins and the thieves, are the prostitutes.'

'That's the best excuse I've heard for a long time,' she said with a scowl.

'We all have our own methods, R'shiel.'

'Funny how all your methods involve consorting with criminals.'

He glanced at her and then smiled. 'Considering you are probably the most wanted criminal in all of Karien and Medalon, I find your attitude rather strange.'

She ignored the jibe. 'I still think Garet is the better option.'

'And I agree, but I want to know that when we confront him he's telling us the truth, not what he thinks we want to hear.'

'You're not a very trusting person, are you?'

'I don't happen to like the idea of having my head decorating the main gate next to poor old Mahina's. If you plan to live long enough to fulfil your destiny, R'shiel, you would be wise to adopt the same outlook.'

After that they rode without speaking through streets that were slowly darkening with the coming night. Squares of yellow light appeared in the windows of the houses that lined the streets, but the silence was heavy and R'shiel could not feel the welcoming touch of the Citadel as she had when she arrived the last time.

It was as if the massive spirit of the Citadel had shrivelled and died – or perhaps he had simply retreated into hiding in the face of the Karien blight that swarmed through him like flies over a dying carcass.

## 36

Garet Warner opened the door to the Lord Defender's office and was greeted by a blast of warm air. Someone must have thought to light the fire, he thought, although he was a little surprised. With the Lord Defender in 'protective confinement' as the Kariens euphemistically referred to his incarceration, Garet used the office rarely, and he had told nobody of his intention to come here this morning.

He pushed the door shut and glanced around, but other than the blazing fire in the small hearth, the room was unchanged since his last visit. The heavy carved desk took up a great deal of space, and the comfortable chair behind it smelled faintly of the saddle soap used to keep the leather supple. The array of Fardohnyan and Hythrun weapons Jenga had collected over the years still hung over the mantle. The aura of the man permeated the room. It was as if he had just stepped out a moment ago and was due back any minute.

But perhaps it was not completely unchanged; the pile of unattended paperwork had grown considerably. Garet groaned as he looked at it. He had his own work to do.

He did not need the added responsibility of the Lord Defender's administrative tasks.

Most of the papers would be fairly straightforward. Requests for transfers, for leave, for permission to marry, for a score of other mundane, everyday matters that required the Lord Defender's approval. But there would be the odd report that needed investigation, disciplinary matters that could not be settled with a mere stroke of a pen – most of them a direct result of the conflicts that arose frequently between the Defenders and the Karien invaders.

There would be orders from the First Sister, too.

Garet was well aware that even though signed by Joyhinia Tenragan, the orders were no more from her than they had been when she was on the northern border, a babbling idiot who would sign anything put in front of her. These orders came from Squire Mathen, and if he couched them in a manner easily digestible to the Medalonians, they were no less the orders of his Karien masters.

He moved towards the desk and then froze as the feeling he was no longer alone in the room suddenly over-whelmed him.

'Garet.'

He started and turned at the voice. R'shiel stood close behind him. She looked much better than when he'd last seen her. He was glad to see her hair had grown out a little and now framed her face in dark red curls. But there was something else different about her: a confidence that he had not seen before. He wondered how she had escaped the Kariens, and why, having managed that remarkable feat, she had so foolishly returned to the Citadel. Standing behind her, wearing an air of lethal calm, was the Harshini halfbreed, Brakandaran.

'R'shiel! Brak! How did the two of you . . . ? Never mind, I'd rather not know.'

He composed himself and walked around Lord Jenga's desk before he looked at them again. They were wearing the close fitting and supple Harshini leathers, which outlined their statuesque bodies, giving a hint of the natural grace and athletic ability that was part of their alien heritage.

'What are you doing here?'

'We have come to put things right,' R'shiel told him.

'And how do you plan to do that?'

'With your help.'

Her declaration did not surprise him. 'I suppose you think I owe you something, for not supporting you at the Gathering?'

'You don't owe me anything, Garet. But as you said when you slipped me your knife, you can't help Medalon from a prison cell.'

'I'm not in a prison cell.'

'I used your knife to kill the Karien Crown Prince. I imagine a prison cell will be the least of your worries if the Kariens learn that.'

Garet was too experienced to let his apprehension show. '*You* killed the Karien Crown Prince? Founders, R'shiel, when you set out to cause trouble, you don't mess about, do you?'

A small smile flickered over her lips. 'Wait until you hear the rest of it.'

He shook his head. 'Thanks, but I'd rather not . . .'

'No!' she cut in. 'That is not an option any longer, Garet. You must decide. You are with us or against us. There is no more sitting on the fence.'

Garet sank down into the Lord Defender's chair – more

to give himself time to think than through any real need to take the weight off his feet. He knew about R'shiel. Knew of her Harshini parentage and her status as their long awaited demon child, but until this moment it had never truly occurred to him that she might actually be as powerful as the pagans believed.

'And if I choose not to follow you?' he asked, wondering how determined she was.

'Then I will remove you from the equation.'

'You'd kill me?'

'I killed a Karien prince. You don't think a mere Defender is going to cause me any grief?'

He placed his hands palm down on the desk and looked at her closely. Her whole being radiated a kind of leashed power, straining to be set free.

'So that's it? Join you or die?'

'Pretty much,' she agreed with a shrug.

'You leave me little choice.'

'Then your answer is yes?'

He nodded cautiously.

In two steps she was across the room. She slammed her hands down over his on the desk and glared at him. 'Then swear it!'

Garet opened his mouth to say what she wanted to hear, but the words wouldn't come. She was doing something to him, something that would not permit him to lie. With a sudden and terrifying flash of clarity, he knew that if he took this oath he would belong to her, body and soul, until he died, and perhaps even after, if one believed the pagans.

'Swear it, Garet,' she whispered. Her face was close to his, her eyes boring through him as though she could read every dark, unsavoury secret he kept hidden in the furthermost recesses of his mind. She wasn't using magic on him, her eyes had not turned black, but whatever it was, he found her impossible to deny.

'I'm yours, R'shiel.'

She studied him for a moment and then stood back. As soon as she released him, Garet slumped back in his chair, light-headed. He closed his eyes for a moment, hoping that when he opened them again, the room would have stopped spinning.

'Sorry, Garet, but I had to be sure.'

He looked up at her, wondering what he had done. It took a moment for him to recover enough to speak.

'So, now what?'

'First, we have to stop the Kariens from hanging Tarja,' Brak remarked, as if it was no more trouble than squashing a flea.

'You know they're blaming him for killing Cratyn, don't you?'

'Well, they can hardly admit the demon child did it. When is his trial?'

'Trial? What trial? The Kariens aren't big on the natural course of justice, Brak. Tarja's scheduled to be hanged next Restday. In the amphitheatre so everyone can come and watch.'

'Then we have to put a stop to it,' R'shiel declared. 'Where's Jenga? Have they killed him too?'

'Not yet. Actually, they haven't interfered too much with the Defenders. Most of their people don't speak a word of Medalonian so they need us. There'd be a mutiny if they tried to kill the Lord Defender and they know it. He's under arrest. They're holding him in the cells behind the Headquarters Building, and it's the Kariens who are guarding him, not our people.'

'Then we have to release him, too.'

'How? Your last attempt at breaking somebody out of the Citadel was spectacularly unsuccessful, as I recall.'

R'shiel frowned at the reminder. 'I intend to plan this a little better. If we're going to do something about the Kariens, the first thing we have to do is get rid of Joyhinia, and replace her with a First Sister who is on Medalon's side, rather than her own, then . . .'

'Who are you planning to put in power? Mahina's dead.'

'I know. I saw the head over the gate.'

'Whose idea was that?' Brak asked.

'The First Sister's.'

'Somehow that doesn't surprise me.' R'shiel's eyes hardened as she spoke, something he did not think was possible. Then she shook off whatever it was that caused such hatred to flare in her and shrugged. 'I was thinking of Harith.'

Garet shrugged. Harith was not popular. But she was, of all the Quorum members, perhaps the one who cared most about Medalon.

'Assuming you manage that, then what?'

'I need to find the Harshini archives. And I'm going to kill Loclon.'

'Loclon? What's he got to do with this? Besides, he's listed as a deserter. Nobody has seen him since the night of the last Gathering.'

R'shiel pulled the wooden chair on the other side of the desk across the rug and sat down facing him. 'Joyhinia didn't recover, Garet. The Karien priests simply borrowed another mind and put it in her body. That's not Joyhinia issuing the Kariens orders. It's Loclon.'

The whole idea was too bizarre for Garet to take in.

'That's absurd . . . it's not possible . . .'

'Of course it's possible,' Brak said. 'You're dealing with powers you refuse to acknowledge, Commandant, but that doesn't make them any less real. Or powerful.'

'Perhaps she simply recovered . . .'

'Tarja destroyed her wit. There is no way Joyhinia could have returned.'

'But Loclon? How did he . . . ?'

'It doesn't matter,' R'shiel insisted. 'All that matters is that we do something about it, about everything – Loclon, the Kariens, all of it. I can't do anything about finding the answers I need until they've been taken care of.'

'Did you ride in here with your eyes shut, R'shiel?'

'I never said I thought it was going to be easy, Garet,' she said. 'But it is necessary.'

The commandant nodded slowly. 'Very well. But if you want me to cooperate, then I ask . . . no I demand . . . two things.'

'You're not in a position to demand anything, Garet.'

'Nevertheless, I will demand them. If you don't wish to heed me, then I'll just throw myself on my sword now, and save the Kariens the trouble of hanging me.'

R'shiel obviously meant to object, but Brak cut in before she could say anything. 'What do you want, Commandant?'

'First, I want your promise that you will listen to me. I haven't been sitting here idly while the Kariens overrun Medalon. I have the men we need in the places we need them and the authority to mobilise them. But if we're to do this successfully, then timing is critical. I don't want anyone – specifically you, R'shiel – going off on a tangent because of some noble pagan purpose I don't give a damn about and ruining it for the rest of us. I don't care about your destiny, the Harshini or the rebels. I don't even want to know what you're looking for in the archives. Is that clear?'

'I think that's fair. And the second thing?' Brak asked before R'shiel could get a word in.

'I want to disband the Sisterhood.'

They both stared at him.

'Disband the Sisterhood? Why?'

'I'm surprised you of all people have to ask, R'shiel. It's a corrupt and destructive form of government. They may have started out with the right intentions, but what drives them now is nothing more than the quest for personal power. The Sisters of the Blade led us into this mess. When we take the Citadel, we take the power out of the hands of the Sisterhood and place it with the Defenders.'

'So you want to replace one form of oppressive rule with another?' Brak asked wryly.

'No. Eventually, we'll hold elections. The people of Medalon should be allowed to vote for who they want to lead them, not leave the choice to a handful of women who are trained from childhood to believe they're better than everybody else. We'll put Jenga in charge until we've cleared out the Kariens and we can organise a vote. He has enough honour to see that it's done properly.'

R'shiel gazed at him suspiciously. 'How long have you been planning this, Garet?'

'The destruction of the Sisterhood? Since the day I learnt of the burning of a small village in the Sanctuary Mountains called Haven,' he told her.

For a moment she said nothing.

'You come from Haven.' It was more a statement of fact than a question; a sudden acceptance of his motives, an understanding of what drove him. He felt as if, on some unconscious level, she had forgiven him.

'Your real family was killed in that raid, R'shiel. So were mine.'

'I never knew you were Mountain Folk.'

'Why should you? I've been a Defender for as long as you've known me.'

'Then you've known all along who I really was?'

He shook his head. 'You were born long after I left Haven. But I knew your mother, J'nel. And B'thrim, her sister.'

'What were they like?'

He smiled, partly in remembrance, and partly because of the expression on R'shiel's face. For all her deeds, for all her awesome power, there was still a part of the child she had been lurking deep inside her, desperate for reassurance.

'B'thrim I remember as being a rather large, overprotective woman who would chase us with a skinning knife if ever she caught us robbing her traps in the woods. J'nel was the complete opposite. She was small and fragile and wild. We used to call her the Snow Child. She was never happier than when she was lost in the woods. As a boy, I was part of more than one search party sent to find her. She was the sort of person who could coax wild rabbits to sit on her lap. I never knew anyone like her. It doesn't surprise me in the least that she caught the eye of a Harshini king.'

R'shiel closed her eyes for a moment and he exchanged a look with Brak.

'When did you leave Haven?' Brak asked.

'I was fourteen. The life of a woodcutter didn't particularly appeal to me so I ran away to Testra. That's when I discovered that knowing how to live off the land in no way prepared one for living in a city. I was caught stealing food by a Defender lieutenant. He gave me the choice to join up or be sent to the Grimfield. So I joined the Defenders. The lieutenant put in a good word for me and I was accepted into the Cadets. I've not been back to Haven since.'

'You were lucky to meet someone so generous,' Brak remarked.

Garet nodded. 'I was. And I still owe him. His name was Palin Jenga.'

R'shiel's eyes opened wide. 'Then you have a debt to pay, as well as vengeance to seek.'

He nodded. 'Which is why I insist on both my demands being met. I don't intend to let your hidden agenda ruin mine. I will never have another chance at this. Do we have a deal?'

R'shiel glanced up at Brak who was standing behind her. The Harshini nodded slightly and she turned back to him.

'Yes, Garet. We have a deal.'

## 37

Garet Warner arranged a meeting with those officers who were with him in his desire to overthrow both the Kariens and the Sisters of the Blade. R'shiel was surprised when she saw them. There were quite a few familiar faces – classmates of Tarja's and other senior officers who she would never have expected to harbour such treasonous ambitions. She was certain every Defender in the Citadel wanted to be free of Karien occupation, but it was a little disturbing to learn how many of these men were willing to destroy the Sisterhood.

They met in a room at the back of the Grey Widow Inn in Tavern Street, slipping in one at a time to avoid raising the suspicions of the Karien soldiers who now frequented the place. The windows were covered against the night with shabby woven curtains and the lanterns that flickered in their yellow glass flutes gave the room an air of conspiracy. When they were finally assembled, Garet locked the door and turned to face them. There were fifteen Defenders present, every one of them an officer and not one ranked below captain. Brak and R'shiel were the only civilians.

'I'm not going to bother with introductions,' he began. 'If you don't know each other's names, then it's probably better that it stays that way. The only people who need introduction are these two. Most of you know R'shiel. Her friend is called Brak.'

'Can we trust them?' an officer asked, one R'shiel did not know.

'They wouldn't be here otherwise.'

The Defender nodded and made no further comment.

'I take it this meeting means that we've decided to make our move,' another man remarked.

Garet nodded. 'We begin at dawn on Restday.'

'That doesn't give us much time,' someone else pointed out. R'shiel knew the voice, but could not put a face to it.

'That's the whole point,' Garet replied. 'Once we leave this room tonight, we will have to take others into our confidence. Every additional person who learns of this plot increases our chances of discovery. The less time between now and when we strike the better.'

'I know we've discussed this before,' a young man near the back of the room commented, 'but even if we can take the Citadel, that still leaves the Karien army camped outside our gates.'

'And there's the priests to contend with, too,' his companion added with concern. 'I don't believe in their tales of magic, but I was on the northern border when their army attacked. I know what I saw there.'

'Take them hostage,' R'shiel suggested.

They all looked at her in surprise, including Brak.

'If you plan it right,' she continued, 'once you take the Citadel you'll have every duke in Karien as a hostage and their priests with them. If you can't negotiate a settlement with Jasnoff, using his entire Council of Dukes as your bargaining chip, you're not going to do it with anything else. It's quite simple, really. You kill them one at a time until he gives in. Start with the priests and work your way up. You shouldn't have to dispose of too many before King Jasnoff gets the message.'

Brak grabbed her by the arm and pulled her close so only she could hear him. 'What in the gods' name are you up to now?' he hissed in her ear.

'Trust me, Brak.' She pulled free of his grasp and rubbed her arm.

'Not this time, R'shiel. I won't stand by while you slaughter innocent men just so you can get even with your mother.'

She let out an impatient, exasperated sigh. Why did he always assume the worst about her? 'I'd hardly call the Karien dukes and their priests innocent. Besides, we're not really going to destroy anyone, Brak; we're just going to threaten it. We're just giving them a reason to go home.'

Brak's faded eyes were burning with suspicion, but he had no chance to question her further.

'You don't seriously expect us to kill hostages in cold blood?' The man who spoke was Rylan, the Citadel's Master of Horse. R'shiel had known him since she was a small child. 'That's not the way we do things in the Defenders.'

'You coped well enough murdering your own people during the Purge, Commandant,' she replied. 'I should think a few enemy heads posted over the main gate would make a nice change.'

The room exploded in a rush of objection. Garet glared at her angrily. 'You're treading on very thin ice, R'shiel.'

'I'm merely stating facts, Garet. The Defenders have much to atone for.'

'The biggest mistake we made was not ensuring we

had completely eradicated the Harshini,' someone called out pointedly.

R'shiel turned on the officer who had spoken. 'You'll make an even bigger mistake if you think you can do this and remain on your high moral ground. Look at you! Hiding in the back room of a tavern, plotting the overthrow of your government while you profess to abhor unnecessary bloodshed. Your precious Defender's honour didn't stop Mahina being killed. It hasn't stopped the Kariens taking control of Medalon and it won't help you get it back. You're fighting fanatics, Captain, not men who think like you do. If you expect to win, you have to play by their rules, not hope they'll play by yours.'

Garet glanced at Brak warningly. 'Shut her up, or leave.'

Brak stepped up behind R'shiel and placed a strong, restraining hand on her shoulder. 'You aren't helping, R'shiel.'

'We can't go ahead with this!' Rylan insisted. 'Jasnoff won't negotiate. He doesn't need to. What does it matter if we control the Citadel? With that army camped outside our walls, we could be under siege for years. There is no army waiting over the next rise to come to our rescue. And even if there were, what army on the continent could rival the number of Kariens out there? It's too dangerous. We should find another way.'

Garet held up his hands to quell the hubbub of agreement that followed the Horse Master's words, then looked at R'shiel and Brak speculatively.

'Rylan has raised a valid point. If this strategy fails and we can't disperse the Karien host, we will be caught in a siege that will be long, painful and ultimately futile.'

'What if you had a chance of being relieved?' Brak

asked. R'shiel glanced over her shoulder at him. Then she smiled in understanding.

'Damin.'

'Who?' someone asked from the back of the room.

'Damin Wolfblade, the High Prince of Hythria. Tarja was taking the men he gathered south to meet him. He has already promised Medalon aid.'

'For that matter,' R'shiel added thoughtfully, 'we could probably get Hablet to join in the fray. And then there are the Defenders who fled to Hythria.'

'How many Defenders?' someone asked. 'A thousand? Maybe two? They'll not be much use against that horde outside.'

'And you seriously think the Hythrun and the Fardohnyans will come to our aid?' Rylan scoffed.

'Damin will come,' R'shiel replied confidently.

'R'shiel's right,' Brak agreed. 'Hythria and Fardohnya will come if she asks for their help.'

'Things must have changed in the south quite dramatically in recent months,' Rylan remarked sourly. 'Last I heard, Hablet was planning to invade us, not come to our rescue. And since when did you hold any sway with the kings and princes of our southern neighbours?'

Garet studied her for a moment then turned to Rylan. He had been on the northern border with them and knew she was acquainted with the Hythrun prince. 'Actually, in this I think she may be right. Wolfblade might come if R'shiel asks him. But are you sure you can trust him?'

'I'd trust Damin with my life.'

'It's not just your life you're trusting him with, R'shiel, but the lives of every man, woman and child in the Citadel.'

Garet studied them both for a moment, weighing the

advisability of placing his faith in their assurances. Eventually he shrugged and turned to face his men. 'As I see it, we go now, or we abandon the idea altogether. Every day the Kariens reside in Medalon makes it all the harder to dislodge them. I'm willing to believe R'shiel if she says she can bring help. I say we do it and then settle down and wait for the Hythrun to relieve us.'

A low murmur ran through the room as the Defenders indicated their cautious agreement. Garet nodded. 'Good. Then let's get down to details.'

There wasn't much R'shiel or Brak could contribute after that. These men had been planning this since the day Joyhinia signed Medalon's surrender. Everything had been worked out: each key position they would take, every weapon they would need and every man they would need to do it. This meeting was simply to sort out the minor details and accommodate any last-minute changes to their plans.

They based their coup on the assumption that every Defender in the Citadel would follow them when the time came, and R'shiel was quite sure their confidence was justified. There was not a Defender who would willingly subjugate himself to the Kariens – with the possible exception of Wain Loclon, and she intended to take care of him personally.

The task of rescuing the Lord Defender and Tarja fell to a young captain whom R'shiel vaguely remembered being a lieutenant when she had been a Probate. He was, she recalled with mild surprise, the young man who had whisked Kilene away to dance, on the night Davydd Tailorson had taken her to meet Tarja in the caverns under the amphitheatre. That night stuck in her memory like the jagged edge of a bottomless abyss, down which she seemed to have been helplessly tumbling ever since, towards a destiny she had never wanted or envisaged. Symin accepted his orders with a serious expression, but she could sense the suppressed excitement that he struggled to hold in check. He worried her a little. This was not an adventure.

It was the early hours of the morning before Garet glanced around the room with a nod of satisfaction. 'Well, that's about it. You all know what you have to do. Any questions?'

'We've not mentioned how we're going to get a message to the Hythrun,' Rylan pointed out.

'R'shiel?' Garet asked, turning to her.

'We'll take care of that.'

'How?' Rylan asked. 'We'll be trapped in the Citadel. How will you get a message out? How will you get past the Kariens? We have no birds here trained to fly to Hythria.'

It was Garet who answered for her. 'I think in this case, we can leave that up to Brak and R'shiel. They have . . . er . . . resources . . . that we don't need to know about. I don't think we need fear on that point.'

R'shiel glanced at Brak who smiled briefly at Garet's cautious acknowledgment of their power.

'Well, if there are no more questions, I think we're finished here. Good luck, gentlemen.'

The Defenders gathered up their maps and plans and began to leave the room, one at a time, slipping out as the young lieutenant, who was surreptitiously guarding the door outside, gave the signal that it was clear. R'shiel and Brak were among the last to leave.

'I'm placing an awful lot of faith in you two, and based on your past history, that's not very encouraging,' Garet said as they waited. 'Can you really get Wolfblade and the Fardohnyans here in time to help?'

'I think so.'

'R'shiel, I'd be a lot happier if you sounded more certain.'

She shrugged. 'It depends on a few things. I have to talk to some of the gods.'

Garet's brow furrowed in concern. 'I can't believe I'm even discussing this, let alone pinning our whole strategy on it.' He stopped and nodded in acknowledgment of a salute from two captains, then waited until they were alone before he continued. 'There's something else I want you to keep in mind. If we kill too many priests and dukes, Jasnoff will seek our destruction out of spite.'

'You won't have to kill more than a few, Garet.'

'That's easy for you to say. It's not you who will be holding the sword to their throats. Or were you planning to do this personally?'

'I couldn't, even if I wanted to. If I caused that much destruction, it would devastate the Harshini, who are linked to the same power source as me.' She glanced at Brak, a little offended by his startled expression. 'You didn't think I knew that, did you? I remember what Shananara said to me about the night that I tried to kill Loclon. If wanting to kill one person could hurt the Harshini that much, killing dozens would destroy them.'

'Then bear something else in mind,' Garet reminded her. 'A hundred thousand rampaging Kariens fleeing through Medalon will be just as destructive as making them die here.'

'Don't worry, Garet. I know what I'm doing.'

He shook his head ruefully. 'I seriously doubt that, R'shiel, and the look of doubt on Brak's face does little to encourage me.'

'Then why are you doing this?'

'Because we have to,' he replied simply.

The Great Hall of the Citadel was now known as Francil's Hall, however R'shiel refused to acknowledge the new name. Joyhinia Tenragan had purchased the name at the cost of a woman's honour, and R'shiel would not give such a base and lowly act any credence by admitting to it. The huge hall was deserted when they slipped inside, cringing as the massive doors boomed shut behind them. It was just on dawn and the hall was shrouded in shadows as the first faint rays of light painted the dancing dust motes pink. The walls below the gallery were just beginning to lighten with the Brightening. Brak stepped into the hall and looked around. His eyes were full of unspeakable sadness.

'The ceiling used to have a painting on it that depicted all the Primal Gods,' he said, looking up at the stark, whitewashed roof. His voice seemed dangerously loud in the silent, cavernous building. 'It took the Harshini nearly half a century to complete it. You could stare at it for a lifetime and still not find everything there was to see.'

'There was a mural in my room like that,' she told him. 'It was so full of detail I never tired of looking at it.'

He did not appear to notice she had spoken. 'Along the gallery up there was a mural dedicated to the Incidental Gods. Their followers would come to the Temple of the Gods and add to the mural as part of their acknowledgment of their gods' existence. Parts of it were magnificent, particularly the panels devoted to the God of Artists. There were sonnets covering the walls devoted to the God of Poets, too. You see the marble balustrade? If you look closely, you'll find each pillar is drilled with holes. Open the windows in the arches at either end of the Hall on a windy day and the whole hall will sing to the God of Music.'

R'shiel wasn't sure what to say, or even if she should say anything. Brak seemed lost in the past. He walked further into the hall, his boots loud on the marble floor.

'See these twenty pillars supporting the gallery? They used to have alcoves set in each one, but they're filled in now. Each pillar was a shrine to one of the Primal Gods.' He frowned at some distant memory and glanced at her. 'The Seeing Stone used to sit up there on the podium. It seemed bigger then, but I guess I remember it through the eyes of a younger man.'

'It must have been spectacular.'

'It was,' he agreed, with a frown at the stark walls. The wall at the back of the podium had been plastered over and whitewashed. R'shiel recalled the impressive Stone in the Temple in Greenharbour and tried to envisage a similar Stone taking pride of place in this Temple, but she could not imagine it. The Hall was filled with too much of the Sisterhood's history for her to really grasp what Brak could see.

'Do you know how much mischief Korandellan and I used to find as children, with the God of Thieves and the God of Chance for playmates?'

'You played with the gods?'

'It was a different world then, R'shiel. There were no Sisters of the Blade. No Overlord. Not much violence at all, to speak of, except in Hythria, but that was the God of War's province and it rarely impinged on our lives.' He shook his head and looked around with regret. 'The Sisterhood has done much to be despised for, but I think this is the worst desecration of all.'

She stared at the stark, empty hall for a moment. She had seen Sanctuary and been overcome by the beauty of it, but she had a feeling it was a pale reflection of what the Citadel had once been.

Brak visibly shook off his nostalgic melancholy. 'Come on. If we're going to do this, we'd better get it over with. The city will be awake soon.'

'Won't the priests feel us?'

'Not in here.'

'You neglected to mention that before.'

'No, I quite deliberately omitted mentioning it,' he told her. 'I didn't want you getting ideas.'

'But they found me here the last time I drew on my power.'

'Only once they were inside with you.'

She scowled at him. 'How many other little snippets of vital information like that have you deliberately omitted?'

'Quite a few. Now get a move on. We haven't got all day.'

This was the Temple of the Gods. To name a god here was to summon him. She hesitated for a moment, wondering if after all this time, the gods would still come to the temple if she called. She glanced at Brak and then shrugged.

There was really only one way to find out.

## 38

Initially, Tarja survived his captivity because nobody recognised him. When he regained consciousness with a pounding headache, eyes glued shut by the blood that had leaked from the wound on his forehead, he found himself in a crowded cell with a score of other men rounded up by the Kariens. He was blue from cold and shivering uncontrollably in his damp clothes, but otherwise unharmed, which surprised him a little. Of Ulran and the others there was no sign. They had either escaped or were being held in a different location.

Tarja's anonymity was aided considerably by the fact that the Kariens had not thought to establish the identity of their prisoners. That was a job for scribes, and they did not consider scribes a necessary part of an advance war party.

The main Karien army arrived in Cauthside the day after he cut loose the ferry. According to his cellmates, who had witnessed the aftermath, the ferry had been destroyed by the river, which had thrown it against the bank like a piece of driftwood. It was now good for nothing more than kindling. The news gave Tarja some small measure of satisfaction. For the time being, the Kariens were stalled.

His good fortune did not last long. A week after he was captured he was reunited with Ulran, who spied him on the other side of the crowded cellar where they were being held and called out to him gleefully, loud enough for every Karien in Cauthside to hear.

Within an hour, Tarja found himself, chained hand and foot, facing Lord Roache and Lord Wherland.

With the discovery of the notorious Tarja Tenragan in their custody, the Kariens obviously felt that the Overlord had answered their prayers. He became the focus of everything that had gone wrong in their campaign: Cratyn's death, Lord Terbolt's death, the fact that their army was facing starvation because there were not enough farms or cities in northern Medalon they could ransack for supplies, that the Defenders had surrendered yet refused to be cowed – even that they still needed the Defenders to maintain control of the civilian population. They blamed him for the squads of roving deserters who harried their flanks and slunk away into the night before they could be captured, and they blamed him for the fact that they were immobilised on the wrong side of the river, a responsibility which Tarja didn't mind shouldering at all, considering he actually was accountable for that.

Everything became Tarja's fault and they intended to see that he paid for it.

The Karien dukes wore the frazzled air that surrounds men whose success comes at a very high price. Lord Roache did not accuse him openly of single-handedly hampering the Karien occupation of Medalon, but he came close. He had spared Tarja a contemptuous glance, then consulted the parchment in front of him.

'You murdered Lord Pieter, Lord Terbolt and His Royal Highness, Cratyn, the Crown Prince of Karien. You also murdered the priest Elfron. You are responsible for countless acts of sabotage, up to and including the destruction of the Cauthside Ferry. You are responsible for the kidnapping of Her Royal Highness, Adrina, Crown Princess of Karien, and for handing her over to the custody of the barbarian Hythrun, where she remains a hostage. You have consorted with demons and pagans and have actively assisted Harshini sorcerers. Do you have anything to say?'

'I think you left out the bit about eating babies,' he had said with the reckless abandon of a man who knows he is condemned and that nothing he said could make the situation worse than it already was.

'You will hang, Captain. Your crimes allow no other course of action.'

'Could you do it sooner, rather than later?' he quipped, enjoying the effect his insolence was having on the Karien duke. 'The food in the cells is terrible.'

'You mock me at your peril, Captain.'

'I say we dispose of him now!' Wherland declared. He was a big man with a big voice and very little patience.

Roache shook his head. 'These Medalonians need to see that even the mighty Tarja Tenragan cannot escape our vengeance. If we hang him here, in this isolated country village, the people will refuse to believe it. He has to die as publicly as possible. We will wait until we reach the Citadel. I want as many witnesses as I can get.'

'Then a little public humiliation will have to do. We'll put him in the stocks.'

'No. The risk of his accomplices trying to free him

would be too great. He'll be confined in the camp. I intend to make an example of him that the Medalonians will not forget.'

They spoke Karien, perhaps not aware that Tarja understood them. He did not react to their words, preferring them to remain ignorant of the fact that he spoke their language fluently. If anything, Roache's determination to hang him in the Citadel gave him heart. It would be a month or more before they could get across the river. A lot could happen in a month.

Roache turned back to Tarja and addressed him in heavily accented Medalonian.

'You will be confined here and transferred to the Citadel at the earliest opportunity. If you wish to prolong your life, you will provide us with the names of your conspirators and the location of your rebel headquarters.'

'You don't seriously expect me to tell you anything, do you?'

The Duke shrugged. 'One is never sure what a Medalonian considers honourable, Captain. You might be willing to barter your friends to save your own neck.'

'A word of advice, my lord. If you expect to hold onto Medalon, you would do well to learn what we consider honourable.'

'Looking at the list of your crimes, Captain, I'm surprised you have the word in your vocabulary.'

While hardly luxurious, Tarja's accommodation proved better than he expected. He was confined to a tent in the centre of the Karien camp, guarded on all four sides by knights who held their loyalty to Karien and the Overlord above even their own mothers, Tarja suspected. They were taciturn to begin with, but as the days merged into weeks, they relented a little and from them Tarja learnt what was happening in the outside world.

The knights told him when the news arrived that Princess Adrina was now in Hythria and married to the Hythrun High Prince. Tarja appeared suitably surprised, not wanting to spoil their outrage by informing them that he had known about her marriage for some time. The news that Damin was the High Prince worried him a little. He wondered if R'shiel had had a hand in it. She had killed twice that he knew of and never shown a moment's remorse over either man. *Had she acquired a taste for murder? Was the blood of the old High Prince on her hands now?* The thoughts ate at him, added to the other memories of her that continued to haunt him. Memories that could not be real. Memories he had no reason to doubt.

Although he had no idea of the fate of Mandah and the rest of his squad, he learnt soon enough what had happened to the Fardohnyans they had found in the abandoned boathouse. When Paval informed the remnants of Adrina's Guard that the Kariens had arrived, instead of fleeing south, which would have been the sensible thing to do, Filip and his men rode straight into Cauthside in a futile attempt to aid the Medalonians. By the time they arrived, there were enough Kariens in the town to outnumber them considerably. The fight had been short and bloody. A number were killed in the skirmish, including Filip and Paval. The remainder were summarily tried and hanged as deserters the following day.

Tarja saw their rotting bodies swinging from a temporary gallows the Kariens had constructed in the town square when he was escorted to his new quarters in the

Karien camp. He felt a pang of guilt and wondered why the Fardohnyans had risked such a fate when they could have gotten clean away. In the end he decided it was some incomprehensible idea of Fardohnyan honour that made them turn back. He had seen the look in Filip's eyes when he had offered their surrender to Damin on the border. Perhaps it was easier to die attempting something heroic against ridiculous odds than return home to Talabar to face the king. The Princess's Guard had not only deserted a battlefield, but had abandoned the princess they'd been sent north to protect. That Adrina had ordered them to do both would not matter to Hablet. Tarja realised the same fate probably awaited these men at home. All they had done was hasten the inevitable.

Tarja spent almost a month in the Karien camp before the rafts were completed and he was transferred across the Glass River to the Citadel under heavy guard. He saw nothing of the journey or the Citadel when the Kariens entered it in triumph. Lord Roache had commandeered a closed carriage in Cauthside, and Tarja was confined to it, night and day, for the entire trip, allowed out only once each morning and evening to relieve himself. He was transferred to a cell in the Defenders' headquarters under cover of darkness, and there he remained, completely cut off from news of what was happening in the outside world.

Tarja did not know if the Citadel had surrendered quietly, or if there had been a pitched battle for it. He didn't know if the Defenders still existed, or if Roache had disbanded them. The guards on his cell in the Citadel spoke no Medalonian and he didn't want to reveal that he spoke their language, so there was no conversation between them. If they discussed the events of the day as they whiled away the hours on duty, they were too far from his cell for him to overhear them.

As he lost track of the days, Tarja found the isolation beginning to wear on him. He had spent enough time behind bars recently to grow accustomed to incarceration – a circumstance that bothered him more than he cared to admit – but he had always had something to occupy his mind. The torturers who had tried to extract the identity of his fellow rebels from him with batons and hot iron pokers had given him some purpose, even if it was merely to resist them. But here, so isolated that he had not seen another soul for days, he began to appreciate the need for human company. He saw no one. Even his meals were delivered anonymously through a hatch in the metal door.

At first he tried to occupy his mind with plans of escape, but with no tools to break out and no contact with anybody who could provide them, he was helpless. He wondered if feigning illness would bring his guards running into the cell, but he had banged on the door until his knuckles were raw and his voice grew hoarse from calling out to no avail. Tarja began to wonder if his isolation was a form of torture in itself. There were worse things than pain, worse than humiliation or defeat. To be forgotten; to be so inconsequential that it mattered to nobody if you lived or died – that was proving to be the bitterest pill of all.

With escape, or even the hope of it denied him, Tarja turned his thoughts inward. Introspection proved a dangerous game. His mind was filled with a past that horrified him, yet he was coming to accept it as real. For some reason – perhaps, as Mandah suggested, on the whim of a god – he had fallen hopelessly in love with

R'shiel. He could remember it all, every thought, every longing, every kiss, every embrace, every moment of intimacy, every time he slept with her curled in his arms. What puzzled him was why it hadn't bothered him at the time – and why it bothered him so much now. He knew, on an intellectual level, that R'shiel was not his sister, but a lifetime of thinking of her as his own flesh and blood was not so easily swept aside. Yet he had loved her, seemingly without regret, until he woke in that wagon on the way to Testra and discovered his world completely changed and no memory or inkling of what had changed it.

When the door to his cell finally opened, Tarja leaped to his feet with pathetic eagerness. The man who opened it was a knight with dark hair and the disillusioned look of a young man who has discovered that war is not nearly as romantic or heroic as he imagined. His tabard was decorated with three stylised pines against a red background.

*Kirkland,* Tarja thought. *He comes from the same province as young Mikel. What happened to him, I wonder? Did he live through this or is he yet another victim of R'shiel's destiny?*

'My name is Sir Andony,' the Karien said in broken Medalonian. 'You come with me.'

Tarja looked down, aware of how bad he smelled. He was unshaved and filthy and his cell reeked, the bucket in the corner long since filled to overflowing.

'Where are we going?'

'Must be clean. You hang tomorrow. Lord Roache say you must look like Defender.'

So, they were finally going to hang him. Roache had

said he wanted as many witnesses as possible and he obviously wanted to remind the citizens of Medalon that he was hanging an officer of the Defenders. The desperate, unwholesome creature he must appear at the moment would threaten no one. Tarja debated resisting for an instant then rejected the idea. There might be some hope of escape once he was out of his cell, although looking at the men arrayed behind Andony it was unlikely.

Tarja followed Andony and resolutely refused to give up hope. He had escaped this fate before. He had eluded death so many times in the past that he had wondered if, like the magical Harshini, he were immortal. As the Karien guards fell in around him, he warned himself not to be so foolish.

He was not invincible. Even the Harshini were not immortal. Barring some unforeseen miracle, in less than a day all his previous narrow escapes would finally catch up with him.

## 39

Dawn broke over the Citadel on Restday to the ring of hammers pounding on wood as the gallows slowly took shape. The sandy floor of the arena was littered with construction debris as the workmen hurried to finish their task before the crowd arrived. Joyhinia Tenragan stepped down through the gate in the white painted barricade and surveyed the progress with a frown as she crossed the arena floor, tugging her cloak closed against the crisp breeze.

'How much longer?'

The foreman turned at her voice and dropped his hammer. He bowed hastily. 'It will be done on time, First Sister.'

Joyhinia nodded with satisfaction. The hanging was scheduled for noon. 'You've done well.'

'I've no need to be doing this at all,' the man complained as he picked up his hammer. 'There's a perfectly good gallows behind the Defenders' headquarters.'

'You don't approve of public hangings?' Joyhinia asked curiously. She probably should have reprimanded him for being so impudent, but she was in a rare mood today.

'It's not my idea of entertainment, no,' the foreman agreed cautiously, perhaps realising the folly of being so outspoken.

'I see. It's not that you harbour sympathies for the criminal, then?'

'No, your Grace!'

'I thought not. Carry on.'

Joyhinia turned away from the workmen with a sour smile. *That should take the lead out of their boots.* A few words from the First Sister and men quivered where they stood. Even the threat of her presence was enough to unman some. It was the headiest feeling. Better than wine. Better than sex. Better even, than watching someone in pain . . .

The First Sister strolled back towards her office in a fine mood. The day was cool but clear, and it would see the last of Tarja Tenragan. That her vengeance had taken so long did not concern the First Sister. If anything, it tasted all the sweeter for the wait.

At the thought of her other enemies who were still at large, the First Sister frowned. She had expected some news by now, but no word had come about R'shiel. She had last been seen in Fardohnya, according to Squire Mathen, claiming to be the Harshini demon child. The news did not overly concern her.

Tarja would draw R'shiel like a water diviner to an underground spring. Joyhinia had made certain that the hanging had been well publicised, surprising even the Kariens with her vehement insistence that Tarja's execution be delayed until the news had reached every corner of Medalon.

R'shiel *had* to come. All this power, all that Loclon currently enjoyed in the guise of the First Sister would be meaningless if she continued to live.

Squire Mathen was waiting when the First Sister returned. He was a thin man with curling black hair, long thin features and a dour disposition. He also had little patience with Joyhinia and it was only the knowledge that this man held the key to the room where Loclon's body lay, empty and alive at Mathen's whim while his mind resided in Joyhinia's body, that kept the First Sister from defying him.

'Where have you been?'

The man was sitting behind the First Sister's desk, going through her papers. Joyhinia bit back her annoyance.

'I was checking on the progress of the gallows. I wanted to be sure everything would be ready.'

'It should be quite an event,' Mathen remarked without looking up. 'Not often one gets to see an officer of the Defenders hanged. I imagine you would have to hang someone as important as the First Sister to get a bigger crowd.'

Even Joyhinia could not miss the veiled threat.

'Tarja Tenragan is a deserter and a miserable traitor.'

Mathen looked up with cold narrow eyes and stared at her. Joyhinia fidgeted under his scrutiny. 'Then it will do the citizens good to see what happens to traitors.'

'And it will bring those who oppose us out of the wood-work,' Joyhinia added.

Mathen finished reading the letter he was holding before he answered. 'Or drive them underground.'

'No, I know these people. Someone will try to rescue him. And when they do, we'll be ready for them.'

'If it was up to me, I wouldn't try to rescue him,' Mathen shrugged. 'If I wanted to ferment rebellion, I would let you hang him unopposed and use his death as a rallying cry for every malcontent in Medalon.'

The implied criticism was clear. 'If you think this is such a bad idea, why are you letting it go ahead?'

'Because Lord Roache wishes it, and even as a martyr, Tarja Tenragan will be less trouble dead than alive. Where is the speech I wrote for you?'

'I gave it to my secretary.'

'Fetch it. I have a few changes I wish to make.'

Joyhinia knew better than to argue with the man. She turned on her heel and crossed the large office, jerking open the door angrily.

'Suelen? Give me that speech I gave you yesterday!'

Suelen jumped to obey. Joyhinia snatched the rolled parchment from her outstretched hand and slammed the door in the young woman's face.

'There!' she said, slapping it on the desk.

Squire Mathen looked up. He seemed amused. 'Temper, temper, First Sister.'

Although it had been the Karien priests who had worked the spell that had put his mind in Joyhinia's body, secretly, the First Sister was no happier about the Karien occupation of the Citadel than any other Medalonian. It had nothing to do with patriotism, however. Loclon simply wanted to be left alone to run things as he saw fit and Mathen's presence was a constant reminder of the limits to his power.

From a purely political point of view, Loclon begrudgingly admired the Duke of Setenton's wisdom in placing Squire Mathen in charge. Even Lord Roache seemed content to let him take care of the day-to-day running of the Citadel. It must have been tempting for the Kariens simply to demand instant conversion of their new subjects to the Overlord; to forbid practices that had been part of Medalonian society for centuries. Mathen was too clever to stir up resistance in such a manner. There had been enough trouble when they threw open the gates of the Citadel to welcome the Karien occupation force. He wasn't going to make Medalon ungovernable by ordering them to change their views on the gods overnight.

With no Quorum to answer to any longer, the First Sister could issue decrees as she wished, although they were written under Mathen's careful guidance. On the surface, the decrees seemed quite reasonable. One had to look closely to realise they were the first insidious steps down the road of Xaphista's worship. Mathen had all but outlawed prostitution, which the Sisterhood had legalised two centuries ago. There were other laws too, which had been enacted in the past months. It was now an offence to wager on anything; a decree that had been met with a great deal of grumbling, but little open resistance. Loclon wasn't a gambler himself, unless he had fixed it so he knew he would win, but he knew enough about the religion of the Kariens to know that this was another of their strict mores that they wished to impose on Medalon.

Illegitimacy was the next target, Loclon knew, but he doubted Mathen would be quite so lucky getting that one accepted. In Medalon, legitimacy was determined by the maternal line – a law set down by the Sisterhood long ago – and one that meant perhaps two thirds of the population had been born out of the Karien definition of wedlock. They would not be pleased to suddenly find themselves considered bastards.

Had he tried to disband the Defenders, Mathen would have had a bloodbath on his hands, so he had wisely made no attempt to disarm them, and had, against Loclon's advice, left Garet Warner in charge, as the senior officer in the Citadel. Loclon didn't trust Garet Warner, although the man gave every indication of accepting the surrender. To Loclon, even wearing the body of the First Sister, the commandant's cooperation reeked of duplicity. Mathen, however, seemed unconcerned. He considered Garet a pragmatist, and while he obeyed orders, he was content to leave him be.

As for the Lord Defender, nobody, from Lord Roache down, was prepared to trust him. He had accepted the surrender unwillingly and actively abetted the deserters who now plagued them with acts of sabotage. There were even rumours that he had dispatched a large force to Hythria, which was massing to attack in the spring. Jenga was locked in the cells behind the Defenders' headquarters and there he would stay until Roache decided what to do with him. The Karien duke was reluctant to kill him out of hand. He may yet prove useful.

They were interrupted by a knock on the door. Mathen looked up and called permission to enter. Garet Warner stepped into the office, saluting Mathen and the First Sister politely when he stopped in front of the desk.

'Good morning, Squire. First Sister.'

'What is it, Commandant? Trouble over the execution today?'

'That's why I'm here. I thought perhaps it might be wise to post extra guards around the Citadel, in case things get out of hand.'

'That's probably a good idea. I'll send out to the camp for some extra men.'

'I was hoping to use the Defenders,' Garet said calmly. Joyhinia watched him with misgiving. Neither Loclon nor Joyhinia had ever liked Garet Warner. He was too clever by half.

'Why?' Mathen asked suspiciously.

'You're going to hang a Defender today, Squire. I'd prefer to have them kept busy. If you leave them off duty, they'll be in the stands as spectators.'

'Then they will learn a salutary lesson.'

'Or they might decide to object.'

Mathen thought on it for a moment, then nodded. 'Very well. Use all the men you need. Preferably away from the amphitheatre.'

'I've made a list of strategic locations that would be at risk if anything were to happen. I'll see my men are sent to all those positions. They'll not think it strange, and as you say, it will keep them away from the amphitheatre.'

'Very good. Is that all?'

'There was one other thing,' Garet added, almost as an afterthought. 'They're having trouble with the main gate. One of the pulleys has seized and they can't get it open. I've got the engineers working on it. It should be fixed some time this morning.'

Mathen looked annoyed. 'A convenient day for that to happen. Are you sure it was an accident?'

The Commandant nodded. 'It's not been tampered with, if that's what you mean. I checked on it myself this morning when I heard they were having trouble with it. You can inspect the problem yourself if you wish.'

'Just get the damned thing open,' Mathen snapped impatiently.

'As you wish, Squire.' Garet saluted smartly and turned towards the door. 'I've taken the liberty of posting some men outside,' he added as he reached it. Then he looked over his shoulder at Joyhinia and smiled. 'And I've arranged a special bodyguard for you too, your Grace. We don't want any incidents.'

Something about Garet Warner's manner screamed a warning to Loclon. He was much too calm, much too accepting of Tarja's hanging. Mathen returned his attention to the speech as Garet closed the door behind him.

'I changed the part here about traitorous deeds. It now reads: "Captain Tenragan is a blight on the honour of the Defenders. His callow and cowardly deeds have shamed every citizen in Medalon" . . . and so on, and so on. It sounds better, don't you think? Calling him a traitor outright might stir up a few passions. Technically, he didn't betray Medalon, only Karien, and that wouldn't bother your people one whit, I suspect. We need to paint him as a coward, a criminal not worth . . . Are you listening to me?'

'He's up to something,' Joyhinia warned.

'Who? Tarja Tenragan?'

'Garet Warner.'

Mathen shrugged. 'Undoubtedly.'

'Well, don't just sit there! We have to stop him!'

'I've taken precautions.'

'What precautions? You moved Jenga, that's all! I'm sure they're quaking in their boots!'

'Jenga is far more dangerous than Tarja Tenragan. The Lord Defender is a symbol of honour to every soldier in the Corps. I don't really care if they try to free Tarja. As you pointed out, this hanging will bring the troublemakers out of the woodwork. Let Warner try something. I've a hundred thousand men on the other side of that gate.'

'The gate is *closed*, you fool!'

Mathen looked at her for a moment and then swore viciously. He jumped to his feet and ran for the door, jerking it open. Suelen was gone. The anteroom was full of Defenders.

A sword pressing into his vest encouraged him to back up. The Defender holding the blade was a captain with the look of a man who wanted nothing more than to plunge his blade right through Mathen's chest.

'You idiot!' Joyhinia screamed at him. 'I warned you!'

'Shut up, Joyhinia!' Mathen moved back far enough that the blade no longer touched him. For a tense moment he watched the Defenders who filed into the office with weapons drawn then addressed their captain.

'You cannot succeed, you know that, don't you?'

'No, actually I didn't know that,' the captain replied pleasantly. 'Thank you for telling me.'

'Even if you manage to take the Citadel, you can't get past our army.'

'We'll see.'

The captain was infuriatingly confident. Loclon had been a Defender and he knew that stupidity was not one of their traits. Nor was Garet Warner a man for taking unnecessary risks. If this man believed they could win, it was because they had something up their sleeve. Something Mathen had not anticipated.

'They've done something!' Joyhinia said with a panicked edge to her voice. 'Look at him! He doesn't care about your army! They've poisoned the water or the food or something.'

'Nothing so crude, First Sister,' Garet Warner remarked as he stepped back into the office. He glanced around and then nodded to the captain. 'Take Mathen down and put him with the others. *Quietly*. Commandant Foren should have control of the administration building by now. Once you've secured the Squire, get over to the guest quarters and see if Cadon needs any help rounding up the priests.'

'What about me?' Joyhinia demanded.

'Ah, now *you* we have special plans for, your Grace,' Garet told her in that calm, annoying and soft-spoken voice that even as a Defender Loclon had always loathed. 'There's someone who is rather keen to deal with you personally.'

'Who?'

Garet smiled knowingly but didn't answer. With a sudden wave of nausea, Loclon guessed who it was. It accounted for the captain's confidence. It accounted for Garet's smug expression. Loclon knew she would come. It couldn't be anybody else. Not today. Not with Tarja's life in danger.

'*R'shiel.*' Joyhinia breathed the name fearfully, as though saying it aloud might cause her to suddenly materialise out of thin air.

'She's not here,' Mathen scoffed. 'We've had priests watching for her. There's no way the demon child could have slipped into the Citadel without us knowing about it.'

'I think you'll be disappointed to learn your confidence in the priesthood is somewhat misplaced, Squire,' R'shiel told him, stepping into the room. Loclon felt the First Sister's knees give way as she turned to him. Behind her was another man he did not know. He had no time to wonder who it was.

He had envisaged her return so often that it didn't seem real. She was not bound and helpless. She was not begging for mercy. She was standing there, staring at him with utter contempt. There was not a trace of fear in her eyes, only a quiet confidence that she finally and unequivocally, had him under her control.

'Get the Squire out of here, Captain.'

Mathen was bundled from the room, leaving R'shiel, Garet, the tall stranger and three other Defenders to deal with Joyhinia. She watched them warily. She knew what would happen next. They would tie the First Sister hand and foot and make her grovel before that Harshini bitch, who would take her vengeance as slowly and painfully as possible.

Loclon knew it was over. His reign as First Sister was done. He had no idea how the Defenders planned to deal with the Karien host, but men like Garet Warner didn't undertake suicide missions. They knew they could win.

The First Sister would die. And R'shiel was standing there, staring at him like she had been planning his suffering almost as long as Loclon had been planning hers.

But Loclon wasn't done yet. His mind occupied the body of the First Sister, but his own body lay empty and waiting in a room in the First Sister's apartments. That was far from this room and probably not worthy of the attention of the Defenders who were taking up arms throughout the Citadel and turning on their Karien masters.

Loclon didn't stop to think about it. With a wordless cry, Joyhinia charged at the nearest Defender. The startled soldier raised his blade in surprise as she threw herself onto it, welcoming the pain as it tore through her body – the old woman's body that Loclon was suddenly desperate to be free of.

'No!' he heard R'shiel scream in anger, realising what he was doing.

But he was too quick for her warning, and perhaps only she truly understood what was happening. The Defender jerked his sword clear and she collapsed on the ground with a smile of intense satisfaction.

'Brak! Help me! Don't let her die!' R'shiel cried, rushing to the First Sister's side. She dropped to her knees beside the body of her foster-mother, her eyes glistening with furious, unshed tears.

Joyhinia didn't die immediately. The old bitch may have been witless, but her body clung tenaciously to life. For a moment Loclon was afraid that the wound had not been fatal. That would have been the ultimate irony – to survive, trapped in an old and ruined body racked with pain. R'shiel grabbed at her shoulders and shook the limp body in fury, but she was fading fast – too fast for R'shiel to stop it; too fast for her to call on her power to save Joyhinia's broken body. Through a red wall of pain Loclon saw her, saw the look of anger and frustration in her eyes as he robbed her of the one pleasure she wanted more than anything else in this life – his death. It made everything worthwhile.

Then he felt a sudden jerk, as if he was being ripped apart – as if some giant hand had reached inside of him and turned his body inside out. Darkness smothered him and he let out a wordless cry of triumph.

Joyhinia Tenragan was dead.

## 40

Tarja slept surprisingly well the night before his hanging. Perhaps it was because he was clean for the first time in weeks. Or perhaps it was just that his fate seemed so inevitable he had given up worrying about it.

Whatever the reason, he woke at dawn feeling remarkably refreshed and far too healthy to dwell on the fact that he would most likely be dead in a few hours. As the small square of sky he could see through the cell's only window changed from pink to blue, he dressed in the uniform Andony had left for him and sat down to wait, feeling nothing but a serene sense of fatalistic calm.

It didn't last long. Voices sounded in the hall outside, followed by the sounds of fighting, then the door to his cell flew open. The young man who opened it was wearing a captain's uniform, panting heavily and grinning like a fool.

'Captain Tenragan, sir! Commandant Warner sends his compliments and wondered if you'd like to forgo your hanging for a good fight, sir? Oh, and R'shiel said to say hello, too.'

Tarja stared at the young captain. He was beyond being

surprised. He had ceased being amazed by his ability to escape certain death some time ago – about the time he had gone to sleep a broken man and woken completely healed in this same cellblock more than a year ago. And he was long past being astonished at R'shiel's ability to appear when he least expected it. She got him out of trouble almost as often as she landed him in it. But he was relieved that she was not the one who had found him. He had been ready to face death, but he wasn't sure he was ready to face R'shiel.

'Find me a sword.'

The captain laughed and tossed Tarja his own blade. He was obviously having the time of his life. Tarja snatched it out of the air and followed him into the hall.

Sir Andony and his men were lined up with their faces pressed against the wall as a score of Defenders expertly disarmed them. The young Karien knight looked stunned. He saw Tarja emerge from the cell and made to turn, but the Defender who stood behind him pushed him back against the wall.

'How far you think you get?' he snarled over his shoulder.

'Far enough,' Tarja replied with a grin, catching the mood of the Defenders around him. Every one of them looked delighted. These men were not trained to deal with defeat and the last few weeks with the Kariens in control of the Citadel had been eating away at them like slow burning acid. Now that they were finally doing something about it, there wasn't a Defender in the room who could hide his glee.

'What are you going to do with them, Captain . . . ?'

'Throw them into the cells for the time being,' the young man replied. 'And the name's Symin. You probably don't remember me. I was a Lieutenant when you . . .'

'When I deserted? It's all right, Symin, you can say it.'

'Well, I just didn't want it to sound as if . . . you know . . .'

Tarja smiled at the young man's discomfort. 'Yes. I know.'

'You not get away with this!' Andony insisted in his broken Medalonian. Tarja looked at him and shook his head.

'Sir Andony, why don't you just shut the hell up,' he said in Karien, 'before I decide to shut you up myself.'

'Kill me if you want,' Andony declared angrily in his own language, lacking the words in Medalonian to express how he felt. 'I will be welcomed into the House of the Overlord! You, on the other hand, will perish and freeze in the Sea of Despair! Don't you think we were expecting something like this? By now the Citadel is swarming with Karien troops. You won't get past the front door.'

'Well, that's our problem, isn't it?' He turned to Symin. 'You do *have* a plan for getting past the front door, don't you?' he asked in Medalonian.

'We're taking back the Citadel,' Symin told him happily. 'The gates are locked and by now we should have control of every key position in the city. Now we've got you out, we have to free Lord Jenga.'

'Where's he being held?'

'We thought he was here with you, but he must have been moved.'

Tarja's brow furrowed. He kicked an overturned stool out of the way, grabbed Andony by the shoulder and turned him around.

'Where have they taken the Lord Defender?'

'Go to hell, you atheist pig!'

Tarja hadn't really expected any other response. Andony

tensed, obviously expecting Tarja to hit him. It would have been a waste of time. Andony *wanted* to suffer for the Overlord. Dying simply meant granting his wish by sending him to meet his god sooner. But if Tarja couldn't threaten his life, he could threaten his soul, and that, he suspected, would frighten him more than any promise of physical violence.

'Symin, did you say R'shiel was here?'

'Yes, sir.'

'Then perhaps we should ask the demon child to have a word with Sir Andony,' he said in Karien to be certain the knight understood him. 'How long do you think it will take her to corrupt his soul?'

Symin looked at him blankly, but Andony paled.

'I cannot be turned from the Overlord by any Harshini witch!'

'This isn't just *any* Harshini witch, Andony,' he said in a low, threatening voice. 'This is the demon child. She is evil incarnate. She can turn you from the Overlord just by looking at you. If she touches you, your soul will belong to her forever. You cannot fight her. Even Xaphista fears her. One look from the demon child and *you* will drown in the Sea of Despair for an eternity.' He watched as Andony's eyes widened with fear. A part of Tarja could not believe that a grown man could be so gullible, while another part of him silently thanked the Overlord for making his followers so vulnerable. 'Do you really care that much about the Lord Defender?'

Andony hesitated. Tarja met his eye and saw the defiance there. He shrugged and turned to Symin.

'Fetch the demon child.'

'No!' Andony cried in horror.

'Where is the Lord Defender?'

The young knight was torn between duty and his immortal soul. The decision was a terrible one. Finally his shoulders slumped and he looked at the floor in shame. 'He's in the caverns under the amphitheatre. They moved him there last night in case there was an attack on the cells.'

'The caverns,' Tarja translated for the benefit of his comrades.

'What did you say to him?' Symin asked curiously.

'I threatened his soul.'

'Clever,' he said with an approving nod, although he clearly had no idea what Tarja was talking about. 'Sergeant Donel! Let's get these Kariens into the cells. The Lord Defender is waiting for us!'

It was not far from the Defenders' headquarters to the amphitheatre. As they ran through the deserted streets the occasional sound of metal against metal echoed between the buildings. A shout of alarm, in Karien, reached them from the direction of the armoury, then suddenly it was silenced. Tarja didn't know if the civilians in the Citadel had been warned of the coup, but they must have instinctively known something was afoot. They did not see another soul on their journey. Even Tavern Street was deserted.

When they reached the tunnel that led into the caverns, Tarja held up his hand to halt the troop. Symin didn't seem to mind that he had automatically assumed command. He studied the entrance for a moment then waved his men forward. The tunnel entrance was deserted, as was the tunnel itself. They moved into the darkness cautiously, listening with every sense they possessed.

The silence of the caverns pressed on Tarja like an

invisible weight. They had once been stables, according to legend; carved out of the natural hill to house the legendary Harshini horses. Reaching far into the darkness, they stretched endlessly in a circle under the amphitheatre like a giant rabbit warren.

Jenga could be anywhere.

He glanced at Symin and silently signalled to him. The young captain nodded in understanding and headed towards the caverns on the left, taking half the troop with him. The other half followed Tarja into the caverns on the right.

Torches mounted in brackets at uneven intervals pierced the darkness with puddles of flickering light. They moved swiftly and silently, checking the caverns as they went. Memories caught Tarja unawares as they inspected the caves. He smiled as the sergeant signalled the all-clear on the cavern where he had stolen his first kiss with a Novice whose name he could no longer remember; frowned as he passed the cavern where he'd broken the news to R'shiel about her true parentage. He knew these rooms well – he'd played here as a child with Georj. It was the best place in the Citadel to hide from Joyhinia. The best place to imagine they were heroes fighting off some implacable foe. They came here to practise their swordcraft, too, away from the critical eye of the Master at Arms. He could remember thinking he was quite a swordsman when he managed to slip his blunted blade through Georj's guard, while R'shiel, barely old enough to keep up with them, had demanded she be allowed to try, even though their practice swords were taller than she was.

'Captain!'

Tarja turned at the whispered call. Symin's sergeant,

Donel, pointed ahead. A pool of light beckoned, brighter than the surrounding caverns. They were almost in the centre of the ring. If Symin and his men had moved at much the same pace, they would be approaching from the other side.

Tarja nodded and signalled the order to move on. They crept like thieves through the darkness. Straining to listen, the silence bothered Tarja. He expected to hear something – the guards talking among themselves, the creak of leather or the scratch of metal armour as the Kariens moved about in the central cavern. But there was nothing. No sound disturbed the silence save for the hissing torches and the sound of his own breathing. He halted the men and waited. Listening intently.

There was nothing to be heard, but Tarja could smell something in the air, something faint, and sweet, and disturbingly familiar. It took him a few moments to identify it. When he realised what it was, he dropped all pretence of stealth and broke into a run. He saw Symin coming from the other direction, apparently having reached the same terrible conclusion. Tarja skidded to a halt as he reached the cavern and let out a wordless cry of despair as the others rushed in behind him.

It was blood he could smell. Fresh blood. The cavern was painted with it. It splattered the walls and pooled on the floor beneath their boots. Jenga lay in the centre of the carnage, his head almost severed from his body. He must have put up quite a fight. Squatting down, Tarja ran his finger through the bloody puddle at his feet. It was still faintly warm. Whoever had done this had done it recently. So recently that they were more than likely still down here in the caverns somewhere. He turned at the sound of someone retching.

'*Why?*' Symin managed to ask in a voice strangled with emotion.

Tarja didn't answer him, although he knew the reason. This was the Kariens' punishment for their temerity. It was the act of a spoiled child who had lost the game then spitefully broken the winner's favourite toy so that nobody else could play with it. For a moment, he couldn't speak. The rage he felt robbed him of any facility other than the desire to seek vengeance for the death of the only truly honourable man he had ever known. Donel looked at him with concern and touched his shoulder to get his attention.

Tarja flinched and stood up so quickly the sergeant drew back from him in fear.

'Spread out. Search the caverns. Whoever did this is still down here.'

Nobody questioned him. The Defenders dispersed quickly, swords at the ready, and began searching again. Tarja stared at the gruesome carnage for a moment then turned away. Symin stood behind him, immobilised by shock. He looked as if he'd suddenly lost his innocence; as if he had only just realised this was not a game.

'*Why?*'

'Because they could,' Tarja told him. 'Because Jenga personified the Defenders. Because they knew they'd lost the Citadel and they wanted to make a point. Take your pick.'

'*Captain!*'

Tarja and Symin both turned at the cry. Donel and two of the Defenders were returning. Between them they dragged a struggling man, but it was not a Karien they had caught. It was a Defender. His uniform was sprayed with a dark pattern of blood. Disbelief warred with a sort of resigned acceptance of the inevitable as Tarja realised who it was.

'Gawn.'

The man stared at him with the wild eyes of a fanatic. Tarja had known him on the southern border and thought him a poor example of the Defenders then. He could not imagine what had brought him to this. Nor did he particularly care. He carefully and deliberately handed his sword to Symin, then as Donel held him, he backhanded the younger captain across the face. All the rage he could not voice was behind the blow.

Gawn's head snapped back and he slumped in the arms of the sergeant, but when he focused his eyes on Tarja again, he was smiling. 'That's your answer to everything, isn't it Tarja? Every time I get one up on you, you have to hit something.'

Tarja flew at him, determined to kill Gawn with his bare hands. It took Symin and two other men to pull him off. Donel hauled Gawn to his feet as the captain wiped away the blood from his nose. Symin flung himself between Tarja and Gawn, forcibly holding Tarja back.

'I know how you feel, Tarja,' Symin said urgently, as he strained to keep them apart. 'But don't let him get to you. He'll hang for this. Justice will be served.'

Tarja took a deep, deliberate breath and relaxed. He shook off the men around him, took a step backwards and held up his hands in a gesture of peace. Satisfied that he had averted cold-blooded murder, Symin nodded with relief and turned to issue his orders.

As soon as his back was turned, Tarja snatched his sword from the young captain's grasp and with one fluid movement he swung it in a wide arc. Nobody had time to stop him, or even cry out in protest. He sliced Gawn's head from his shoulders, barely missing Donel as the sergeant ducked under the blow. Blood sprayed the room in a fountain of death as Gawn's head landed with a sickening thump and rolled to a stop at Symin's feet.

Donel threw the headless body away from him in disgust and stood there, drenched in blood, staring at it in stunned disbelief. The other Defenders did not move, frozen in shock. Symin wore a look of absolute incredulity.

Tarja threw the sword atop Gawn's headless, twitching body.

'Justice has been served,' he said.

Without waiting for an answer, Tarja turned and walked back into the darkness of the caverns.

## 41

R'shiel reluctantly let go of Joyhinia's limp body as the full repercussions of her death hit. She slumped against the body and closed her eyes. Every muscle trembled and she was sweating profusely in the stuffy room. Brak squatted beside her.

'Are you all right?'

'No.'

She waited, expecting some snide remark, but he said nothing. She opened her eyes and looked at him curiously. 'What's this? No reprimand?'

'There was nothing you could have done.'

'At least we won't have to worry about deposing the First Sister,' Garet remarked, as he looked down dispassionately at the body and the spreading stain on the rug.

'It's far from over, Garet,' R'shiel warned.

'It is for the First Sister,' he shrugged. 'Now, if you will excuse me, we have some rather angry Karien dukes to take care of. Lieutenant, see that the body is removed and get that rug out of here, too.' He stepped back as the Defenders hastened to obey.

Brak stood up and held his hand out to her. 'There's nothing more you can do here, R'shiel.'

With a last look at Joyhinia's body, R'shiel took his hand as he pulled her to her feet. Garet led the way out of the First Sister's office and down the broad staircase into the street. When they emerged into the sunlight, they discovered that pandemonium had broken loose in the city. The streets were crowded with people being held back by a line of red-coated Defenders who strained against the surging mob. Garet Warner walked into the centre of the small clearing that his men had forced, to confront the six dukes of Karien who had invaded the Citadel. Their faces were pale, their eyes glazed with shock. The crowd was shouting at them. R'shiel could only make out some of the words but their mood was ugly. There were quite a few Sisters of the Blade among them who were stirring up the passions of the mob. Through the raucous melee she heard the words 'Karien pigs!' 'Murderers!' and a few other insults that shocked her with their crudeness.

She glanced at Brak who shrugged with resignation. 'You can't really blame them. The Defenders may have taken back the Citadel, but there's still a Karien army camped outside and a lot of people have lost a great deal since Medalon surrendered.'

A captain stepped forward to report to Garet. He spared R'shiel and Brak a curious glance then turned to the commandant.

'So it worked then?' Garet ask. There was no need to be specific.

'Yes, it worked,' the captain told him. 'Almost everything went according to plan.'

'Almost?' Brak asked with a raised brow.

'I'll explain later.'

Garet nodded and stepped forward to address the Karien dukes.

'What do you hope to achieve, Commandant?' one of them yelled before Garet could utter a word. 'You cannot hold out against our army.'

The man who shouted the question was a slender knight standing at the front of the Kariens with a canny look in his eyes. He seemed a little less overawed than his companions.

'Who's that?' she asked Garet.

'I am Lord Roache,' the duke announced, in answer to R'shiel's question. 'And you cannot imagine the destruction you have brought down on Medalon by your actions.'

'The Overlord will protect us!' another duke blustered, but his words lacked conviction. He was a large man, but he carried more flab than muscle on his big-boned frame. He looked ridiculous standing in the street in a long flowing red nightgown. The Defenders must have dragged him from his bed.

'I hope for your sake your king is as keen to keep you alive as you seem to think your god is,' Garet remarked. Then he turned to the captain in charge of the squad guarding the dukes. 'Put them in with the others for now.'

The officer saluted as R'shiel turned away from them, too tired and stunned by Joyhinia's death to care much about what became of the Karien dukes. She looked around for Brak and found him standing near the edge of the crowd, waiting for someone to push through to the front. For a moment the line of Defenders broke to let another officer through. R'shiel's disappointment fell away from her as she realised who it was.

'Tarja!'

She ran to him, but stopped short when she saw the expression on his face. He was splattered with blood and his eyes were haunted. He showed no evident pleasure at the sight of her.

'R'shiel.'

'Tarja, I . . .' She couldn't think of anything to say. He was whole, and unharmed, despite the blood which she guessed was not his, but there was nothing welcoming in his demeanour.

'You killed Joyhinia, I hear.'

'She killed herself,' Garet corrected, coming up behind them. 'That's not your blood, I hope, Captain.'

'No.'

'Good. Then let's get these streets cleared.' He turned to another officer and began issuing orders to push the mob back. It was a futile gesture. There were too many people and not enough Defenders.

R'shiel watched their useless efforts as the crowd shouted obscenities at the Kariens. Someone hurled something at Lord Roache. He ducked instinctively as a piece of rotting melon landed harmlessly against the steps. Hurt from Tarja's cold reception and distressed beyond belief by the fact that Loclon had eluded her, she felt her ire rising. Impatiently she grabbed at the power and turned on the crowd.

'*Go back to your homes!*' she shouted, using the power to amplify her voice. '*Leave now, before I show you what the Harshini are really capable of!*'

The crowd was stunned into silence. Faced with her Harshini black eyes that blazed with rage, the citizens of the Citadel had a sudden change of heart. With barely a muttered protest, they began to melt away. The Defenders took advantage of the impetus she had provided to push the rest back. Her eyes still fiercely burning, she turned to Tarja and Garet. Tarja took an involuntary step backwards as if she repelled him.

She could not believe how much that one small step hurt.

Perhaps Brak sensed something of her pain, or perhaps it was because he was linked to the same power. He stepped in front of her, blocking her view of Tarja.

'Let it go, R'shiel,' he said softly. 'There's no need for it.'

Reluctantly, she did as he bid. He smiled at her. 'Good girl.'

'Don't treat me like a child, Brak.'

'Then don't behave like one.'

She glared at him for a moment, then nodded. 'It's all right. I'll be fine.'

'Are you sure?'

Taking a deep breath, she squared her shoulders. 'Yes. I'm sure.'

He waited until he was satisfied that she had her emotions – and more importantly, her power – under control, then stepped back. Tarja was talking to Garet Warner. He seemed determined not to look at her. Garet turned as they approached, his expression concerned for the first time since they had begun this coup.

'What's wrong?' Brak asked.

'As the captain said, *almost* everything went according to plan. The Sisters are demanding they take control, but we can deal with them. Unfortunately, Jenga's dead.'

'And what about Loclon?' R'shiel demanded. 'Did they find him?'

'I told you days ago that no one has seen him since the last Gathering. He's a deserter. He's probably halfway to Fardohnya by now.'

'No! You don't understand!' She turned to Brak desperately. Only he could fully appreciate what she feared.

'We have to find him,' Brak agreed.

'I've got a lot more to worry about than one miserable deserter, R'shiel. This,' he pointed out with a wave of his arm that encompassed the chaotic street before them, 'is just the beginning.'

'Then I'll find him on my own!'

'I can't allow that.'

'I don't recall asking your permission.'

'Let her go, Garet,' Tarja said. His voice was dull, as if the life had gone out of him. 'She needs to do this and there's nothing at present that requires her help.'

'Very well, go look for Loclon, if you must. We've more important things to take care of. If you tire of such a fruitless task and you wish to join us later, we'll be in the First Sister's office.'

Garet turned away in annoyance. Tarja followed him without looking back. R'shiel wasn't sure if he'd spoken up because he supported her, or was simply trying to be rid of her.

At that moment, she didn't care. Joyhinia was dead, which meant Loclon was free to return to his own body. Somewhere in the Citadel, he was on the loose. She was determined that he would not escape her this time. Not if she had to tear the Citadel apart stone by stone to find him.

d. Garet could deal with them. The commandant
ood at that sort of thing.

'e've moved all the Kariens we rounded up into the
iitheatre, sir,' the officer reported.

was Symin, the young captain who had rescued him
en? Only this morning?

've assigned enough men to see they don't escape, but
e pretty thin on the ground elsewhere because of it.
e priests have been separated from the others. We're
ding them in the caverns.'

'What did you do with their staves?'

'We piled them up in one of the caverns. I posted a
uard on them. They look pretty valuable.'

'A priest doesn't like being separated from his staff,'
Tarja remarked, still staring thoughtfully out of the dark
windows.

'That's true enough,' Symin agreed. 'They made quite
a fuss when we confiscated them. But the rest of the
Kariens are docile enough. I think the weather has damp-
ened their spirits somewhat. I told them they'll be released
in the morning if they want to go home.'

'Who's in command there now?'

'Captain Grannon.'

'Then go and get some sleep, Captain. You've earnt it.'

'Thank you, sir. Goodnight. Goodnight, Tarja.'

'Goodnight Symin,' he said.

The captain saluted without meeting Tarja's eye and
left the office. Tarja watched him go with a frown.

'He doesn't know whether to worship you or run like
hell,' Garet remarked.

'I'm glad you think it's funny.'

The commandant leaned back in the First Sister's chair
and stretched wearily. 'Stop feeling so bloody remorseful,

# 42

Tarja leaned his head tiredly against the cool pan
on the long windows of the First Sister's offic
would have to think of another name for it s
thought idly. The position of First Sister no longer

The Citadel was quiet. A light rain blurred the
and trickled down the small panes of glass, distortin
world outside. He could see nothing in the darkness
squares of yellow light from the windows of the libi
building across the street. There were Defenders on gu
there tonight to prevent the Sisters of the Blade gainir
entrance and destroying documents they didn't want t
fall into the hands of the Defenders.

Harith had already been to see them, demanding that
Garet hand over the Citadel, now that the Defenders
had control. She had been shocked beyond words when
he refused. It had been a fairly ugly confrontation, and
although they had won this round, Tarja knew the
Sisters of the Blade would not fade into oblivion quietly.
In a way, they were liable to be more trouble than the
Kariens.

He heard the door open but didn't turn to see who

Tarja. Gawn deserved to die. I'd have done the same thing in your place. No . . . actually, that's not true. I'd have tortured the miserable little bastard for a month or two before I killed him. That's the difference between you and me. You prefer pure, uncomplicated justice. I'm more of "the end justifies the means" ilk. And I'm very patient. I can wait a very long time before I get my vengeance.'

'Time is one thing we don't have,' Tarja reminded him. 'The Kariens outside will attack as soon as they realise what's happened, and then we're going to be facing an even bigger problem.'

'That's where your Harshini friends come in,' Garet mused. 'I hope R'shiel remembered to get a message to Hythria before she went chasing off on her damned fool quest to find Loclon.'

There was no point trying to explain to Garet why R'shiel thought finding Loclon was so important, so Tarja let the matter drop. He moved away from the window and took one of the deep leather chairs on the other side of the desk, stretching his feet out. He rubbed eyes that were gritty with exhaustion and looked at Garet questioningly.

'So, what happens now? With Jenga gone, we've no one to take command – unless you fancy the job.'

The commandant shook his head. 'Not me. I have neither the ability nor the presence to hold Medalon together. We need someone the people know. I've made a career of keeping a low profile. If you issued a decree in my name, the entire population would stare at you blankly and say "Garet *who*?"'

'Then who else is there?'

'There's you.'

'That is not even remotely amusing, Garet.'

'I wasn't joking.'

'Nobody would follow me, even if I wanted the job, which I don't.'

'You underestimate yourself, my friend. You are the most notorious Defender that has ever lived and your reputation is that of a fearless—'

'Don't be absurd!'

'Hear me out, Tarja. You deserted the Defenders because you refused to serve under Joyhinia, and she turned out to be the most savage, uncompromising bitch that ever put on the First Sister's mantle. You publicly defied her. You helped the rebels who challenged her. You got caught. You escaped. You fought the Kariens and then led the resistance against them, too. Every ill-advised, impetuous, accidental thing you've done since you refused to swear that oath to Joyhinia has made you a hero, like it or not.'

'That's ridiculous!'

'As a matter of fact, it is, but it doesn't make it any less real. You are the only man in Medalon the Defenders, the people and the pagan rebels will follow. You count the High Prince of Hythria as a friend and we're going to need him. He'll come to our aid because *you* asked him. I'm damn sure he wouldn't come if I did.' Garet smiled then and added, 'Even half the damned Sisterhood will fall in behind you – at least the younger ones who devoted a good part of their Novitiate to trying to catch your eye.'

Even Tarja allowed himself a smile over that. As a Cadet, Garet Warner had once called him in to his office to inform him that he and Georj were no longer permitted to study in the library when the Novices were in class, as Sister Mahina considered their presence 'disruptive'. His smile faded and he shook his head.

'I don't want to rule Medalon, Garet. Not even temporarily.'

'I know. That's why I'm offering you the job. If I thought for a moment that you had your eye on the post, I would never have mentioned it. We need someone who cares about setting things right. I've had enough of people who hunger after power for its own sake. That's the whole point of getting rid of the Sisterhood.'

'You can't make me do it.'

'Fine. Then give me a name. Find me one man in the whole of Medalon that can do what you can do, and I'll never bring the subject up again.'

Tarja sighed. 'Let me think about it.'

'We don't have time. Tomorrow morning, when the Citadel wakes up, we'd better be damned sure we know what we're doing or Harith will have the Sisters of the Blade back in charge so fast your feet won't even touch the ground between here and the nearest gallows.'

Before he could answer, the door banged open and R'shiel stormed into the office with Brak on her heels. She barely even glanced at him, for which Tarja was grateful. The inevitable confrontation between them had once more been delayed. Her quest to find Loclon had kept her out of his way all day.

'How nice of you to join us, demon child,' Garet remarked.

R'shiel did not seem to notice the sarcasm. 'I just spoke to Symin. He said you're going to release the Kariens tomorrow.'

'That's always been our plan.'

'You can't open the gate. I haven't found Loclon yet.'

'I'm not going to hold two thousand Kariens prisoner on your whim, R'shiel. The priests and the dukes will be enough.'

'This is not a whim. He's more dangerous than you know. We have to find him.'

'Then I'll post extra men on the gate to see that he doesn't slip through, but the Kariens are going, R'shiel, and that's final.'

She looked over her shoulder at Brak, seeking his support. She did not look at Tarja.

'I can appreciate your desire to get the Kariens out of the Citadel, Commandant,' Brak agreed reasonably. 'But R'shiel is right. Loclon poses a danger that you would be unwise to ignore.'

'A danger to whom, exactly?' Garet asked. 'He's your enemy, not mine.'

'Don't you *understand*?' R'shiel cried in frustration. 'Loclon was the one controlling Joyhinia's body! It was Loclon who was aiding the Kariens ever since we tried to remove Joyhinia at the Gathering. Founders, Garet, he's the single, most heinous traitor ever to draw breath in Medalon!'

Suddenly she turned on Tarja. 'Tell him, Tarja! Tell him I speak the truth!'

The pain in her eyes almost broke his heart. She needed his support. But finding Loclon in the Citadel would be like sifting through a pile of sand looking for one particular grain.

'She's right,' he admitted. 'He's a traitor, and if we can find him, we should.' R'shiel smiled at him gratefully, which made him feel even worse, knowing what he was going to say next. 'But we can't afford to hold those Kariens. We don't have the men to guard them, or the resources to feed them. Until we're relieved, every mouthful of food in the Citadel is going to be rationed. I'm sorry, R'shiel. I know what this means to you and I want to see Loclon brought to justice as much as you do, but I agree with Garet. We open the gates tomorrow.'

She stared at him, stunned by his response. Brak stepped forward and placed his hand on her shoulder, as if preparing to restrain her. Tarja wondered for a moment about the half-breed Harshini. For all his laconic scepticism, he seemed to truly care for R'shiel. There was a time when Tarja thought Brak loathed her.

'There! You have it from the Lord Defender, himself. The Kariens leave first thing tomorrow.'

'From *who*?' R'shiel demanded, shaking Brak off.

'The Lord Defender,' Garet repeated calmly.

'*Tarja* is the Lord Defender? When did *that* happen?'

'Just now. The position became available, and as the ranking officer in the Citadel, I decided to appoint him.'

'You're going to let Loclon get away with everything he's done to you, to me, to Medalon, just so you can be the Lord Defender?' She was trembling with suppressed rage. Her violet eyes glistened with unshed tears.

'It's not like that, R'shiel.'

'Isn't it?' she asked bitterly. 'You've been marked as the next Lord Defender since the day you joined the Cadets, Tarja. Everybody in the whole damned Citadel knew you'd eventually get the job. Well, I hope the title makes you happy. I never thought you would stoop so low to take it.'

She turned and fled the room. Tarja expected Brak to follow her, but he didn't move.

'Sort this out now, Tarja,' he advised. 'It'll only get worse if you don't.'

Tarja stared at him for a moment then swore softly as he rose to his feet to follow her.

\*　　\*　　\*

'R'shiel!' he called as she ran down the wide marble stair-case leading to the dark deserted foyer. 'Damn it, R'shiel! Wait!'

She turned to look up at him. The torches set high in the wall sconces cast deceptive shadows over her face. He stopped several steps above her, panting from the chase.

'I didn't mean to hurt you, R'shiel. I'm sorry.'

'No, you're not.'

'Then what do you want me to say? Don't you think I want Loclon as much as you do? But Garet's right, and you damned well know it. We can't hold the Kariens here.'

'There was a time when you would have done anything for me.'

He found he couldn't answer her. Memories flooded through him, reminding him that she spoke an awful truth he was not prepared to face. She studied his face, reading the conflict, the confusion, and even the self-loathing that had plagued him since he recovered from the wound he received trying to save her from the Kariens.

'That time is past, now, isn't it?' she said softly, bitterly. She knew about the geas, he realised. And that he was no longer bound by it.

'R'shiel . . .' he murmured helplessly. He had no idea what to say. No words to express what he felt.

She nodded, as if accepting the inevitable. 'The irony is, I saved your life because I couldn't bear the thought of being parted from you and I ended up losing you, anyway. Did you ever truly love me, Tarja?'

For a long, dreadful moment, he didn't answer her. In the end, he settled for the truth. 'I don't know.'

She looked away for a moment, perhaps to prevent him seeing her pain. When she turned back to him, her eyes were cold.

'Free the Kariens if you must, Tarja. I'll just have to keep a watch on the gate for Loclon myself.'

'We'll find him, R'shiel,' he promised.

She shook her head sadly. 'No, Tarja, *we* won't be doing anything together any more. I'll find Loclon and deal with him on my own. You're the Lord Defender now. You have Medalon to rule.'

Like a man donning chain mail before a battle, she had surrounded herself with an impenetrable shell, constructed of bitterness and pain. Relief warred with a sense of inexplicable loss as he watched the transformation. He knew then that the R'shiel he had known was gone forever. In her place was a hard, determined and powerful young woman who would never let anyone close to her again.

As she turned and slowly walked down the stairs away from him, Tarja felt he was staring at a stranger.

## 43

For a long time, R'shiel walked blindly through the deserted streets of the Citadel, paying no attention to where she was going. She was calm – even serene – uncaring of the light rain that fell softly on the glistening cobblestones. Her mind did not seethe with grief for her loss, or rail at the tragedy of unrequited love. She was numb; totally devoid of any human emotion that could rise up and cause her anguish.

R'shiel wondered if this was what it felt like to be fully Harshini.

After a while, she discovered that her wandering had led her to the Lesser Hall of the Citadel. Without any conscious decision, she climbed the steps and pulled open the massive bronze door, letting it swing shut behind her with a hollow boom that echoed through the empty darkness. Night was trapped within its walls, the whitewashed ceiling lost in the shadows. She tried to recall the picture Brak had painted in her mind of the Great Hall, the Temple of the Gods, when it had dazzled the world with its glory and wondered if this smaller temple once dedicated to the Goddess of Love had been just as impressive.

She couldn't do it. The Lesser Hall was nothing more than a big, cavernous room with no life or beauty to recommend it.

'Why, Kalianah?' she asked the darkness.

A pillar of light pierced the shadows as she named the goddess. Assuming the form of a child, the Goddess of Love crossed her arms and glared at her. R'shiel stared at the goddess, oblivious to the aura of adoration that surrounded the pale little girl whose feet hovered just above the ground.

'Why?'

'Don't you know that it's extremely ill mannered to summon the gods as if they were—'

'Why did you make Tarja fall in love with me?'

'Oh!' the Goddess said with the guilty air of a child caught playing with something she was forbidden to touch. 'That.'

'Yes, *that*! Why did you do it? What gives you the right to interfere in my life?'

'I was only trying to help.'

'You're supposed to be the Goddess of Love. How can you cause such pain?'

'Well, whose fault is *that*?' the Goddess asked petulantly. '*You* destroyed the geas, not me.'

'How?'

'You asked the demons to substitute for Tarja's blood. How was I supposed to know what you were planning?'

'You sent Dace with a message, reminding me I could use the demons to heal him.'

'Yes, but I didn't expect you to use them like that! Any Harshini could have told you something like that would break my geas.'

'Perhaps they would have, if they'd known about it.'

'Well, Brak certainly knew. He was there when I did it. Why don't you ask him why he didn't say anything?'

The news surprised her. He had never warned her, never even hinted that something was amiss.

'I want your promise, Kalianah, that you will never, *ever*, do anything like this to me again. Or to Tarja.'

'You can have that!' she sniffed indignantly. 'If this is what you call gratitude, I'll never even think of trying to help you again. Then you'll see how hard it is to love anybody without my blessing!'

'I don't want to love anybody, Kalianah, so I don't mind at all.'

Kalianah's eyes narrowed and she began to change form. A tall, fair-haired young woman suddenly took the place of the little girl.

'You can live without love?' the goddess asked. 'Is that what you think? You might be able to tame the God of War with your meddling, R'shiel, but my power is beyond your reach.'

'What makes you think I'm trying to tame the God of War?'

'I am not blind, demon child. Hythria and Fardohnya are united for the first time in centuries. Zegarnald already grows weaker. But don't think that by hardening your heart you can do the same to the Goddess of Love. Humans prosper without war. They will shrivel and die without me.'

'Do you personally take a hand in every romance? Do you make every mother love her child, every man love his brother?'

'Of course not!'

'Then why do they need you?'

'They need the hope I represent.'

'What hope?' she demanded. 'You're a spoiled, petulant child who helps or hinders the course of love on nothing more than impulse. You interfere because you can, Kalianah, not because some human petitioned you for aid and you found his cause worthy.'

Kalianah was incapable of real anger, but she was as close to it as her essence allowed. 'Your task is to destroy Xaphista, demon child, not impose your own atheist bigotry on the rest of us. Do what you are destined for and leave the Primal Gods to do what we are meant for.'

'And once I've destroyed Xaphista, what then?'

The goddess looked away, unable to meet her eye. 'That is not for me to decide.'

'You decide who will love me easily enough.'

'It is not for me to decide,' Kalianah insisted stubbornly. 'And you should not waste time dwelling on such things. You must turn your attention to Xaphista. If you devoted as much time to defeating him as you do to making things difficult for the Primal Gods, he'd be as weak as a newborn pup by now.'

'Xaphista will weaken.'

'Not in your lifetime,' Kalianah scoffed. 'You have to tackle the core of his power, not nibble at the edges like a terrier trying to chew up a mountain. If you don't, then the moment Xaphista realises what you're doing, he will fight back with every iota of power at his disposal.'

'Then what do you suggest I do, *Divine* One?'

'If I knew that, demon child, I would have done something about Xaphista myself!'

Kalianah vanished, plunging the hall back into darkness. R'shiel stood unmoving, staring at the space where she had been. Something Kalianah said bothered her, but the thought was too elusive to grasp. Something about tackling the core of Xaphista's power . . .

With a flash of inspiration, R'shiel knew what she had to do. Kalan had given her the first inkling in Greenharbour. She had no idea exactly *how* she was going to do it, but the secret of bringing Xaphista to his knees was suddenly so obvious that she could not believe she had taken until now to realise it.

R'shiel pounded on Brak's door until he opened it.

'What is it? Have you found Loclon?'

'There's something I need to ask you.'

'Do you have any idea what time it is, R'shiel?'

'What do you care?' she asked, pushing past him into the apartment that Garet had allocated him. 'You're Harshini. You don't need to sleep.'

He closed the door and turned to look at her with a frown. 'We don't need as much sleep as humans, R'shiel. That doesn't mean we don't need to sleep at all. A point you would do well to remember. When was the last time *you* slept?'

'I can't remember.'

'Well, I can. It was four days ago. I'm seven hundred years old. I need my rest.'

She smiled at him. He was fully dressed and alert and every candle in the room was alight. The fire was crackling cheerfully and an open book lay on the table beside the large chair near the hearth. He had not been sleeping.

'Well, demon child, what is so damned important that it can't wait until morning?'

'I have to destroy Xaphista.'

'Really?' he asked with wide-eyed astonishment. 'And

it's taken you exactly *how* long to come to this startling conclusion?'

'Don't make fun of me, Brak. You know what I mean.'

'Yes, I do, but I can't understand why it's so important at this hour of the night.'

'I think I've figured out a way to do it.'

'How?' he asked, with no trace of mockery.

'I was just talking to Kalianah. She said I had to tackle the core of his power, not nibble at the edges like a terrier trying to chew up a mountain.'

Brak smiled. 'That sounds like Kali. What else were you two discussing?'

'We had words,' R'shiel admitted, 'about what she did to Tarja.'

'That must have been interesting.'

'She said you knew about it,' she accused.

He nodded and moved away from the door. R'shiel followed him with her eyes, but he was impossible to read when he didn't want her to know what he was feeling.

'Why didn't you tell me?'

'It wouldn't have made a difference.'

'How do you know?'

'Because I've seen it before. A geas is no small thing R'shiel. Tarja was smitten and there was nothing to be done about it.'

'What about me?'

'You were never under Kalianah's geas. Not even the Goddess of Love would have risked such a thing for the demon child.'

'But I loved him,' she said, afraid her voice had allowed some hint of the pain she was trying so hard to deny.

'You didn't need Kalianah for that R'shiel. You grew up worshipping the ground Tarja walked on.'

'If she hadn't interfered, would he . . . ?'

'Would he have truly loved you in return?' Brak finished for her with a shrug. 'I don't know.'

'He despises me now.'

'No, he doesn't. He just doesn't know how to cope with what's happened. The fact that he doesn't actually believe in the gods who did this to him won't make it any easier on him, either.' He poured two cups of wine and crossed the room, holding one of them out to her. 'He'll get over it eventually. Drink up. Lost love always looks better through the bottom of a glass.'

'I don't want a drink.'

'Well I do, and it's bad form to drink alone. Humour me.'

She took the cup and sipped the wine sullenly, letting its warmth spread through her. Despite Brak's assurances, it made absolutely no difference to how she felt. Brak resumed his seat by the fire and took a long swig from his glass.

'So, are you going to tell me what this brilliant idea is, or do we have to keep rehashing the story about poor old Tarja for a few more hours?'

'Why do you take such delight in ridiculing my pain?'

'Because you're a lot tougher than you realise, demon child. I know you're hurting, but deep down you knew this would happen. As soon as Xaphista told you about the geas, you knew that Tarja didn't love you willingly. For all your human failings, you have an innate sense of what is right. It's part of being Harshini. You might lament losing him, but you know, in your heart, that it's better this way. The sooner you admit it openly, then the sooner you'll get over it.'

'Better?' she asked bitterly. 'How could it be better?'

'Tarja was the chink in your armour, R'shiel. Xaphista would have exploited that weakness to its fullest. Don't you remember what you told me about Xaphista when he tried to seduce you into joining him? He used Tarja then, and you almost gave in.'

R'shiel had no wish to be reminded of that dreadful journey through Medalon, but she could not deny the truth of what Brak told her. She sank into the chair on the other side of the fire and stared at the flames, not wanting to give him the satisfaction of seeing that she knew he was right. She need not have bothered. Brak knew her too well.

'A moment ago you were bursting to tell me how you could bring Xaphista down. Do we really have time for you to sulk?'

She hurled the goblet at him. He ducked it easily and the glass shattered harmlessly against the far wall.

He smiled. 'Feel better now?'

'I hate you.'

'No, you don't. You just hate the fact that I'm right.'

'It's the same thing.'

Brak sighed, as if his patience was wearing thin. 'Ask me what you came to ask, R'shiel. I really do intend to get some sleep in what's left of this night.'

'I have to attack the core of Xaphista's power,' she told him with considerably less enthusiasm than she had had when she burst into his room earlier.

'So you said before.'

'We have to go after his *priests*.'

Brak frowned. 'You won't turn a single Karien priest, R'shiel. Even if you managed to win their minds to your cause, Xaphista owns their souls. Each priest is linked to the Overlord through his staff.'

'Then that is their weakness. If I can use that link, I can reach every priest in Karien and cripple Xaphista overnight.'

'In theory, yes, but how are you going to do it?'

'Kalan had an idea that set me thinking. I have to get a close look at a staff, though. I want to see how it works.'

'I'll tell you how it works, R'shiel. Very, very well. Don't you recall what happened the last time you had a close encounter with a Staff of Xaphista?'

'I'm never likely to forget. But you told me the staff *destroys* magic. Well, if it can do that, then the staff has to *use* magic, too. And if it can use magic, maybe I can do something to change its purpose.'

Brak sighed and climbed to his feet. 'Come on then.'

'Where are we going?'

'You want to take a look at a Staff of Xaphista? Garet Warner has more than a hundred of them piled up in a cavern under the amphitheatre.'

She jumped to her feet in astonishment. 'You think it'll work?'

'No. I think it's the most misguided excuse for a plan that you've ever come up with, but I know you won't let it go until you've discovered that for yourself.'

She hugged him impulsively. 'I knew you'd help me.'

He pushed her away gruffly. 'Don't get too excited, R'shiel. I'm doing this to prove you wrong.'

'I'm not wrong. I know this will work.'

He picked up his cloak from the back of the chair where he had discarded it earlier and looked at her sceptically. 'A few more burns from touching those staffs might convince you otherwise, demon child.'

\* \* \*

Two determined-looking Defenders barred the entrance into the tunnel that led into the caverns under the amphitheatre. R'shiel demanded entry to no avail, but the ruckus brought out the officer in charge to see what all the fuss was about. He recognised R'shiel and frowned. Shorter than the average Defender and prematurely grey, he was renowned for his organisational abilities, rather than his fighting skills. He was also an old friend of Tarja's.

'You can't see the prisoners, R'shiel.'

'We don't want to see the Kariens, Captain Grannon. We just want to have a look at the staffs you took from the priests.'

He frowned, but could see no harm in her request. As far as Grannon was concerned, the staffs were just useless, if rather valuable, religious frippery.

'Very well. Go with them, Charal. And stay with them,' he added with a disturbing lack of trust.

The sergeant took a torch from the wall and led them through the tunnel into the caverns on the left. The staffs were piled in a careless heap in a room near the entrance. There were another two Defenders posted outside, who stood aside to let them enter. Charal went in first and held the torch high. The flames reflected off the staff heads like myriad tiny jewels. R'shiel and Brak stared at the pile, careful not to get too close.

'Can you pick one up for me?' she asked Charal.

'Captain Grannon didn't say you weren't allowed to touch them.'

'We can't touch them.' Brak explained. 'They're specifically designed to harm anyone with Harshini blood.'

Charal looked sceptical, but he turned to the wall and dropped the torch into a metal bracket before bending down and picking up a staff at random. He thrust it at R'shiel, who took an involuntary step backwards.

'Careful!'

Swallowing a sudden lump of fear, R'shiel stepped closer and studied the hated symbol of Xaphista's power. The shaft had been treated with something that stained it black and made the metal suck in the light around it. The head of the staff was made of gold; shaped like a five-pointed star and intersected by a lightning bolt crafted of silver. Each point of the star was set with crystal and in the centre of the star was a larger gem of the same stone.

Charal looked at the staff curiously, his eyes alight with greed. 'Are they real diamonds, do you think?'

'No,' Brak said. 'They're crystals of some sort.'

'They look like the Seeing Stone.'

Brak stared at her. 'What?'

'I said they look like the Seeing Stone. You know, the big crystal they have in the Temple at Greenharbour?'

'I know what the Seeing Stone is. Bring it closer to the light.'

Charal moved the staff until it caught the flames of the torch. R'shiel stepped closer, studied it for a moment, and then tentatively reached out towards the staff head.

'What are you doing?' Brak cried in horror.

'Putting a theory to the test.'

She lightly brushed her fingertip over the centre crystal. No bolt of agony shot through her, not even a whisper of pain.

'How . . . ?' he gasped in astonishment.

'I didn't touch the staff, just the crystal. Try it yourself.'

Reluctantly, Brak reached out to touch the sparkling

jewel, jerking his hand back instinctively in anticipation of the torture he was certain awaited him. When nothing happened, he gingerly laid his finger on the stone and looked at R'shiel in wonder.

'I don't understand.'

'Watch,' she commanded. He stepped back as she reached for the staff once more, this time with her eyes blackened by the power she drew. She placed her finger on the centre crystal and the room flared with light as every stone in every staff on the floor began to glow in response to her touch. Charal dropped the staff with a cry of alarm. Brak jumped clear of it as the room was plunged back into relative darkness as soon as her contact with the crystal was severed.

'But how . . . ?' Brak asked, looking at the now quiescent pile of staffs that lay on the floor beside them.

'I think they're chips off one of the missing Seeing Stones.'

'I hate to admit it, R'shiel, but you may have been right, after all.'

'I can use the staffs to influence the priests, can't I?'

He glanced at the pile. 'That's what you came to ask me? I suppose. Provided you can access a Seeing Stone to control them.'

'The Citadel's Seeing Stone is lost,' she reminded him, glancing at the pile of staffs. 'But Kalan said it couldn't be destroyed. It has to be somewhere.'

He did not seem to share her optimism. 'I suppose, although where you would hide something as large as a Seeing Stone is beyond me. And have you considered the possibility that these crystals might be all that's left of the Citadel's Stone?'

'I'm guessing if a Seeing Stone was broken down into

smaller stones, it's the one from Talabar. The Sisterhood would only care about destroying it or hiding it. Only the Fardohnyans would think of selling it.'

Brak nodded thoughtfully. 'Which would explain Hablet's determination to keep the Harshini out of Fardohnya. He wouldn't want us to realise what had happened to it.'

'And only a god would have the power to break the Stone up. It makes sense, I suppose, although it must have cost Karien a fortune. I always wondered how Fardohnya got so rich so quickly. But what about Loclon?'

'We'll look for him, but without help we're not going to find him.' Her expression hardened. 'The new Lord Defender has other priorities.'

Brak studied her determined expression and shrugged. 'All right then, that just leaves one rather pertinent question to be answered.'

'What's that?'

'Where does one hide several tons of magic crystal?'

# 44

Loclon jerked back to consciousness with a start, and for a long time could not decide where he was. His mind was filled with so many images, so much pain, that he could not gather his thoughts into anything remotely resembling coherent thought. He stared at the strange room, at the heavy drapes over the bed and the softly glowing walls, trying to recall how he came to be there. His head was weighted down with pain and he could not move his limbs. He could not even remember who he was.

It came to him, after a time, although how long was impossible to judge. He gradually remembered being Joyhinia Tenragan. He remembered the power he had wielded in her name. He remembered R'shiel standing over him, demanding that he live.

And he remembered dying.

The feeling stayed with him like a shadow looming over his soul. The pain seemed almost irrelevant when compared with the overwhelming terror he experienced when he recalled throwing himself on some nameless Defender's sword in the First Sister's office to escape the fury in R'shiel's eyes.

In hindsight, it was the most courageous thing he'd ever done – perhaps the *only* courageous thing he'd ever done.

He did not lament the death of Joyhinia, and his grief was inspired more by annoyance than guilt. He had lost the only true taste of power he was ever likely to have. Now he was nothing more than a fugitive.

As that thought occurred to him, he experienced a moment of blind panic. A fugitive was exactly what he was and he knew that R'shiel would not rest until he had been found. He had to get out of here, out of this room, out of the Citadel.

Loclon tried lifting his head and was appalled to find the task almost beyond him. His body had lain dormant for months and the muscles had wasted almost to the point of atrophy. He had no strength, no control, not even the ability to push himself off the bed.

It had never occurred to Loclon that his body might be wasting away in his absence. He knew it was alive – and as long as his body lived, so did he. Mathen had assured him the priests were taking care of it, but he had never been permitted to view the body himself, the priests claiming such a confrontation would undo whatever magic they had worked to transfer his mind into Joyhinia's body. To awaken, in this thin, emaciated body, with barely enough strength to lift his head from the pillow, seemed the ultimate irony.

R'shiel could not have planned it better if she tried.

A sense of urgency overwhelmed him, for a moment swamping even his despair at finding his body so useless. R'shiel was looking for him. She would not rest until she had him in her power.

Anger warred with fear as he thought of R'shiel. She

had no right to come back, he decided, even though, as Joyhinia, he had done everything in his power to ensure that she would. If the Kariens had done as they promised she would have been dead by now – burned at the stake in Yarnarrow for the Harshini sorcerer she was. But not even the Karien god could hold her, and Loclon was not so foolish as to think that if she possessed the strength of purpose to face down a god that he could escape her wrath.

That thought finally spurred him to action. With a panic-driven burst of strength, he threw himself off the bed, landing heavily on the floor. He lay panting, exhausted by even that small effort. He could see the door, a mere five paces from where he had fallen. The distance stretched before him like a vast canyon.

For a long time, he simply lay there, gathering what little strength he had to cross the gap. He didn't think of anything but the urgency of his mission. He had died once already today. He did not intend to let it happen again.

Loclon pushed himself up onto his elbows and began the painstaking task of dragging his useless body towards the door. He had barely moved a pace across the floor when he heard footsteps in the hall outside. Terror lent him another burst of strength. He slithered painfully over the polished floorboards, filled with an unnamed dread. His arm slipped out from under him and he banged his chin, making black lights dance before his eyes. The door loomed in the distance, seemingly no closer, despite his desperate efforts. The footsteps drew closer, louder. Sweat beaded his brow and left clammy handprints on the floor as he clawed his way painstakingly forward.

He collapsed in exhaustion, his breathing ragged. Tears

of fear and frustration blurred his vision. The door might as well be on the other side of Medalon. He would never make it. Any moment now it would open and R'shiel would be standing there, ready to even the score for every insult, real or imagined, that he had inflicted on her. He sobbed with terror and stared at the panelled door; watched it open with a feeling akin to having hot lead poured into his stomach. The door slammed against the wall. Loclon let out an unintelligible cry for mercy; tasted the acrid smell of urine as his bladder let go.

'Oh, for the gods' sake, stop blubbering!' Mistress Heaner declared impatiently. 'Pick him up, Lork.'

The old woman looked down on him, staring at the spreading stain on the front of his loincloth in disgust. As usual, she was dressed in black, clutching an expensive cape around her shoulders. Her small eyes set amid the folds of her thin, leathery face were filled with distaste. Lork stepped forward and scooped Loclon up from the floor. Even he screwed up his nose.

'You should be grateful, Captain. They're turning the Citadel inside out looking for you.'

Loclon did not reply. He was too relieved by his rescue and too frightened by its source. Owing Mistress Heaner anything was dangerous in the extreme. She demanded a finger for an unpaid gambling debt. Loclon was afraid to think of what she would charge for his life.

Bathed and fed, Loclon began to feel better now he knew he was safely within the walls of Mistress Heaner's house. His only care was to hide until he could escape the Citadel.

Later that evening, Mistress Heaner came to his room. When she opened the door Loclon noted, with some alarm, that Lork was on guard outside, standing there with that implacable, witless expression that seemed to respond only to Mistress Heaner. There was a boy of about twelve with her, with sandy hair and a sly, but beautifully innocent face. Loclon remembered him as one of Mistress Heaner's more exotic playthings. Lork closed the door behind them and the boy carried the tray he was holding to the small table beside the bed. The tempting smell of roasted meat escaped from under the domed cover on the plate.

'The Defenders have control of the Citadel,' she told him as she lit the lamp. 'They've imposed a curfew until tomorrow at sunrise. You can go now, Alladan.'

'Who's the new First Sister?' he asked with a twinge of professional jealousy as the boy slipped silently from the room.

'There isn't one,' the old woman shrugged. 'Nor will there be, if you believe the rumours.'

'You mean the Defenders have taken over the Citadel? Without the Sisterhood?'

'So it would seem. I hear Garet Warner masterminded the whole thing. That's not surprising. He's a slimy little bastard. Jenga's dead though,' she added, with no more emotion than she might tell him of a change in the weather.

Loclon felt no remorse over the loss of the Lord Defender. 'So Warner's in charge?'

'He'll probably name himself Lord Defender in the morning.'

'I have to get out of the Citadel.'

Mistress Heaner nodded. 'Squire Mathen left instructions in case something like this happened. You're to be taken to Karien.'

Loclon's eyes narrowed suspiciously. 'Why?'

'Because you were the First Sister. You have information the Kariens will need to take back the Citadel.'

'There's a hundred thousand men outside the walls. They don't need me.'

'The Defenders are holding all the dukes hostage. There is an army out there, certainly, but no one to lead them.'

She spoke matter-of-factly; as if she were repeating some idle gossip about a neighbour, not telling him that his entire world was falling apart.

'Then she's still here?'

'Who? R'shiel? Oh yes, she's still in the Citadel.'

'She wants to kill me.'

'So would every Defender in the Corps, if he knew what you'd done,' Mistress Heaner pointed out with infuriating smugness. 'Fortunately for you, your brothers-in-arms don't believe in magic, therefore they're not likely to seek vengeance for an act they cannot conceive.'

'Can you get me out of here?'

She smiled. It was a cold, calculating smile. It made him shudder.

'For a price.'

'How much?'

'It's bad manners to discuss such things over a meal,' she replied, glancing around to ensure everything was to her satisfaction. She had put him in the Blue Room. The hint was not lost on Loclon. This was where he had killed that whore . . . what was her name? Peny? This was the room where Mistress Heaner found the leverage she needed to turn him into a traitor. 'We'll talk about it later.'

'How am I going to get out of the Citadel?' he asked, lifting the cover off the platter and nodding appreciatively. He was starving.

'Through the gate, how else?'

'But isn't it closed against the Kariens?'

'For the moment. They're opening it in the morning to let the Kariens go.'

Loclon looked up from the plate with astonishment. '*They're letting them go?*'

'They seem to think we're going to be under siege for quite some time,' Mistress Heaner shrugged. 'They've told the Kariens they can leave and anyone else who would prefer to go with them. I doubt they're planning on releasing the dukes, but they want to be rid of the rest of the Kariens. Clever thing to do, actually. A lot less mouths to feed.'

'R'shiel will be there,' Loclon predicted with dread certainty.

'Probably.'

'She'll recognise me.'

'Don't worry, Captain, we'll give the demon child something else to think about.' She walked back to the door and knocked on it twice. Lork opened it with a key. He was a prisoner, he realised with despair, but a prisoner with some value at least.

The question was: how much was Mistress Heaner going to charge?

## 45

Tarja assigned a squad of Defenders to aid R'shiel in her search for Loclon. He even made a point of picking men who knew Loclon on sight. It was a thoughtful gesture, but not enough for R'shiel to forgive him for opening the gate. Particularly when she learnt he had ordered the men to look for Loclon, but not hinder the Karien exodus. R'shiel wanted to stop every man leaving the Citadel. She wanted to examine each soldier and knight closely, search every wagon, every sack, and every woman's purse, to ensure that Loclon didn't get past her. When the officer in charge of the squad repeated his orders, R'shiel turned on her heel furiously and made her way straight to the First Sister's office.

Tarja met her rage with silent fortitude. He was wearing a new red jacket bearing the sword and shield insignia of the Lord Defender. Despite the fact that it was before sunrise, the First Sister's office was full of Defenders. They cleared a path for her warily and avoided her gaze. None of the Defenders in the office appeared concerned that Tarja had been promoted over them to the Lord Defender. They acted like men who were glad that the ultimate responsibility for their fates had been shifted to someone else. A small part of her understood how they felt. This coup was still very new, and although they controlled the Citadel, Medalon was a long way from being secure. If it fell apart on them, Tarja would bear the brunt of any reprisals.

'Garet said we could check everyone leaving the Citadel!'

'Actually, he said that we'd post extra men on the gate to see that Loclon doesn't slip past. There was never any suggestion that we would allow you to stop and search every single person trying to get through the gate.'

'There are thousands of people down there! We'll never find him!'

'Then I'm sorry, R'shiel. I've given you all the men I can spare.' His tone was implacable. It was as if he had assumed some of Jenga's dignified gravity along with his rank.

'And if I find Loclon? Your men *do* have orders to arrest him, don't they, my Lord Defender? Or did you want me to just give him a friendly pat on the back and wish him a safe journey?'

He frowned, impatient with her sarcasm. 'Take the men I gave you, or not, R'shiel. I've neither the time nor the inclination to argue about it.'

'Is this your idea of helping me?'

'Would you care to discover what *not* helping you feels like?'

They glared at each other for a tense moment.

'If he gets away from me, I'll never forgive you, you know that, don't you?'

'It's getting light out there,' he said, turning his attention to his men. 'If you want to be at the main gate when it opens, I suggest you get a move on.'

\*    \*    \*

The wind was biting when she emerged into the light on the broad ledge that circled the towering white walls of the Citadel. R'shiel had not been up here since she was a child, when Tarja had brought her to the walls to show her the rare spectacle of the high plains covered in snow. She was only five or six years old at the time and snow on the plains, while not unheard of, was unusual enough that she had cried out with delight at the sight of it. That Joyhinia had beaten her afterwards for sneaking out with Tarja had not lessened the thrill, and she had held on to the memory as she sobbed in her room, hungry and cold, her legs throbbing from the cane. She could remember thinking that it had all been worth every savage blow. It didn't matter that she had been sent to bed without dinner. She didn't even care when Joyhinia had declared that as she seemed to like the cold so much, she could get a taste of what it really felt like in the snow and had the fire in her room extinguished and the blankets removed. It didn't matter that her legs were black and blue. She had stood on the wall-walk in the still, cold air and looked out over the countryside blanketed in white, the shallow Saran River frozen with a thin coating of ice, and thought she was standing on top of the world.

A trace of the same feeling came back to her as she looked down, but this time no peaceful layer of snow softened the view. The plain crawled with humanity as far as the eye could see, even as far away as the small village of Kordale, whose smoking chimneys R'shiel could just make out in the distance. From this high up it was impossible to make out individual details, rather the ground below rippled like some strange, poisonous ocean that lapped at the walls of the Citadel.

'Are you all right?' Brak asked with concern.

'Why wouldn't I be?'

He didn't answer for a moment. He was sitting with his back to the wall with his booted feet stretched out in front of him on the ledge, cleaning his fingernails with the tip of his dagger. Scattered clouds left over from the rain during the night hung motionlessly in a sky tinted the colour of washed-out blood.

'If you happen to find Loclon, just be careful, will you?'

'What do you mean?'

'I mean that if you're planning to use your power to restrain him, try to do it as quickly as possible. You'll be drawing on the same power as Korandellan. He'll have to fight you for his share of it.'

Brak did not need to add that if she drew too much, Korandellan's ability to hold Sanctuary safely out of time would be compromised. She had seen his weary face in the Seeing Stone in Greenharbour. R'shiel knew how close to exhaustion he was.

'You make it sound as if I actually have control over it.' She closed her eyes, letting the chill air clear her mind then looked down from the wall-walk over the mass of humanity swarming to be let out of the Citadel. 'This is hopeless!'

'You knew that before you came here,' Brak pointed out.

'Aren't you going to help?'

'What do you want me to do?'

She muttered something unintelligible and looked back over the crowd. The Defenders were pushing the people back to clear a path for the gates to open. On the other side of the wall, the plain was littered with the Karien army. There was a sizeable gathering outside the gate, waiting for their comrades inside the Citadel to be released.

A truce had been arranged the previous day, although with their leaders now hostages in the Citadel, it had taken some time to sort out the Karien chain of command and find someone capable of making a decision. The wall-walk was lined with archers to discourage the Kariens from attempting to break the truce. The Defenders could not hope to fend off a well co-ordinated attack, but they were enough to deter the disorganised and bewildered Kariens from trying anything stupid. They seemed incapable of understanding that the Citadel was lost to them, or that their leaders had been taken prisoner. The Overlord would not allow such a thing.

'Isn't there something magic we can do?' she asked, turning her back to the Kariens.

He raised a brow at her. 'Something *magic?*'

'You know what I mean.'

Brak sighed with long-suffering patience. 'You still have no idea what you're dealing with, do you?'

'I don't want a lecture, Brak. I just want to know if there is anything we can do to find Loclon more easily.'

'You could make every person leaving tell the truth then ask their names as they pass through the gate,' he suggested.

'That won't work. Tarja won't let us stop them.' She was scanning the crowd and did not see Brak's smile.

'I was joking, R'shiel.'

'I'm beside myself with mirth. Do you have any other brilliant suggestions?'

'No.'

'Good.'

Brak sheathed his dagger then climbed to his feet and came to stand beside her. The gates swung open ponderously as the Defenders shouted orders to the crowd. The first to leave were the troopers that had been posted around the city, and they made up the bulk of the occupation force. They looked cold and miserable, having spent a night in the damp weather confined to the amphitheatre. Most of them were simple peasants dragged into this war because their masters owed a fealty to the Karien king. They were at the mercy of their god, their king and their dukes.

'They don't look very happy, do they?' Brak remarked.

'Can you blame them?'

'You're not feeling sorry for them, are you?'

'A little bit. Most of them would much rather be at home getting ready for the spring planting, I think. Not stranded here in a foreign country fighting a war they probably don't even understand.'

'Well, if you think the peasants are unhappy, imagine what that lot must be feeling.' Brak pointed up the street.

The next group waiting to be let through was the knights. Tarja had permitted them their mounts, but other than that, they were leaving empty handed. Their faces were cold and haughty, as if they were leaving of their own free will, not being forced out like beggars who couldn't pay the rent. Sir Andony sat at the head of the small column. R'shiel could not make out the others from this height. She watched them curiously, wondering what they were thinking. *Were they plotting revenge? Were they already planning to return?*

'My lady! My Lady R'shiel!'

R'shiel glanced down at the street and discovered an urchin waving up at her. She did not know the child, but he was panting heavily, as if he had run all the way to the gate.

'What is it?' she called.

'That man you're looking for? The one with the scars? I saw him!'

'Wait here!' she told Brak, heading for the stairs that led down into the gatehouse at a run. When she reached the street, she had to push through the crowd to find the child. The boy was waiting for her by the gatehouse wall. He had the most beautiful face R'shiel had ever seen on a child.

'Who are you? Where did you see Loclon?' she demanded.

'My name is Alladan. I work for Mistress Heaner.'

'Who is Mistress Heaner?'

'She's . . . she's . . . my employer,' the boy said, a little uncertainly. 'But I saw the man you're looking for. He was at Mistress Heaner's last night.'

'Is he still there?'

Alladan nodded. 'I think so. Did you want me to show you?'

She glanced up at the wall-walk where Brak was looking down at her and debated calling him. Although she was certain he was telling the truth, the child might be wrong, and she could not risk letting Loclon slip past her. She waved reassuringly to Brak then turned back to Alladan.

'Show me.'

As she pushed through the crowd behind the boy, she faintly heard Brak calling her back, but she ignored him. The idea that she might have found Loclon consumed her, swamping caution and common sense. They broke through the crowd after a great deal of pushing and shoving, turning towards the warehouse district. The boy ran ahead, looking back over his shoulder occasionally to ensure she was still with him.

When the boy finally reached his destination, it proved

to be a narrow gate with a small hatchway at eye level, jammed between two dilapidated warehouses. He stopped and waited for her to catch up and then jerked his head in the direction of the door.

'He's in there.'

'Are you sure?'

'He was this morning.'

'How did you know I was looking for him?'

Alladan shrugged innocently. 'The whole Citadel knows, my lady.' Then he grinned and added, 'Is there some sort of reward for finding him?'

She smiled at the boy's expression. 'We'll see.'

'I was . . . well, I was hoping I could get it now,' he said. 'I mean, you never know what's going to happen . . .'

'Go back to the gate and ask for Lord Brakandaran. He'll see you're rewarded.'

Alladan looked a little disappointed, but he didn't press the point. He ran off without another word. R'shiel watched him leave with a shake of her head. He certainly was an enterprising lad.

Turning back to study the small gate, R'shiel carefully drew on her power and pushed at the gate with a thought. It creaked open to reveal a lane strewn with litter. She could not sense anyone in the lane, so she stepped through cautiously, gagging on the smell. She stepped silently over the rubbish towards another doorway at the end of the alley. It stood open and inviting. When she entered the room beyond she gasped with astonishment.

It was sumptuous – decorated with no thought to expense, or good taste. There were velvet-upholstered couches scattered about the room, each one sectioned off by diaphanous sheer curtains. The carpet was as thick as the grass in the garden behind the infirmary. Fardohnyan crystal chandeliers hung unlit from the ceiling. There was a smell about the place, too, something she could not identify, although it was annoyingly familiar. R'shiel looked around her wide-eyed, wondering what such a place was doing hidden down here in the warehouse district – and who would frequent it.

The answer came to her as she checked the deserted rooms along a narrow passage leading off the main room. The first was innocent enough – simply a room with a large double bed, decorated in blue to match the colour of the door. But as she opened each door along the hall, the purpose of the rooms became clear enough. There was one room sporting a huge tub, another with a bed big enough for six and then another containing nothing more than two velvet-lined, metal cuffs hanging from the ceiling by chains and enough instruments of torture to make the Defenders' interrogation chamber look positively inadequate. Feeling a little queasy at the thought of what might go on in this place, R'shiel wondered about Alladan. *Was he part of the entertainment?* The idea made her sick.

At the end of the hall was a smaller door, which opened at a touch and led down into the darkness. Stepping through, R'shiel called up a finger of flame to light her way, rather pleased with herself. When Brak had tried to teach her how to call fire one evening on their journey here from Vanahiem, she'd almost consumed them both in a ball of flame. The short steps opened into a cellar with an earthen floor. She made the flame brighter and stared at the altar by the far wall, letting out a yell of outrage as the star and lightning bolt of Xaphista stared back at her.

With a sudden thump, the cellar door slammed shut

behind her. She ran to the door and pounded on it, but it was shut fast, locked from the other side. Furiously, she called on her power and blasted the door out of her way, only to discover her way blocked by a wall of fire. She remembered now, what that smell was. Oil. Whoever had set this trap had soaked the building in it, hoping to send her to a fiery death.

R'shiel took a step back from the roaring flames. If this fire spread, here in the warehouse district, it would destroy the city. Even if it only spread a little way, all their supplies, all the food they had stored to see them through the coming siege would be destroyed. Without thinking, she drew even deeper on the Harshini power, pulling as much as she could handle and sent it outwards from the cellar. The blast of air shook the surrounding buildings and almost brought the roof of the cellar down on top of her. But the flames were blown out like candles in a strong draft.

Panting with the effort of her exertions, she clambered through the debris until she reached the ground floor. The building was flattened, its roof gone, the walls blown out and laying flat on the ground. The warehouses on either side were in no better shape, and beyond them she could see the broken windows and fractured walls of the other buildings that had been in range. There were shouts in the distance and voices yelling orders. The Defenders come to investigate the source of the explosion, no doubt. She looked around at the devastation she had caused with a sigh. She had simply meant to blow out the flames. She hadn't expected to level everything in sight.

It was Brak who reached the scene first. She was still standing there, dazed and bewildered as he leapt over the rubble to get to her.

When he reached her, Brak helped her sit down, his expression a mixture of anger and concern. 'What, in the name of the gods, do you think you're doing?'

'It was a trap,' she told him dully.

'No kidding.'

'I didn't mean to . . .' she said, looking around her at what was left of the warehouse district.

'You never do, R'shiel. That's what makes you so bloody dangerous.'

'You're mad at me, aren't you?'

'Yes.'

R'shiel took a deep breath and held out her hand to see if it had stopped trembling, then looked up and smiled wanly at Brak.

'I'm sorry.'

'You and I need to have a little talk about restraint,' he said with a frown. 'You can't go drawing on that much power every time you want to do something. There is such a thing as overkill, you know.'

'But I had to put out the fire. I didn't know how much it would take.' For that matter, even if she had known, she still lacked the finesse to limit what she drew on, but she decided not to remind Brak of that.

'I feel exhausted, but somehow more aware. Isn't that odd?'

'What do you mean?'

'I'm not sure. It's as if I can feel everything more clearly. I can even feel Sanctuary like it was right here.'

'That will be with you wherever you go, R'shiel.'

'I know. I've felt it ever since I left the place, but this is different. It's stronger somehow . . . I don't know . . . clearer . . . Brak?'

She blanched at the expression on his face. Suddenly,

He l

'But why is it so stro
impression in the back of my mi
notice any more.'

'That's because normally, Sanctuary i
time.'

'Then it's back? Why would Korand

'He wouldn't. Not willingly.'

He glanced at her grimly and she
what he meant. Korandellan had brou
real time because he was no longer ca
back. R'shiel stared around her with h
on the magic of the Harshini with
amount that she was consuming.

It was her fault the Harshini we

'Oh Founders, Brak,' she said v
'What have I done?'

By mid morning the last of the
civilians who did not want to sta
through the gates and they wer
outside. The Defenders had du
for Loclon's familiar face, but

he wasn't listening to her. He rose to his feet slowly and turned to stare blankly towards the west, reaching out with his senses, rather than his eyes. R'shiel struggled to her feet and stood beside him, following his gaze, seeing nothing but the flattened buildings and the Defenders coming towards them, demanding to know what had happened.

'What is it? What's wrong?'

'I can feel it too.'

'Sanctuary?'

He nodded.

Normally it's just like a vague ... that I hardly even ...

'What happened at the warehouse district?' Tarja . . . as soon as R'shiel appeared in the doorway of the Fi . . . Sister's office. He was alone with Garet Warner and a . . . young woman that she did not recognise at first. The woman had long blonde hair and was dressed in home-spun trousers and a rough linen shirt, with a Defender's cloak, of all things, thrown carelessly back over one shoulder. The fire burned brightly in the hearth and the room was almost uncomfortably warm. For a fleeting, gut-wrenching moment, R'shiel remembered this office, so hot and stuffy, when Joyhinia had ruled here. She shook off the feeling impatiently. Joyhinia was dead.

'There was a bit of an altercation,' she shrugged as she stepped into the office with Brak on her heels. The woman with Tarja turned as she spoke and studied R'shiel curiously.

'Hello, R'shiel. Hello, Brak.'

'Mandah!'

'You sound surprised to see me, demon child.'

'Don't call me that,' she snapped automatically. 'What are you doing here?'

'What I've been doing since long before I met you, R'shiel. Helping my people.'

Her people, R'shiel knew, were the pagan rebels. 'I didn't expect to see you here. You were supposed to be heading into Hythria with the Defenders.'

'I chose to stay and help Tarja,' Mandah told her with a smile in Tarja's direction. R'shiel recognised the look and felt an unexpected spear of jealousy pierce her chest.

'How convenient for you that the new Lord Defender is someone sympathetic to your cause.'

'There's nothing convenient about it, R'shiel,' Garet remarked, looking up from the map spread out over the desk. 'It's one of the reasons Tarja got the job. What exactly do you mean by an *altercation*?'

'Someone tried to set fire to the warehouses. I . . . caused a bit of damage, but the fire is out.'

'Did you find Loclon?' Tarja asked.

'No. And I don't think we will. But that's not why I'm here. We have another problem.'

'What now?' Garet asked, folding his arms across his chest.

'The Harshini are in danger.'

'The Harshini have been in danger for the past two centuries.'

'This is more than just the threat of discovery, Garet. Sanctuary is no longer hidden. The Kariens can find them now.'

'I'm heartbroken,' the commandant told her unsympathetically, returning his attention to the map.

Tarja frowned at Garet. He appeared a little more sympathetic. 'How long have they got?'

Brak shrugged. 'Before the Karien priests locate Sanctuary? They've probably pinpointed it already. It will

---

the huge, simple-looking man hauli
the gate piled with old blankets, o
eyed old woman who walked b
inspect the cart. The rugs sm
openly wore the symbol of X
her neck. Another fanatic l
all of them, they decided
attention to the crowd,
distinctive scar.

The huge man with
boy and the old wo

take them some time to get there, though. A few weeks, maybe.' He noticed Garet's sceptical look and continued his explanation looking straight at the commandant. 'The reason the Sisterhood could never completely eradicate the Harshini was because Sanctuary was taken out of time. I won't try explaining how – you probably wouldn't believe me, anyway. Suffice to say that the strain of keeping it hidden has finally taken its toll on King Korandellan. Sanctuary is back in real time and the Kariens will be at its gates within weeks.'

'That would be convenient,' Garet remarked. 'It might get them away from ours.'

'But can't the Harshini simply hide Sanctuary again?' Mandah asked, with a glare at Garet. She was a pagan and worshipped the Harshini along with their gods. R'shiel found herself with an unexpected ally.

Brak shook his head. 'If Korandellan let it return, then he's exhausted. Keeping Sanctuary out of time takes a lot less effort than actually sending it there.'

'I can't spare the men to go trekking off into the wilderness, or wherever Sanctuary is to help them, R'shiel,' Tarja told her. 'Even if we could get past the Kariens.'

'Then we have to bring the Harshini here. To the Citadel.'

They all turned and looked at her.

'*What*?' Garet demanded in horror.

'The Harshini can't be killed here. The Citadel won't permit it.'

'And you think we're going to let you bring the Harshini into the Citadel? Absolutely not!' Garet snapped before anyone could say a word.

'But you must!' Mandah cried. 'The Harshini will be slaughtered if you deny them shelter.'

'Young woman, every Defender in Medalon has been trained to hunt the Harshini down and kill them on sight. And you expect us to let them back into the Citadel?'

'Tarja?' Mandah begged, her green eyes moist. R'shiel watched her with interest, and more importantly, Tarja's reaction. He seemed decidedly uncomfortable. Was Mandah the reason Tarja found it so easy to deny the geas? She forced the thought from her mind. She had other, more important things to deal with.

'Even if I agree, what makes you think the Harshini will want to come?' Tarja asked.

'It's that or die in Sanctuary. They can't willingly take their own lives and staying at Sanctuary would be tantamount to doing that, if there was a chance they could return here to safety.'

'What about Loclon?'

'He'll keep.'

'You were burning with vengeance a couple of hours ago.'

'A couple of hours ago I hadn't inadvertently put several hundred innocent lives in danger.'

'You bring the Harshini back in here and we'll be neck deep in pagan rituals within days,' Garet warned.

'We have a common enemy, Garet,' Tarja pointed out. 'I'm inclined to let them come, simply to frustrate the Kariens.'

'If you don't let them come, you'll have the blood of the Harshini on your hands,' R'shiel added.

Garet laughed sourly. 'Do you know how many Harshini the Defenders have killed in the last two hundred years, R'shiel? There's plenty of blood on our hands already. A bit more won't make that much difference.'

'Then it is time to undo some of the damage,' Mandah

declared. 'You must let them back, Tarja! If you want the pagans to follow you, you can do nothing else.'

'It didn't take you long to learn the art of political blackmail, did it?' Garet snapped at Mandah, and then turned to Tarja. 'It's your decision. You're the Lord Defender now. Just so long as you understand the trouble you're bringing down on us if you agree.'

Tarja nodded, but did not answer. Instead, he turned to Brak. 'Where is Sanctuary, exactly?'

'In the Sanctuary Mountains.'

Tarja glared at him.

'It's north-west of Testra,' Brak added. 'That's about as specific as I'm willing to get.'

'Then how are you going to get them out of there? I wasn't kidding when I said I don't have the men to spare, and it's too early in the spring for the passes to be cleared of snow, in any case. Even if we didn't have half of Karien camped around our walls, I have a list as long as my arm of Sisters we need to arrest before they can get organised against us. I don't know that I can help you, even if I was inclined to.'

'They can fly,' R'shiel said. 'On dragons.'

'Oh, well that should reassure the population,' Garet remarked sourly. 'A few hundred dragons landing in the Citadel loaded with a race we've spent two centuries convincing them we've eradicated.'

'Tarja, please,' R'shiel asked, ignoring Garet's sarcasm. She needed him to agree. She needed the Harshini safe. Her conscience would not permit anything else.

'I don't suppose there is any way you can do this discreetly?' he asked.

'You mean try to avoid a few hundred dragons landing in the Citadel loaded with a race that you've spent two centuries convincing your people you eradicated?' Brak asked drily.

'That would be a good start.'

R'shiel glanced at Brak, who thought for a moment then shook her head. 'Not with the Kariens blocking their path.'

'Even if you can get them here in one piece,' Garet pointed out, 'chances are they'll be attacked on sight, once our people see them.'

'Then you'd best make sure they're protected,' R'shiel warned. 'You claim you want a different world from the one the Sisterhood left you. Learning to live with the original inhabitants of Medalon seems like a good place to start. You never know, Garet, you may even learn something from them.'

'I'm learning where your loyalties lie pretty quickly,' he accused.

'My loyalty is to Medalon.'

'You've an interesting way of showing it.'

'Enough, Garet,' Tarja sighed. 'Arguing will get us nowhere. The Harshini can return, R'shiel, but only if you can promise me that they will not try to reclaim the Citadel or cause any more trouble than they have to.'

'Interesting that you suspect the Harshini of trying to reclaim the Citadel,' Brak said with a smile. 'Have you considered what will happen if the Citadel tries to reclaim the Harshini?'

'What do you mean by that?' Garet asked suspiciously.

'He doesn't mean anything,' R'shiel cut in, before Brak could say anything further. 'Do I have your word on this, Tarja?'

He nodded, but he didn't seem very pleased with the decision.

'Then I'll summon Dranymire and the demons.'

'Will you send the Divine Ones a message?' Mandah asked. Her eyes were alight at the prospect of seeing a real demon and of meeting the fabled race that she so admired.

'No. I'm going to have to return to Sanctuary myself to convince the Harshini that any asylum they are offered in the Citadel is genuine.'

'Can't Brak go alone?' Tarja asked.

He shook his head. 'I'm not the one who brought this on, nor I am going to be the one to convince Korandellan and his people that you have opened up the Citadel to the Harshini. It will have to come from R'shiel.'

She nodded and looked at Brak. 'Will you come with me?'

'Don't I always?' he said.

'R'shiel!'

She stopped and turned, waiting for Mandah to catch up with her. The young rebel closed the door of the First Sister's office and hurried towards them along the carpeted hall.

'What is it, Mandah?'

'Could I speak with you?'

R'shiel shrugged. 'I suppose.'

'About Tarja.'

'What about him?'

Mandah stopped before her, taking a deep breath, as if preparing herself mentally for what she planned to say. Brak walked on ahead, leaving them some semblance of privacy. 'You know what happened, don't you? About the geas?'

'Yes, but how did you know about it?'

'You forget that I'm a pagan, R'shiel. I know more about the gods and the Harshini than you do.'

'That's not difficult,' she agreed with a wan smile.

'It's just . . . well, I wanted to know . . .'

'What? If I still have some claim on him?'

'I didn't mean it like that.'

'No, but I've seen the way you look at him. You've done it since we first met. Remember that night in the stables in Reddingdale, when you helped us escape the Defenders? You could have found a dozen other ways to hide Tarja, but you had to throw yourself down on top of him and start kissing him.' R'shiel smiled suddenly. 'He's yours if you want him, Mandah. He certainly doesn't want me any more.'

'R'shiel, I don't want you to think that . . . well, that I'm benefiting from your misfortune.'

'Don't worry, Mandah. Tarja is yours if you can hold him. He's not mine. He never really was.'

Mandah studied her for a moment, as if trying to detect some glimmer of falsehood in R'shiel's assurance.

'You've changed, R'shiel. There was a time when you would have denied me out of spite.'

'There was a time I would have done a lot of things, Mandah,' she said. 'But I know when I'm beaten. I won't stand in your way.'

'Then I have your blessing?'

'I wouldn't go that far.'

Mandah impulsively hugged R'shiel and then ran back towards the First Sister's office. And Tarja. R'shiel watched her disappear inside and turned to find Brak leaning on the banister at the top of the stairs, staring at her thoughtfully.

'What?'

'That was very noble of you.'

'You shouldn't have been listening.'

'Are you kidding? I wouldn't have missed that for the world.'

She stalked past him in annoyance. 'Are you coming?'

'Of course, demon child,' he replied mockingly, as he followed her down the stairs. 'Although, I have to say, you were wrong about one thing.'

R'shiel stopped and glared over her shoulder at him. 'What was I wrong about?'

'You do *not* know when you're beaten, R'shiel.'

# PART 4
# DESTINY

## 47

Damin's coronation as High Prince was a subdued affair, for which he was grateful. He had no wish to indulge in the orgy of excess that normally accompanied such an event. Greenharbour was still getting over the siege and the battle that had raged through the city streets. There were thousands of homeless and some foods were still being rationed. It would have been asking for trouble if he had sanctioned such indiscriminate waste. Adrina had agreed with him, although Marla had been rather put out. She had spent her life imagining the day when her son would finally be crowned High Prince and was rather annoyed that her grandiose dreams were to be so easily dismissed.

Kalan had placed the crown on Damin's head with a wink that only he could see, then placed the High Princess' crown on Adrina's dark hair with only the faintest hint of reluctance. There had not been a High Princess in Hythria for more than fifty years and the last one had been a small, timid girl who had struggled through two pregnancies and then finally given up on life when she delivered a healthy girl. She had not lived long enough to learn that the baby had been named Marla. In fact, since the death of one of her twin boys she had delivered the year before, she had not paid much attention to anything. Damin glanced at Marla and wondered what she was thinking as her mother's crown was placed on his Fardohnyan wife's head. Her expression was unreadable.

Following the coronation, they retired to the banquet hall for a moderately extravagant feast, at which all the Warlords of Hythria lined up to pay their respects and renew their allegiance to the House of Wolfblade.

The four Warlords who had supported him during the civil war approached the high table one by one, and repeated their oaths without hesitation. Tejay Lionsclaw was jovial, Rogan Bearbow grave and respectful. Narvell could barely contain his glee. Only Toren Foxtalon appeared a little wary, no doubt still thanking the gods that he had changed sides before it was too late.

Once the oaths were out of the way, Damin stood up and silence fell over the gathering. The hall was full, crowded with the Hythrun nobility he could not afford to offend, his new Fardohnyan allies and the Defenders who had arrived in time to save them all. He cast his gaze over them, wondering if ever a High Prince had addressed such an oddly assorted gathering before.

He raised his cup. 'To Hythria!'

'Hythria!' the guests responded dutifully.

'It is customary, when a new High Prince takes the throne, to reward those who deserve it, and to punish those who deserve it also. I think we can dispense with the latter. Most of the punishments that needed meting out were taken care of *before* the coronation.'

A smattering of laughter wafted through the hall. Damin had been ruthlessly efficient in dealing with his enemies. He had no intention of bringing his child into a court riddled with potential assassins. If there were any souls left who wished him harm they were keeping very quiet about it.

'It now falls to me to name the Warlords of the provinces that find themselves without a ruling lord. The first province I wish to award is Krakandar, and I gift it to the man who deserves it better than I did. Step forward Lord Almodavar Krakenshield.'

Almodavar had been warned, of course. One did not hand out entire provinces on a whim and the Convocation already had ratified in secret every decision he would announce tonight. But Almodavar still looked stunned. He had worn the same look of blank surprise since Damin had told him about this three days ago.

The condition for Almodavar's acceptance had been that he take the name Krakenshield, so that Laran's name might live on. Almodavar had been his father's closest friend and had not objected to the condition. No one but he and Almodavar knew of the other condition that Damin had imposed. It made him smile with immature, vengeful delight – his only regret that he would not be there to see the look on Starros' face when Almodavar finally acknowledged him as his son and informed the head of the Thieves' Guild that he was now the heir to Krakandar.

Almodavar had guarded Krakandar as if it were his own since before Damin was born, and if his son could manage an organisation as volatile as the Thieves' Guild, ruling an entire province should prove easy by comparison. He had given Almodavar a message for Starros, which his old captain had promised to deliver when he returned home.

'Tell Starros he did *not* beat me. I let him win.'

'Is that it?' Almodavar had asked curiously.

'He'll know what I mean.'

Almodavar stepped forward and swore his oath of allegiance with pride and then moved to the empty seat on the high table with the other Warlords. Applause followed him to his seat. Nobody present doubted either Almodavar or his ability to rule Krakandar. More than a few mothers eyed him speculatively, aware that he was unmarried. More than a few young women present saw the look in their mothers' eyes and cringed – Almodavar might be capable, but he was *old*.

'The next province I wish to award is Dregian.'

The crowd stilled, wondering who would win the province of the man who had led the coup against the Damin. Many eyes turned on Garina Eaglespike and her three-year-old son Tav, who had been invited to attend. Her elder daughter Bayla sat next to Valorian Lionsclaw with a look of quiet terror in her eyes. If Damin took it into his head to destroy the Eaglespikes completely, she had only her marriage to Valorian to protect her, and Tejay was notoriously intolerant of her daughter-in law. Damin had it in his power to ruin her and there were many wondering why he had allowed her brother and mother to live.

'I grant Dregian Province to Tav Eaglespike, to be held in trust for him by Lord Bearbow. Tav is to be fostered with his sister at the court of Lady Lionsclaw until he comes of age. Lady Eaglespike may continue to reside in Dregian Province at Lord Bearbow's pleasure. She may see her son and daughter at Lady Lionsclaw's pleasure.'

The decision met with a relieved round of applause. Damin had avoided future trouble by leaving the province in the hands of the Eaglespike family, which had held it since time began, but with Tav raised under Tejay's watchful eye, he would grow up far differently from the way he would with an embittered mother to poison his mind. Nor would Dregian suffer until the child came of age. Rogan Bearbow's province was close enough to Dregian that he could easily administer both. Garina had accepted the decision with mixed feelings. She had lost her home and her son, but she would be permitted to keep her life and her position, such as it was. It was more than she could have hoped for and more than most people thought she deserved.

'That just leaves Greenharbour,' Damin announced as the applause dwindled away to nothing. He glanced across the table at Tejay Lionsclaw. Although she knew what he was about to do, and had even voted for it in the end, she wasn't particularly happy with the idea when he first proposed it. There were no heirs to the Falconlance name. Conin was a distant cousin and had been awarded the province on the death of the previous Warlord. There were no other cousins to placate and no heirs to object to his decision. Adrina sat beside him, unsuspectingly.

'I grant Greenharbour Province to my brother-in-law, Gaffen of Fardohnya on the condition that he renounces his Fardohnyan citizenship and swears his loyalty to Hythria. He must also renounce any claim to the Fardohnyan throne, and choose a Hythrun name for his House.'

Stunned silence met his announcement. Adrina stared up at him in astonishment, understanding immediately what his declaration meant. By adopting a Hythrun name and renouncing his Fardohnyan ties, Damin was removing Gaffen from the line of Fardohnyan succession, even indirectly. If Hablet followed tradition and had his bastard sons murdered once he had a legitimate heir, her half-brother would be spared.

'Thank you,' she mouthed silently, a wealth of emotion in her eyes.

Damin smiled at her briefly then turned back to face the gathering. They were still staring at him silently. It was Tejay who broke the tension, leaping to her feet as she banged her tankard on the table.

'Damn it! If I can live with this, the rest of you can!' she declared. 'Here's to Gaffen! None of you would be sitting here if it wasn't for him and the Defenders who came to our rescue and thank the gods no more of us got killed or we'd have had to appoint a few Medalonian Warlords, too!'

Someone laughed. Then someone else started clapping and then the whole room joined in. Gaffen stepped forward and swore the oath, just as conscious of its ramifications as his sister.

He took his place beside Tejay, who appeared to have had something of a change of heart about the big blond Fardohnyan since the Convocation. She was probably ten years his senior, but Tejay liked big men and Gaffen was endowed with a great deal of his *court'esa* mother's charm when he wanted to be disarming. Damin shook his head with a smile and resumed his seat.

'Why didn't you tell me?' Adrina asked.

'I wanted to surprise you.'

'My father is going to be furious.'

'I know,' he replied with a grin.

'You're really enjoying this, aren't you?'

'I'm starting to,' he admitted. 'Provided I can keep my head on my shoulders and stop having to go to war every time I turn around, I think I might actually get to like being High Prince.'

'I thought you liked going to war?'

'I like a nice clean fight, Adrina. If I never see another siege as long as I live, it will be far too soon.'

It was too soon, he learnt later that evening, when Glenanaran strode purposefully through the hall to stand before the high table, his black eyes filled with concern. The Harshini bowed before the High Prince and spoke in a voice laden with regret.

'I am sorry to disturb your celebrations, your highness, but I have a message for you from the demon child and I'm afraid it cannot wait.'

Glenanaran said nothing further until they had gathered in the throne room. Everyone had scrambled to follow when Damin left the banquet hall, but in the end he had restricted the meeting to include only the Warlords, the two Defender captains, Denjon and Linst, Adrina, Marla and Kalan.

'R'shiel is at the Citadel,' Glenanaran informed them, when they were finally gathered. 'At least she was when I spoke to her demons.'

'I thought she was in Fardohnya?' Tejay remarked. 'She certainly gets around, this demon child.'

'What makes you think she's not there now?' Adrina asked.

'King Korandellan has collapsed. Sanctuary is back in real time. She may have gone there to render what aid she can.'

Damin glanced around at the others, certain his own face was just as concerned as the other Warlords were.

'What's the situation at the Citadel?' Denjon demanded impatiently.

'The Defenders have taken back the Citadel, Captain,

and are holding the Karien dukes and a number of priests as hostages, but the Karien host still surrounds the city. I believe you call such a situation a . . . stand-off?' Glenanaran turned to Damin then, his expression grave. 'The demon child asks that you gather up the Defenders and whatever Hythrun you can muster and come to their aid. I have already dispatched Joranara to Fardohnya to request King Hablet's aid.'

'You think he'll come?' Tejay scoffed sceptically.

'He'll come,' Gaffen assured her. 'When he heard what happened to Tristan and his Guard, he was ready to attack Karien the next day.'

'How many men do the Kariens have surrounding the Citadel?' *Another siege*, Damin thought. *Damn, how I hate siege warfare!*

'At least a hundred thousand, I'm led to believe.'

The High Prince swore under his breath then looked around at his Warlords. 'Counting the Fardohnyans, how many can we put in the field?'

'Fifty thousand, perhaps, maybe sixty, if Hablet is serious,' Rogan replied. 'But it will take months. The logistics of moving such a force are unthinkable.'

'How long can the Citadel hold out, Divine One?'

Glenanaran shrugged. 'The demon child did not say, your highness. But she did say that the gods have agreed to expedite your journey.'

'What does that mean?' The question came from Linst, the other Defender. He looked singularly unimpressed by the assurance.

'It means that if Hablet sails up the Glass River, he'll have fair winds all the way,' Glenanaran explained. 'Sickness will not plague you, nor lack of fresh water. The bounty of the land will be at your disposal.'

'That doesn't help us much,' Toren Foxtalon complained. 'The gods can't make the roads any shorter, or make our troops eat any less.'

'Pity we can't sail to Medalon, too,' Almodavar remarked.

'I'm not sure the gods had rearranging the geography of the entire continent in mind when they offered their help, my Lord,' the Harshini told him with a thin smile.

'Then how do we get there?' Gaffen asked. 'I'll take every man I have, but it won't do them much good if we can't get to the Citadel before next winter.'

Damin studied Glenanaran's serene expression for a moment then turned to Gaffen. 'We'll get there the same way I got to Medalon the last time.'

The Harshini smiled. 'I see you understand, your highness.'

'Well, I'm glad he understands, because I certainly don't,' Tejay grumbled.

'When his highness crossed into Medalon to aid the demon child at Lord Brakandaran's request, we called on the power of the gods to expedite our journey,' the Harshini explained unhelpfully.

'That tells me nothing.'

'Don't worry about it, Tejay. Just get your Raiders mustered.'

'And what happens to my borders while we go chasing off to Medalon?'

'I will send Farandelan to Sunrise Province and she will see that your Fardohnyan neighbours do not try to take advantage of your absence.'

'I appreciate the offer, Divine One, but Farandelan cannot kill.'

'There is no need to kill, my lady. Her presence will

be enough. She will not permit any killing at all. That is how it was in the past and how it will be again.'

'And assuming we manage to get to the Citadel before it falls?' Denjon asked. 'What then? We're still outnumbered two to one.'

'The demon child was of the opinion that your numbers would be sufficient, Captain. I can tell you no more than that.'

'And we all know what a tactical genius R'shiel is,' Linst muttered sarcastically.

'Captain, I cannot ease your mind or tell you what I do not know. All I can do is ask that you heed the demon child's request and gather your forces as quickly as possible. Other Harshini will join you to aid your journey north.'

'Other Harshini?' Kalan asked.

'With Sanctuary no longer hidden, our people will be safer with your forces than they will be at home. We will do what we can to help, High Arrion.'

'I guess that settles it then,' Damin said, looking around at the others. 'We're going to Medalon.'

## 48

Mikel helped Adrina pack for the journey to Medalon, quite certain that he would have to unpack it all again once Damin Wolfblade discovered she was planning to join him. Her condition was plainly visible now, although it didn't seem to bother her. The fatigue that had plagued her previously had passed. Her skin glowed with health; her emerald eyes were bright as jewels and her dark hair shone with lustre. Having spent much of the early months of her pregnancy in the saddle, she carried little extra weight other than the child. She was full of restless energy and had been, for the past few weeks at least, quite easy to get along with. Mikel had even overheard Princess Marla complain that a woman had no right to look so damned healthy in her condition.

Mikel had fallen back into the role as her page after R'shiel vanished. With Tamylan gone, Adrina had worked her way through a score of slaves since then, none of them meeting her exacting standards. The latest had fled in tears this morning when Adrina accused her of being a fumble-fingered half-wit. Mikel didn't blame his princess, and had his suspicions about the slaves sent to wait on her. Marla hand-picked them and he suspected that the Dowager Princess was not going out of her way to be accommodating. For some reason, perhaps because of their previous history, Adrina found Mikel to her liking. Although his earlier innocent worship of her had been replaced by something a little more realistic, he still admired her and was happy to be of service.

'Is it cold in Medalon, Mikel?'

He dumped the pile of clothes he was carrying on the bed and looked at the princess. She was holding a fur cloak in front of her, studying her reflection in the mirror.

'I don't know, your highness. It will be nearly summer by the time we get there.'

'Maybe just the woollen cloak then. I want to travel light.'

Mikel cast an eye over the mammoth pile that Adrina had already labelled her 'essentials' and frowned. 'Your highness, I'm not sure that Prince Damin will consider that "travelling light".'

She looked at the heap of clothes and sighed. 'You're right. I'm lost without Tam. I wish she were here.'

He didn't know how to answer that. He had liked the Fardohnyan slave, but was not so attached to her that he could empathise with Adrina's grief. His earlier guilt about her fate had faded with the passage of time. He was saved from answering by the appearance of Damin Wolfblade, who stopped at the door and looked around suspiciously.

'What's all this?'

'I'm trying to decide what to pack,' Adrina told him. 'I wish Tam were here. She was so much better than me at this sort of thing.'

'What happened to the slave Marla sent you?'

'She was an idiot. I sent her away.'

Damin stepped into the room and examined the chaos scattered around the room more closely. 'Why are you packing?'

'For Medalon, of course.'

He stared at her as if his hearing had suddenly failed him. 'You're *what*?'

'Packing for Medalon. Do you think I'll need the fur?'

'No, Adrina, you won't need the fur. Or anything else, for that matter. You're staying here.'

She looked at him in astonishment. 'Of course I'm not staying here! I'm coming with you.'

'In case it's escaped your notice, Adrina, you're having a baby.'

'I'm only pregnant, Damin, not terminally ill.'

'I'm not going to risk you or our child by taking you into a battle.'

'Oh for the gods' sake, Damin. If I was a peasant I'd be working in the fields until I dropped the brat and then I'd be back in the fields the very next day.'

'That *brat*, as you so eloquently put it, is the heir to Hythria.'

'Then travel will be good for him. It will broaden his horizons.'

'Neither are you a peasant,' he added, not at all impressed by her attempt at levity. 'I forbid you to come.'

'I don't recall asking your permission.'

'That's because you knew damned well I wouldn't give it.'

Adrina threw down the fur cloak and put her hands on her hips. Mikel shrank back a little, having seen Adrina in a similar mood before. Her eyes glittered dangerously.

'Damin, I think we need to settle something. I am your wife. I am not your *court'esa*, or your lackey, your slave or your possession. I am going with you. If you refuse me, I'll simply find my own way there, but one way or another, I *will* go to Medalon.' Then she smiled suddenly, as if making her declaration had settled the matter. 'Besides, you need me.'

'Why do I need you?'

'Because my father will be leading the Fardohnyans and you really don't want to confront him without me there to calm him down.'

'I can manage.'

'Don't be too sure about that,' she warned. 'You don't know my father.'

Damin took a deep breath. He did that a lot when he argued with Adrina, Mikel noticed. 'Adrina, even if I conceded the point about your father, the fact is, the Hythrun heir must be born on Hythrun soil. If you come to Medalon with me, you will deliver the child before we can get back.'

'Is that your only objection? Mikel, come here!'

Damin turned to stare at him as he edged his way around the High Prince to reach his mistress. Although Damin rarely paid him any attention, he was still more than a little afraid of the Hythrun prince.

'Your highness?'

'I have a job for you, Mikel.' She marched over to the bed and pulled one of the pillows from it, shaking it out of its silk cover. She handed Mikel the pillowcase. 'Take this out to the gardeners and ask them to fill it.'

'With what, your highness?'

'With Hythrun soil, of course.' She looked up at Damin and smiled triumphantly. 'If it's Hythrun soil you want so badly, Damin, then I'll simply take some with me. Off you go, Mikel! There's a good lad.'

Damin shook his head. 'There's no way I can talk you out of this, I suppose?'

'No.'

They stared at each other, debating who was likely to give in first. Damin Wolfblade finally threw up his hands in defeat. He wasn't happy with the idea, but he seemed to admire her spirit. Cratyn would have hit her, Mikel thought with a twinge of guilt.

'Go on then, Mikel. Get us a sack of Hythrun soil. And guard it with your life, boy. We may need it in a hurry.'

Although the fighting had not reached this far, Gaffen's Fardohnyans had used the palace gardens as a shortcut from the dock below the palace and trampled everything in sight in their haste to join in the fray. The statuary was pushed over, the shrubbery bent and shredded, and even the large fountain in the centre was broken, its water dragons cavorting in a dry pool with snapped-off noses and missing fins. Mikel wandered through the vast gardens for quite a while, looking for someone to fill the pillowcase with soil. The gardeners were nowhere in sight.

'A sad sight indeed, don't you think?'

Mikel glanced across the broken fountain and discovered the old man sitting on the edge of the pool. He hadn't seen him for a while, but he seemed to pop up in the strangest places. Although he looked a lot like the old man he had seen in the stables in Roan Vale, Mikel had convinced himself it could not be the same person. This man roamed the Hythrun palace at will. He was, so Mikel figured, a retired slave or old family retainer, who had been given the freedom of the palace in return for a lifetime of service. Mikel often bumped into him in quiet, out-of-the-way places, and had come to think of the old man as a friend, although if pressed, Mikel wasn't sure he even knew the old man's name.

'They'll fix it eventually, I suppose. They're too busy rebuilding the houses to think about fountains.'

'Ah, yes, the ever practical Hythrun,' the old man chuckled. 'They were always like that. One of the reasons I could never get much sense out of them.'

'What do you mean?'

'Nothing. So, are you off to Medalon with the others, then?'

He nodded and walked around the fountain to sit beside the old man. 'I'm going with Princess Adrina. I'm her page now.'

'That's wonderful!' the old man cried, patting Mikel on the back. 'You must be very proud. Imagine the things you will do, the places you will see, the important people you will meet.'

'I suppose. I'll probably meet the King of Fardohnya. He's going to Medalon, too.'

'Is he now? Won't he have trouble getting there in time?'

'The Harshini Glenanaran said the gods are going to help.'

The old man's expression grew fierce for a moment, as if some uncontrollable anger had suddenly consumed him. Then it was gone; so quickly that Mikel thought he had imagined it.

'Well, he should be fine then. And what of you, my young friend? Will you see the demon child again, do you think?'

'I suppose so.'

'That is excellent news. I shall have to give you a message for her.'

'Do you know the demon child?'

'Very well,' the old man said. 'Very well, indeed.'

Mikel looked at him curiously, not sure what it was about the old man's tone that unsettled him. 'What did you want me to tell her?'

'Ah, I shall have to compose my message most carefully. I will see you before you leave. I'll let you know then. Now, what *are* you doing strolling the gardens of the palace clutching an empty pillowcase, my lad?'

He glanced down at the pillowcase and shrugged. 'Princess Adrina wants me to fill it with Hythrun soil in case she has her baby in Medalon.'

The old man laughed. 'A wise precaution. Well, don't let me keep you from such an important task, Mikel. We'll meet again, never fear. And I will give you my message for the demon child.'

Mikel stood up and turned to say goodbye, but the old man was already gone.

## 49

Sanctuary glittered in the dawn as R'shiel and Brak flew over the mountains, sitting proudly atop the ranges where for so long it had remained hidden. Brak watched it draw closer through eyes that watered from the cold wind, feeling as if he had stepped back in time, rather than Sanctuary coming into real time to meet him.

It was almost two hundred years since he had ridden on the back of a dragon towards Sanctuary. The last time it had been to warn Lorandranek that he must hide the settlement or risk the Sisterhood finding it – a mission the Sisters of the Blade had pursued for decades after the First Purge. Lorandranek had conceived the idea of hiding the settlement out of time, a burden that he found trying, but not unbearable. In those days he had shared the task with his nephew, the young Korandellan, and between the two of them, Sanctuary had been able to appear and disappear at will, safe from the Sisterhood, the Karien priests and the odd marauder who stumbled into the mountains trying to escape justice.

But since the madness and death of Lorandranek and the arrival of the demon child, that luxury had been denied them. Sanctuary had stayed hidden as Xaphista grew stronger and more desperate to find his nemesis. Korandellan had carried the burden alone, although why Shananara had not taken up some of the load concerned Brak. She was just as much a té Ortyn as the king, and just as capable as her brother of wielding the power such a feat required. He planned to ask that of the princess when he saw her. His relationship with Shananara té Ortyn was such that he had no qualms about demanding an answer. They had been lovers once, in a distant past.

Brak glanced across at R'shiel, smiling at her awestruck expression. She had never seen Sanctuary like this before and it obviously left her breathless. Or perhaps it was the altitude, he thought cynically. R'shiel wasn't impressed by much these days.

Without any prompting from Brak, his dragon began to bank to the right, circling over the slender towers of the Harshini settlement with Dranymire and R'shiel close behind. With surprising gentleness, the dragons beat their massive wings and lowered themselves down onto a high terrace circled by a balustrade that appeared dipped in silver in the soft dawn light. A solitary figure waited for them, dressed in the customary long white robes of the Harshini.

Brak jumped down from the dragon and squinted into the rising sun as the figure approached. As soon as he was clear of the dragon, the meld crumbled and the demons spilled over the terrace, delighted to be home.

'You're a bit late, Brakandaran,' Shananara said, side-stepping demons as she approached. 'And you've brought the demon child.'

'Hello, Shananara.'

The princess glanced over Brak then turned her attention to R'shiel. 'You're still alive, I see. Amazing.'

'We felt Sanctuary return.'

'That's hardly surprising. Every god, every sorcerer, every priest and every village charlatan on the continent probably felt it. You'd better come with me. Korandellan wants to see you.' She turned on her heel and walked towards the tall doors that opened off the tower, expecting them to follow.

'What's the matter with her?' R'shiel asked as they followed.

'She's angry.'

'I thought the Harshini couldn't get angry?'

'They can't.'

'She's doing a pretty good imitation.'

Brak shook his head and said nothing. He understood what Shananara was going through. Denied the human outlet of anger or fear or recrimination, she was boiling inside with emotions she did not have the luxury of being able to voice.

They followed the princess through the halls of Sanctuary, past a subdued and cautious population, to the king's chambers. When they finally reached the broad white doors, Shananara waved them open then looked at R'shiel.

'You must speak with the king. Alone.'

R'shiel glanced at Brak, as if she wanted him to confirm the instruction. He nodded imperceptibly, and he watched as she took a deep breath, visibly bracing herself for what she would find within. He watched her walk through the tall doors, watched Shananara wave them shut behind her.

'What happened?' he asked, as soon as the doors were completely closed.

'Not here,' the princess replied, with a glance around the empty hall. 'Let's go to my chambers.'

He did not try to hide his surprise. This was Sanctuary. There were no secrets here. But he followed her wordlessly down to the next level where she lived. Stepping across the threshold, Brak decided that her rooms had not changed at all since he had last been here. They were still large and airy and filled with the clutter of her many forays into the human world. She closed the doors by hand and stood leaning against them, watching him as he looked around the room.

'Why did you bring her here?'

'R'shiel? She has a plan to save the Harshini,' he said, picking a small statue from the table near the hearth. It was a small horse, exquisitely carved in jade. It looked Fardohnyan.

'If it's anything like her plan to deal with Xaphista, we'd be better off without her help.'

Brak replaced the tiny statue and smiled at her. 'Cynicism does not become you, Shananara. Actually, you sound ridiculous. You need a bit of human blood in you to make it really effective.'

'The demon child should thank the gods I *don't* have any human blood. If you could see Korandellan . . .'

'How bad is he?'

'Bad enough.' She moved away from the door and walked to the tall open window. The rising sun touched her dark red hair with flecks of gold and lined her perfect Harshini features in crimson. She crossed her arms, as if she was cold, although the temperature in Sanctuary was constant and always pleasant. 'He's dying, Brak.'

'How . . . ?' he asked, too stunned to ask more.

'How do you think? The demon child draws on our power like it has no end. She threatens, she cajoles, she coerces, and she contemplates violence with every breath she takes. Korandellan has been linked to the power without a break since R'shiel was born, and may the gods help me, I taught her to tap into it. Do you know what it's done to him? Can you imagine what it must have been like for him to try to hold Sanctuary out of time while the demon child is on the loose, throwing her anger around without a care for anything or anybody? It has destroyed him.'

'Can't Cheltaran help him?'

'It's the power of the gods that has hurt him, Brak. More of it will simply make him worse.'

'But Cheltaran has helped others in the past who've drawn too much. He did it not so long ago in Greenharbour.'

'Glenanaran and the others drew too much of one strand of the power. Cheltaran could heal them because he was using a part of it they had not touched. Korandellan has been drawing on all of it. If the gods intervened, any one of them could kill him.'

'Then why didn't you help? You could have taken some of the load off him.'

'You think I didn't try? I've begged him, Brak, time and again. But he believed R'shiel would prevail and that she would do it before he faltered. An idle wish, as it turns out.'

'He's not dead yet, Shananara, and the Harshini are still safe. At least until Xaphista's minions can find a way into the mountains. There is time yet.'

'Time for what, Brak? For Korandellan to die? And you know what will happen if he dies, don't you? R'shiel is Lorandranek's daughter. She is the rightful heir.'

Brak stared at the princess, aghast at the mere sugges-tion. 'You're not seriously considering letting R'shiel take the throne? That's insane! Doesn't Korandellan have a child?'

'There are no children, Brak.'

'Then it must be you.'

'I cannot step forward unless R'shiel refuses the crown.'

'Then I'll make damned sure she does refuse it,' he promised. The idea of R'shiel ruling the gentle Harshini was too bizarre, too horrible to contemplate.

Shananara smiled at him fondly. 'I believe you would, Brakandaran. But it is not my decision, or yours. It is between Korandellan and the demon child.'

'She won't do it.'

'Perhaps. But the crown is hers for the taking should she ask for it.'

'She won't ask for it. R'shiel is driven by anger, not power for its own sake.'

'Your opinion of her has improved somewhat, I notice.'

'She's learning.'

'Yes, but what exactly have you been teaching her?'

He shrugged. 'Only what I have to. But she's a quick study. She sees a thing once and remembers it.'

Shananara nodded. 'Her tutors here said much the same thing. Unfortunately, she lacks wisdom and wisdom is something gained through experience, not learnt by rote, no matter how well meaning the teacher.'

R'shiel was gone for hours, leaving Brak little choice but to impatiently pace Shananara's chambers, waiting for news. Samaranan came to visit for a while, delighted to see her half-human sibling, but even his sister's smiling presence had a fragile edge to it. They spoke of inconsequential things, both of them avoiding the real reason Brak was here. The Harshini were averse to violence, but they were not blind to the consequences of Korandellan's collapse. They knew the demon child had returned and that Xaphista was as strong as ever. Their future was bleak and for a race unable to imagine such desolation, it was a trying time indeed.

Eventually, Dranymire materialised in the apartment, startling Brak with his sudden appearance.

'Lord Brakandaran. Your highness. The king wishes to see you both.'

They hurried upstairs to Korandellan's chambers and found the doors open and waiting for them. Brak entered the room hesitantly, afraid of what he would find. R'shiel was waiting for them by the door to Korandellan's bedroom. She looked pale and rather chastened. Without a word she stood back to let them enter, and then followed them inside, closing the door behind her.

Brak was shocked by the king's appearance. Korandellan lay on the bed, his golden skin sallow and almost as pale as the sheets beneath him. He was as thin as a man who had not eaten for a month and his once bright eyes were dull and lifeless.

'Thank you, Brakandaran, for bringing the demon child home.' His voice, once so vibrant and resonant, was barely more than a hoarse whisper.

'It was her idea, your majesty. I merely showed her the way.'

The king smiled weakly. 'It is good that you did . . . Shananara?'

'I'm here, Koran,' the princess said, moving to her brother's side. Brak stepped back to let her pass. R'shiel had not moved from the door.

'R'shiel has come to lead our people home.'

'We are home, brother.'

'No. Sanctuary has been our prison these last two hundred years. The Citadel is our true home.'

'The *Citadel*?' Shananara's eyes flew to R'shiel in astonishment, then she looked back at the king. 'You don't mean you want us to return to the Citadel?'

'We cannot be harmed there. The Citadel will protect us.'

'But what of the Sisterhood and their Defender henchmen?'

'There is no more Sisterhood,' R'shiel said from the door. 'The Defenders are in charge. Tarja is the new Lord Defender. I have his word that the Harshini may return unmolested.'

Shananara glanced at her in disbelief then sat down beside Korandellan on the bed, taking his clammy hand in hers. 'Don't worry about it now, Koran. We can discuss this when you've recovered.'

'I'll not recover, Shanan. You know that as well as I do. Take our people home. I charge you with their welfare.' Korandellan closed his eyes, as if the effort of so much conversation had exhausted him.

'Are you mad?' she asked R'shiel, softly. 'How can you come here and offer him such false hope?'

'It's not a false hope, Shananara. The Harshini may safely return to the Citadel.'

She turned to Brak. 'Is this true?'

He nodded. 'I told you she had a plan.'

'You might have warned me what it was!'

The king's eyes opened again and he smiled at his sister. 'You were always the practical one, Shanan. Do this thing for me. Our people need you.'

'They don't need me, Koran. The demon child will be their queen once you are gone.'

'I've already told Korandellan I don't want the job,' R'shiel said.

'You see, sister, the demon child is wiser than you think.' Korandellan smiled wanly and held out his hand to R'shiel. She crossed the room and took it in hers. Brak was astonished to see that her eyes were filled with tears. 'Do not regret what you have done, demon child. Think only on the good you will do in the future. You have what you need to defeat Xaphista, so remember what I have told you about the Seeing Stones. Do what you are destined for and be at peace with yourself.'

R'shiel nodded wordlessly then looked across at Brak. The king looked at him too, his dull eyes filled with forgiveness. 'I give you the same advice, Brakandaran. Do not regret what you have done. Everything is as it should be. You have more than made amends for your mistakes. Face Death secure in that knowledge that your sacrifice was not in vain.'

'I will.'

'And you, Shananara. You are the last of the té Ortyn. It is up to you to see that we continue. Once you have returned to the Citadel, you should speak with Glenanaran. It is time you two had a child.'

Shananara smiled fondly at her brother. 'If I wanted a child, what makes you think I would pick Glenanaran?'

'I know you too well, my dear.'

'That you do, brother. That you do.'

Brak looked up suddenly, as he felt a presence in the room. Although he could see nothing yet, he knew who it was. With a sharp glance at R'shiel, he waved her away from the bed. She could feel it too, but didn't recognise it. Shananara leaned over and kissed Korandellan on the forehead, and then stepped back.

'What . . . ?' R'shiel began to ask, but Shananara glared at her so fiercely that she fell silent.

Death materialised slowly at the foot of the king's bed. He had chosen the benign aspect of the Harshini to welcome the king into his realm, although his robes were translucent and his black eyes hollow orbs, rather than the bright eyes of the Harshini. Korandellan smiled when he saw him, unafraid.

'You will sup with me this night, your majesty.' Death's lips did not move, but each of them could hear him, as if his voice spoke directly to their souls.

'You do me a great honour, my lord, to escort me personally.'

'You do *me* the honour, sire. It is not often I am able to welcome one of your people into my home.' Death turned then and stared at R'shiel, who took a step back from him in fear. 'There is no need to be anxious, demon child. You and I will not meet again for quite some time.' R'shiel did not answer him. She appeared frozen in shock. Death swivelled his head to stare at Brak. 'But you and I will meet, Brakandaran, and soon, I suspect. Our bargain is almost fulfilled.'

'Well, don't get too excited,' Brak warned disrespectfully. 'It's not done with yet.'

'I will be waiting, Brakandaran.'

'I never doubted that for a moment, my lord.'

The spectre turned his attention back to Korandellan. 'Are you ready, your majesty?'

'I am ready.'

Death raised his arm and pointed at Korandellan. As he did so, the king appeared to change. He began to fill out and his colour returned. His aura glowed with strength, pure and unmarked by fear or pain. This was

Korandellan in his prime. His eyes brightened and he assumed such an aura of wellbeing that Brak expected him to leap off the bed. Instead, he rose slowly until he was standing, his weight making no impression on the down-filled mattress.

Then with a smile of serene happiness Korandellan walked into the arms of Death and they both disappeared from the room.

## 50

'I don't understand.'

'That's not unusual for you.' Brak smiled at R'shiel's scowl.

She waved her arm to indicate the gathered Harshini who were busily preparing to depart. Demon-melded dragons could be seen on every terrace, although some apparently preferred to travel by large and improbable birds who beat their vast wings slowly, as if warming them up for flight, and hissed impatiently at the dragons. The dragons varied in size and colouring. Some were massive, like Dranymire and his brethren; others more delicate, their metallic scales touched with fire as the sun set over the mountains.

'Why are they so damned happy?'

The whole atmosphere in Sanctuary had changed since Korandellan's death and Shananara's announcement that they were to return to the Citadel. The fragile cheerfulness that had permeated the fortress had been replaced by a sense of optimistic anticipation. The Harshini preparing to leave were so buoyant, R'shiel was surprised they didn't whistle while they worked. Some of them were heading for the Citadel; others for Fardohnya and Hythria. Shananara had also called for volunteers to fly to the aid of the relieving army that was heading for Medalon.

'They're going home.'

'To the Citadel? I didn't realise it meant so much to them.'

'The Citadel is part of the Harshini, R'shiel. It's been very trying on them being away from it for so long.'

'Don't they realise what's waiting for them there? The Defenders . . . the Kariens . . .'

'Of course they do. But you've assured them they'll be safe and they trust Tarja to keep his word.'

She noticed his smile and narrowed her eyes suspiciously. 'Why are you smiling like that?'

'You remember what I said about the Citadel reclaiming the Harshini?'

'Yes.'

He laughed softly. 'I can't wait to see what happens when they arrive.'

'Is this another one of those vital details you neglected to mention?'

'The Citadel has been hibernating for two hundred years, R'shiel. He's liable to wake up when the Harshini come home.'

'What do you mean?'

'I'm not certain myself,' he told her with a grin. 'But it's bound to be interesting.'

Annoyed with Brak's smirking, R'shiel turned her attention back to the departing Harshini. They were sitting on the balustrade of the same terrace they had landed on, watching the demons melding. Dranymire and a dozen other prime demons were fighting for space on the crowded terrace, trying to pull their brethren into their melds. Occasional squabbles broke out among the younger demons, but they were put down swiftly and sharply by the older ones. They reminded R'shiel of unruly children.

'Look at them!' she scoffed. 'Their King just died and they're being kicked out of their homes. You'd think they'd spare a thought for poor Korandellan, at least.'

'Grief is a human emotion. Besides, the Harshini are delighted. Korandellan didn't die. Death came for him personally.'

'Oh? You mean there's a difference?'

'Of course there's a difference. Death took Korandellan body *and* soul. That's a rare honour.'

'He's still dead, Brak.'

'Yes, but you saw him before he vanished. Death restored him. And there's always the chance that he'll come back.'

'*What?*' she said, turning to him, her eyes wide.

'It's happened before.'

'When?' she demanded sceptically.

'Well, it's a theoretical possibility.' He smiled at her doubtful expression. 'Put it this way: if you die, and Death only takes your soul, then that's the end. You're gone. It's the reason your people cremate their dead, did you know that? Pagans believe in burial, so that Death can still claim the body if he has a mind to.'

'But if you burn the body, then there's no hope of resurrection?' she asked, nodding in understanding. She had never wondered why Medalonians practised cremation, or really cared why the pagans preferred to be buried, but it made sense now she knew the reason.

'That's right. If your soul ever comes back, it'll have

to be in another body. But if Death takes your soul *and* your body, then he can send you back again, if the mood takes him.'

'And does it?'

'Not often. He doesn't like to disturb the natural balance of things. He's a real stickler for the rules.'

'He seemed to know you pretty well.'

'We've had dealings in the past,' Brak said abruptly. She could tell he didn't want to elaborate.

'What did he mean about—'

'Here comes our new queen,' Brak cut in, before R'shiel could frame the question she was certain he didn't wish to answer. There was an inexplicable edge in his voice. 'We'd best say goodbye.'

Shananara approached them, dressed in dragon-rider's leathers, her long-legged stride and easy grace marking her as Harshini, even more than her totally black eyes. She smiled as she neared them, then glanced over her shoulder to check on Dranymire and the demon-meld before turning to R'shiel.

'As soon as we have reached the Citadel, I will send Dranymire and Elanymire back for you both. Do you know what to do?'

R'shiel nodded. Although the Harshini were abandoning Sanctuary, they had no intention of leaving it empty to be pawed over by the Kariens and defiled in the same way the Citadel had been defiled by its new tenants. Shananara had shown R'shiel how to remove it from time, but on this occasion there would be nobody inside to suffer from it. The fortress would be completely empty of life. Every animal had fled. Every Harshini was preparing to leave. Even the insects had been advised to move out. Once the Harshini were gone, she would send

Sanctuary so far out of time that only she or Shananara would have any hope of retrieving it.

'Then let the Kariens come. There will be nothing here for them to find.'

'I hope I do it right,' R'shiel said, suffering a momentary pang of uncertainty.

'You will,' Shananara assured her. 'Korandellan was right about you, you know. You are not nearly as unreliable as I first thought.'

'Thank you . . . I think.'

'Things are as they should be, R'shiel.'

'Even though Korandellan is dead?'

'My brother was honoured by Death. There is no greater reward for a lifetime of service. Now, I must bid you farewell. I will try to ensure that our return does not wreak too much havoc on the residents of the Citadel.'

Shananara and Brak exchanged a look that was full of amusement.

'You both keep saying that! What are you talking about?'

'You'll see,' Shananara replied with a cryptic smile. 'Will I see you again, Brak?'

'Yes. It's not over yet.'

'Then there is no need for goodbyes. I will see you both at the Citadel. Hopefully, Tarja will be a little more reasonable than the last time we met.'

'He wasn't unreasonable, Shanan. He was under a geas.'

Suddenly serious, Shananara nodded. 'I know. And now the geas is gone. It's strange, but when we sat around that fire beside the Glass River trying to coax the demon child home, I never imagined that a couple of years later I would be returning to the Citadel as the Harshini queen and Tarja would be the Lord Defender. Even destiny can play tricks on us at times.'

'Go easy on him, Shanan,' Brak advised. 'He's had a rough time lately.'

'Never fear, Brak. I know how to handle humans, even testy ones.' She turned to R'shiel and hugged her briefly. 'As for you, little cousin. Do this thing for us then return to the Citadel to fulfil your destiny. I will help you locate the Seeing Stone.'

'Why not use the Stone here?' Brak asked. 'Now that Sanctuary is back in real time, does it matter?'

'Korandellan told me that only the Seeing Stone of the Citadel is capable of what I need. I must find that or find another way, I'm afraid.'

'We'll find it, R'shiel. The High Arrion was right. No human could have destroyed it. If it's still in the Citadel, we'll locate it eventually.'

Shananara then turned on her heel and walked back towards her dragon. She leapt aboard with practised ease and the dragon lifted into the sky with a powerful beat of his massive wings. Her departure was the signal for the other Harshini to take off, and within minutes the sky was dotted with dragons climbing towards the red-tinted clouds. There were too many for R'shiel to count. She watched them dwindle into the distance until they were little more than specks in the sky. The sight both cheered and saddened her. The Harshini were abroad once more, but they were facing a world they had been removed from for centuries and it was radically different from the one they had left behind.

'Will they be all right, Brak?'

'Yes. Shananara is right, you know. Things *are* as they should be.'

She turned to look at him, puzzled by the sadness in his voice.

'Korandellan was a good king, but he never stepped foot outside Sanctuary. Shanan has been walking among humans since she was a child. She'll rule the Harshini much more effectively now that they have gone back among humans than Koran ever could.'

'But you still grieve for Korandellan, don't you?'

He nodded. 'He was a good friend.'

'How many good friends have you lost for me, Brak?'

'More than you will ever know.'

She had no answer for that and darkness was falling rapidly over the deserted fortress.

Brak jumped down from the balustrade and held out his hand to her. 'We'd better make sure this place is empty before you send it away.'

She took his hand and jumped down beside him and together they walked back into the silent, empty halls.

## 51

The last room they checked was Brak's. R'shiel looked about in fascination, seeing a side of him she never suspected. There was an easel by the window with a half-completed landscape resting on it. Leaning against the wall near the bed was a beautifully crafted lyre, and beside it a thick pile of music. She picked the lyre up and strummed the strings thoughtfully. Brak looked up from papers he was sorting through on the table on the other side of the room and frowned.

'Please don't touch anything, R'shiel.'

'I didn't know you played.'

'I used to.'

'I didn't know you painted, either.'

'There's a lot you don't know about me.'

She replaced the lyre carefully and sat on the bed. 'Why did Death say he would meet you again soon?'

Brak shrugged. 'He's a sociable sort of fellow.'

'I noticed,' she said with a smile, hoping to lighten his mood. He had grown ever more morose the longer they spent in Sanctuary's echoing, silent rooms. 'Korandellan told you to face Death secure in that knowledge that your sacrifice is not in vain. Shananara asked if she would see you again, too. Why would she say that?'

'Ask her.'

Brak was shifting papers across the table without purpose. She had angered him and couldn't understand why.

'Did I say something wrong?'

'No . . . look, why don't you go and see if there's any other rooms on this level we haven't checked? I'll meet you on the terrace when I'm finished here.'

She rose to her feet, a little hurt that he was dismissing her so coldly. 'Can't I help?'

'No.'

'Brak . . .'

'Out!'

R'shiel jumped at the anger in his voice. 'What did I do to deserve that?'

'Right now, you're breathing!' he retorted. 'That's enough.'

'What's gotten into you, Brak? This isn't my fault, you know.'

'Actually, R'shiel, it is your fault. Now, if you don't mind, I'd like to be alone while I sort out my things. I'm not likely to get another chance.'

'Fine!' she declared. 'Take all the time you want. I'm not going anywhere!'

R'shiel stormed from the room and ran down the long hall, her footsteps loud and discordant in the dark, silent halls. She stopped when she reached the balcony overlooking the valley, angry and hurt by Brak's sudden rejection. The waterfall tinkled musically down the rock face on the other side of the valley, although the perpetual rainbow had been swallowed by the half-light that passed for night here. The sound soothed her. She had done nothing to deserve Brak's anger that she could recall. No more than usual, at any rate.

His sudden intolerance mystified her. She tried to recall everything that had happened since they arrived at Sanctuary. Nothing sprang to mind that would make him turn on her like that. Except when she questioned him about Death. He'd been rather touchy about that up on the terrace, too. *And why, in the name of the Founders, did he suddenly decide to sort his papers out? Anyone would think . . .*

With the thought only half completed, R'shiel ran back to Brak's room and threw open the door. She glared at him accusingly, tears blurring her vision, anger and grief battling each other for dominance.

'It's *you*!'

'What?'

'It's you, isn't it? The life you traded for mine? "A life of equal value," that's what you said. You told me you traded someone's life for mine when Joyhinia almost killed me. You bargained with Death and offered your life to save mine, didn't you? That's why Death said your deal was almost done. It's why Shananara asked if she would ever see you again. You damned, sentimental, self-sacrificing, half-breed, bastard idiot!'

Brak stared at her for a moment and then looked away. His anger had faded. He looked simply resigned. 'It doesn't matter.'

She crossed the room and grabbed his shoulder, forcing him to look at her. 'How *could* you?'

'How could I not?' he asked her softly.

She wiped away her tears angrily and punched his arm. 'You can't do this to me! You can't do it to yourself. I don't deserve it. Founders, Brak, what am I supposed to do? Spend the rest of my life – all ten thousand years of it – knowing I'm alive because you squandered your life on me?'

She tried to hit him again but Brak pulled her close and held her while she sobbed. She could not believe what he had done, or the guilt such knowledge had burdened her with.

'There, there,' he said, as if he was comforting a small child. 'It's too late to do anything about it now.'

'Why did you do it?' she cried, her face buried in his chest.

'I only had one life to bargain with, R'shiel. To offer another life would have been murder.'

'You could have let him take me.'

Brak kissed the top of her head and lifted her chin with the tip of his finger. With his thumb he gently wiped away a tear. 'No. That I couldn't do.'

For a timeless moment he looked at her. Then he kissed her, lightly, his lips just brushing hers, as if he expected her to pull away from him. It sent an unexpected shiver down her spine. There was a world of promise behind his kiss, so different from Tarja's artificially imposed desire that it left her unable to breathe. R'shiel stared at him in wonder, suddenly understanding the source of her anger, the reason for her grief. This moment had been long in the making, she realised, simmering at the back of their often-volatile, strangely dependent relationship, waiting for an opportunity to catch them unawares.

R'shiel reached up, running her fingers through his dark hair and pulled his head down towards hers, with the certain knowledge that no god had interfered in his desire, no geas had imposed feelings for her that he did not want to own. He pulled her even closer, the slow burning heat of his desire searing away her doubts. He kissed her neck, her ear and then her mouth again, then broke away from her embrace suddenly and took her face in his hands.

'Look at me.'

She met his gaze evenly, unafraid, wishing he would stop talking.

'You know this changes nothing, don't you?'

She shook her head wordlessly, wanting to deny him, not trusting herself to speak.

'Nothing can be altered, R'shiel. Whatever happens, if you succeed or fail, I cannot alter the bargain I made.'

'But—'

'There are no buts. No loopholes. No way out. Do you understand that?'

R'shiel felt fresh tears prick her eyes as she nodded her reluctant agreement.

'Then understand this, too. You are part-human, R'shiel, but you are also part-Harshini. There is so much you don't understand. So much you have yet to learn. You can't send Sanctuary out of time until sunrise. We have one night. I can show you a part of being Harshini that you cannot possibly imagine. But I'm not doing this for payment and I don't want you doing it out of guilt, or to get even with Tarja. Tomorrow, you will still be the demon child, he will still be the Lord Defender, and I will still be the half-breed who will die as soon as you succeed. There is no future. There is only now. The choice is yours.' His eyes bored into her, demanding an answer. Then he added huskily, 'Stay, or stay out of my way until morning.'

The decision was harder than she imagined. But

tomorrow was a lifetime away, and deep down, despite everything she had seen, everything she had done, R'shiel was still not convinced that she was ruled by her destiny.

'I want to stay.'

He searched her face, looking for some sign that she was uncertain. When he found none, he smiled briefly and his eyes began to darken as he kissed her again, harder, and more hungrily. R'shiel followed his lead and kissed him back, opening her mouth to his and her mind to the power. Her eyes blackened until they were orbs of glittering ebony as the intoxicating sweetness filled her. Brak reached for her, not with his hands but with his mind. The space between them blurred as he wove an enchantment around them that left no room for anything but a sweet, seductive desire that had no parallel in the human world.

This was what the legends spoke of. This was the gift of the Harshini that ruined humans for any other lover. She'd heard stories about it. The Novices had whispered about it in the dormitories late at night, fascinated and repelled by it. The Sisterhood had tried to destroy the Harshini for fear of it. All the violence they could not contemplate, all the conflict they could not confront was transformed into this offering, this all-consuming, passionate inferno that consumed every thought, every fibre of one's being in the pursuit of mutual pleasure. It was the ultimate expression of the Harshini quest for happiness.

R'shiel lost all sense of time; could not separate reality from fantasy. She did not know how they got to the bed or how long the night lasted. She could not distinguish touch from desire, or pleasure from pain. Nothing she had experienced in the past had prepared her for this and nothing would ever come close to it in the future.

It was the first time she truly understood the meaning of magic.

Brak shook her awake at sunrise. She turned in his arms, a little surprised that she was still holding onto the power. It filled her with a heavy, languid weariness.

'Time to get up and do your good deed for the day, demon child,' he reminded her with a smile.

'Brak, I . . .'

'No,' he said, placing a finger on her lips to silence her. 'Don't say it.'

She smiled and nodded. 'I was going to ask if there's anything to eat. I'm starving.'

'I'll find something while you're getting dressed.'

By the time Brak returned with a platter of impossibly perfect fruit, grown here in Sanctuary where even the grubs were considerate of others, R'shiel was dressed and ready to leave. They ate as they walked through the silent halls. Brak made no attempt at conversation and R'shiel didn't try to engage him. There was nothing to be said. He had laid down the conditions of their one night together and they bound her, despite what it would cost her in the future. There was nothing to be gained by talking about it.

The sun was almost over the peaks as they stepped through the Gateway and out into the chill, snow-covered mountains. They walked some distance from the fortress before R'shiel stopped and turned to look back at Sanctuary.

'I wonder how long it will have to remain hidden?'

'Not as long as the last time, I hope.'

She frowned. 'If I get this wrong, we may never be able to find it again.'

'Then don't get it wrong,' he suggested dryly.

She hesitated a moment, framing her next question carefully. 'Can I ask you something, Brak, about last night?' When he did not answer, she chose to take his silence as permission. 'When we . . . well, could the other Harshini feel it?'

'Yes.'

She felt her face redden with embarrassment, but that was not what she wanted to know. 'What about the demons?'

'If they were paying attention.'

'And the gods?'

'Certainly.'

'So Kalianah would know?'

'Oh, yes, Kalianah would know.'

'Would Xaphista have felt it?'

'Undoubtedly.'

She tossed her apple core to a curious squirrel come to investigate them. 'Good.'

He stared at her curiously.

'I *want* that bastard to know I was having a good time.'

'If it's any consolation, he was probably squirming the whole night. When he rose to power the first thing he did was forbid his people to indulge in anything so wantonly pleasurable. They call all sex a sin now in Karien, but his original intention was to stop his people consorting with the Harshini. He had that in common with the Sisterhood. They too were afraid of the effect it had on humans. It's like a drug, in some ways. As the only way to get more of it is to have a relationship with a Harshini who can't abide violence, the end result was a fairly peaceful and very happy community – back in the days before Xaphista and the Sisters of the Blade.'

'And a lot of half-breeds,' she added with a grin.

'That too.'

'So Xaphista despises pleasure.'

'He's afraid that it will distract his people from him.'

R'shiel nodded, filing the information away for future reference. Then, unable to delay what she was planning any longer, she drew even more of the power she was still channelling and turned her attention to Sanctuary. The fortress glittered in the sunrise, as if it had put on its best face to bid them farewell.

With infinite care, R'shiel wove the glamour Shananara had taught her, sending the threads of power over and around Sanctuary. In the background, she could feel Brak linked to her, guiding her hand. He had the training to help her envelop Sanctuary, but only she and Shananara had the strength to fling it beyond the reach of mortals.

When she was certain she had wrapped every part of the settlement in her magical cocoon, she hesitated. She felt Brak sever the link that joined them as he let go of his power. What she was about to do would destroy him if he stayed coupled to her.

She glanced at him, saw his eyes had returned to their usual faded blue and then gathered her strength. With a mighty push, she flung every ounce of power she was holding towards Sanctuary. It shimmered for a moment, almost as if it was fighting to stay put, and then, with a boom that rolled over the mountains like a distant thunderstorm, Sanctuary disappeared from sight.

R'shiel was sagging from the effort, but Brak caught her before she could fall. She let go of the power with relief.

'Did I do it right?'

'I guess we won't know that until you try to bring it back.'

She smiled wanly. 'You're a real comfort.'

'I do my best.'

Suddenly she laughed. Whether from relief or amusement she didn't know. There was a lightness in her that came from more than just the knowledge that she had successfully hidden Sanctuary. It came from somewhere inside her. It was as if she had stepped over an invisible wall that she hadn't known was holding her back.

'What's so funny?'

'I know this is going to sound crazy, but I think that for the first time in my life, I'm actually happy to be alive.'

Brak smiled slowly. 'So am I.'

Sitting close together for warmth, they settled down with their backs to a large pine tree and waited in companionable silence for the dragons to return.

## 52

'Oh Tarja, they're beautiful!' Mandah breathed reverently.

He glanced at her and smiled. She was staring up at the sky as though seeing something from her dreams. He had allowed her to come to greet their new guests because he could think of no way to stop her. And besides, of all the people in the Citadel, Mandah was the least likely to offend the Harshini when they arrived.

Tarja watched the dragons settling on the sandy floor of the amphitheatre, almost as awestruck as Mandah and the Defenders who stood behind him. He hadn't expected there to be so many of them. Or so many dragons. Garet Warner studied the swarming sky with a frown, then turned to him with a shake of his head.

'I hope you know what you're doing, Tarja,' he murmured.

'My lord! Sir!'

Tarja turned towards the urgent voice. A cadet was running towards him across the sand. Garet had pulled all the cadets out of training and was using them as messengers and for minor administrative tasks to free up as many Defenders as possible. The lad was no more than fourteen and seemed torn between fear and pride that he had been chosen for such an important task as he skidded to a halt in front of the Lord Defender.

'What's wrong?' Tarja asked.

'It's the Kariens, sir. Captain Symin sent me to fetch you.'

'What are they up to now?' Garet asked.

'It's the dragons, sir. Ever since they appeared the Kariens have been going wild. Some of them are even fleeing the field.'

Garet glanced at Tarja in surprise. 'Well, that's an unexpected bonus. I'll check out what's happening at the gate. You'd better stay here and keep your new friends under control.'

Garet followed the boy back to the tunnel entrance, as a tall Harshini with dark red hair slid gracefully from the back of the dragon that looked like the one who had accosted Tarja at the vineyard near Testra. He walked forward to greet her, pushing back a momentary wave of apprehension. She looked so much like R'shiel.

'Hello, Tarja.'

'Shananara.'

'Thank you for letting us come home.'

'You may not thank me in a few days. We're under siege, and you're not exactly welcome here. This isn't going to be easy.'

'I know.' She noticed Mandah, who had followed Tarja cautiously, and smiled at the young woman. 'Aren't you going to introduce me to your friend?'

'Of course. Shananara, this is Mandah Rodak. Mandah, this is her highness, Princess Shananara té Ortyn.'

'I'm *Queen* Shananara now, but we can talk about that later. The gods' blessing on you, Mandah.'

'Your majesty. Divine One,' she gushed, falling to her

knees in the sand. The young pagan woman looked set to faint with happiness.

Shananara smiled indulgently. 'Arise, child. We have no time to stand on ceremony.' She looked at Tarja then, and her smile broadened mischievously. 'I fear I have an apology to make, my Lord Defender. Childish and petty as it may seem, I'm afraid I could not resist taunting your besiegers. We strafed the fields surrounding the Citadel on our approach. I fear I've caused something of a panic among the Kariens.'

Tarja tried without success to hide his amusement. 'I'm sure I can find it in myself to forgive you.'

'I thought you might.'

He glanced over her shoulder at the other Harshini, who were climbing down from their dragons and looking about them with expressions ranging from happiness to rapture. There were no children among them, which surprised him a little.

'I've made arrangements for you to be accommodated in the dormitories. As we've no Sisterhood any longer, there didn't seem any point keeping the Novices and the Probates.'

'What did you do with them?' Shananara asked with a hint of concern.

He was tempted to tell her he'd murdered them all in their beds, just to see what her reaction would be, but thought better of it. 'We sent them home.'

'May we visit the Temple of the Gods?' When Tarja looked at her blankly, she smiled. 'I believe you call it your Great Hall.'

'Tomorrow, perhaps, and I'd prefer you did it in small groups. Hundreds of Harshini marching through the streets of the Citadel might cause a riot.'

'We shall be discreet, my lord.'

'Thank you. Mandah will act as liaison between us. She's a pagan, and a number of her people are here. I thought you might be more comfortable dealing with them, rather than the Defenders.'

'Your consideration of our feelings is both unexpected and appreciated, Tarja,' she told him with a slight bow. 'It seems R'shiel was correct when she said you could be trusted.'

'She's not with you?'

'She and Brak had something else to take care of, but they should be back by nightfall. Which brings me to a rather delicate matter. I cannot ask the demons to stay melded in dragon form, and you have nowhere to accommodate them in any case. But if I dissolve them, I cannot guarantee their good behaviour.'

Tarja groaned silently. He hadn't thought about that when he'd told R'shiel the Harshini could return. On the other hand, she had conveniently neglected to mention that the demons were a part of the deal.

'Can't you just . . . disappear them, or something?'

Shananara laughed. 'A demon you can't see is likely to cause a lot more trouble than one you can keep an eye on, Tarja. I'll do what I can, but I really should dissolve the melds.'

'Just try to keep them out of trouble.'

'I will. And now, if you would be so kind as to let us find our accommodation, we'd like to settle in. It has been a long night.'

'Mandah will show you the way.'

Shananara looked at him with a sad little smile. 'We know the way, Tarja.'

Tarja refused to acknowledge the unspoken accusation. 'These men will escort you.'

'Are we prisoners?'

'They are for your protection, Shananara. I'm not worried about what you'll do to the citizens of the Citadel; I'm worried about what they'll do to you.'

'Then once again I thank you for your consideration. Will we meet again later? There are things we need to discuss.'

'Of course.'

Shananara bowed and returned to her people, who had patiently gathered behind her, waiting for their queen to finish her discussion. Mandah followed her, still wearing that same look of awe that she had acquired when the dragons first appeared over the Citadel this morning. Tarja called over the lieutenant in command of the escort, gave him his orders and then headed for the tunnel.

As he entered the cool darkness he felt the ground tremble faintly under his feet. He stopped, curious, waiting for it to happen again, but when no further tremors eventuated, he shrugged and kept on walking, certain that he must have imagined it.

'The Kariens are frantic,' Garet informed him later that day.

'Shananara did more than just fly over them, Garet,' Tarja told him with a grin. 'She strafed them. They must be having quite a crisis of faith at the moment. How many priests do you think they have left out there?'

'Not many. The priests liked their creature comforts. Most of them were billeted in the Citadel.'

'Then they lack spiritual guidance as well as leadership. How many fled?'

'A few thousand at least,' Garet informed him. 'Any word from King Jasnoff yet?' Their demands had been sent in a carefully worded message to the Karien king. They'd dispatched a dozen birds carrying the same message, to ensure that at least one got through.

Tarja shook his head. 'It's far too early to expect a response. The birds we sent may not have reached Yarnarrow yet.'

'What about our relief forces?'

'Maybe R'shiel will be able to tell us something when she gets back.'

Garet nodded and took a seat on the other side of the desk. Tarja was too restless to sit. There was too much to be done.

'I've had the lads check the stores. We've enough here to hold out for years. Mathen was looting the country-side, but he was rather considerately storing it all here in the Citadel. He was expecting to use it for the troops outside.'

'Which means they'll get hungry soon.'

'That'll thin their numbers some more. Desertions are always a problem when your army isn't being fed.'

'Well, between the Harshini scaring the wits out of them and their bellies grumbling, hopefully, by the time help arrives they'll be down to a manageable number. Has there been any trouble in the city?'

'No more than usual. Once again, thanks to Squire Mathen, the people are getting quite used to living under martial law. And we reopened the *court'esa* houses, so that's eased the tension, somewhat.' Garet smiled faintly. 'I did it in your name, of course. You're very popular at the moment.'

'I wonder how long that will last?'

The walls trembled faintly again before Garet could answer. The tremor he had felt in the tunnel under the amphitheatre had not been his imagination. They had been going on all day, growing steadily stronger and more frequent. He frowned and glanced at Garet, who looked just as concerned.

'That's all we need,' he muttered. 'First a siege, then the Harshini, and now a bloody earthquake.'

'It's not an earthquake, Tarja,' Shananara informed him, stepping into the office as Mandah opened the door for her. 'It is the Citadel awakening from his slumber.'

'You talk as if the Citadel is alive.'

'The Citadel may not be "alive", by your definition, Tarja. But it is sentient by ours.'

'This is where I leave,' Garet announced, rising to his feet. 'You can sit here and swap pagan fairytales with the Harshini, Tarja. I have better things to do.'

Shananara turned her regal gaze on the commandant. 'You are Garet Warner?'

'You've heard of me?'

'Brakandaran speaks quite highly of you, sir. For a human.'

'Does he now?'

Tarja recognised the dangerous edge to Garet's soft-spoken reply and inwardly cringed. This could get very ugly if he didn't head it off, and quickly.

'Are your people settled in, your majesty?'

'Yes, thank you, although we took the liberty of removing the tapestries and other . . . impediments, that you have used to disguise the Citadel's origins. I hope you don't mind. It looks almost like home again, now.'

As far as Tarja was aware, most of the dormitories had been whitewashed to conceal the Harshini frescoes that had once decorated the walls. He sighed; they had been here barely more than a few hours and already they were redecorating.

'You didn't do any structural damage, I hope?'

'The Citadel is not that easy to harm, my lord.'

He wasn't sure what she meant by that and decided he really didn't want to know. 'Garet was just telling me that your rather dramatic entrance this morning has caused quite a stir among the Kariens.'

She shrugged. 'We cannot fight with you, my lord, but we help where we can. Xaphista's believers either deny our existence or consider us the essence of pure evil. Either way, they do not know how to react when they see us.'

'We deny your existence, too,' Garet pointed out. 'Yet our people aren't panicking.'

'No, Commandant, you have never denied our existence. You tried to eradicate us and thought you had succeeded. There's a distinct difference.'

Garet glared at her, but made no further comment. The building trembled again, hard enough that Tarja clutched at the desk for support. Shananara looked around the room thoughtfully for a moment then turned to Tarja.

'I really should do something about that, I suppose.'

'Exactly what did you have in mind?'

'I need to speak to the Citadel. It can feel our presence, but the humans here are disturbing it. Once I've reassured it that you mean us no harm, things should settle down.'

Garet muttered something that sounded suspiciously like a curse.

'How can you speak to . . . it . . . him . . . whatever the hell it is?'

'It will have to be in the Temple of the Gods. The Citadel's presence is strongest there.'

'I'll have someone escort you.'

'Founders, Tarja! You don't seriously think sending this woman down to talk to a building is going to stop an earthquake, do you?'

Shananara turned to Garet with a serene smile. 'Perhaps you and the Lord Defender would like to accompany me, Commandant?'

'Why? So we can watch you talking to the walls?'

'No, Commandant,' the Harshini Queen replied with solemn dignity. 'You should come because you and your people have occupied our home for two hundred years. You have vandalised and defiled it, with no thought to the consequences. It is time you understood what you have done.'

## 53

Like R'shiel, Tarja had never been able to refer to the Great Hall as Francil's Hall without choking on the words. At least now he could change that, if nothing else. The Great Hall would be known as the Great Hall once again, although, as he escorted Shananara up the broad steps with Garet, he wondered how long it would be before the Harshini convinced everyone to refer to it by its original name: the Temple of the Gods. If they were as determined to do that as they were to return the dormitories to their original condition, he figured it would only be a matter of days.

It was almost sunset and the chill of the coming evening was settling rapidly over the Citadel. A score of Defenders stood on guard outside the Hall, causing Tarja to glance questioningly at Garet. He'd ordered no detail to guard the Great Hall, and there was no need he knew of to protect it. Shananara strode on ahead, anxious to do whatever it was she was planning. The ground trembled under their feet.

'Why the guards?' he asked the commandant curiously.

'We've confined the priests in there. Couldn't think of anywhere else to put them.'

Tarja cursed softly and hurried after the Harshini queen. The guards on the doors, seeing the Lord Defender and Commandant Warner were escorting the Harshini, made no effort to prevent her from entering. She disappeared inside before Tarja could stop her.

He pushed open the door to find Shananara frozen in shock. She was as pale as the whitewashed walls and looked as if she had forgotten how to breathe. More Defenders lined the walls, watching the Karien priests warily. The hall itself was littered with bedrolls and the milling priests who had been confined within. They were still dressed in their dull brown cassocks and all but a few had stubbled heads and the beginnings of scraggly beards.

Nobody was foolish enough to give these men a razor.

Robbed of their staffs and their dignity, they were a sorry lot. The priests turned at the sound of the doors opening, showing no interest in the new arrivals, until someone noticed Shananara's eyes.

And then all hell broke loose.

The priests began shouting hysterically. Some of them rushed towards the Harshini queen while others backed away in fear. The building trembled, as if in outrage. Shananara cried out, but it was a cry of despair, rather than a scream. The Defenders reacted immediately, calling for the guards outside to reinforce their numbers as they drove the priests back. Tarja drew his sword and stepped in between Shananara and the oncoming priests, whose eyes burned with fanatical hatred.

He felt, rather than saw, Garet take a stand beside him, just as ready to carve a few priests up as he was. The priests who had thought to attack the Harshini backed off sullenly, as wary of the dangerous look in Tarja's eyes as they were of the blades he and Garet wielded.

Once the other Defenders were inside the Hall, the ruckus was put down quickly. The Kariens were no match for the armed Defenders, particularly men who were itching for any excuse to cause them harm. Garet Warner issued his orders with a few hand signals and the priests were herded into a loose circle in the centre of the Hall, surrounded by the Defenders. Tarja studied them warily for a moment then slowly sheathed his blade before turning to face Shananara. She was shaking all over, and although he had no ability to detect it, he had a strong feeling that she was channelling her power. For a moment he was very glad it was not R'shiel standing there. The priests would be splattered all over the walls if it had been Shananara's half-breed cousin under attack.

'I'm sorry, your majesty. I didn't know they were being held in here. I'll have them removed at once.'

Shananara shook her head. 'No. Leave them. Just keep them out of my way.'

'Are you sure?' He studied her warily. He knew the Harshini were incapable of doing harm, but right at that moment he wasn't that certain Shananara could be trusted.

The Queen nodded then took a deep breath and walked past Tarja towards the centre of the Hall. The Defenders cleared a path for her, pushing the priests back, being none too gentle about it.

Shananara looked about her, ignoring the priests and the Defenders, then she closed her eyes and the Citadel began to tremble in earnest.

Silence descended, fractured only by a whimper that came from one of the priests as the Harshini queen stood in the centre of the Hall, her head thrown back, her eyes closed in concentration. Certain he was imagining it, he thought he saw a faint glimmer of light surrounding her in a soft, white nimbus. Small white flakes began to fall from the whitewashed ceiling.

The Citadel rumbled beneath his feet.

It was only a few at first, and Tarja thought them simply the result of the building's movement. But soon the flakes of whitewash began to fall faster, until he felt as if he was caught in a snowstorm. A sudden popping made him jump as a plug of plaster burst out of a small alcove in the pillar on his right. It was followed by a dozen or more tiny explosions as the plastered-over niches spat out their fillings, which shattered into powder as they hit the floor.

The Hall shook so hard it rattled his teeth.

The paint on the ceiling was coming away in strips now, and he could just make out the first signs of the paintings underneath. The walls blistered and their white-wash began to fall off, too. He was powdered in flaking whitewash and plaster as he glanced at Garet, who looked as if he'd been dipped in flour. The commandant's eyes were dark sockets of incomprehensible horror set in a bone-white face. The priests began to wail in terror as the building shuddered so hard that Tarja could barely stand upright.

Shananara did not move.

Then a splintering sound echoed loudly through the hall. Tarja looked in the direction of the sound through the swirling white storm and noticed a large crack had appeared on the wall at the back of the podium. Another crack appeared and then another, sundering the painted symbol of the Sisters of the Blade that decorated the far wall. Shananara had claimed the Citadel was not easily harmed, but she appeared to be bringing the building down on top of them. The wall cracked even further and began to crumble, but amazingly, the half-cupola over the podium held fast.

As the wall tumbled down in a shower of plaster and white dust, taking with it the last vestige of the Sisterhood's imprint on the place, Tarja saw the reason why. The wall had been nothing more than a false front, concealing the rest of the podium behind it. Red light from the setting sun flooded the circular alcove, turning the falling white dust into glittering motes of fire. The cupola was tiled in an intricate pattern, resting on a curved wall that was painted with a glorious fresco, although from where he was standing, he could not make out the detail.

But it was not the fresco, or the gilded dome that made him stare in wonder. In the centre of the podium was a massive crystal, taller than a man, mounted on a block of polished black marble. He had no idea what it was, or what its purpose might be, but it obviously held pride of place in the Temple of the Gods. He realised then why the wall had been built to hide it. Too massive to move and probably indestructible, there would have been no way to get rid of the Stone when the Sisters of the Blade had tried to remove all vestiges of the Harshini from their new home.

They had done the next best thing and hidden it.

The shuddering slowly trembled to stillness and Tarja looked about him in awe. Shananara had restored the Hall to what it had been during the reign of the Harshini. Although it was almost nightfall, the pillars shone as bright as day. The ceiling had a painting on it that depicted the Primal Gods. Along the gallery was a mural dedicated to even more gods. It looked as if a hundred – maybe a thousand – different craftsmen had added to it over the years. The parts of it he could see were magnificent. There was writing – songs perhaps – covering some of the walls, too. The pillars supporting the gallery now had alcoves set in the side of each one and he wondered for a moment at their purpose.

Then he noticed the priests and forgot all about the Hall.

To a man, they were on their knees. Some were sobbing like broken-hearted children. A few others were tearing at their robes, howling with despair. One man was clawing at his own face until the blood flowed. Then a shattering scream pierced the sudden silence as one of the priests leaped to his feet and ran blindly towards him.

Tarja felt his stomach churn and had to forcibly stop himself from vomiting. Where the priest's eyes had been was nothing but two bloody sockets. In his hands he held his own eyeballs. The fool had clawed his own eyes out rather than witness the return of the Harshini.

Tarja caught the man and wrestled him to the ground. The man was howling in pain and outrage. Tarja looked up angrily at Shananara, who had finally lowered her head and opened her eyes. If she was distressed by what the priests were doing to themselves, she gave no indication.

Garet helped Tarja hold the hysterical priest down as Shananara approached. The commandant looked as pale as the powdered paint that coated him.

'Is *this* your idea of doing no harm?' he snarled at the queen.

Shananara looked down at the blind priest for a moment before she answered. 'This is Xaphista's work, not mine, Commandant. To heal him would mean forcing him to break his faith and he holds that more dearly than his eyes. Even if I could restore his sight and remove his pain, he would just claw his eyes out again as soon as your back was turned.'

There was a strange twisted logic in what she said. A Karien priest would rather suffer and die than acknowledge the existence of the Harshini or the God of Healing. Tarja had no doubt that she could heal him – he had seen the Harshini ability. He also had no doubt that she was right when she claimed the man would simply try to harm himself as soon as they let him out of their sight. They were a sick breed, these priests. The sooner R'shiel did something about Xaphista the better.

'Get him to the infirmary,' Tarja ordered, standing back to let two of the guards pick up the struggling, howling priest.

Tarja looked at the other priests, who had been stunned into silence by the courageous action of their brother. They wore the look of men who thought he had done something to be proud of. *How many more of them were contemplating the same thing?* Suffering for Xaphista was more than just a hopeful wish for these men; it was damned near a job requirement. He had to put a stop to it. Now.

'The next one of you that tries to harm himself,' he announced loudly, 'will be delivered to the Harshini for healing. And he'll stay there until he denounces Xaphista and swears allegiance to the Primal Gods.'

Shananara looked at him in surprise then nodded approvingly as she realised what his threat would mean to these men.

'How long is that going to last?' Garet asked, ineffectively brushing the white dust from his jacket.

'Tarja's threat is very real to these men, Commandant.

They will avoid stubbing a toe rather than risk being touched by one of my people.'

Garet stared at her coldly then looked around the Hall. 'Did you make this much mess redecorating the dormitories?'

'Not quite.'

'And what the hell is that thing?' he asked, pointing at the crystal on the podium.

'It is the Seeing Stone.'

Garet stopped trying to clean his jacket and stared at the crystal with a thoughtful expression. 'I thought that was in Greenharbour?'

'There is also a Stone in Greenharbour. This one belongs here.'

'What does it do?'

'It channels the power of the gods, among other things.'

Garet absorbed that piece of information silently and then looked at the priests. 'I suppose we'd better get them out of here. I'll move them to the Lesser Hall.' He looked at Shananara and added frigidly, 'Unless of course, you're planning to do this to every building you walk into, Your Majesty?'

'I will not disturb your prisoners again, Commandant,' she assured him.

Garet obviously doubted her word, but did not voice his scepticism. He looked at Tarja and shook his head. 'Look at this place, Tarja. They haven't been here a day yet.'

'I'll get everything sorted out,' Tarja promised, not at all certain he believed his own words.

'Well, you can start by making the Harshini clean up this mess. After all, she caused it.' With a pointed and very unfriendly glare in Shananara's direction, Garet

Warner moved off to organise moving the Karien priests from the Great Hall.

'I'm sorry, Tarja,' Shananara said as soon as Garet was out of earshot. 'I thought only to help by calming the Citadel.'

The Harshini could not lie, so legend claimed, but he wondered if she was bending the truth a little. She must have known what making the priests witness her power would do to them. Or perhaps she really didn't understand. If she couldn't contemplate the thought of violence, how could she imagine a man willing to put his own eyes out?

'The damage is done now. At least the tremors have stopped.'

'That's because the Citadel is awake.'

'Is that going to cause problems?'

She smiled suddenly. 'Come and see.'

Grabbing his hand she pulled him towards the doors. He noticed that the bronze sheathing had peeled away and they were now carved with unbelievably intricate knot-work designs that chased themselves across the doors in a complex pattern.

They stepped out of the Hall into a street that was crammed with people. The sun had set, but it was as bright as day. The walls of the Citadel had brightened and dimmed with metronomic precision for two centuries, but now, when they should have faded to darkness, they were burning with vibrant light. Every building he could see was ablaze, banishing the night.

'Founders!' he murmured in awe.

His sentiments were reflected in every face he saw. Although crowded, the street below the Great Hall was strangely silent as the people tried to make sense of what they were witnessing.

Then he heard the noise, like a distant wail of despair, coming from the distance, from the other side of the walls. *The Kariens.*

'Come with me,' he ordered abruptly, running down the steps. Shananara followed him as he pushed through the crowd. It took a while and a great deal of elbow work to get to the main gate, and he didn't stop when he reached it, or bother to check if Shananara was still with him. He bolted into the gatehouse and up the stairs to the wall-walk to look down over the plain. .

The camp below was in chaos. The Kariens seemed to have moved from their earlier panic to utter desperation. Some cried out in horror at the sight that transfixed them. Others were fleeing in terror. Tarja glanced back over his shoulder at the tall towers and then looked down at the walls.

The whole Citadel was glowing like a beacon in the darkness, casting its benign light as far as the bridges over the Saran.

## 54

Without consulting him, or giving him a reason, R'shiel announced that rather than return directly to the Citadel, she wanted to check on the progress of Damin and Hablet and the armies they were bringing to relieve the Citadel. He wondered at her decision but did not question it, suspecting that it had much to do with the night they had spent in Sanctuary. She did not want to face Tarja so soon, he guessed, or the Harshini who would know what they had done.

He wanted to explain to her that the unique Harshini way of sharing pleasure was not riddled with the same emotion-laden guilt that humans insisted on attaching to sex. For the Harshini it was a celebration of life; simply another way to express their joy for living. Harshini did not marry and the concept of jealousy was unknown to them. They shared their bodies and their irresistible, magical gift with no thought to the consequences, or any real understanding of the importance humans attached to it. Among them, it was never a problem: For the Harshini there was no need to explain and nothing to justify.

But when they shared that gift with humans, things got complicated. He had told R'shiel that life had been peaceful and happy before the Sisters of the Blade, but it was jealousy of that peace and happiness that had given rise to the Sisterhood. Their whole sick cult had grown out of the fear of a handful of human women afraid they could not compete with the impossibly perfect, magically gifted Harshini. The original First Sister, Param, had been a bitter old woman whose younger husband had had a fling with a Harshini woman and never recovered from the experience. Param never understood that what had driven her husband away was not the loss of love, but the fact that no human coupling could ever compare with the magic a Harshini could weave.

Only Brak knew that the Harshini woman who had so thoughtlessly shared her body and her gift with the handsome young human who took her fancy was actually Shananara té Ortyn.

She had told him about it a few days after it happened, afraid that she might have conceived, aware that any half-human child of hers would be a demon child. He understood her predicament a little better than her full-blooded kin. She was fearful of explaining what she had done to her uncle, Lorandranek – or worse, the gods, who, back then, would never have contemplated such a child being allowed to exist. Xaphista wasn't as strong then and the other gods paid him little mind. When her moontime came and went a few weeks later, Shananara swore off humans, claiming they weren't as satisfying as Harshini in any case, and thought nothing more of it. None of them had.

Until Param and her Sisterhood overran the Citadel and set about destroying the Harshini.

He glanced across at R'shiel as the dragons flew southward, following the silver ribbon of the Glass River, and decided not to tell her. She had too much going on inside that head of hers already. She would cope with what had happened in her own way, and if he had done nothing else, he had freed her from the last vestiges of her grief over Tarja. Although she did not realise it, her Harshini heritage was strong. Her conversation with Mandah in the hall outside the First Sister's office sprang to mind. Letting Tarja go like that, being so willing to stand back and let Mandah have a clear field, was probably the most Harshini thing he had ever seen her do.

They were a few hours north of Bordertown when they spied the Fardohnyan fleet. Brak was amazed they had come so far so quickly, even with Harshini help. The ships were strung out in a line, their oars dipping and rising in perfect unison.

Maera, the Goddess of the Glass River, and Brehn, the God of Storms, were assisting their passage. While Maera hadn't gone so far as to make the river flow backwards, the strong currents that characterised the river were now so mild that the oarsmen could keep up their steady pace for hours. Between Maera's help, the winds that Brehn provided (which conveniently changed direction with every bend in the river) and the Harshini, who had flown south to join them, the Fardohnyans were likely to be in Brodenvale within a couple of weeks.

Satisfied that the Fardohnyans were on their way, they did nothing more than swoop down over the fleet and wave before turning south-east towards Hythria.

It took them nearly a week to find Damin. His call to arms had been answered, but the same problem that had plagued Damin when Greenharbour was under attack was still causing trouble. The Warlords' armies were scattered throughout Hythria and it was taking a mammoth effort, both logistical and magical, to gather them all in one place.

They found him eventually, still in Hythria, but close enough to the border that he would be over it in a few days. They landed on the edge of Damin's camp at sunset. The High Prince was waiting to greet them, with Adrina at his side. She was noticeably pregnant, but was glowing with good health. Brak frowned when he saw her. Damin should have had more sense than to let a woman in her condition ride into battle. Then again, when it came to Adrina, he guessed Damin probably didn't have much say in the matter.

'Nice of you to drop in, demon child,' Damin said as he stepped forward to greet them. His good mood no doubt had as much to do with the fact that he was off to war again, as it did with his pleasure at their arrival. Brak had always liked Damin, but he was a warrior at heart. The responsibilities of a High Prince, a wife and a child on the way weren't likely to change him.

R'shiel smiled, just as pleased to see her friends as they were to see her. She eyed Adrina with a slight frown and shook her head. 'Adrina, what are you doing here?'

'Not much, if the truth be known. Damin won't let me do a damned thing.'

'He shouldn't have let you come at all.'

'As if I had any say in the matter,' Damin complained. 'Hello, Brak. How was Fardohnya?'

'Interesting.'

Damin laughed. 'I want to hear all about it. We're waiting for Rogan and his Raiders to catch up with us at the moment so we've a day or so to spare before we get moving again. Are you here to stay?'

'No,' R'shiel answered for him. 'We have to get back to the Citadel.'

'Well, we might as well enjoy the evening, then. Will the dragons be all right out here?'

'They'll be fine. Is Glenanaran with you?'

'He's resting at the moment. It's taken a lot out of him to get us this far so quickly.'

'Did the others arrive safely?' He wasn't sure who among the Harshini had volunteered to join the Hythrun, or even how many there were.

Adrina nodded. 'They arrived a couple of days ago. I've never seen so many Harshini before.'

'Neither has anyone else,' R'shiel agreed. Then she caught sight of a small figure half hidden behind Adrina. 'Mikel! What are you doing hiding back there?'

The Karien boy stepped forward with a hesitant smile. 'My lady.'

'Look at you, Mikel! You've shot up like a weed! What are you feeding him, Adrina?'

'Hythrun army rations,' Adrina told her with a grimace. 'I'm glad they have such a beneficial effect on small boys. They do absolutely nothing for my taste buds.'

'Always complaining,' Damin sighed, but he was smiling at Adrina, who glanced back at him warmly. The change in them was astounding. Adrina had never looked better, and Damin, who had always been a cheerful sort of fellow, appeared ready to burst with happiness. 'Come on then. Let's go sample the culinary delights of Hythrun army rations, and you can tell me how the hell you managed to get Hablet to send his fleet to our rescue.'

R'shiel slipped her arm through Damin's and the three of them turned back towards the tents, as R'shiel began to relate how she had blown the doors off Hablet's palace in Talabar.

Damin's tent proved to be more luxurious than he normally preferred – no doubt a concession to Adrina, who made no secret of her desire for life's creature comforts. Despite the dire warnings about Hythrun army rations, dinner was delicious, the wine excellent and the company entertaining.

The High Prince and his princess sat close together on the low scattered cushions and once Mikel cleared the remains of dinner away from the low table, Adrina leaned against Damin unselfconsciously as they shared their news from the past weeks. Damin draped an arm over her shoulder in a gesture that seemed as much possessive as affectionate. They still argued a lot, but it lacked the vicious edge of their earlier encounters – although Adrina's caustic wit had not dulled, and neither had Damin learnt to take anything seriously.

Watching Adrina and Damin together, Brak wondered if Kalianah had taken a hand in their romance. He decided she hadn't. They were too well suited to each other. Kalianah's interference was required only when a couple would never fall in love unless she stepped in. She took a perverse pleasure in doing that, too. It gave her a sense of power. But the Hythrun High Prince and the daughter of the Fardohnyan king were obviously kindred spirits. He wondered idly whether if Damin had not been so keen to avoid Adrina earlier, their obvious attraction – which, according to what he'd heard in the Defender's camp in Medalon, was apparent from the moment they laid eyes on each other – would have caused trouble sooner.

It might be a very different world if it had.

Damin was relating the tale of Greenharbour's dramatic rescue by the unexpected appearance of the Defenders when Brak caught sight of Mikel out of the corner of his eye. He turned and watched as the child approached R'shiel. He was holding a goblet – a plain, metal cup with nothing to distinguish it from any other in the tent – but he held it reverently, as if it was an offering to the gods.

'So, there we were,' Damin was saying, 'ready to burn Greenharbour to the ground and I hear trumpets in the distance. I thought I was going mad.'

'But why did the Defenders head for Greenharbour?' R'shiel asked. 'I thought the plan was to muster them in Krakandar.'

'It was,' Damin agreed. 'But somehow the messages got mixed up and the Defenders thought I'd left orders for them to move south. The irony of it all,' he added with a laugh, 'was the reason they got there so damned quickly. Denjon and Linst were so furious that I'd left such high-handed orders, they pushed their men south as fast as they could move, just so they could tell me off.'

R'shiel laughed and glanced up at Mikel. She accepted the cup and turned back to Damin and Adrina. 'I wish I could have seen the look on your face when you realised the Defenders had come to your rescue. How did the rest of your Warlords take it? It must have irked them no end.'

'By the time the Defenders arrived, I think they would have accepted help from just about anybody,' Adrina told her with a smile. 'They'd already had to swallow their pride and accept my brother's help, but grateful though they seemed, I think the Defenders were like rubbing salt into an open wound.'

R'shiel chuckled and lifted the cup to her lips. Mikel had remained standing behind her. His eyes were wide, his body tense.

'*R'shiel*! No!'

Brak threw himself across the low table, knocking the cup from her hand before she could take a swallow. Adrina screamed. R'shiel was thrown backwards by the force of his sudden weight and struggled to push him away, more startled than frightened. Damin was on his feet, his sword in his hand before Brak had rolled clear. Mikel froze with panic for a moment then ran for the entrance. Still on his hands and knees, Brak reached out and snatched at the boy's ankle, bringing the child down. Mikel cried out in protest, but Brak's vice-like grip allowed him no escape. Damin stepped over the cushions and picked up the discarded cup, sniffing it suspiciously.

'Jarabane,' he said. 'It's poisoned.' He hurled the cup to the ground then he turned his attention to the boy.

Mikel was stretched out face-down on the floor of the tent, trying to kick his way free, but unable to escape while Brak held him.

Damin nodded to Brak, who released him as Damin grabbed the child by his shirt and hauled him to his feet. He pressed the point of his sword into Mikel's neck.

'Damin! No!' Adrina cried, reading the murderous look in her husband's eyes. 'He's a child!'

'He's an assassin,' Damin corrected.

Brak climbed to his feet, offering R'shiel his hand to help her up, and they exchanged a worried glance. There was no trace of humour left in the High Prince, and no trace of mercy.

'Damin, Brak and I need to take care of this,' R'shiel said. She sounded calm and reasonable, just as aware as

Brak that at that moment, Damin was dangerously close to – and more than capable of – cold-blooded murder.

'This child is a member of my household. He tried to kill a guest under my roof. Even if you weren't the demon child, R'shiel, the penalty for such a crime is death.'

Mikel had not uttered a sound. He was paralysed with fear. A small trickle of blood oozed from his neck where Damin held the point of his sword with his right hand, his left gripping the boy by his shoulder.

'If you kill him, Damin, we won't be able to question him.'

'What's to question? The child is Karien. He obviously follows the Overlord. What more do you need to know?'

R'shiel turned to Brak, her eyes silently begging him to reason with him.

'We need to know why he turned from Dacendaran,' Brak added. 'The God of Thieves took a personal interest in this boy, and somehow he's been subverted. I don't want to interfere with your idea of justice, Damin, but if you harm that boy before we have a chance to talk with him, you'll regret it.'

Damin glared at Brak. 'Are you threatening me?'

'Yes, Damin,' he replied softly. 'That's exactly what I'm doing.'

For a moment, Brak wondered if that had been a wise thing to do. He may have just said the one thing guaranteed to push Damin beyond reason. For a long, tense moment, the High Prince stared at Brak defiantly, then he lowered the sword and thrust Mikel at Brak.

'You have an hour, Brak. Ask him what you want, do what you want. But in one hour that child dies for what he's done. R'shiel, I hope you will forgive this grievous insult.' He sheathed his sword as Brak caught the boy who was shaking so badly he could barely stand. 'Oh, and by the way, don't think to leave this camp with him,' he added with an icy glare at Brak. 'If you do, I will simply turn around and go home. I'll call off my Warlords, and the Medalonians can face the Kariens on their own and to hell with them.'

Damin strode out of the tent without another word. Brak pushed Mikel down onto the cushions and looked over at Adrina.

'Can you talk him out of this?'

She shrugged helplessly. 'I don't know. I've never seen him so angry.'

'You've got an hour, Adrina,' R'shiel pointed out coldly.

The princess nodded. 'I'll do what I can, but he may not listen to me. I was the one who brought Mikel here.'

'Then you'd better do something about keeping him alive, hadn't you?' the demon child said unsympathetically.

## 55

The God of Thieves appeared at R'shiel's summons, although he looked rather put out by the call. R'shiel had told Brak that Kalianah thought Dace was sulking about something and he wondered if the reason had been Mikel.

The child was a study in abject despair. He sat huddled on the cushions, his knees drawn up under his chin, tears streaming silently down his face. He had said nothing. In the warm glow of the candlelight he was an island of misery and dejection.

'What do you want, demon child?' Dacendaran asked sullenly as he materialised behind R'shiel.

'What's the matter with you?' she demanded as she spun around to face him. Although she knew he was a god, R'shiel had known Dace as a simple thief in the Grimfield first, and she often made the mistake of still thinking of him that way. Brak wished she were a little more cautious. He might look cute and adorable and wear an air of guileless innocence, but Dacendaran was still a god, and a powerful one at that.

'I'm busy,' Dace muttered, scuffing the rug with a boot that did not match the other he wore.

'I want to know what happened to Mikel.'

'You stole him from me,' Dace accused with a petulant scowl.

'*I* stole him from you? Don't be ridiculous! I'm not a god! How could I steal him?'

'You gave him to Gimlorie.'

'Oh,' R'shiel said, suddenly looking guilty. 'That.'

Brak glanced at R'shiel for a moment and then looked at Mikel. 'Why did you give him to the God of Music?'

'I needed to make sure the Kariens would leave, so I asked Gimlorie to help.'

'What *exactly* did you do, R'shiel?' Brak asked suspiciously.

'I asked him to teach Mikel a song that would instil an irresistible longing for home in the Kariens. I knew it might be a little bit . . . dangerous . . . so I asked Gimlorie to make his brother Jaymes his Guardian. That way, if he got lost in the song, Jaymes would be there to pull him back.'

Brak muttered a curse. 'R'shiel, have you any idea what you've done? A Guardian is only effective if he's in touch with his ward. Once Jaymes left his side Mikel was vulnerable to this sort of manipulation.'

'Hey, how come suddenly this is all my fault? *He* tried to kill *me*!'

Neither Brak nor Dace answered her.

'I needed to turn them back,' she added defensively. 'It seemed like a really good idea at the time.'

'Gimlorie's songs are dangerous, R'shiel. They can twist men's souls around. You should never have taught one to this boy.'

'I didn't teach it to him. Gimlorie did. He didn't seem to mind when I asked him.'

'Of course he wouldn't mind. Every soul who hears it hungers for him. But it's what it has done to Mikel that you should be concerned about.'

'Are you saying Gimlorie is the one who turned Mikel into an assassin?'

'No,' Dacendaran said. 'Gimlorie wouldn't do that. But what you *did* do was leave Mikel vulnerable to Xaphista.'

'Humans need faith to believe in the gods, R'shiel,' Brak added in a lecturing tone. 'What you did was take away Mikel's freedom to believe or not believe. You destroyed his free will and made him a creature of the gods. Any god.'

R'shiel turned to the boy and stared down at him impatiently. 'Is that what happened, Mikel? Did you go back to worshipping the Overlord?'

Mikel shook his head silently, too distraught to speak.

'Then why? Who told you to do this thing?'

'The old man,' the child replied in a voice so low even Dacendaran had to strain to hear him.

'What old man?' Brak asked.

'The one in Hythria. At the palace. He told me to give the demon child a gift. He said it would help her see the truth.'

'What old man is he talking about?' R'shiel asked Brak.

'It was probably Xaphista himself,' Dace shrugged.

'Can he do that?'

The God of Thieves gave the demon child a withering look.

'Oh, well, I suppose if you can do it, so can he.' She turned and studied the miserable figure hunched on the cushions for a moment then turned to Brak. 'Why Mikel?'

'Because he's young, he's impressionable, he's feeling guilty for turning away from his god in the first place, and,' he added with a frown, 'you left him wide open to manipulation when you opened his mind to Gimlorie's song.'

'Well, how was I supposed to know it would do that? The Harshini sang it all the time in Sanctuary. It didn't seem to bother them.'

'The Harshini are already a part of the gods, R'shiel. But even they will only share it among themselves. No Harshini would ever share the song with a human.'

'So what do we do with him?'

'I don't know, but we've got about half an hour to make up our minds,' he reminded her grimly.

'Dace? Can't the gods do something?'

The god shook his head. 'You can't *un*teach him, R'shiel, and he's done the Overlord's bidding. None of the gods has any interest in saving this child.'

'But he was your friend, Dace!'

The god stared at her. His smile faded and for a moment he let R'shiel see the true essence of his being. The lovable rogue was gone and there was simply Dacendaran, the God of Thieves, powerful, implacable and concerned only with his own divinity. Brak had seen it before and the knowledge of what the gods were truly capable of was at the core of his distrust of them. But R'shiel had never been confronted with it until now and it stunned her.

She took a step back from Dacendaran in fear.

'Do what you want with the child,' Dacendaran said in a voice that chilled Brak to the bone. 'His fate is of no concern to the Primal Gods.'

Dace vanished, leaving them alone in the tent. R'shiel appeared to be having trouble breathing. Mikel had still not moved, resigned to his fate – perhaps even welcoming it. He would soon be dining at the Overlord's table.

Damin Wolfblade would see to that.

They came for him on the hour, three heavily armed Raiders who were there to stop them from trying anything heroic, Brak suspected, rather than any real need to escort an eleven-year-old to his execution. They didn't try to prevent the men from taking the boy, even with magic. It would simply have angered the High Prince. The bind that Damin Wolfblade had placed them in was untenable: go to the rescue of those in the Citadel or stand back and watch a child put to death for the crime of being easily manipulated.

Adrina was waiting outside with Damin. Her eyes were swollen and she had obviously been fighting with him. Damin's eyes were bleak and unforgiving. Behind Adrina were the Harshini who had come to aid the Hythrun in their quest to relieve the Citadel. Glenanaran stood at the front of the small gathering of Dragon Riders. Brak could feel their pain from the other side of the clearing. This was a vicious way to reintroduce them to the world of humans.

One look at Damin and Brak knew that Adrina had not changed his mind.

'You can't order this, Damin,' R'shiel told him as Mikel was escorted across the clearing to stand before the High Prince of Hythria. 'You can't ask a man to execute a child!'

He looked at her. 'I don't ask anything of my men I wouldn't do myself.'

'Damin, *no*!' Adrina cried in horror. She ran forward and grabbed his arm, but he shook her off impatiently.

'You don't have to watch, Adrina. Nor do you, Divine Ones,' he added, looking over his shoulder at the horrified Harshini. 'This is none of your concern.'

'Damn it, Damin, be reasonable!' R'shiel yelled angrily as he began to walk away with Mikel and the guards in his wake.

Damin stopped and turned to her, then he walked back to confront her, his eyes blazing in the torchlit clearing among the tents.

'Reasonable?' he snarled. 'Define "reasonable", demon child. Is it reasonable that I let this child live so he can turn on you again? It is reasonable that I let an assassin reside in the heart of my family? Suppose Adrina had taken that cup? Suppose Brak hadn't noticed something was wrong? What the hell do you expect me to do?'

'You cannot murder an eleven-year-old boy for something that wasn't his fault. He's a child, Damin, a tool. If anyone is to blame, it's me.'

Her calming tone did nothing to deter him. 'R'shiel, I have lived with assassins all my life. I grew up afraid of the dark, because for me, the darkness *was* likely to conceal danger. I will not have *my* child raised the same way. I will not have him sleep with armed guards standing over him. I want him to grow up playing with children his own age, not learning how to take down men twice his size in case he's attacked. I want the whole damned world to know what I'm capable of if they dare to threaten me or mine. This ends now.'

'He didn't threaten *you*, Damin, or your wife and child. He was trying to kill me.'

'You're my friend, R'shiel, and he did it under my roof. It amounts to the same thing.'

'Do this thing and we won't be friends any longer, Damin.'

Brak watched him hesitate for a moment, but the implacable rage that consumed the Warlord was not something so easily swayed. Even faced with the horror of what he was about to do, Brak found himself sympathising with Damin. He'd been alive for seven hundred years and seen worse things done for lesser reasons. He didn't know how many men had tried to kill Damin as a boy, but he could see now the scars that it had left on him. He was willing to do anything, literally, to save his unborn heir from the fear he must have lived through as a child, not realising that in order to slay the monster, he would become a monster himself.

Brak saw the look of horror in Adrina's eyes and the pain of this confrontation emanating from the Harshini like waves of desperation. And he could see in Damin's eyes the weight of the decision he had been forced to make. For Damin it boiled down to a simple decision: the life of a Karien child or the life of his own child.

'I'll do it,' Brak said, stepping forward into the torch-light.

R'shiel rounded on him in horror. 'Brak!'

'I'm sorry, R'shiel, but Damin has a point. If he doesn't deal with this, he'll never put an end to it. The child needs to die. He has to make an example of him.'

Damin looked stunned to find such an unexpected ally. 'I cannot ask a Harshini to do this. I won't even ask it of my own men.'

'I'm a half-breed, Damin, and it won't be the worst thing I've done.' He turned to the Harshini and met Glenanaran's black eyes evenly. 'Take the others away from here, Glenanaran. Just pray to the gods that watch over this child that Death comes quickly for him.'

The Harshini stared at him for a moment, while Brak silently willed him to understand. Then Glenanaran nodded solemnly. 'We will pray for the child.'

*Then do it quickly*, Brak urged silently.

The Harshini turned and vanished into the darkness. R'shiel watched him with dismay as he walked across the clearing and took Mikel by the hand. Damin stood beside her, surprised and a little suspicious of Brak's willingness to kill.

'How do I know this isn't a trick?'

'This is no trick, Damin.'

He grabbed Mikel by the arm and pulled him clear of the guards, then drew the dagger from his belt. He turned it for a moment in his hand as if testing the weight, then he glared at Damin.

'Are you planning to watch?'

'Yes.'

'You're a sick son of a bitch, aren't you?'

'No, just a distrustful one. I don't believe you'll do it.'

*He's calling my bluff.* But he could not draw on his power to create an illusion. Damin would notice what he was up to as soon as he saw his eyes darken. R'shiel stood with Damin and made no move to stop him, either. She too was calling his bluff.

He looked into the eyes of the confused child. Mikel had moved beyond fear and stepped over into paralytic terror.

'Are you ready to meet Death, Mikel?' he asked softly, almost gently. Adrina choked back a sob in the background and the torches were hissing loudly in the unnatural silence.

Almost as soon as the words left his mouth, he felt the presence of a god and almost sagged with relief. All around them, the air was suddenly filled with unnatural, crystalline music as the figure of Death appeared in the clearing. He wore a long hooded cloak, blacker than the night surrounding them. His face was a pale skull, his hollow eyes radiated light and he actually carried a scythe in his left hand.

*Theatrical bastard*, Brak thought sourly.

'This is the child you wish me to take?' the spectre asked in a musical voice that boomed through the clearing.

'Yes, my lord.'

'You presume a great deal, Brakandaran.'

'This is necessary, my lord.'

The being glanced around the clearing until his eyes alighted on R'shiel. Brak noticed, with some relief, that she was more suspicious than frightened. She was a smart girl. She would work out what was going on sooner or later. He just hoped that when she did figure it out, she kept her mouth shut.

'Demon child,' he said, with a slight bow in her direction.

'Divine One.'

The creature swivelled his fearsome head towards Mikel then and held out a skeletal arm to the child. 'Come.'

As if in a trance, the Karien boy walked towards the spectre unresistingly. There was no fear in his eyes now, only quiet acceptance. Death took the child by the hand, cast a withering gaze over the stunned humans and disappeared, taking Mikel with him.

The silence that followed was chilling. Adrina screamed.

The sound broke Damin out of his trance and he ran to her, but she pushed him away and turned on Brak savagely.

'Get out! Get away from here! You murderous, cold-blooded bastard!'

'Adrina . . .' Damin said, trying to take her in his arms.

'Don't touch me! This was your idea and now look what you've done. Leave me alone!' She fled from the clearing sobbing loudly. Damin spared Brak a helpless look and followed after her.

Brak turned to find R'shiel standing alone in the clearing, her arms crossed, staring at him disapprovingly.

'Why?'

He shrugged. 'Less blood this way.'

She crossed the space between them in three strides and punched him painfully in the shoulder. 'What the hell was all that about?'

'Damin was going to kill him, R'shiel, make no mistake about that. It might have seemed like a good idea now, but I suspect it would have had long-term consequences he hadn't thought about. Don't worry about the boy. Gimlorie will keep him out of harm's way for the time being.'

She looked ready to hit him again. 'You got Glenanaran to call Gimlorie, didn't you? That's why the Harshini didn't object.'

'Clever girl.'

'But why pretend he was Death?'

'Damin had to believe Mikel was dead, or he would have finished the job himself. Actually, I thought Gimlorie did a fair imitation of Death myself, although the scythe was a bit over the top.'

'Is Mikel dead?'

'He's residing with the gods, temporarily.'

'Will you stop being so bloody cryptic!'

He smiled at her anger, which did nothing to help. 'I'll explain later. In the meantime, I think we should get out of here before Adrina decides to have me hung, drawn and quartered.'

'Where are we going to go at this time of night?'

'Back to the Citadel. I'm getting a little fed up with Xaphista. I think it's about time you fulfilled your destiny, demon child.'

## 56

R'shiel was surprised by the number of Kariens camped around the Citadel as they flew towards it. The invading army had now pulled back behind the shallow Saran River. They had blocked the bridges with overturned wagons and there was clear ground between the Citadel and the Karien troops. There seemed to be fewer Kariens, although they still numbered in the tens of thousands. The combination of dwindling supplies, no spiritual or military leadership and, she learnt later that day, the news that the Harshini had returned, had played havoc with the siege army.

She had no time to dwell on it, though, as she noticed the Citadel. It was just on dusk, and she had expected to see the Dimming begin as the walls paled and lost their radiance with the coming night. But the Citadel shone like a lantern in the gathering gloom, casting its soft light out towards the Saran. It made sense, then, why the Kariens had pulled back behind the water. They were hiding in the darkness where the Citadel's illumination could not touch them.

The dragons settled on the sandy floor of the amphitheatre as the sun set completely, but even here the night was banished by the radiance. A Defender R'shiel didn't know came out to greet them, casting his eyes over the dragons with the world-weary air of a man who had seen it all before, and informed them that the Lord Defender was expecting them, and required their presence immediately.

'Where have you been?' Tarja demanded as soon as they appeared in the doorway. 'We expected you back days ago.'

'We were checking on Damin and the Fardohnyans.'

'How close are they?' Garet asked. He and Shananara were sitting in the heavy leather chairs facing the desk. Tarja paced behind it like a restless cat.

'The Fardohnyans should reach Brodenvale late next week. Damin's not far behind them. Another few days I suppose.'

'That's impossible!' Garet exclaimed. 'There is no way they could have covered that much distance in such a short time.'

'You forget the Harshini and the gods are actively helping them, Commandant,' Shananara reminded him.

'I don't care who's helping them, your majesty. It is simply not possible to sail upriver so quickly, even in oared warships. Or march an army through anywhere at that speed.' He turned to Brak and R'shiel, shaking his head. 'You must be mistaken.'

'We're not mistaken, Garet. Believe it, or don't believe it. It makes no difference to us.' R'shiel stepped into the office, took the seat beside Shananara and turned her gaze on Tarja. He looked tired. 'The Defender who met us in the amphitheatre said you wanted to speak to us.'

'We got a reply from King Jasnoff.'

'What did he say?'

'It was pretty long-winded, but the essence was, "Kill my dukes and I'll turn Medalon into a graveyard".'

'What are you going to do now?' R'shiel asked.

'That's what we were just discussing,' Garet informed them. 'Tarja wants to wait until the relief forces arrive, and then attack the Kariens outside. I think we should stick to our original plan: kill one of the dukes and send Jasnoff his head to prove we're not bluffing. Her majesty here wants us to lay down our arms, put flowers in our hair, and swear eternal peace and brotherhood with our enemies.'

R'shiel smiled, not at all sure that Garet was joking. 'Well, I happen to like Shananara's idea better.'

Tarja frowned at her. 'This is no joking matter, R'shiel. Do you have anything constructive to offer? If not, we don't need you here.'

'Actually, I do. I want you to give the priests back their staffs and let them go.'

Even Shananara baulked at that suggestion. 'You can't be serious.'

'She's serious,' Tarja said, studying her intently. 'It was your idea to take them hostage, so I'm told. Now you want to let them go. You have a reason, I suppose?'

'We need them outside, where they can influence their troops.'

'I was under the impression that the whole purpose of confining them here was to *stop* them influencing their troops,' Garet remarked. Oddly, he had not objected to the suggestion. R'shiel thought his would be the loudest voice raised in protest.

'That was before *I* figured out how to influence the priests.'

'So, we let a hundred fanatical priests loose among the

currently leaderless and uncoordinated troops outside, who outnumber us about seven to one, on the off chance that you can make them act the way you want?' Garet asked. He nodded thoughtfully. 'That sounds reasonable. Perhaps we could just throw all the people in the Citadel off the walls, too, so our enemies won't have to go to the bother of putting them to the sword.'

'Your wit is exceeded only by your blindness, Garet,' R'shiel retorted impatiently.

'At least I *have* my wits. You seem to have lost yours.'

'Garet . . .' Tarja said warningly, in an attempt to head off the argument. He turned to R'shiel with an expression that left little doubt of his reaction if she continued to bait the commandant. 'How can you influence the priests?'

'Their staffs are made up of pieces of the missing Seeing Stones. They're like a conduit. If I can find the Seeing Stone here in the Citadel, I can use it to channel whatever I want through it to the priests.'

'But how is that possible?' Shananara said.

'Well, if *you* don't know, that hardly fills me with confidence,' Garet muttered.

'My guess,' Brak interjected, understanding what Shananara was asking, 'is that either the Fardohnyans or the Sisterhood sold their Stone to the Kariens and they broke it up. They're the only two that are missing.'

'Well, it wasn't the Sisterhood,' Tarja informed them. 'We've found the Citadel's Seeing Stone.'

'You found it? Where?'

'In the Great Hall. There was a false wall at the back of . . . R'shiel!'

She did not answer him or even hear what else he had to say.

R'shiel was on her feet, out of the office and barrelling down the stairs with Brak on her heels before anyone could stop them.

'What happened here?'

R'shiel's voice echoed through the Great Hall, although it seemed strange referring to it by that name. This was the Temple of the Gods in all its majestic glory. This was the place that Brak had described to her with such melancholy longing. She understood now, what he had been trying to tell her.

'My guess is Shananara,' Brak said, his voice filled with awe. 'If the Citadel needed placating, she would have done it here.'

'It's fantastic! Look!' She walked the length of the Hall to the podium. The Seeing Stone stood before them, twice the size of the one R'shiel had used in Greenharbour. It reflected the radiant pillars with a soft light that filled the hall, banishing the shadows, highlighting the exquisite artwork. 'Oh, Brak, why did they ever try to hide this?'

'Because they were human, and humans have a tendency to destroy anything they don't understand.'

R'shiel reached up and ran her hands over the cool surface of the Stone, then turned to him doubtfully. 'Do you think this will work?'

'It's theoretically possible.'

'That's what you said about coming back from the dead.'

He shrugged. 'Well, that relies on the whim of Death, so it's not that cut and dried. This, however,' he said pointing at the Stone, 'is a lot more straightforward. The problem is not if it's possible, though.'

'Then what is the problem?'

'R'shiel, you have raw power to burn. You threw Sanctuary into hiding like it was a child's toy. But that required brute force, not finesse. What you want to do to these priests is going to call for a delicate touch that you are a century away from achieving.'

'Then perhaps I should wait? That gives you another hundred years to live.'

He smiled at her. 'I doubt the Primal Gods would be so patient. Besides, you'd be pretty sick of me in a hundred years, R'shiel.'

'How do you know?'

'Even the Harshini don't stay together that long. It's why they don't get married. There's only so much you can take living with another person before they start to wear on you.'

'Will I be as cynical as you when I'm seven hundred years old?'

'You're worse than me already.'

She smiled and sat down on the steps of the podium. He sat beside her for a moment in silence as she took in the monumental Temple. All of this was her legacy, her inheritance. She laid her head on Brak's shoulder, trying not to let the knowledge of his impending death distract her.

For a moment, she closed her eyes and let the silence and the memories of Sanctuary overwhelm her. She wished Brak had not put conditions on it – wished he would wrap them in that unbelievable cocoon of magic again and transport her to that other plane where pleasure and indulgence were the only things that mattered . . .

'Founders!' She sat bolt upright and stared at him wonderingly.

'What?'

'I don't need finesse, Brak.'

'You don't?'

'No! I need *pleasure*!'

'Here? *Now*? A bit public, don't you think?'

'Don't be an ass!' she said, leaping to her feet, giddy with the knowledge that she knew, with absolute certainty, how to bring Xaphista undone. 'Don't you see? The other night the Harshini could feel us. You said even Xaphista could feel it. You said he made his people turn away from pleasure because it distracts them from him.'

Brak looked at her askance. 'What are you suggesting we do, demon child? Have an orgy here in the Temple of the Gods and channel it through to the priests via the Seeing Stone?'

She laughed. 'You'd be surprised how close you are to the truth, Brak. Come on!'

She grabbed his hand and pulled him to his feet then headed down the Hall, dragging him in her wake.

'R'shiel!'

'What?'

'Where are you going?'

'You'll see,' she said with a laugh.

He stopped and pulled her back. 'Enough! I'm not taking another step until you tell me what you're up to this time.'

'Don't you trust me?'

'Not in the slightest.'

She sighed heavily. 'Brak, I'm going to distract the Kariens. I'm going to take their minds off Xaphista for a while.'

'Is that all?'

She nodded. 'That's all I *have* to do, Brak.'

She saw the dawning light of comprehension in his

eyes and smiled. Brak shook his head ruefully. 'You're a sneaky little thing, aren't you? I'm glad you're on our side.'

'It'll work, won't it,' she said. It was a statement, not a question.

He nodded slowly. 'Yes. It should work.'

'Then let's go see Tarja.'

'Gods, you're not going to tell him what you're planning, are you?'

'Of course not. I'm going to ask him to throw a party.'

## 57

The following day, Tarja relented and agreed to let the priests go. Garet objected vehemently, but once she had spoken to Shananara and had her support, his advice was overruled. Tarja doubted her, she could tell that from the way he looked at her and the edge of scepticism in his voice. But with the knowledge that the Fardohnyans were close, and Damin Wolfblade not far behind, he seemed to think that she couldn't do their cause much harm and was prepared to indulge her. Up to a point.

The priests were herded from the Lesser Hall towards the gate at dawn the next day. Two of them led another priest whose eyes were bandaged, although R'shiel did not know what had happened to him. Parked near the entrance to the gatehouse was a covered wagon, inside which were the confiscated staffs. Once she'd talked her way around Tarja's objections, and the Defenders realised the stones were mere crystals rather than diamonds, avarice gave way to apathy. But she was not so foolish as to stand in range of a priest wielding his staff, which was the reason she had chosen this vantage on the wall-walk, high above the main gate.

As they neared the wagon, a Defender threw back the tarpaulin. The tonsured men swarmed over it, grasping for the security of the symbols of their rank. One of the priests glanced up, caught sight of her and shook his staff, mouthing some insult she couldn't hear. Others followed his gaze as they reclaimed their sacred sceptres. An uneasy prickle of apprehension washed over R'shiel as she watched them.

'Brak, was it such a good idea to let so many of them gather like this armed with their staffs?'

'You can't influence the Overlord's priests through their staffs if they don't have them,' he shrugged. 'Don't worry. I don't think they can—'

His words were cut off by a loud explosion, as the merlon near R'shiel shattered into a shower of flying pebbles. R'shiel ducked for cover as another explosion buffeted her with flying debris. Screams of terror, and the Defenders' cries of alarm, suddenly filled the street below.

'You don't think they can *what*?' she shouted over the commotion.

Brak saw her eyes darken and laid an urgently restraining hand on her arm. 'They destroy magic, R'shiel. You're not linked through the Seeing Stone here. Don't try to fight them.'

'Watch me,' she snarled angrily.

R'shiel stood up and looked down over the street. Defenders were rushing heedlessly to fight an enemy they could not comprehend, while the citizens who had come to watch the priests being released milled about in panic, looking for a way to flee the sudden carnage, too afraid to approach the gate. All other escape routes were blocked by the Defenders.

She spied the cause of the trouble quickly enough.

Three tonsured priests held their staffs above their heads, chanting in unison as they called on the power of the Overlord to strike down the demon child. The other priests were not yet organised enough to join in the Watching Coven, but it would not take them long. Three priests she could handle. She knew that from experience. Any more and she could not predict the outcome.

Turning her attention to the first priest, she hurled a burst of raw power at the staff, understanding now what she had done by accident on the northern plains of Medalon. Whatever spell made the staff drain magic, its focus was the small chip of Seeing Stone at its core. The power she threw at it overloaded the crystal and the conflict between the force at its centre and the staff's ability to absorb magic created an explosion that threw the priest to the ground with bleeding eardrums. She repeated her effort at the next man, and then the one beside him, careless of the power she was drawing.

Several others defiantly held up their only protection against her, only to find themselves lying prostrate on the ground, their staffs shattered, the gold star and silver lightning bolt fused into a glob of worthless metal. R'shiel could feel rather than see Brak beside her. He shouted something at her that she couldn't understand. Something about using restraint, but all he could do was stand at her side, ready to catch her if she fell.

It took a dozen or more explosions for the priests to be dissuaded from any further attempts to destroy the demon child; much longer for the Defenders to restore some semblance of order. R'shiel clung to the power, standing over the gateway, her eyes burning black as she dared them to try her again. She was trembling and exhausted and felt Brak's arm slide around her waist gratefully. If she appeared to be a tower of strength to the Kariens below, then let them think that. There was no need for them to know that he was holding her up.

'You've come this far. Don't give up now, demon child,' Brak whispered as she slumped against him.

'I think I'm going to faint.'

'No you're not,' he told her sternly. 'You're going to stand up here and watch every last one of them leave.'

'Don't let me go, Brak.'

'I won't.'

She stood there for a long time, leaning into Brak's solid strength as the Kariens picked up their staffs and filed through the gate beneath her. Towards the end of the line, another small commotion broke out as the three priests left discovered they didn't have a staff they could claim.

'Seems someone decided to collect a few souvenirs,' Brak remarked.

'Looks like it,' she agreed distantly.

R'shiel watched the last of the priests leave. She heard the gate close behind them, then turned to watch as they ran towards their forces on the other side of the Saran. She did not let go of the power until they had crossed the bridges and put the shallow river between them and the Citadel.

The celebration that was organised to mark the departure of the priests had been harder to arrange. R'shiel had eventually convinced Tarja that it would be good for morale, but more than that, it would annoy the Sisterhood. Even Garet didn't mind annoying the Sisterhood, and with the strict rationing the Defenders had imposed, they were in no danger of running out of food. A bit of largesse would go a long way to easing the minds of the population, she pointed out reasonably, and there were still a lot of Sisters of the Blade in the Citadel, looking for any excuse to stir up trouble. She had listed all her reasons calmly and didn't even try to pick a fight with Garet Warner. Tarja eventually agreed and had given Captain Grannon the task of organising such a mammoth affair. All R'shiel had to do now was convince the Harshini to do their part.

The dormitories where the Harshini were quartered were nothing like those R'shiel remembered living in. The whole building glowed with light and colour. She walked the corridors with her mouth agape at what had been hidden under the whitewash, until she reached the place Shananara was using as a dayroom. It had been the Mistress of the Sisterhood's office until recently.

'I hear there was some trouble at the gate,' Shananara remarked as R'shiel knocked on the open door.

'The priests took exception to my presence,' R'shiel told her with a shrug. 'But I discouraged them from doing anything about it.'

'I know,' the Harshini queen replied with a grimace. 'I have the headache to prove it. I really wish you would learn some restraint, R'shiel. You can be very exhausting at times.'

'I'm sorry.'

Shananara smiled and indicated that R'shiel should sit. The heavy furniture seemed out of place now. With the walls restored to their former glory, these rooms needed light, airy pieces, not the cumbersome dark furniture the Sisterhood favoured.

'Brak tells me you have a plan.'

'I need your help,' she said, taking the seat opposite the queen.

'We cannot help you destroy Xaphista, R'shiel. For that matter, I could not help you if you wanted to step on a bug.'

'I know that. And I won't ask anything of the Harshini that goes against their nature – but I need to distract his believers for a while.'

'Distract them? How?' Shananara asked suspiciously.

R'shiel explained what she had in mind. The queen listened to her, nodding occasionally, then finally laughing delightedly. 'And you honestly think this ploy will work?'

'Brak seems to think it will.'

'Yes, well Brak is half-human. It would probably appeal to his rather skewed sense of humour.'

'Then you'll help me?'

'Yes, demon child, the Harshini will help you.'

'Even knowing it may result in the destruction of a god?'

'I don't know that will happen for certain, R'shiel. For all I know, this will do nothing but annoy him.'

R'shiel nodded, aware that the queen was right. Brak thought it might work, but none of them could be sure. 'I have another favour to ask.'

'I'll grant it if I can.'

'I need you in the Temple of the Gods with me. I don't have the skill to do this alone.'

'I cannot take a direct hand in this, R'shiel.'

'No, but you can show me what I have to do.'

'Very well,' Shananara agreed with some reluctance. 'But don't count on my help. I don't mean to sound like I'm threatening you, but I simply cannot do anything that goes against the nature of the Harshini. I will do what I can, but you may find, at the point where you need my help the most, I will be useless to you.'

'I'm prepared to risk that.'

'Then I will be there, demon child. And may the gods guide our hands.'

R'shiel had one other task to perform before she was ready, and when she left Shananara, she hurried through the streets to the Defenders' blacksmith shop. They had finished the job she had asked them to do and she examined their handiwork closely, careful not to brush against it, until she was satisfied that it was exactly what she had asked for. The sergeant in charge of the forge smiled as she looked over it.

'You can touch it, lass. It doesn't bite, you know.' He was shouting to be heard over the ringing of hammers on metal. The smiths and the fletchers had been working non-stop for days, turning out weapons and arrows to be stockpiled in case of a Karien attack.

'Actually, Joulen, it does bite.' She straightened up and nodded in satisfaction. 'Can you get one of your men to take it over to the Great Hall for me? Ask them to put it near the Seeing Stone.'

'Aye, if that's what you want.'

'It is, thank you.'

It was late afternoon when R'shiel left the blacksmith's forge, satisfied she had done all that she could for the time being. All that was needed now was for Xaphista to walk into her trap.

## 58

Music from the amphitheatre drifted on the night as musicians warmed up their instruments. The Citadel blazed softly under a cloudless, blue-velvet sky. R'shiel looked down over the Karien camp from the wall-walk at the scattered fires that pierced the plain like dollops of hot blood in the darkness. The fires stretched as far as she could see. She had done everything she could think of, covered every contingency.

There was nothing left to do now but wait.

'It's been pretty quiet down there since we let the priests go.'

She glanced at Tarja, aware that he was rather uncomfortable. This was the first time they had been alone since her return. She had brought him here to talk to him undisturbed. That was never going to happen in his office. There were things she needed to say to him, for her own peace of mind, if nothing else.

'They're probably down there plotting our downfall,' she remarked, trying to sound lighthearted.

'I'd say that was almost a certainty.'

She glanced at him, but he was staring down at the

plain with determination. His profile was guarded.
'Tarja.'

'Yes?'

'I'm sorry.'

He turned to look at her. 'For what?'

'For what Kalianah did to you. For all of it, I suppose.'

Tarja shrugged, not comfortable with either the subject
or her apology. 'R'shiel, there's really no need . . .'

'Yes there is, Tarja. At the very least, it eases my guilt
a bit.'

'In that case, apology accepted,' he said, smiling faintly
to assure her of his sincerity.

There were ten thousand other things that R'shiel
wanted to say to him, but Tarja seemed satisfied that the
subject was painlessly closed. He turned back to watching
the plain in silence. R'shiel sighed and decided to let the
matter drop. There was nothing to be gained from
opening old wounds. Tarja had obviously been at pains
to put the past behind him.

R'shiel's thoughts turned to the coming confrontation.
She tried to calculate how much longer she had to wait.
It was the evening of Fifthday. Tomorrow was Restday
and, at dawn, every Karien would be crammed into the
village churches, every city dweller would be crowded into
the nearest temple. Even the soldiers below would turn
their backs on the Citadel to listen to their priests. And
that's when she would make her move. When every Karien
voice would be raised in worship of their god.

It was when Xaphista would be at his most powerful.

It was also when he was most vulnerable.

'If this works,' she said, breaking the silence, 'all Damin
and Hablet are going to have to do is mop up.'

'Mopping up tens of thousands of Kariens and getting

them back across the border will be a job in itself, R'shiel. And don't forget that we still have to gain control over the rest of Medalon. The Sisters of the Blade here in the Citadel might appear to be toeing the line, but I suspect it's only because of the siege. They're happy to let us fight their battles for them, but the moment we're rid of the Kariens, they'll start trying to regain their position. We've a very long road ahead of us.'

'You'll make a good Lord Defender, Tarja.'

He shrugged. 'I never wanted to be Lord Defender, you know, not even when I was a Cadet. I knew what people were saying about me. I knew everyone thought I was being groomed for the job and the idea terrified me. The responsibility terrified me. It still does. I was much happier as a simple captain on the southern border fighting Damin Wolfblade. Life was a lot less complicated back then.'

'I think Damin would agree with you. He's finding some of the decisions required of a High Prince a bit more than he bargained for.' For a moment she recalled Damin's unforgiving eyes as he sentenced Mikel to death. Tarja would be confronted with similar dilemmas, she was certain. She envied neither of them. Then she smiled, as something else occurred to her. 'He has Adrina with him.'

'Oh, wonderful,' he groaned.

'Don't worry, Tarja,' she assured him, laughing softly at the expression on his face. 'You'll be safe. She only has eyes for Damin, these days. Besides, she's due to give birth soon. You never know . . . she might have the child here in the Citadel and decide to name it after you. But I think you'll find her too preoccupied to worry about flirting with you.'

He looked very relieved. 'I like Adrina, but she can be very . . . trying.'

With a sympathetic smile, R'shiel turned her back on the Kariens and leaned against the softly glowing wall. She folded her arms across her body and studied the pattern in the stonework beneath her feet for a moment, working up the courage to say what she had brought him up here tell him.

'Tarja, when this is over, I'm leaving.'

He looked at her in surprise. 'Where are you going?'

'I have some things to take care of. Loclon is still out there somewhere, for one thing. I won't rest until I've dealt with him.'

'I'm sorry we didn't find him. No, worse than that, I'm sorry I didn't kill him. You were right. You warned me years ago that I should have put an end to him that evening in the arena when he killed Georj. Do you know how often I wish I had?'

'Probably nearly as often as I do.'

For a moment, he couldn't meet her eyes. The memory of what Loclon had done to her was too dreadful to confront. He glanced back over the plain before he answered.

'We didn't see any sign of him when we let the Kariens out. He may still be in the Citadel.'

'No, Tarja. He's long gone. But it doesn't matter. I'm half Harshini. I have several lifetimes to fill. I don't mind using one of them to find Loclon.'

He nodded silently, needing no further explanation.

'I have to get Mikel back, too.'

'Mikel? That Karien boy who crossed the border with Adrina? What happened to him?'

'The God of Music is minding him for a time. I have to go and get him back.'

'A god is *minding* him?' Tarja repeated doubtfully. 'I don't really want to know what that means, do I?'

She laughed softly. 'No.'

'Will you come back when you've finished?'

'I don't know,' she shrugged. 'There's something else I have to do, but I don't think it's going to be that easy, and I don't know how long it will take. You can keep a lantern burning for me, Tarja, but don't wait up.'

He smiled then, perhaps even a little relieved that she would not be around to remind him of a past he thought better forgotten. Kalianah's geas was not yet a distant memory. Time would make the past easier to come to terms with. He was no longer her brother and would never again be her lover, but she could count him a friend.

'I'll miss you.'

'No you won't. You'll be glad to see the back of me. So will Garet. And Mandah.' He turned from her, and it took R'shiel a moment to realise that it wasn't anger that turned him away, but embarrassment. 'Oh, Tarja, don't be so foolish. I know I've never been friendly with her, but Mandah adores you. I worked that out when we first met in Reddingdale. I suppose that's why I never liked her. That, and the fact that she's so insufferably nice. She's probably one of those Novices who grew up in the Citadel lusting after you and Georj. It doesn't bother me, and you shouldn't let it bother you.'

Tarja suddenly grinned at his own foolishness. 'That's very noble of you, R'shiel.'

'Actually, Brak said the same thing.'

Tarja's grin faded at the mention of Brak. There was still a degree of residual distrust between them, R'shiel knew. Brak had done a great deal that Tarja found hard to forgive. 'Is he going with you when you leave?'

She shook her head sadly. 'No, Tarja. Where Brak is going, I can't follow.'

He was silent for a moment then looked at her strangely. 'Do you love him, R'shiel?'

'Not in the way you think. It's something else. You wouldn't understand. The Harshini would.'

'The Harshini,' he sighed heavily. 'I don't suppose there's any chance the Harshini will want to leave the Citadel too, once this is all over and done with?'

'Not much,' she agreed with a grin.

He shook his head ruefully. 'Well, wherever you go and whatever you do, R'shiel, spare a thought for me every now and then. Things are going to get a lot worse before they get better, I fear.'

R'shiel smiled sympathetically, but didn't answer him. They stayed on top of the wall for a while longer, until the discordant notes of the distant musicians ceased. Then the air was filled with the strains of a cheerful melody as the party in the amphitheatre got under way. By unspoken agreement, they turned and walked back down the spiral staircase in the gatehouse to the street and headed towards the music.

## 59

R'shiel had feared that allowing the Harshini to mingle with the people of the Citadel in the amphitheatre would be inviting trouble, but she need not have worried. Although the Medalonians had spent two hundred years reviling their race, when confronted with one in person, the Harshini were almost impossible to dislike. They did not share the human frailties of shyness or self-doubt, and assumed everyone was as happy to meet them as they were to meet others. Their wide-eyed joy at being invited to share the celebration was infectious. After a moment's awkward silence when the Harshini first arrived, the party settled down again and the citizens of the Citadel set about enjoying themselves as if the Karien army outside did not exist.

'Isn't it amazing what a bit of free food and alcohol will do for a city's morale,' Brak remarked as he found R'shiel sitting high up in the tiered seating of the amphitheatre watching the party.

'You think *that's* going to help morale? Just wait till they find out that the *court'esa* have been laid on free of charge for the evening.'

'How did you get Tarja to agree to that?'

'Ah, well . . . come to think of it, I didn't actually mention it to him. He's pretty busy at the moment. I didn't want to burden him with details.'

'I'm sure he'll appreciate your consideration when the *court'esa* houses send him their bills for this evening's entertainment.'

'He'll get over it.'

'You spoke to him, then?'

'Yes.'

'*And*?'

'And what? There's nothing much to tell, Brak.'

'No more guilt? No more pain?' he asked gently.

'No.'

'Then all that is left to do is wait, demon child.'

She nodded silently. Brak slipped his arm around her shoulder against the cold and she leaned against him as they watched the party in silence, waiting for the dawn.

The party was still well under way when R'shiel and Brak rose from their seats high in the amphitheatre and made their way to the Temple of the Gods. The sky was still dark, but R'shiel could feel the morning approaching. The Citadel was ablaze with light, adding its own unique essence to the celebrations. They walked through the almost-deserted streets in silence, aware that the overwhelming atmosphere in the Citadel was not one of fear or tension, but – temporarily at least – one of joy.

Shananara was waiting for them in the Temple of the Gods, her expression serene and hopeful. She smiled as they walked across the echoing floor to greet her.

'For the first time since I've been back, the Citadel almost feels like it used to,' she remarked.

'Let's hope it lasts,' R'shiel said, suddenly plagued with doubt.

'Have faith, demon child.'

R'shiel didn't bother to answer that. Faith was something she had been raised to scorn. Instead, she looked at Brak and Shananara questioningly. 'What time is it?'

'Almost dawn.'

'Then there's no point in putting this off any longer.'

She turned to face the Seeing Stone and opened her mind to the power. Drinking in the intoxicating sweetness, she let it fill her until her eyes burned black and she trembled with the raw force of it. She could feel Shananara reach for it too, and then Brak. His eyes darkened until they were as black as ebony. The torrent that she and Shananara could channel was vast compared to the mere stream he had access to, but his touch was that of the maestro next to her ham-fisted grasp. At the edge of her awareness, she felt him call to the Citadel. The mammoth awareness was slow to respond. But Brak knew the Citadel and the Citadel knew Brak. It was a relationship that was centuries old and beyond her comprehension.

In the distance, inside the Citadel, she heard shouts of alarm and the sound of a woman screaming. The walls began to pulse with light. They throbbed as the Citadel responded to Brak's call. R'shiel felt him stir. She felt the Citadel's touch and it almost brought her to her knees. Once before he had reached out to welcome her. She realised now that the last time he had merely glanced over her with mild interest.

R'shiel turned her attention to the Temple of the Gods and called out silently for Brehn, the God of Storms. He was waiting for her. Clouds began to gather over the fortress with unnatural speed, blotting out the rising sun and casting a pall of fear over the army outside.

She called out to the other gods. Jagged lightning split the awakening sky as Dacendaran appeared beside her in his motley garb, and beside him Jondalup, the God of Chance materialised. Further along the hall Kalianah appeared, but for this occasion she chose to appear as a young woman, rather than the child she normally preferred. She stood there in all her radiant glory, blinding any man foolish enough to look upon her. One by one, the other Primal Gods appeared, many of whom R'shiel could not even name. But every one of them she had summoned had answered her call. They couldn't help it. She was drawing on so much of their essence that even they were under her compulsion for a time. Finally Zegarnald appeared, curiously smaller than normal, although he still stood as high as the gallery.

Through the link she shared with Shananara she had no need for words. By mutual agreement they reached out to embrace the Citadel. Every thought, every mood, every happy laugh, every bawdy song and dancing couple, every lover's caress was drawn into their net. R'shiel drew it to her, relying on Shananara's skill to filter out the odd discordant thought – a fight between two drunken Defenders over an insult from their Cadet days. Two women squabbling over whose baby was the prettier. A lover's quarrel. All of it swirled through the net they wove, and with the skill of a master, Shananara refined it and filtered it until it was almost a concentrated essence of joy and happiness and pleasure.

But mixed in with the joy was more than just simple human pleasure. The Harshini were here and they willingly lent their essence to the emotions R'shiel and

Shananara were distilling. Passion, pleasure and a hint of the wonder R'shiel had experienced in Sanctuary with Brak were added to the potent blend. The feel of it was enough to make R'shiel's spine tingle, and she had to concentrate hard to avoid losing herself in the sheer ecstasy of it.

R'shiel had no concept of time, no idea if it was fully dawn yet, or if a whole day had passed. She opened her eyes, seeing nothing but the crystal that loomed in front of her, and placed her hands on the Seeing Stone.

Taking a deep breath, R'shiel hurled everything she had gathered at the Stone, not attempting subtlety or finesse. She had only her strength to rely on, and the knowledge that every Seeing Stone would respond to her sending. *Every Seeing Stone and every part of one.* Every staff that contained chips of the broken Stone absorbed the elixir of joy that she threw at it greedily. Every drop of pleasure that she could wring from the Citadel she hurled at them, then sent her mind out to follow.

She had unleashed chaos.

The Seeing Stone in Greenharbour pulsated with light, and she caught a glimpse of Kalan, standing before the Stone, her face alight with rapture as she tried to fathom its unaccountable behaviour. With a blurring, gut-wrenching twist, R'shiel found herself looking down over another Stone in a dank cave, surrounded by tonsured priests, who wailed with despair as the pleasure emanating from the Stone began to draw them from their god. In the back of her mind she felt the Stone in Sanctuary, hidden far out of time, trying to answer the call. She gathered her thoughts that were rapidly being torn apart by the maelstrom and threw her mind northward towards Karien.

She reached for any part of any Seeing Stone that she could touch, and the chips of crystal responded immediately. She saw a large temple with a ceiling covered in mother-of-pearl tiles, a priest in glorious robes gripping his staff with wide, terrified eyes as his congregation fell under the spell she was weaving. Another place, another temple. Another terrified priest. Another congregation caught in the thrall. An orgy of rapturous pleasure. Everywhere she cast her mind the response was the same. Her own savage joy suddenly swelled the link and she turned from the Stone.

It didn't matter now. The damage was done. The power flowed through the Seeing Stone like a dam that had broken under the weight of too much rain. All the pleasure, all the joy, all the sin denied to his believers hit the Overlord's people like a wave of bliss that made them forget everything for a brief moment in time . . . including their god.

She felt a surge of power from the Citadel as it reached out to embrace her, to bolster her resistance – and not a moment too soon. She had barely taken her hand from the Stone when Xaphista appeared, striding through the other gods, his eyes burning with anger.

'*Stop this abomination!*'

Although she well knew the seductive touch of his spirit, R'shiel had never seen Xaphista in material form. She found the sight a little disappointing. He chose to appear as an old man, with long white hair that flowed around his broad shoulders, although the physique he affected belonged to a much younger man. His dark cassock rippled in the breeze of his passing and in his hand he carried a staff that almost brushed the ceiling, topped by a small sun that radiated beams of blinding light through the Temple.

'*How dare you! These are my people!*'

The ground trembled with his wrath.

'I'm just reminding them of what you've made them forget!'

Xaphista's answer was to hurl a blast of rage at her that almost knocked her off her feet. But the Citadel surged to meet it, adding his implacable will to her own, so it merely buffeted her like a sudden gust of magical wind.

The Primal Gods did nothing. There was nothing they could do but grant her open access to their power. Xaphista was stronger than them combined. That was the danger of him. It was the reason they created the demon child, and the reason they could do little but rail helplessly against him. Individually, they did not have the strength to fight him, and their own, inviolable laws did not permit them to kill him. The demon child was their only hope.

'*You defy me at your peril, demon child!*'

'You threaten me at yours!'

And then, like a tap suddenly turned off, she felt Shananara let go of her power. R'shiel felt it go, and staggered under the weight of Xaphista's wrath, but the Harshini queen could not hold her power against the might of the God's anger. But as the torrent through the Seeing Stone dwindled to nothing, Xaphista let out a cry of unimaginable pain. Although she wasn't certain, R'shiel guessed that across the length and breadth of Karien, the thrall was slowly being shaken by his followers. In the aftermath of R'shiel's storm of pleasure and joy, one over-riding, overwhelming feeling now consumed the hearts of his believers.

Doubt.

'It's over, Xaphista. The Kariens have begun to doubt

you. How long will they belong to you once Kalianah or Zegarnald walk among your followers? They are yours no longer!'

'*You will never be strong enough to defeat me, demon child.*'

'I'm not trying to defeat you, Xaphista. I just want your people to doubt you.'

The Overlord looked down on her with blazing eyes. '*You cannot take my people from me!*'

'You think not? You've spent centuries convincing them the others gods don't exist. Every time a Karien turns round now, there will be a Primal God waiting for them. I'll flood the world with miracles. I will have Jondalup turn every human who games into a winner. I will have Dacendaran turn every person into a thief. Cheltaran will heal every wound, every sick child, every dying old woman. I'll make the Primal Gods answer every single prayer your people utter. You'll be so deep in divine intervention that there won't be a Karien left who can deny the presence of the Primal Gods within a month.'

'*Such recklessness would destroy the natural balance of the universe.*'

'I don't care.'

She truly didn't, and Xaphista knew she wasn't lying. R'shiel had not been raised among the Harshini. Despite everything they had tried to teach her at Sanctuary, despite everything Brak had explained to her since, she still did not quite understand the place the gods held in the scheme of things. It was her ignorance that lent her threat its power. No full-blooded Harshini could have contemplated such a course of action. R'shiel did not appreciate the consequences of her behaviour. She was a child who had accidentally stumbled over a weapon of mass destruction and wanted to use it to get her own way, totally oblivious to the fact that it would destroy her along with her foes.

The Overlord glared at the other gods, who had remained silent for the entire exchange.

'*You cannot hide behind this child. Each one of you will fade into nothing as I grow in strength.*'

'*You cannot destroy us, Xaphista,*' Zegarnald boomed, unable to contain his anger. '*Look at you! Already the doubt begins to take its toll.*'

Zegarnald was right. In the short time Xaphista had been in the Hall, he had visibly diminished. R'shiel wasn't sure how long she had before his priests restored order. Not sure how long the doubt and uncertainty of his believers would last, or how long the pleasure she had swamped them with would distract them from their god.

'*We will have an accounting for this, demon child.*' The statement was as close to an admission of defeat as Xaphista was likely to get. He was not conceding victory and he wasn't going to quit without a fight. He turned on the God of War savagely, even as he dwindled a little more. '*I have no need to destroy you, Zegarnald. When the whole world lies prostrate at my feet there will be no wars and you will be obsolete . . . Each of you represents a vice that my believers eschew. You, Kalianah, and you, Dacendaran – when every human believes it is a sin to love or steal, there will be no need for you, no need for any of you . . . Enjoy your dying moments, Primal Gods. Before long you will be nothing more than sad, forgotten legends.*'

Xaphista's defiant words were at odds with his stature. He was no taller than Brak now, and he no longer had the power to assume the form he chose. A demon stood before them, larger than normal, but still raging defiantly.

It was not a smooth transition. He surged up in size every now and then as pockets of his followers denied what they had seen and felt, but he was dwindling fast. But how much longer did they have before doubt gave way to habit? Before wonder gave way to fear? Before his people shrugged off what they felt, or worse, attributed it to the Overlord and their belief in him came surging back, like the backdraft after a savage explosion?

Not long, R'shiel knew. Not very long at all.

'Go!' she cried to the Primal Gods. 'Go out among his people! Now! While you have the chance!'

Most of the gods vanished abruptly and R'shiel became aware of the noise. A wailing arose that seemed to be coming from everywhere at once. She discovered she was rigid with tension. The Citadel and the plain surrounding it were filled with incredulous, panicked shouting.

She turned to Xaphista, looking down at him as he shrank back to a demon no larger than Dranymire.

And then she felt it.

On the very edge of her awareness.

The backlash.

'*Brak!*' There was more than a little panic in her voice as she cried out to him. She did not have the skill, or even the energy, to do what was needed now. Brak did, however. The crude iron cage built by the Defenders flew through the air, guided by Brak's mind, rather than his hands. He could no more touch it than R'shiel could. It landed with a clatter over the cringing demon that had once been a god – and would be a god again, as soon as the racing wave of belief hit them. Xaphista howled his outrage and then his pain as he snatched at the bars of the cage. The three staff heads welded to the bars absorbed his power as easily as they had tortured the little demon caught by his priests when R'shiel had tried to fool the Quorum into believing that a demon meld was really the First Sister.

And then it hit her.

R'shiel fell hard, only vaguely aware of Brak calling out to her, only dimly seeing Shananara as she collapsed beside her. Xaphista leapt at the bars of his cage, but the force of the backlash hit her and she plunged into unconsciousness before she could discover if her trap was sufficient to contain him.

## 60

When R'shiel finally awoke, it was to find Death standing over her.

The Hall was quiet; even the gods were gone. Daylight, splintered by the stained glass windows, striped the floor in coloured light. Her head was pounding, her body wrung out and weak. R'shiel felt like she had been hit by a falling building.

'Am I going to die now?'

Death looked down at her and shook his head. He was once again in the form of a Harshini, the same benign form he had assumed to escort Korandellan into the Underworld.

With a start, R'shiel realised what that meant. She pushed herself up painfully and looked around the temple. The gods were gone. The temple was just a huge, empty hall once more, devoid of life, devoid of power. On her left, Shananara lay at the base of the Seeing Stone, only the faint rise and fall of her chest indicating she was still alive. R'shiel turned her head, feeling every aching muscle complain in protest. Brak lay not far from her on the right, his skin pallid.

He wasn't breathing.

'*No . . .*'

Pushing herself up painfully, R'shiel scrambled on her hands and knees to his side.

'No . . .' she whispered frantically. 'No, Brak . . . gods no . . . not like this . . . *please* . . .' She shook him by the shoulders, but he showed no sign of life. Urgently, she took his limp body in her arms and held him to her, hugging him tightly, as if her mere presence could draw him back. 'Please, Brak . . . don't do this to me . . . not now . . .' she begged, ignoring the looming presence of Death a few feet away. 'Don't pay any attention to him . . . you never listened to a damned god your whole life . . . please, Brak, don't start now . . .'

'There is no point to this,' Death pointed out, a little impatiently, taking a step closer. 'It is time he came with me.'

'You've taken him already!' she accused, tears spilling down her face.

'It was our agreement.'

'It's my life he was bargaining for. Don't I get a say?'

'No.'

'But why now?' she sobbed, rocking him back and forth, her vision blurred by tears of inconsolable grief seasoned with intolerable guilt. 'Couldn't you have waited even a little longer?'

'It was the backlash, demon child. It affected all the Harshini.'

She glanced over at Shananara, who also lay unconscious on the floor of the Hall. 'Are the other Harshini dead?'

'No. The Citadel will not permit a Harshini to die within his walls. They were protected. The Harshini outside the Citadel would have been too far out of range to suffer more than the edges of it.'

'Being Harshini didn't help Brak much.'

'In death, as in life, Brakandaran was a Halfbreed, child. Like you, he was ever caught between both worlds and the two sides of his nature never sat well together. Perhaps you will fare better in life than he, but I have always known his torment would eventually bring the Halfbreed to my realm.'

'It wasn't that. It was me. I caused the backlash. I killed Brak.' She wiped away her tears impatiently and looked down at him, brushing a stray lock of hair out of his lifeless face. She felt numb with guilt. And overwhelmed by what she might have unleashed. She was almost afraid to ask what had happened beyond the walls of the temple.

'What about the humans?'

'The backlash would not have affected them. Not physically. Only a halfbreed would be in danger.'

'I didn't die.'

'You are far stronger than he was.'

She shook her head. 'No. I might be more powerful, but there was nobody stronger than Brak. And I killed him.' she said dully. 'One way or another, he was going to die because of me.'

'Brak offered his life in exchange for yours some time ago, demon child. He did not die unwillingly.'

R'shiel stared down at Brak, unable to comprehend, unwilling to accept it. All she really understood was he didn't deserve to die for her, not after all she had put him through, all the trouble she had caused. It simply wasn't fair. He deserved better.

She looked up at Death, wondering why she no longer feared his presence. 'Have you come to take him?'

'That was my intention, demon child. But you sent his soul on its way without the body.'

'But you can take his body now, can't you?'

Death stared at her but didn't answer. R'shiel was suddenly frightened that the answer would be one she didn't want to hear. She leaned forward and gently placed a kiss on Brak's rapidly cooling forehead, then climbed slowly to her feet and staggered past Death, falling on her knees near the cage that held Xaphista.

The trap had held. Xaphista cowered in the centre of the cage, trying to stay clear of the magically charged bars. He was whimpering. The magic of the staff heads had shielded him from the blast but his own magic had prevented him from drawing strength from the backlash when he needed it most. She had been afraid the trap would not hold. But the power that had washed over the cage was unfocused. There was no Seeing Stone to direct it, no determined will behind it. Xaphista the God was vanquished. All that remained in his place was Xaphista the demon. And he was a small and rather pathetic looking demon at that.

'I have come for this one too,' Death told her, gliding to her side. 'He will cause less trouble in my keeping.'

'Just his soul,' R'shiel said, glancing up at Death. 'Not the body. I don't want you getting bored one day and deciding to send him back.'

'You presume much, demon child.'

She glanced around the Hall at Brak's body and Shananara's prone form, then looked back at Death. 'I've earnt it, don't you think?'

'Perhaps.'

'And you have to take Brak's body. All of him.'

'His soul has already fled, demon child.'

'You're Death. You can reunite them.'

'To what purpose?'

'Because the gods owe me that much.'

'Was there anything else?' Had she not been so exhausted, she might have detected a slight note of impatience in his tone.

'Is there any way I can get Brak back?'

'I am Death, demon child. I do not run an inn. Lives do not come and go as they please through my realm.'

Significantly, Death hadn't said no. R'shiel climbed to her feet and faced him, willing for the moment to let the matter drop. 'Then can I ask you a question before you go?'

'You may.'

'How many hells are there?'

If he was surprised by her question, he gave no outward sign. 'As many as there are creatures to imagine them, demon child. I do not create them. Each soul creates its own hell. Whether they suffer the afterlife or enjoy it is entirely up to them.'

'So if I want someone to suffer, how do I make sure?'

'Evil is its own reward, demon child.'

She nodded, thinking she understood what he meant. Death turned away from her and looked at Xaphista. The demon trembled under his scrutiny and then suddenly slumped against the bars. The withered grey body no longer cared about the shielded cage. Its soul was gone. Death then turned and opened his arms. Slowly, almost tenderly, Brak's lifeless body rose from the ground, as if cradled like a child. As he gently floated across the hall, R'shiel involuntarily reached out to him, pulling back when she realized what she was doing. She watched silently as Death gathered Brak into his embrace.

Then, without a word, Death vanished. R'shiel stood

alone in the cavernous, empty Hall, wrapped in a cocoon of numbness, struggling to hold the grief and pain at bay.

They stumbled out into bright sunlight. The Citadel was in chaos. The streets were crowded, and the sounds of shouted orders overlaid the general panic. They stood at the top of the steps, looking down over the confusion. R'shiel had her arm around Shananara, but she wasn't really certain who was holding up whom.

'You certainly know how to create a riot, cousin,' Shananara said with a wan smile.

She helped Shananara down the steps and they pushed their way against the panicked crowd towards the dormitories. R'shiel had to push them flat against the walls on several occasions as troops of mounted Defenders galloped by. The last troop to pass them stopped as their officer called a sudden halt. He flew from his saddle and ran to them. It was Tarja.

'What happened?' he demanded as R'shiel collapsed against him.

'Xaphista is dead,' she told him weakly.

Tarja looked at her in concern then waved his men forward. A lieutenant jumped down from his mount and caught Shananara before she fell.

'Get her back to the dormitories,' Tarja ordered the man holding the queen. 'Get her own people to help her. And take an escort.'

The young officer saluted with his free hand and scooped up the Harshini queen into his arms. He lifted Shananara up into his saddle, swung up behind her, and then, waving a few of the troopers forward, pushed his way through the throng and headed back towards the dormitories. Once Shanan was safely out of harm's way,

R'shiel sagged with relief. Now she only had herself to worry about.

'Can you stand?' Tarja asked.

'I think so.'

'Where's Brak?'

'He's dead.'

'I'm sorry.' Tarja sounded like he meant it, but R'shiel knew he would not grieve his death for long. Not like she would. 'Let's get you out of here.'

'Is everyone all right?'

He glanced over his shoulder for a moment at the chaos in the streets and smiled. 'You mean this?'

She nodded.

'Oh, yes, everyone is fine, as far as we can tell. Just after dawn there was some sort of . . . well, I don't know what it was, but it knocked most of the Harshini unconscious and everybody else just seemed to go berserk for a while. We're getting it under control, but it's taking time, and now the Kariens are attacking.'

'Attacking?'

'Don't worry, it's nothing serious. They're fighting amongst themselves as much as they're aiming at us, but we still have to do something to put it down. Sergeant!' A Defender hurried forward and saluted. 'See that she gets back to her rooms and post a guard. I don't want anybody disturbing Lady R'shiel while she's resting, is that clear?'

'Yes, my Lord.'

'Tarja, I don't need—'

'Shut up, R'shiel. You can hardly stand. Sergeant, once the Lady R'shiel is in her rooms, find Mandah Rodak and send her to keep the lady company.'

'*Tarja!*'

Tarja grinned at her, knowing full well what his order meant. Mandah would not let her budge until she was convinced she was fully recovered. Worse than that, Mandah would insist on calling her 'Divine One'. He thrust her into the arms of the waiting sergeant and ran for his horse, yelling orders as he leapt into the saddle and resumed his push to the main gate. R'shiel watched him leave with a furious snarl, but she was too tired to resist and let the Defender lift her onto his mount and take her away from the bedlam that filled the streets of the Citadel.

## 61

The Defenders beat back the attack on the Citadel with little effort. The Kariens were too disorganised to mount a serious campaign, despite their numerical superiority. By mid-morning they had withdrawn to the other side of the Saran. A significant number withdrew even further. Desertions were decimating the ranks of the Karien army on a regular basis. Garet estimated there were less than seventy thousand left.

By the time Tarja returned to his office to confront the remainder of the aftermath of whatever it was that R'shiel had unleashed, he was exhausted. He had not been immune to the party atmosphere last night and had consumed far too much wine. When all hell broke loose at dawn he had woken with a head as thick as a door, his bed a tangle of sheets and Mandah curled in his arms, her thick blonde hair spilling across the pillow and tickling his nose. He had pushed her away impatiently, annoyed at himself. He had not intended to get caught up in the celebrations. He had certainly not intended to take Mandah to his bed, and he couldn't shake the feeling that he had done so because R'shiel had given him her blessing. *Damn her. Damn all Harshini.*

Seeing that she was wounded by his rejection, Tarja had kissed Mandah soundly, promised to see her later and fled the room, getting dressed on the run. He was hopping on one foot, pulling his boot onto the other when Garet knocked on the door and opened it without waiting for an answer.

'We appear to be under attack, my lord,' Garet said calmly. He looked over Tarja's shoulder towards the bedroom door. Mandah stood there wrapped in nothing but a sheet, yawning sleepily. 'Good morning, Mandah.'

'Commandant.'

Tarja glared at Garet, waiting for him to say something, anything, about finding the young pagan woman in his room. He was in a foul enough mood to react rather badly if Garet even looked at him askance.

But the commandant's composure didn't waver for an instant. 'Oh, and the population appears to be rioting, too.'

'What the hell happened?'

'I assume it has something to do with R'shiel, but I can't be certain. I suggest you get a move on, my lord. We've a busy day ahead of us.'

That had proved to be a vast understatement. Tarja yearned for a day that was *merely* busy. The Kariens had been pushed back and the population in the Citadel would calm down eventually. Already many had returned to their homes with sore heads and puzzled looks. But there was still more to be done.

There was always more to be done.

When he finally pushed open the door to his office, he found several Harshini waiting for him. Three were dressed in the long white robes they favoured. The other two were dressed in Dragon Riders' leathers. All five of them bowed solemnly as he entered the office and walked cautiously to his desk.

'My Lord Defender.'

'How is Shan . . . your queen?'

'She is recovering, my lord,' one of the white-robed Harshini informed him. 'We are most grateful for your assistance this morning.'

'And the rest of your people?'

'They are well, my lord. Thank you for your concern.'

The Harshini's constant thanks were starting to wear on him. 'Is there something I can do for you?'

'We are here to do something for you, my lord.' The Harshini who spoke was one of the Dragon Riders. She stepped forward with a smile. 'I am Pilarena and this is Jalerana. I have been honoured to aid Prince Damin in his journey north and my companion has been with King Hablet and his navy. We have come to coordinate your forces, my lord.'

Tarja slumped back in his chair in astonishment. 'Coordinate my forces?'

'We will relay messages, my lord,' the other Dragon Rider explained. 'If they are verbal, then we will carry messages of goodwill. If you want to communicate anything . . . else, then we must ask that the messages are written and sealed and that we are not advised of their contents.'

Tarja nodded in understanding. The Harshini could do nothing to aid their attack. If they knew the messages they carried were likely to cause death, they would not deliver them. He smiled faintly, thinking that they were very easy to underestimate. This race had survived for thousands of years without being able to lift a finger in their own defence. He was beginning to understand how they had managed it.

'Can you show me where they are now?' he asked, indicating the map laid out on his desk. He and Garet had been poring over it yesterday, trying to guess where Damin might be.

Jalerana nodded and stepped forward. 'The High Prince is here, my lord. He has with him approximately forty thousand men. The King of Fardohnya is here and has another ten thousand. His majesty asked that I pass on his apologies that he could not bring a larger force. In the time available it was all he could gather, and there are only so many ships he could carry them in.'

'Then we have fifty thousand men ready to attack?'

'*You* have fifty thousand men, my lord. What you do with them is not our concern,' Pilarena remarked sternly.

'I'm sorry, I didn't mean to offend you.'

She bowed slightly. 'You are forgiven, my lord.'

'How did Damin get here so fast? With an army that big?'

'With the aid of the gods,' Jalerana told him serenely.

Tarja shook his head, deciding he would be better off if he didn't know the details. 'I'd like to send a message to both Hablet and Damin. Written messages. How soon before you can leave?'

'We will be ready when your dispatches are completed,' Jalerana assured him.

'Then if you would excuse me, Divine Ones, I have a lot of work to do.'

Four hours later, Tarja sealed the letters he had written to Damin Wolfblade and King Hablet. Garet watched him pressing the Lord Defender's seal into the warm wax and frowned.

'You know, those letters could cause us a lot of grief if they fell into the wrong hands.'

'The Harshini will deliver them safely.'

'Suppose they decide to *deliver* them into the wrong hands?'

Tarja shook his head at Garet's suspicions. 'Haven't you seen enough yet to know that they're on our side?'

'They're not on our side, Tarja. They are on their *own* side. And you would do well not to forget it. Just because their queen is stunning and they smile a lot, it doesn't make them harmless.'

Tarja grinned at the commandant. 'Shall I tell Shananara you think she's stunning?'

'Not if you want to see the sun come up tomorrow,' Garet warned with a faint smile. 'Any news on R'shiel?'

'Mandah says she's sleeping like the dead.'

'Any idea what she actually did in that Hall?'

'No, and I don't want to know.'

'Neither do I.' Garet rose from his seat and walked to the map, frowning as he noted where the troop placements were marked. He still thought the Harshini were lying about how far they had come. 'Speaking of Mandah . . .'

'It's none of your business, Garet.'

'You're the Lord Defender, and she's a pagan.'

'Then you've got nothing to complain about. A few months ago I was sleeping with a Harshini. If I keep going at this rate, I'll have worked my way up to a Quorum Member by next spring.'

'This is no joking matter, Tarja. Once we clear out the Kariens, we still have the rest of Medalon to secure. As it is, we've got half the damned Sisterhood confined to their quarters. It's not going to help our cause with you flaunting a pagan lover.'

'You were the one who claimed I was the only one the pagans would follow.'

'Yes, but I didn't expect them to follow you into the bedroom.'

Tarja leaned back in his chair and studied Garet. 'Is that your only concern?'

'Yes.'

'Then mind your own damned business.'

Garet shook his head and bowed mockingly. 'As you command, my lord. It's your neck.'

'Garet, you wanted change. You wanted the Sisterhood gone. You can't have just the bits you like and discard the rest.'

'True,' the commandant conceded reluctantly. 'But you can't blame me for hoping.'

They were interrupted by a knock on the door. Tarja called permission to enter and Jalerana and Pilarena entered the office. They bowed politely and accepted the letters Tarja handed them, not even glancing at the packets they held.

'Do you have any other messages, my lord?'

'Just tell Prince Damin and King Hablet that we anxiously await their arrival. With joy, of course.'

Jalerana smiled. 'Of course, my lord.'

Garet watched them suspiciously as they left the office then shook his head. 'You're too trusting, Tarja.'

'They can't knowingly cause harm, Garet.'

'Perhaps not, but they can do a hell of a lot of damage *unknowingly*. Besides, I never trust anybody who is always so damned happy.'

## 62

Damin Wolfblade and his army arrived at the Citadel within an hour of the appearance of the first of King Hablet's Fardohnyans. The constant flow of messages delivered by the Dragon Riders between the Citadel, Hablet's ships and Damin's Warlords had allowed an unprecedented level of coordination. Their forces were in place, their strategy worked out to the finest detail, their victory almost a foregone conclusion long before the Citadel came into view.

The only thing that irked Damin as he rode out to meet his father-in-law was that Hablet had got here first.

Hablet proved to be a short, heavy-set man with a greying beard and a scowl that was reserved for the man who had run off with his daughter. Adrina had been left back at the camp, despite her protests. The Harshini had stepped in to aid him in restraining her, no more willing to let a pregnant woman near a battlefield than he was.

Hablet waited on a small rise overlooking the Karien army. The enemy was aware of their presence. One could hardly move an army this size in secret, but they were milling about aimlessly. The Karien dukes were still hostages in the Citadel and their forces lacked any sound leadership.

Damin frowned as he saw Hablet sitting astride a magnificent black stallion, waiting for the High Prince to approach. It was deliberate, Damin was certain. Hablet wanted him to be the supplicant. With a quick glance at Narvell, who rode on his left, Damin bit back his annoyance and galloped forward.

'Your majesty,' Damin said, with a slight bow as he reined in beside the king. His own stallion sidestepped nervously as he caught the scent of the king's mount. The irony was not lost on Damin as he fought to keep the beast under control. Two territorial stallions, indeed.

'You're Wolfblade, I suppose?'

'That's very observant of you, your majesty.'

'Where's my daughter?'

'She's safe.'

'Married to you? That's debatable.'

Damin suddenly grinned at the Fardohnyan king as he realised Hablet was more afraid of meeting him than he was of meeting Hablet. This man had tried to have him assassinated any number of times, and had been planning to invade his country until recently. It would not be unreasonable for Damin to have called him out for it the moment he laid eyes on him.

'Your majesty, I'm sure you've a lot to say to Adrina and I *know* she has quite a bit to say to you. But let's put aside our differences for the time being and do something about these Kariens, shall we?' He didn't wait for Hablet to answer. 'This is Narvell Hawksword, the Warlord of Elasapine. He'll act as my liaison. Once the battle is engaged the Harshini will be forced to withdraw, so I thought it might be easier this way. As my force is four times the size of yours, and includes a couple of thousand Defenders, we'll be bearing the brunt of the attack, but any advice you offer will be welcome. If you wish to join us in the command tent, just let Lord Hawksword know, and he'll have someone show you the way.'

Hablet sputtered something in Fardohnyan at Damin's high-handed manner, but he didn't wait to find out what it was. He wheeled his stallion around and galloped back towards his own lines, laughing at the look on the King of Fardohnya's face.

Once the attack was sounded from the walls of the Citadel the gates opened, and rank upon rank of depressingly well-disciplined troops marched forth, followed by the Defender cavalry. As they formed up in front of the walls on the other side of the Saran River, Damin gave the signal to move forward. His advance forces were mostly mounted, and they moved onto the plain like a wall of impending death. He gave another signal and the Fardohnyan infantry moved in from the west.

And then they waited.

Shananara had insisted that the Kariens be given the opportunity to surrender. It was a condition of using her people to relay their messages back and forth between the Citadel and the armies coming to relieve them.

Damin took out his looking glass and focused on the Citadel as Tarja emerged through the main gate. Mounted beside him was a bearded Karien, one of Jasnoff's dukes, no doubt. Tarja let him take a long look at the forces arrayed against his men. The two men spoke at some length, the Karien gesticulating angrily, and then the duke wheeled his mount around and returned to the Citadel. Damin swung the looking glass up to the flagpole mounted over the gate. The white flag of truce was hastily pulled down and battle colours were raised in their place. A whoop of glee sounded along the Hythrun lines.

'It appears the Kariens aren't planning to surrender, my lord,' Damin remarked to Almodavar with a grin.

'What a shame, your highness,' Almodavar said insincerely.

'Then I suppose we'd better go and kill them all.'

'That would seem to be the only option left open to us, your highness.'

Damin glanced over his shoulder. 'Have the Harshini withdrawn?'

'They're clear of the field, your highness. They withdrew as soon as they saw the battle flags being raised.'

Damin nodded and passed his looking glass to an aide and unsheathed his sword. The sound of the Defender trumpets reached him faintly on the breeze and he raised his arm to lead his troops into battle.

The battle, once it got under way, was almost as bad as the one on the northern border. The Kariens were not acting under a coercion, but they were demoralised, hungry and leaderless. Their god was dead, their leaders held hostage in the enemy fortress. They put up a fight, certainly, but there was no need for strategy. It reminded Damin of quelling the riot that had stormed the gates of Greenharbour during the siege. All they did – all they needed to do – was draw inexorably closer, pulling an ever-tighter circle of steel around the Kariens until there was no escape and no quarter given.

The knights put up the best fight. Their code of honour would allow them no other course of action, but even they fell eventually to the unstoppable advance. By the time Damin thought to look up, bloodied and exhausted, he was surprised to discover the sun high overhead. The ground behind him was littered with more bodies than he could count, and in the distance the Saran River ran red as the Defenders splashed through its shallow waters to meet their foes.

Looking about him and realising there was nobody left to fight, Damin rested his sword across his saddle and looked up at the Citadel. The fortress seemed to glow, even in the bright sunlight. The archers on the walls had stopped loosing their arrows, as the only men within reach now were their own troops.

Then he heard another trumpet blare out and saw the battle colours come down, replaced with the plain blue flag that they had agreed they would hoist in the case of victory.

A cheer rose from the field, muted but heartfelt. Damin surveyed the battlefield, feeling strangely let down. Like the battle on the northern border it had been as much a cattle cull as it was a decent war. The only enemy worth fighting these days, he realised, were probably the Defenders, and he'd allied himself with them. Maybe he should have stayed at home, or planned to invade Medalon. Then at least he would have been guaranteed a decent fight.

'Your highness? Prince Damin?'

He turned in his saddle to find a Defender riding towards him. 'I'm Damin Wolfblade.'

The Defender saluted sharply. 'Your highness, the Lord Defender sends his compliments and requests that you join him in the Citadel.'

'Very well.'

'Would you happen to know where I could find the King of Fardohnya, sir?'

'Back that way,' Damin said, waving in the general direction of the command post some leagues distant. He was in no hurry to have Hablet join them in the Citadel. He wanted to speak to Tarja first. 'He's in the command tent.'

'Thank you, sir.'

'Oh, Lieutenant!'

'Your highness?'

'Once you've delivered your message to King Hablet, could you ask Lord Hawksword to fetch my wife and bring her to the Citadel, too?'

'Of course, your highness.'

The Defender galloped off towards the command tent and Damin turned his stallion towards the Citadel.

'You look like hell,' Tarja announced by way of greeting.

Damin smiled wearily as he dismounted, handing his reins to a waiting cadet. The boy led the stallion away cautiously. 'Well, some of us have been out fighting, you know, not sitting here in the Citadel playing Lord Defender. How in the name of the gods did they talk you into accepting that job?'

Tarja grimaced. 'It's a long story. You're wounded.'

Damin glanced down at his blood-soaked sleeve and poked at it curiously, then shrugged when he felt no pain. 'Must be someone else's blood. Any chance you can find me a clean shirt before Adrina gets here? I *will* be wounded if she sees me like this. I promised her I wouldn't get involved in the fighting.'

'She didn't really expect you to stay out of it, did she?'

'Who knows with Adrina,' he shrugged.

He followed Tarja up a broad set of sweeping steps to the front of an impressive building that looked vaguely like one of the temples in Greenharbour. Tarja pushed open the massive door and Damin stepped inside, gaping in wonder.

'The Temple of the Gods,' he whispered in awe.

'We prefer to call it the Great Hall,' Tarja said with a thin smile.

'I can't believe you left it so untouched.'

'We didn't. The Harshini queen rearranged things a bit when she got here.'

Damin grinned at Tarja. 'That must have been hard for your poor little atheist heart to cope with. Will you introduce me to the queen?'

'Of course. She should be here soon.'

'And the demon child? I half expected her to be standing on the walls hurling lightning bolts into the enemy.'

Tarja's face clouded. 'R'shiel has been asleep for days now.'

'Asleep?'

'She says she destroyed Xaphista.'

'Yes, well that would take it out of you, wouldn't it?' He slapped Tarja's shoulder to remind him he was joking. 'You said she was asleep? Not unconscious? What do the Harshini say about her?'

'They don't seem to be worried.'

'Then neither should you.'

They walked the length of the Temple to where a long polished table had been set up in the shadow of the massive Seeing Stone. It would dwarf the one in Greenharbour. For a moment Damin wished he'd brought Kalan with him. She would have been awestruck to stand here in the fabled Harshini Temple of the Gods facing the Citadel's Seeing Stone.

As they approached the table, the Defenders on guard snapped to attention. Tarja sent one of them to find

Damin a clean shirt as he pulled at the laces on his leather breastplate and lifted it over his head.

'Have you got anything to drink, or is this going to be one of those long, boring *dry* affairs?'

Tarja smiled and ordered a Defender to bring wine. He came back with a carafe, two goblets and the clean shirt he'd requested. Damin drank the first one down without taking a breath, changed his shirt and then poured another drink down his throat, before collapsing into one of the high-backed chairs around the table.

'So, I take it we're having this little chat in here to intimidate the Karien dukes?' he inquired as he poured himself another drink.

'That thought did cross my mind, yes.'

'Good idea. Where are they?'

'I want to wait until Hablet and Shananara get here before I let them in.'

Damin nodded approvingly. 'You're getting very good at this, aren't you?'

'I suppose. How do you like being a High Prince?'

'I loathe it. I had to kill that Karien child a few weeks ago. He tried to poison R'shiel. I've never had to make a worse decision in my life.'

'R'shiel never mentioned it.'

'She wouldn't. Not after Brak stepped in. Where is he, by the way? Watching over the demon child?'

'He's dead.'

The news surprised Damin almost as much as Tarja's obvious lack of remorse. 'Well, that will make Adrina happy. She was planning to kill him herself.'

The doors opened at the far end of the Hall and a woman stepped through. At first, Damin thought it was R'shiel. As she drew closer and he saw her black eyes and her air of serene calm he knew it could only be the Harshini queen. He jumped to his feet and bowed low as she approached.

'Your majesty.'

'High Prince,' she replied graciously, then turned to Tarja. 'I hope you don't mind, Tarja, but I have sent my people out to help the wounded.'

'Of course I don't mind, but won't they be distressed roaming a battlefield?'

'We abhor violence, my lord, but we abhor suffering even more. Don't fear for my people. They are not as fragile as you think.'

'Tarja!'

The man who called out from the entrance of the Hall was Garet Warner, the commandant the Sisterhood had sent to investigate the goings on when they were on the northern border. Tarja excused himself and hurried to speak to him and then walked back to the table. His expression was thoughtful.

'What's wrong?'

'We've just received a bird from Yarnarrow. Jasnoff is dead. He killed himself the same day R'shiel claims she killed Xaphista.'

Shananara took the news stoically. 'He ruled Karien by divine mandate. With Xaphista gone, so is his crown.'

'So who's in charge now?'

'With Cratyn dead, the next in line is someone called Drendyn. He's Jasnoff's nephew. Apparently, we're holding him here. He's one of the dukes.'

'*Drendyn?*' Damin asked with a laugh. 'Oh, Tarja, are you in for an interesting time! He's a boy. And I can promise you he wasn't raised to rule a nation the size of Karien.'

'Well, we'd better break it to him gently. I'm not sure how he's going to take the news that he's now their king.'

'If you want my advice, talk to him alone and leave the other dukes out of it. They'll just try to manipulate him. Maybe, with a bit of guidance, we can mould him into a half-decent king.'

'It is not for you to manipulate other nations to suit your own purposes, your highness,' Shananara scolded.

'Actually it is, your majesty. We've just spent thousands of lives out there for no good reason. If we can take this boy and turn him into a king, one who thinks before he attacks, we'll all benefit.'

The Harshini queen suddenly smiled. 'Perhaps we should consider returning to the old custom of Harshini advisers at court, your highness. You saw how effective it can be when scattered parties can communicate quickly with each other.'

'And that would include my court, I suppose?' he asked, admiring her quick mind – and her own blatant manipulation.

'We would not want to be seen playing favourites, your highness,' she replied ingenuously.

'Of course not,' he agreed with a wry smile and then turned to Tarja. 'It's not a bad idea, you know. With Xaphista gone, the Collective will move in to Karien. But with a Harshini looking over his shoulder, we should be able to keep young Drendyn out of trouble while he grows into his crown.'

'The plan has merit,' Tarja agreed hesitantly.

'I do have one condition, though, your majesty,' Damin added, turning to the queen.

'And what is that, your highness?'

'I want to be there when you break the news to Hablet,' he said with a malicious grin.

## 63

R'shiel was awake for some time before she opened her eyes. She waited, feigning sleep until she heard Mandah leave the room. Once she was certain she was alone, she swung her feet to the floor and rubbed her eyes. The remains of what must have been a mammoth headache lingered behind her eyes, but other than that she bore no obvious evidence of her battle with Xaphista.

Climbing out of the bed, she padded barefoot to the door and opened it a crack. Mandah was talking to Tarja. She couldn't make out what they were saying, but when he was finished telling her what he had come to say he kissed her, hard and hungrily, before letting her go. Mandah shut the door behind him with a smile and headed back towards the bedroom. R'shiel raced back to the bed and pulled the covers over herself, closing her eyes and forcing her breathing into a deep rhythm. She heard Mandah cross the room, felt a cool hand on her forehead and then heard the door open and close, followed by the fainter sound of the apartment door closing.

So Mandah had gone; perhaps to join Tarja. It hopefully meant they were going to be occupied for a while. She hunted around the room for her clothes, finally finding them pressed and folded in a drawer under the window. Typical, she thought with a frown. Not only was Mandah insufferably nice, but she was neat as well. She shook out her clothes and dressed quickly, throwing the nightgown onto the floor.

There was a hairbrush on the dresser and she picked it up, running it through her tangled hair. She glanced in the mirror and froze mid-stroke. An alien reflection stared back at her. She was not drawing on her power, yet her eyes were Harshini black. The whites of her eyes were gone and her skin was as golden as a full-blooded Harshini. Whatever she had done in the Temple of the Gods had left an indelible mark on her. R'shiel slowly replaced the brush, aware that she would never be counted as human again. For some reason the thought didn't bother her as much as she thought it would. Along with the change in her eyes came a sense of rightness, a sense that she was somehow complete.

She was Harshini.

R'shiel glanced around the room and realised there was nothing here that belonged to her. Nothing she need take. Her life was headed in a different direction and nothing here in the Citadel offered her any sense of ownership. Feeling suddenly cast adrift into an unknown future, she turned her back on the mirror and headed into the next room.

When she reached the outer door she pressed her ear against it and heard faint male voices in the hall. Tarja's guards – there to see that she wasn't disturbed. R'shiel reached inside herself cautiously and drew on her power. She surprised herself with the control she now had.

Perhaps being linked so closely with Shananara she had absorbed some of her cousin's skill and knowledge. It was how the demons learnt from each other.

With a skill she hadn't known she possessed, she drew a glamour around herself and opened the door a fraction. The guard in the hall turned towards the sound, studied the door curiously for a moment before opening it wide. When he found no one, he shrugged and pulled it closed.

R'shiel ran down the corridor, still wrapped in the glamour that hid her from the notice of anyone who happened to pass her. She didn't remember learning how to do it so easily, but she seemed to know instinctively how to hold it in place. The last time she had tried such a thing, when she and Damin rescued Adrina from Dregian Castle, it had taken all her concentration.

R'shiel took the stairs to the ground floor and walked out into the street, amazed to find the city going about its business as if nothing was wrong. Wagons trundled down the street laden with produce and the roads were crowded with soldiers – but they wore Hythrun and Fardohnyan colours and looked more like tourists than warriors.

*So the siege is over*, she thought, beginning to wonder, a little uneasily, how long she had been asleep. If there had been time for the siege to be lifted and the city to regain some semblance of normalcy, it must have been quite a while. She walked down to the end of the street and out onto the main thoroughfare. It was even more crowded here, and there were Harshini on the streets, too. She wondered if they would notice her, or even feel the minimal power that she was drawing amidst the sights and sounds and smells of the city.

Crossing the road, R'shiel headed for the Temple of

the Gods. She stopped on the corner as she saw Damin and a heavily pregnant Adrina climbing the steps. Behind them walked Tarja and Garet Warner, Shananara and a young Karien that R'shiel recognised but could not immediately name. On their heels strode a richly dressed man with a barrel chest and a greying beard. Hablet of Fardohnya.

R'shiel followed them into the Temple of the Gods, still wrapped in the glamour, and watched curiously as they took their places around the conference table.

Shananara remained standing as the others took their seats. She held a scroll in her hands and studied the others carefully for a moment before she spoke. Then she looked up, stared straight at R'shiel and smiled. Shananara knew she was watching, but she did not reveal her presence. She acknowledged R'shiel with a faint nod and turned her attention back to the table.

'It has taken quite some time, but I have here the treaty that you have all agreed to sign. If one of you breaks it, they must face the other three.'

R'shiel looked around the table curiously. Tarja and Garet looked satisfied. Adrina was positively smirking. Damin appeared relieved and a little smug. Whatever the treaty contained, it obviously hadn't done Hythria any harm. Hablet wore a look of wounded resignation. The young Karien, who R'shiel realised was the knight who had travelled with Cratyn to hunt down Adrina, looked caught somewhere between terror and relief.

'I won't go into details, but it boils down to this: all of you will withdraw your troops to the borders as they were set down prior to the Karien invasion of Medalon. No nation has gained territory and no nation has lost it. You, King Drendyn, will open your borders to the

Sorcerers' Collective. Your god is dead and your people will suffer if they are not given an opportunity to find another god to believe in. King Hablet, you will also grant free access to the Collective, as will Medalon. No more arrests. No more gaols. No more persecution.'

Hablet muttered something inaudible, but he did not openly react to the rebuke. Tarja appeared unconcerned by the condition.

'Each monarch, and whatever government Medalon finally decides to adopt, will accept a Harshini adviser in their court,' Shananara continued. 'The Harshini will act as final arbiters in case of disputes between the nations.

'The succession in each nation will remain as it is now, with two exceptions. In the event that King Hablet dies before his unborn son reaches maturity, then High Princess Adrina of Hythria will assume the role of Regent until he comes of age. The other change also concerns the Fardohnyan throne. The condition that requires a Wolfblade heir in the absence of a legitimate male heir is no longer valid. In the absence of a legitimate male heir to the Fardohnyan throne, it will fall to the eldest legitimate female.'

'Now, wait on!' Hablet objected. 'I never agreed to that. If I die, Adrina only has to kill my son and she gets to be queen.'

'Just because *you* don't think twice about eliminating members of your family, Father,' Adrina retorted frostily, 'doesn't mean I share your sentiments. I give you my word; I will *not* kill my brother. Any of them.'

'It makes no difference in any case, your majesty,' Shananara explained. 'Adrina is excluded from the succession by virtue of her position as Regent. If anything should happen to your son, the throne would fall to your next eldest daughter.'

'Cassandra?' Hablet laughed. 'Gods preserve us from such a fate! Well, at least I know that Adrina will fight to keep her brother alive. I'm sure she'd rather die than see Cassie sitting on the throne.'

*Peace.*

R'shiel moved away from the pillar she was leaning against with a frown, as it dawned on her how superfluous she had become. Zegarnald would not die; he was a Primal God and truly immortal. But he would not walk into Karien and step into the vacuum left by Xaphista, either. He had wanted her tempered so that she was strong enough to face Xaphista. Well, he had what he wanted, but she had also gained a measure of revenge for the suffering he had condoned. The gods would rise and fall, gain strength and weaken as life rolled on, but the God of War would not have the strength to bully the other gods into doing his bidding. The balance had been restored.

There was no need for the demon child now. No destiny awaited her. No nation needed her counsel. That they had done all this while she slept left her feeling so inconsequential that it actually hurt.

Inkwells were being brought out, along with a number of quills, for the formal signing of the treaty. She left them to it.

There was nothing more to be done.

R'shiel slipped through the doors and out into the sunlight, realising that for the first time, she had nobody to please but herself. No destiny loomed over her like a shadow. She was beholden to no one – human, Harshini or god.

The glamour still wrapped around her protectively, R'shiel turned towards the Main Gate. She walked through it unseen by the Defenders on duty and out onto the busy road. The battlefield was still being cleared and troops were piling bodies into mass graves dug by the countless Karien prisoners that had been taken after the battle, but the Saran ran clear, its shallow waters tripping happily over the rocks beneath the surface. It was a bit grand calling it a river, actually. It was not much more than a wide stream. She stopped on the bridge and glanced back at the shining Citadel. It had been her home and her prison. Her ruin and her salvation.

Impulsively, she sent out a thought to the massive fort, a farewell of sorts. She didn't know when, or even if, she would be back. She had to find Loclon. And she had an appointment with Gimlorie. Maybe she could find a way to convince Death to release Brak, too.

The Citadel responded with a benevolent wave of affection that washed over her gently. Smiling to herself, R'shiel glanced down and discovered she was not alone. The little demon she had last seen with Mikel in Greenharbour was sitting on the ground at her feet, looking at her with its huge black eyes.

'Where have you been?' she asked, squatting down.

The creature chittered something incomprehensible and jumped into her arms.

'Is that your way of saying sorry about Mikel?' she chuckled. 'It wasn't your fault, little one. You'll be a few hundred older before you can protect someone from the likes of Xaphista.'

Mention of the dead god's name set the demon off again. R'shiel stood up with the demon's skinny arms wrapped thightly around her neck. With a final glance at the Citadel, she released the glamour and crossed the bridge.

'I suppose,' she said to the demon, as she walked away without looking back, 'we'd better do something about finding you a name.'

## 64

Loclon tossed and turned on the hard ground as the nightmare took him again. It haunted him in his dreams and he lived it in his waking moments. It never left him. It never gave him a moment's respite.

It had begun as they left the Citadel. He was expecting to be smuggled into the Karien camp and treated like a hero – until they took the fortress and slaughtered everyone in it. But Mistress Heaner, her thug Lork and the chillingly beautiful boy Alladan had kept on going. They had not stopped until they reached Brodenvale, and then they had bundled him onto a small river boat and sailed downriver to Bordertown. When they reached the port town they stayed only long enough to arrange another boat, and before he could raise an objection, he found himself heading for the Isle of Slarn.

It hadn't been too bad at first. The island was dank and miserable, and the priests were a strange bunch, but they tended his malnourished body and helped him regain his strength and even began talking of letting him travel to Yarnarrow.

He had done the Overlord a great service, the priests assured him, and his reward was waiting for him.

For a time, he had foolishly believed their promises – until he remembered that for the followers of the Overlord, the rewards for service were not to be found in this life, but the next.

His first escape attempt had been treated as an unfortunate misunderstanding. His second earnt him a savage whipping. His third and last attempt had almost succeeded. It would have, had not the island begun to tremble as if in the grip of an earthquake, and the priests suddenly gone mad.

Something drastic had happened.

Loclon had been at the back of the Karien chapel for the Restday dawn service, waiting for the chance to slip out the door, when the staff belonging to the priest conducting the service had flared with light, and a wave of intense pleasure had washed over the congregation like a warm breeze. It took hold of him for an instant and held him in a thrall. There was a promise of so much in that wave. A hint of joy. A breath of sexual fantasy. A promise of paradise. Even a glimpse of the other gods. It had taken his breath away.

It had almost destroyed the priests.

They had fled the chapel and run towards the cavern where their sacred rock was hidden, howling with terror at whatever it was that it was doing. It only lasted for a few moments, then the feeling had faded abruptly and Loclon shook his head to clear it and bolted for the door.

His original plan had been to head for the small dock near the keep, but with the priests running everywhere like lunatics, he discovered that route no longer open to him. So he ran the other way, pulled himself over the wall that faced the leeward side of the island, cursing as he fell down the long drop on the other side, and ran until he collapsed onto the boggy ground. He was terrified, and at the limit of his endurance, expecting to hear the priests coming after him, not really believing he had succeeded in getting clear of them.

It was then that the nightmare truly began.

They found him that evening, shivering and exhausted, and in the darkness he could not make out their faces. They weren't priests. All he knew was that someone wrapped a blanket around him and someone else thrust a cup of cool water in his hands. He drank it greedily and grasped at the mouldy bread they offered him. They led him through the darkness to a rough hut so close to the shore that he could hear the waves crashing below him as he fell into a fitful sleep.

At some time during the night he woke to find a body pressed against his, warm and young and unmistakably female. He smiled to himself, thinking that before he left this place, he might have some fun. If he was careful, and didn't leave any marks, they wouldn't know he had hurt her until after he had gone. With a smile and a contented sigh, Loclon pulled the girl closer and went back to sleep.

With daylight came the horror.

He had opened his eyes slowly, enjoying the feel of the naked body pressed against him. He ran his hand over her small breasts and her slender hips and then over her belly, reaching down between her thighs to pull her legs apart. He felt something sticky against his hand and cursed. He pulled his hand away and held it up to the light.

It wasn't blood on his fingers – it was pus.

He screamed, leaping from the rough pallet as the girl turned over. She was grotesque. Her face was ruined, half of it eaten away by the disease that devoured a person from the inside out. Her whole left side was covered with open sores that wept pus, and a clear sticky fluid that stained the rough sheets beneath her.

'Please . . .' the girl cried, tears streaming from her one good eye. Her pathetic cries made him want to vomit; the idea that he had touched her made him want to die.

He had leapt the wall into the colony of Malik's Curse sufferers.

Loclon screamed again, and he kept on screaming until a big man with a huge fist and half his face eaten away by the Curse burst into the hut and knocked him out cold.

He had been in hiding ever since. He avoided the small settlement and its disgusting inhabitants, sneaking in at night to find whatever scraps of food he could scavenge. The others knew he was out there, and the grotesque girl from the hut sometimes left scraps for him, perhaps in an attempt to coax him back into her bed. She had been quite pretty once, he supposed, but now she was just a husk that was being slowly consumed by a disease that had no cure. A disease that ate at the extremities and left the body covered in ulcers, and ate through one's internal organs until there was nothing left and the victim died an agonisingly painful death.

He peeled off his ragged clothes and checked his body every day, looking for some sign that he had contracted the disease, but so far he showed no symptoms. All he could do was prowl the island looking for a way off.

There was none.

It was the reason the victims of Malik's Curse were confined here.

He made one attempt to get back into the Karien compound, but the wall, which had been so easy to clamber over from the inside, was much steeper on the leeward side. A deep, empty moat surrounded it that made it impossible to climb without a rope. There was no rope to be had. So he had returned to his prowling, scavenging existence and gone back to trying to find another way off the island.

Loclon tossed restlessly and then sat up, unsure what had wakened him. He looked around in the darkness but could see nothing, so he scrambled on his hands and knees to the entrance of the small cave where he sheltered and looked out over the rocky beach. He saw a figure standing in the moonlight on the beach and scuttled out to get a closer look. Whoever it was, it appeared to be a woman, but he could not make out her identity from this distance. A bubble of excitement began to build in him.

The figure saw him stumbling across the beach and began to walk towards him. He raised his hand in greeting, certain that he had been rescued. The woman was tall and walked with an easy grace that showed no hint of the wasting disease. She wasn't one of them.

'Hello, Loclon.'

He froze at the sound of her voice as she stepped closer. '*R'shiel!*'

'You sound surprised, Captain. You should have known I'd come for you.'

He studied her warily. She must have been drawing

on her power – her eyes burned black as the night surrounding them. Her hair had grown out and was almost on her shoulders, ruffled gently by the sea breeze. It took him a while to work out what else was different about her. It wasn't her quiet air of confidence, or the power that radiated from her.

It was her lack of fear.

Loclon cautiously took a step back from her. 'You've come for me?'

'Did you doubt that I would?'

Hope flared in him as he realised rescue was at hand. She would take him from this place. He would probably be dragged back to the Citadel in chains, but that was better than being here. Better than a slow, lingering death while he was eaten alive by his own body. He could escape eventually. Either along the way or once they got to the Citadel. It didn't really matter.

He nodded and held out his hands to her. 'I'll come quietly. I won't resist.'

R'shiel studied him for a moment and then smiled. It chilled him to the core.

'Death told me once that evil is its own reward, Loclon. I understand what he meant now.'

'What are you talking about? I'm surrendering to you. Take me!'

'I don't want your surrender.'

'*Then what do you want?*' he screamed desperately.

'Vengeance,' she said softly.

'Then take it! Take me away from here! Take me back to the Citadel! Put me on trial! I'll confess. I'll tell them everything I did to you. They'll hang me R'shiel, you know that. Rape is a capital offence. You can stand there and watch me swing! You can gloat over my corpse! Take me back! *GET ME OUT OF HERE!*' He was blubbering and didn't care.

'No, I don't think so, Loclon.'

She turned away from him and began to walk back along the shore. The waves shone with phosphorescence as they slapped at the pebbly beach. He fell to his knees, sobbing with despair.

*'You can't leave me here! Have mercy!'*

She stopped and looked over her shoulder, her black eyes reflecting the shimmering waves. 'Mercy?'

'Please, R'shiel. Take me back with you. I'll do whatever you want. I'll suffer as much as you want. *Just get me off this damned island before the disease gets me!*'

R'shiel stood there watching him on his knees, begging her for mercy. She had done this to him before. She had made him grovel like this at the Grimfield and once they were gone from this place, he would make her pay for that insult, too. But for now . . .

She was wavering. He could tell. She walked back towards him. Hope burned bright in his eyes. She was part Harshini, wasn't she? They were supposed to be unable to kill. Deep down, she didn't have what it took to make the killing stroke. That he was alive at all was proof of that. She'd been raised by the Sisterhood. She believed all that stuff about law and honour. She would not be able to turn her back on him.

But when he saw her face, he realised how wrong he was. There was no mercy in those alien black eyes. No pity. No compassion.

Nothing but cold, unrelenting contempt.

'I came here to send you to hell,' she said. 'But I don't have to, do I? You're already there.'

He wasn't sure how to answer her; he wasn't even sure

what she meant. She just stood there, staring at him with those alien black eyes . . .

Then the itching started. It was barely noticeable at first. He was too consumed by his fear of her to pay attention to it. It began in his fingertips, a niggling, annoying sensation that barely even distracted him. He rubbed his hands against his tattered trousers to relieve it, but it simply made the itching worse.

R'shiel didn't move.

The itching spread up his left arm. He scratched at it with his right hand and discovered his arm covered in small hard lumps. He tore his eyes from R'shiel and glanced down. The lumps were growing larger. As he watched, one of the lumps on his forearm began to develop a pus-filled head. The itching progressed beyond annoying into true pain. The lumps were spreading. He could feel them forming on his back and across his belly. His trousers chaffed as the sores began to form in his groin. His face was swelling with them, too. He tore at his clothing as another sore erupted, the burning itching growing more and more relentless; his breath came in gasps as he realised what was happening to him. The sores kept spreading.

'No!' he panted, as he tore at his own flesh in a futile attempt to relieve the burning. 'No! No! . . . *Noooo!*'

R'shiel stood there watching him.

'What have you done to me?' he wailed. 'Make it stop! Don't do this to me! Not this! Kill me if you must, R'shiel, but not like this! Let me die like a man!'

That evoked a reaction from her. She laughed.

'Like a man, Loclon?'

'Stop it, R'shiel! *Please. I beg you!*'

'It takes years to die from Malik's Curse, did you know that?' she asked in a conversational tone. 'Of course, a few years being slowly devoured by your own body doesn't seem sufficient to repay all you've done, but it will have to do, I suppose.'

'I'll . . . kill myself before . . . I let this thing . . . eat me alive,' he gasped, unable to stop scratching at the spreading sores.

'No, Loclon, you won't kill yourself. For one thing, you're too big a coward, and for another, I won't let you.'

'How are you . . . going to . . . stop me?'

'Magic.'

R'shiel turned and walked away, until eventually she was swallowed by the darkness. She didn't look back.

*I'll kill myself,* he decided silently. *I won't die this way.* He staggered to his feet and turned towards the ocean. *That's all it will take. Just wade into the water and let the sea take me.*

The salt water stung the sores on his legs as he splashed into the foam. He plunged into the sea until it was waist high, then suddenly found he could go no further. He wanted to live, he realised with despair. Even though he had consciously made the decision to die, there was another voice in his mind that wouldn't let him. He found himself unable to take another step.

Loclon staggered back to the beach and threw himself down on the sand, rubbing against the grains to ease the itching, but the sand merely aggravated his already inflamed skin. He was sobbing with frustration. He couldn't relieve the itching. He couldn't stop the pain. He couldn't even die . . .

A hand reached for him and hope flared bright for a fleeting moment! He knew she couldn't walk away from him! She had to come back! This was just a game, she was just tormenting him for revenge . . .

'Mister?' the voice said gently. 'It's all right, Mister. The itching goes away after a few days . . .'

He looked up to find the girl from the settlement with her pathetic smile and her ruined face staring down at him, her eyes filled with pity.

Loclon's howl of despair echoed across the empty beach.

Then he forced himself up and looked around urgently, but it was as if R'shiel had never even been here. There was no sign of her.

Not even footprints in the sand.

*Look out for the next series, beginning with*

# <u>LION OF SENET</u>

The Second Sons Trilogy: Book One

Jennifer Fallon

Life has been good on the world of Ranadon, illuminated both day and night by the light of its greater and lesser suns. The dark ages were banished by Belagren, High Priestess of the Shadowdancers and her political position seems unassailable. However, a series of events escalate, breaking old alliances and breeding new and deadly rivalries.

A volcanic eruption divides the seas between the kingdoms of Senet and Dhevyn, and an ill-omened sailor is thrown onto the island of Elcast. His arrival is a catalyst - baring old hatreds and secrets best left hidden. He brings fear to the Duke of Elcast and Antonov, the influential Lion of Senet is drawn to the island.

The second sons of these powerful individuals develop a strong friendship, but it may not survive events set in motion by their ambitious families . . .